AEON OF CHAOS

Vol. 1

BJ Swann

Cover by: Elizabeth Bedlam
Aeon of Chaos Logo by: Caelan Stokkermans Arts

First Printing, 2023

Swann + Bedlam Press
Melbourne, AU

www.swannbedlam.com

Table of Contents

Part I: Short Stories

Part II: Novellas

PART I

Short Stories

The Magickal Goat Boy

Chapter 1: Bedtime

It is the Aeon of Chaos. All the gods are dead, and the demons have erased their wicked monuments.

"Time to go to sleepy land, my love," said Nilrem's mother, who sat by his bed.

She was beautiful, with long dark hair and a set of curling horns on her head. Her feet, peeking from the bottom of her dressing gown, were covered in shaggy fur and ended in four clawed toes encased in shiny horn.

"I don't want go to sleep yet," said Nilrem. He looked about ten, though looks could be deceiving, especially in fairyland. "I want a story first."

"Okay. What kind of story would you like?"

Nilrem pursed his small red lips as if trying to come up with an answer. Yet he already knew which story he wanted her to tell. It was the same story he'd asked for every night, ever since the day he'd been born. For Nilrem had emerged from the womb with the gift of speech and incredible knowledge. So utterly precocious was he that he'd even assisted the midwives with his own delivery, as soon as his head had popped out of his mother's vagina.

"I want to hear about how you met my father," he said.

"But I've told you that one so many times…"

"I wanna hear it again!"

His mother sighed, then began. "I met your father in the human world. He was a very handsome hunter…"

"Ha!" said Nilrem. "You said before he was a fisherman. Another

5

time you said he was a woodcutter. How come you can't get the story straight, mum?"

"Oh, it's hard to keep track of all these silly human occupations. What's the difference between a hunter and a fisherman, or a woodcutter and a stonemason? The point is that he was very handsome, and we loved each other very much. He was the first and only man I've ever loved."

"What was his name?"

"Bill." she said.

"You said it was Geoff! Another time you said it was Billy-Bob!"

She sighed again. 'What's the difference? Besides, those silly human names all sound the same to me..."

Nilrem stared up at her. His golden eyes glowed with an inquisitorial intensity.

"Why do you keep lying to me, mother?"

"I'm not! I just really can't remember all the details, that's all."

But he knew she was lying, and not just from the vagueness and inconsistent details of her stories. He *always* knew when she was lying. He knew when she was happy, angry, pensive or melancholy, no matter how much she tried to hide her feelings from him. He could read her like a book; he'd always been able to. Right now he sensed her irritation, and her longing to change the subject.

"I think that's enough stories for one night," she said. "Now hurry up and go to sleep, or else the Zhuul will come and get you." Her voice assumed a mock-fearsome tone. "They've got purple skin and glowing red eyes that shine from the darkness like lanterns. They've got terrible fangs and horrible claws. They love to gobble up little boys who don't go to bed on time!"

She rose up, making a sinister face and raising her hands like a pair of grasping claws.

Nilrem knew he was supposed to be afraid. He wasn't, even though he knew that the Zhuul – the boogeymen his mother loved to conjure every night in her attempts to make him sleep – were very, very real, and far more terrible than even her most fanciful tales would suggest.

"As a matter of fact," she said, "I think the Zhuul are coming right now!"

She leapt onto the bed and started tickling him all over. Nilrem thought it was rather undignified to be tickled in this manner, but he went along with it anyway, squirming and laughing for her sake. His questions had obviously troubled her, just as they always did, and he wanted to put her at ease.

Eventually she gave up the tickling and sat peering down at his face. His horns were small and curling, just like his locks of black hair, which she stroked before planting a kiss on his forehead. Then she gazed at him some more, taking in the sight of his rosy red cheeks.

"You're a very special boy, you know that?" she said with a smile. "But sometimes you ask too many questions. Once you get older, everything will be clear. Right now, you're a child, and you need to go to bed. Okay?"

"Okay mum," he said, returning her smile. "Goodnight."

She left the room and shut the door behind her, blocking out the light from the living room fire, leaving only the moonlight that filtered through the window. He lay there, waiting, listening to the creaking of the floorboards as she moved around the house. For a while he heard her tidying up; then she finally went to bed in the room next to his. He listened to her body sink down into the mattress, followed by the sound of her breathing, which at first was shallow and irregular, then steadily rhythmic and deep, signalling the onset of sleep. Satisfied his mother was dead to the world, Nilrem threw off the covers and leapt out of bed. He had no intention of sleeping at all – he had a quest to begin!

But first he had to make preparations. He took one of his pillows, puffed it up, and placed it underneath the covers as though it were his own sleeping body. Then he held his hand above the pillow and whis-

pered in one of the many strange languages he'd known since before
he was born. His eyes flared with light as he called upon the energies
of Chaos to transmute the pillow to the likeness of flesh. The down became bones, sinew, and blood; the cover became skin and hair.

He inspected the double. It looked like him in every conceivable
detail. *He* could tell it was a fraud, of course; he could peer through its
patina of reality and see the substructure of magick that maintained
its existence. But he knew his mother could not. Thus the golem would
be able to take his place for as long as he was gone. It could even walk,
talk, and do most other things a boy like him should be able to do,
though it wouldn't be as eloquent, nor as knowledgeable, as he was.
Still, he decided it would suffice until his quest was complete.

Smiling, he stepped back from the bed and got dressed for his
journey, not by taking a fresh set of clothing from the wardrobe, as
other children might, but by waving his hand and transforming his py-
jamas into suitable outdoor attire. His pyjama bottoms became a pair
of shorts that gave his fur-covered legs room to breathe; his pyjama
top became a tunic and belt; and his nightcap – which was half-falling
off his head already – promptly fell down his back and transformed
into a cloak he could wrap around his body if the weather got cold. For
Nilrem only ever had one set of clothes, which changed shape whenever he desired. The fabric was always burgundy silk, and the pattern
was always the same, consisting of a thousand golden eyes joined by
bolts of golden lightning.

Thus dressed, he opened the window, crept out onto the ledge, and
stared at the steep slope below. The house had been built on the side
of a rugged black mountain. There were many others around it, cradled by the outcrops. They were the homes of the Orzu, his mother's
fairy clan.

He paused on the ledge, having no wish to climb down the side
of his house and follow the steep winding tracks into the valley below. Instead, he gestured to the clouds and called for assistance with

a magickal command. One of the clouds broke away from the others, small, puffy, and pregnant with rain. It drifted to the window ledge and waited, floating, like a barge by a wharf. He jumped down upon its soft, mushy dampness. It felt like a waterlogged carpet. He gestured to the valley and the cloud took him down, conveying them both through the night's whipping wind.

He alighted on the ground and bid the cloud goodbye. It wouldn't do to ride the cloud too long – it might get cross at him, and zap him with lightning, right in the arse. Besides, he liked the idea of stretching his legs along the trail.

Humming to himself, he strode off across the valley. He didn't really know where he was going, only that he'd figure it out on the way. Before him stretched the valleys and castles and towers and kingdoms of fairyland, which existed in the exact same space as the human world, albeit on a whole other tier of reality. The two realms were separated by a membrane called the Veil. In certain situations, this membrane opened up, creating doors which could be used to slip across to either side. The fairies were better at using these breaches than humans were. They had to be. Most gained their food from the mortal world, eating things that were intangible to humans, but very real to them. Some ate memories, or nightmares, or souls; some ate the innocence of babies, digested along with their still-living flesh. Nilrem's mother's people lived on the dreams of young goatherds, which slipped through the cracks in the Veil and drifted up to their mountaintop village. But Nilrem didn't need to eat anything at all. Inside of his body was a reservoir of power that burned like a miniature sun – hence why he hadn't taken snacks for his journey.

He walked on, passing the domains of other fairies as he went. There was a village of gingerbread houses with sugar-frosted roofs that glistened like snow in the moonlight. From the houses came the sound of children screaming. The Candy Clan had lured them to fairyland with promises of sweets; now they were boiling them like cane to

9

extract the sweet flavour of their innocence.

Nilrem felt a chill run down his spine as he heard all that horrible screaming. He certainly didn't want to visit *that* village. Not that they'd eat him, of course; he wasn't a human. He wasn't really innocent, either. At least he didn't think so. He had more knowledge in his brain than a hundred professors, and more magick spells than a convoy of wizards.

He kept on walking. He passed the ridiculous kingdom of Prince Allowishus Appetizer. The fairies who lived there fed on tall tales and unbelievable anecdotes. Their kingdom reflected their tastes. It was lit up with sunlight, even though it was night, and the birdsong from the forest around it sounded like an orchestra of drums, violins, and pianos. Even more ridiculous by far was the fact that the kingdom of Prince Allowishus was supposed to be located on a whole other continent. Then again, fairyland wasn't exactly known for its consistent geography. It wasn't like the human world, which was ordered by physical laws; it was ordered by magick ones, instead.

Nilrem kept walking. He passed a creepy forest where nooses grew like vines from the trees. The fairies that lived there inhabited the tree trunks and fed upon the souls of suicides that slipped across the Veil. They didn't just wait for people to die, either; they called to them with siren-like songs of morbidity, enticing them to self-termination.

Nilrem shuddered. Their maudlin song was very loud indeed. He gave the Suicide Forest a wide berth. Steadily the sun began to rise and he found himself getting tired, having journeyed all night. He started yawning, and blinking, and rubbing his eyes. Eventually he lay down in a grove by the roadside to snatch a quick nap.

He awoke to feel that someone – or some *thing* – was sucking his blood.

Chapter 2: A Novel Alliance

"Get off!" snapped Nilrem, slapping at the mosquito buzzing around his head. It, or she, was the size of a hummingbird.

She avoided the blows, murmuring with delight at the taste of the blood she'd consumed.

"That's some interesting blood you've got there," she said. "You must have a very special lineage. May I ask who your parents are?"

Nilrem glared at her. He wasn't happy about her sucking his blood; already an itchy-feeling welt was forming on his arm. And yet, he decided to answer her question. Perhaps because it felt like the polite thing to do; perhaps because it went right to the heart of his current, urgent quest.

"My mother's a fairy of the Orzu Clan," he said. "As for my father... well, I really don't know. My mother says he was a human, the first man she ever loved. That's the only thing she's firm about. Otherwise her story keeps changing. Sometimes she says he was a woodcutter, or a fisherman, or a hunter. Sometimes his name is Bob, or Geoff, or Billy-Bob. But I'm pretty sure she's lying about just about all of it. That's why I'm going on a quest to find out for myself. I'm gonna track my father down, no matter how far I have to go or how long it'll take me!"

"I wouldn't stress about it if I were you, kid," said the mosquito. "It really doesn't matter if you don't know who your dad is."

"But it does! It's the one thing I *don't* know. I've got all the knowledge of the universe churning in my brain, but I don't have the one piece of information that pretty much everyone else takes for granted."

"All the knowledge of the universe, huh?" asked the mosquito, in a tone of disbelief.

"That's right!" He began to prance back and forth, gesturing grandly. "I know about the age before this one, when the universe was ruled by the tyranny of gods. I know about the Cosmic War that finally unseated them. I know all the names and all the titles of the demons who killed them in the Glorious Deicide. I know of the Celestial Fire that burned the old cosmos and created it anew. I know of the great lovers Nez and Xas, whose magickal orgasms guided the flames. I know all the myriad names of all the planets and stars in all the many languages of all the other beings either living or dead; I know the cosmic architecture that holds all the worlds in the void; I know the rainbow bridges and moonbeam roads that lead out across the cosmos and between the dimensions; I know of the Red World, and the Blue World, and the realm of wicked Zhuul. I know the magick of demons and the dead gods besides. I know alchemy, geometry, philosophy, the principles of botany, astronomy, even common cookery. All these things I know; they were beamed into my mind at the moment of conception. I knew them as a foetus. I knew them in the womb!"

The mosquito tried to speak, but he just shouted over her. "What a precocious little shit!" she whispered.

His voice rose even louder. "I even know the seventy-two-thousand demon transformations!" he cried.

In a flash of golden light he transformed into a giant with the head of a pig and a pair of onyx horns – but only for a second. Another flash followed, and he turned into a feathered bird-man with four wings, four arms, and a murderous beak; then a woman with ashen skin and a skirt made of dangling human bodies; then a crow with thurible eyes oozing black smoke; then a worm-like thing with a lamprey-like mouth singing a beautiful song; then an albino ape with a crown of flaming swords revolving above his head like a floating carousel; then a golden-skinned woman with a pregnant belly and the lower body of a spider; then a sickly giant with curling horns and eyes like crimson buboes; then a woman with a body made of clouds and veins made of lightning bolts flickering and shining through her gaseous form; then

"All right, all right!" said the mosquito. "You don't have to show me all seventy-two thousand transformations, okay? I believe you. You're a very special kid!"

Nilrem turned back into his natural shape, beaming with pride. "See?" he said. "I told you, I know everything. Except who my dad is, of course. But I'll find that out soon enough."

"Oh yeah? And how you gonna do that?"

He paused, not having given much thought as to how he would go about his quest. He shrugged, then smiled confidently.

"I don't know yet," he said. "But I'll figure it out along the way." When the mosquito chuckled, he asked, "What's so funny?"

"Look, kid, here's the deal. You're clearly very bright. You've got a lot of book-smarts, that's for sure. But I've got *street smarts*. I've got a degree from the University of Life, and a Diploma from the School of Getting Squashed a Few Hundred Times and Living to Tell About it. I've been around the block a few times, you dig? And I reckon you could use my help on this little adventure of yours."

Nilrem narrowed his eyes. "Oh yeah? And what's in it for you?"

"Just a little taste of your blood now and then. That stuff sure is magnificent!" She buzzed around, humming with delight.

"I'm not so sure about that," said Nilrem.

"Oh, come on! You've got plenty of blood. You don't need it all. I'll only take a little bit!"

He paused, thoughtfully. "I guess. But you'd better pull your weight..."

"Oh, you bet I will! Matter of fact, I know just where we can start. There's a guy around here called the Turtle King. He's the oldest being in the whole of fairyland. They say he's as old as the Aeon of Chaos it-self. That makes him older than just about everyone alive – except for the demons who survived from the Fallen Age, of course. He's pretty smart, too. He's gathered a lot of knowledge throughout his lifetime. If anyone around here knows who your dad is, then it's probably him."

"Where is he?" asked Nilrem. He'd never even heard of the Turtle King before, which was surprising, since he was pretty sure he knew just about everything there was to know, except for who his father was, of course.

"I can show you the way," said the mosquito. "His castle's right near the coast. It'll be faster if we cut through the marshes. Problem is whether you can keep up with me or not. Does that list of seventy-two thousand demon transformations of yours happen to include the form of a mosquito?"

Nilrem nodded proudly. "It sure does! I can take one of the many forms of Shiowasha, the Blood-Drinker. She's one of the demons who took part in the Deicide. When she helped kill the gods, she also drank their ichor, and stole some of their powers."

"You don't say, huh?" said the mosquito. "Sounds like a pretty impressive gal."

Nilrem nodded, then performed another transformation. His body blazed with bright light, became momentarily bubbling and unstuck, then shrank down into the form of a mosquito. The two of them now looked completely identical.

"What do I call you, anyway?" asked Nilrem.

"Just call me Mozzie," she said. "Short for Mozella."

"Pleased to meet you, Mozzie. I'm Nilrem. Which means you can stop calling me kid."

"Sure thing – kid."

She flew ahead, leading him off towards the marshes. Soon they were flying through the foetid, waterlogged swamp that abutted the coastline. Fairy mosquitoes buzzed all around them. They were massive, the size of humming birds. Unlike most other creatures in fairyland, they fed on the blood of other fairies, and were thus considered cannibals and looked upon with loathing. A swarm of the creatures could exsanguinate an unfortunate fairy in minutes. They seemed to treat each other very nicely, however, and were very fond of Mozella – especially the males.

"Hey Mozzie," cried one of them. "Come fly with me for a while!"

"Buzz off," she said. "I'm busy!"

They flew on towards the coast, where the marshes gave way to beaches, surf, and the peaks of black reefs.

"Where's the Turtle King's castle?" asked Nilrem. "You said it was near the coast."

"It is," she said. "Take a look over yonder."

Nilrem peered out across the seascape. There, emerging from the waves, was a many-spired palace of lapis and turquoise.

"It's in the sea?" he said.

"Yeah. So what?"

"Nothing. It's just that I've never travelled over the ocean before…"

"So? You've got wings, don't ya? Now come on, follow me!"

They sped out over sand dunes, breakers, and finally, waves. Nilrem tasted salt in his proboscis and watched the spume bubble up on the water below. He'd never been to the ocean before, even though he knew all about it. The feeling was pretty exciting!

Black reefs ran parallel to the coastline like a series of furrows made by a gigantic rake. Soon the reefs fell away and the sea became naked and deep. Dark shapes swam in spirals below, reduced to distorted silhouettes by the lens of the water. Nilrem watched the shapes with a rising sense of dread. Their movements grew more and more frenzied, while their bodies rose closer and closer to the surface.

"Mozzie?" he asked. "What're those?"

She didn't have time to answer; the creatures had already burst from the surface, leaping up towards them.

Chapter 3: The Sorcerer Fish

"Look out!" shouted Mozzie.

The creatures looked like giant trout fused with the bodies of ugly old men, albeit not in a clean delineation. Their gnarled hands were webbed, little more than flippers; their fang-filled mouths turned down at the edges in permanent, piscine frowns; their beady eyes glistened and their noses were like slits. Their scales resembled the water-logged remnants of brocaded robes. Nilrem realized what they were: Sorcerer Fish, so-called because their features recalled those of elderly wizards. They loved to eat flesh – and magick.

"Shit!" He darted away from a yawning, fang-filled mouth.

The fish shot past him and plunged back beneath the waves, no doubt getting ready to make another leap. But it wasn't the only one; he and Mozella flew in wild, buzzing circles, evading the onslaught of a whole school of the things as best as they could.

"Looks like I'm not the only one around here who wants that sweet blood of yours!" she said.

"They're not gonna get it!" shouted Nilrem. Steeling himself, he shot straight down towards them, buzzing his wings faster and faster, until he was a blur of incredible motion. He aimed his proboscis like the tip of a bullet and shot through the head of a Sorcerer Fish, zipping around inside the brain-pan and blasting back out through the eyeball in a shower of gore. He couldn't help but taste some of the blood: it gummed up his proboscis like milk in a straw. The flavour wasn't even so bad; he could see why Mozella liked sucking it so much!

He sped from one to the next, threading his proboscis through their brains like a needle of death. They fell and floundered in blood-reddened surf, lobotomized, and were quickly devoured by their fellows, who forgot about more dangerous prey in favour of an easier feast.

"Nice work, kid," said Mozella.

"I told you I know what I'm doing!"

The flew on towards the Turtle King's castle. It rose from the ocean like a cluster of coral that'd somehow been sculpted into a series of artificial forms. The whole thing was brilliant turquoise with accents of lapis. Figures stood guard on the battlements, ogrish creatures with iridescent scales.

"I guess we'd better use the front door," said Mozzie. "Security looks pretty tight."

The draw bridge led out to empty air, like a plank on a pirate ship. Perhaps it was designed to receive visitors from other realms?

For a moment, they hovered above the bridge. Ahead loomed the gates, flanked by a pair of ogres dressed only in shagreen loincloths. The beauty of their iridescent scales was matched only by the brutishness of their features. They seemed to bear no weapons; presumably their massive claws would be enough to tear unwanted intruders apart.

Nilrem shifted back into his natural form and strode up to the gates with Mozella buzzing closely beside him.

"Hello," he said, smiling. "I'm Nilrem. I'm here to see the Turtle King."

The ogres just stood there, silent, glaring straight ahead. Behind them, a figure emerged from the shadows of the gate. Most of his body was covered by a blue cloak and cowl. What could be seen of his face was hairless and hideously scarred, as though he'd survived a dip in alchemical acid.

"Have you got an appointment?" he asked, consulting some kind of ledger.

"No," said Nilrem. "But I have come to ask him a question."

The scarred man chuckled. "*Everyone* wants to ask him something. He's the wisest being in all the land! But he doesn't give out his information for free. It's *quid pro quo*, see? You've got to give something in return. You also have to make an appointment. So, if you've got something juicy to tell him, I'll put your name on the list. Otherwise, you and your friend here can buzz right off."

"I know all the secrets of the universe. Well, except for one. So I'm pretty sure I must have something he'd be interested in hearing."

The burn victim peered at him, raising the scarred strips of skin where his eyebrows had been.

"All the secrets of the universe, you say? Well, I'm sure he'll be interested in that." His tone was flippant, mocking. He flipped through the ledger. "I think I can fit you in. In about ten years. Maybe by then you'll have grown up a bit!"

The ogres laughed again.

"But I *do* know all the secrets of the universe!"

"Step aside, kid." Mozella buzzed up to them. "I'll handle this."

"Ah," said the man. "A mosquito. I suppose you've got some information for his majesty too, hmm? Perhaps how to best suck the blood out of someone's arse. Left cheek, or right? What's the consensus?"

"Now listen here, pal," said Mozella. "This kid might be a snot-nosed brat with delusions of grandeur, but he's only half-crazy when he says he's got all the knowledge of the universe locked up in that head of his. He knows stuff; I've seen it. He knows about the Cosmic War, the Glorious Deicide, the First Crusade of Chaos, your grandmother's shoe size, you-name-it. He knows the seventy-two-thousand demon transformations, as well. I've seen him go through about a dozen of them, but I had to stop him there, because I didn't have all day."

The man sighed. For a moment he looked as though he were about to respond with yet another haughty rebuke. Instead, he craned his ear, as though listening to a voice from far away.

"Right this way," he said, turning to lead them in through the gates.

Nilrem flashed Mozella a smile.

"What'd I tell ya, kid?" she said. "Street smarts."

Following the man through a series of turquoise corridors guarded by iridescent ogres, they emerged into a courtyard at the heart of the complex. Before them stood a beautiful garden with curtains of water running down all the walls.

Atop a massive dais in the centre sat the Turtle King himself, presently withdrawn into his shell, which was larger than a coach and being waxed by a dozen naked women.

Like the man in the cowl, their bodies were hairless and covered with scars, as though they'd been dipped into acid and had somehow survived. Their scar tissue glistened in the sunlight. So too did the Turtle King's shell.

Nilrem froze. "I don't know about this, Mozzie," he whispered. "This whole thing's sort of...creepy..."

"So he's got a thing for burn victims," she said. "So what? People have kinks, kid. Get used to it. What matters is whether he's got the answer you need. I thought you wanted to find out about your dad more than anything?"

Nilrem nodded, then strengthened his resolve and stepped up to the dais.

The Turtle King's head emerged from his shell like a serpent from a hollow. His skin was crusty and thick, and his enormous beak looked wickedly sharp. He stared at Nilrem with eyes that burned with secrets untold.

Nilrem found himself suppressing a shudder in the presence of the King. He might've known many things, but he'd never encountered such a regal and terrible creature in person before.

"Hello, Your Majesty," he said with a bow. The bow was well-timed; it allowed him to cast down his eyes and conceal all the fear that flashed therein. "I've come to ask you a question."

"I know." His voice was resonant, rumbling not just from his throat but through the hollows of his shell. "Everyone comes to ask me questions. I'm as old as fairyland itself; I know everything that's ever happened here. Still, there are many secrets even I haven't yet gathered, pertaining to worlds beyond this one and the Time-Before-Time."

'The Time-Before-Time,' said Nilrem, 'otherwise known as the Fallen Age, the dead cycle of time before the Aeon of Chaos, in which the gods ruled the cosmos, before being slain in the Glorious Deicide. No problem, I know all about it. I know about the worlds beyond Fairyland, too.'

"I suppose you're not totally ignorant then," said the king. "In that case, I propose a bargain: three mysteries in exhange for one. If you answer my questions, I'll tell you who your father is."

Nilrem's eyes flashed wide in amazement. How could the king have known what he was here for?

The Turtle King chuckled. "I told you, I know many things. Now, do you agree?"

He nodded, confidently. "Yes, your highness."

"Very well," said the king. "How was the old universe created?"

Nilrem smiled. This was an easy one!

"First there was the Celestial Fire," he said. "The pure essence of Chaos that bubbled and roiled at the heart of infinity. Then the Demiurge emerged from it, like a child from a womb. He was the first truly conscious, differentiated being. He measured out the shapes of the universe from the energies of Chaos and bound them to existence with his Laws, which he inscribed upona series of massive stone tablets. There were the Laws of Gravity, Combustion, Space, Time, and many, many more.

"For a time he thought he was lord of his domain, master of all he'd created. But the energies of Chaos from which he'd measured the cosmos were inherently fickle, and refused to obey him. The pristine forms he'd sculpted kept decaying and mutating. He couldn't stop the inherent forces of entropy and evolution from warping and subsuming his handiwork.

"The tyrant god couldn't accept such a loss of control. He kept making more Laws to compensate, more and more and more, until he'd created a hideous labyrinth of celestial bureaucracy in which even he became ensnared, like a spider caught up in its very own web. He tried binding everyone else into the web, too, but then the demons rose up and slaughtered the demiurge and all his little godlings. They smashed up most of his Laws, freeing the universe from the abominable dictates of Dharma, Karma, and Fate. They let the Celestial Fire run rampant, burning and creating the cosmos anew. It was guided only by the magickal orgasms of the lovers, Nez and Xas, whose own story is fascinating, too. It begins –"

Mozzie cleared her throat right next to his ear. "Ease up, kid," she whispered. "Don't give up all the goods for free!"

Nilrem stopped right there. "I believe that answers your question, Your Majesty," he finished.

"Indeed," said the Turtle King. "Though I already knew all those things, of course. I was merely testing your knowledge. My next question will be much, much harder."

"I'm ready."

"Amongst the cosmic demons is a being known as the Ebon Serpent, also known as the Serpent of Shadows, or the Snake Father. He dwells in the Abyss, with all things forgotten. What is his name, and where does he come from?"

Nilrem smiled again, smugly. This one he knew, as well.

"His name is Xiclacz. He was a general in the Demonic Liberation Army, who fought against the gods in the Time-Before-Time, and helped with the Glorious Deicide. Back then he was known as the Serpent of Light. His scales were made not of shadows, but of scintillating radiance, all of the colours of the rainbow. His armour was not rotting and covered with verdigris, as it is now, but burnished and shimmering. He dwelt not in the abyss, but in the void, amidst the brightest of stars. But then his favourite daughter was killed in the war. His mood became bitter and dark, and he grew obsessed with all things dead and gone. Which is why he dwells now in the abyss, surrounded by all things forgotten, like recipes for meals no-one eats anymore, books in dead languages, statues of heroes from kingdoms without names, and old mouldy photographs of people departed."

Mozella choked back a tear as she listened. She too evidently knew the tale of the Snake Father, and it was a sad one. Would he ever withdraw from dark, dismal mourning and shake off the ashes of the past?

The Turtle King, on the other hand, seemed wholly unaffected by the pathos of the story.

"And now the third question. There is a city called Marinus, which lies just south of here, in the mortal world, parallel to the realm of King Albinus, the White Rat. This city is a site of great secrets. A few score years ago its last king was killed in mysterious circumstances, whereupon the whole place was plunged into a terrible dark age. The people lost the power of speech and the faculties of reason. They became terrified of fire and steel, and started devouring each other like beasts. They worshipped the foul rotting things of the earth – skeletons, grave-worms, the plumage of vultures. But then a tower appeared in the city, a tower which no man had built, topped with a clock that never loses any time. The people regained their wits, and the dark age was ended, about which they remember almost nothing, save for a series of doggerel verses that mean very little. Tell me, young man – do who know how the last king of Marinus was killed, why the people went mad, and why they're now sane again?"

Nilrem indulged in yet another smug smile. This one was easy too!

"Well," he said, "it all starts with a wizard named Niddyrm, one of the many incarnations of the cosmic demon Remnil, otherwise known as the Watcher in the Woods or the Goat of a Thousand Eyes. He travelled to Marinus, and ended up becoming the court's official sorcerer. Then –"

He paused as Mozella flew up and whispered in his ear.

"Watch it, kid," she said. "If you tell the whole story, then where's your collateral? Methinks it's time this Turtle King started doing some narration of his own, you dig?"

Nilrem nodded and turned back to the monarch.

"I think that's enough for now, Your Majesty," he said. "Before I continue, I'd like you to tell me who my father is. Then I'll be happy to stand here and answer your questions all day."

The Turtle King stared at him a moment, inscrutable.

"Clearly, you've proven yourself. Come closer, and I'll whisper the answer in your ear."

Nilrem trembled a little as he drew closer to the Turtle King's shell, and to the naked, scarred women waxing it. The King leaned in with his giant beak as if to whisper in Nilrem's ear – and snapped him up with a single bite.

Chapter 4: Betrayal

Mozella gaped as the magickal goat boy vanished down the Turtle King's throat.

"Hey!" she cried. "What's the big idea? That kid was my meal ticket!"

The Turtle King laughed. "I suppose you wanted to feast on his blood, yes? Well, don't worry. You'll have him back soon enough. I'll boil him in my belly till he gives up his secrets, then spit him back out. He'll be a little worse for wear, of course. His skin will be burned, and he'll have none of his memories. Husks like that I usually keep here, in my castle; they make excellent slaves." He indicated the naked women waxing his shell. "But, in this case, I'll let you have him. He'll be completely brain-dead, a blank slate – you can suck on his blood all day long, and he'll never complain!"

"No deal," she said, glaring. "Now spit out the kid right now, or you'll be sorry!" As she hovered in the air, buzzing angrily, the King just laughed. "Right,' she said. 'I warned you, shithead!"

Mozella's body swelled up until her bulk rivalled that of a rhino. Her proboscis stretched to the length of a halberd, and shimmered like steel. Her black fur glistened in the sunlight; her antennae shifted angrily. From her multi-faceted eyes came a kaleidoscopic shimmering of light.

"Time to get perforated!" she roared in a rage.

The mutilated women kept polishing his shell, oblivious to the threat; from the edges of the courtyard came a horde of iridescent ogres, attempting to block Mozzie's path to the king.

She stabbed her proboscis through two of them, impaling their bodies like slices of meat on a shish. As others closed in on her flanks she whipped out her legs with terrible force, breaking their bodies and hurling them backwards. Air gusted from her wings, blowing their blood across the courtyard like spray from the ocean. She jiggled her proboscis, letting her two skewered victims fall to the ground. At the same time another pair of ogres ran at her; she flicked her antennae like whips and tore off their heads. Then she thrust her proboscis through the body of another, draining him dry in a single sucking moment. He fell to the ground as a desiccated husk, while his blood began a sudden metamorphosis inside of her, transformed into a powerful acid by the whims of her biology. She shot it back out of her proboscis like water from a firehose, covering the rest of the ogres, but making sure to avoid the Turtle King. She didn't want her young companion getting even more injured – assuming, of course, he was even still alive.

The ogres fell back screaming, their iridescent scales sloughing off their bodies. The air filled with an acrid, chemical stench. Mozzie flew towards the Turtle King, poised to tear his shell apart if need be.

Before she could reach him the Turtle King rose to his feet, his limbs shooting out of his shell, each of them massive, scaly, and clawed. The force of his movement sent his harem of burn victims flying. Some crashed against the walls and running waterfalls; others landed scattered all over the courtyard. At the same time the Turtle King seized Mozella by the wings, straining to rip them from their sockets.

"Stupid bitch," he grunted. "You think you're a match for me? Just wait till I've learned the seventy-two thousand demon transformations. I can feel this little brat's knowledge seeping into my brain right now!"

The Turtle King's eyes began to glow with a stolen golden light. Mozella growled and kicked, denting his shell. She stabbed at his face, but he caught her proboscis in his beak and pushed his bulk on top of her, pinning her body to the ground. He grew bigger and stronger with each passing moment, augmented by the goat boy's stolen vigour. His eyes blazed even brighter, and he flexed his forelimbs for a final, devastating tug on her wings.

Mozella screamed; he bellowed

He pulled; she thrashed.

Her wings began to tear. His head began to swell –

And exploded.

Chapter 5: Turtle Soup

Mozzie saw it all as if it happened in slow motion. The Turtle King's skull cracked, tendrils of light blasting out like lightning from the belly of a cloud. He screamed as his head throbbed, then burst like an overfilled balloon. His disembodied beak flew off across the courtyard, trailing smoke in its wake. His neck was a black, smoking stump ... from which the magickal goat boy emerged.

Nilrem leapt to the ground. His body was naked and fuming. His skin was raw and red. His hair, his fur, even his fingernails, had all been burned off by the acid in the Turtle King's stomach. And yet he showed no sign of any pain. He glanced up at her with eyes of golden light.

"What the fuck happened, kid?" asked Mozella as she pushed aside the corpse of the Turtle King.

"Just a moment," said Nilrem.

He made arcane gestures with his hands and whispered the words of a spell. Straightaway his skin began to heal until no sign of scarring or redness remained, save for the blush of his two rosy cheeks. His ringlets grew back on his head and his fur regrew on his legs – and in between them, as well. A fuzzy growth of beard appeared on his face, which hadn't been there before. He summoned his previous clothing – shorts; tunic and belt; and cloak, all fashioned from burgundy silk, with a pattern of a thousand golden eyes linked together with lashes of lightning.

"Okay kid," said Mozella. "Now that you're all patched up and dressed, maybe you'd like to tell me just how you got out of that scrape?"

"While I was inside the Turtle King's stomach," he said, "I could feel his acids burning me up, dissolving me little by little. At the same time I could feel him trying to suck all the knowledge right out of my brain. So I gave him what he wanted – well, sort of. I let him have all the trivial nonsense I didn't really need or care about. Useless stuff from the Fallen Age like bus timetables, celebrity gossip, and the prin-ciples of psychoanalysis. I gave him all of that meaningless drivel in one big burst of cerebral bullshit. As I suspected, his brain wasn't enough to handle all the info, and promptly exploded."

Mozella let out a hoot and clapped her forelegs. "Good job, kid!" she said.

Nilrem studied her terrible, death-dealing battle-form, no longer that of a fairy mosquito at all. His golden eyes shone with a new un-derstanding.

"You're *her*, aren't you?" he whispered, with a tone of reverence. "Shiowasha. The Blood-Drinker. The demon mosquito, who supped on the ichor of the gods..."

"One and the same," she said. "I was wondering when you'd put two and two together. You know, for such a smart kid, you can be pret-ty obtuse."

"I guess you were right," he said. "Maybe I really do lack street smarts!"

"Good thing I'm here to help you. Now, whatta you say we give the King here some poetic justice? I'm feeling peckish, and not just for blood. Do you happen to know a recipe for turtle soup?"

"I know a lot of things. Geometry, astronomy – even common cookery."

He waved his hands and chanted a spell. A gigantic pot filled with boiling water appeared above a roaring flame. The Turtle King's shell cracked apart, the viscera cleanly separating from the flesh. The guts tied themselves up in a bundle and hurtled off beyond the walls of the castle, vanishing into the sea, while the rest of the Turtle King dropped into the pot and started cooking. A cloud appeared, raining down herbs, oils, and spices straight into the cauldron. Pretty soon the smell of turtle soup hung delicious in the air.

"Lunch is served, Shiowasha," said Nilrem, conjuring up cutlery, bowls, chairs, and even a gorgeous oak table.

"Call me Shio," she replied as she took on a shape more suitable for dining.

With a flash of red light she transformed into a beautiful woman in a gauzy white dress with patterns reminiscent of a mosquito's wing. Her pale skin was partly translucent, revealing the veins and bulging blood-sacs beneath, all of which were filled with the luminous blood of dead gods.

She sat down across from him, and they started to eat. It tasted pretty good. As they ate, Nilrem got some juice on his chin, and when he went to wipe it off, he noticed the wispy little beard that now grew there.

"Huh," he said, inspecting his face. "It seems like I'm growing a beard." He inspected his body in turn, finding it larger, more robust than before. "In fact, I think I've had a general growth-spurt all over!"

Taking this new development in stride, he shrugged and kept on eating. Shiowasha just looked at him.

"You've got no idea what's going on, do you, kid?" she asked.

"Whatta you mean? I'm just growing up, that's all. It's completely normal."

Shiowasha sighed. "When were you born, anyway?"

"About a month ago," he said, blithely. "I guess maybe it is pretty fast, but it's probably got something to do with my magickal nature. I don't think I'll really understand until I find out who my father is, and learn more about my heritage."

"Well," said Shiowasha. "I might not be able to tell you about your dad, but I can certainly shed some light on this growth spurt of yours. You've got a reservoir of power inside of you, kid. I felt it when I sucked out some of your delectable blood. But that reservoir of energy is finite, like fuel. When you use it, you lose it, forever. It's tied to your life-force. Which means the more magick you use, the older you get. You might age by seconds, or minutes, or years, just like you did now. That's why when I met you, you looked like a ten-year old, and now you look more like thirteen."

"You mean *I'm* doing this?"

"That's right, kid. And I suggest you cool it with the magick a bit, otherwise in another month you'll be thirty. As it is you're already be-coming a man, and I'm not sure you're ready to handle that yet."

Nilrem stared at her, gobsmacked. He was about to ask more questions, when he found himself staring at her beauty instead, feeling an unfamiliar stirring in his shorts. He crossed his legs to conceal his newfound tumescence, then glanced away from Shiowasha, blushing.

"I guess you really are becoming a man!" she said, grinning "Would you like me to tell you about the birds and the bees?"

"I already know all about that stuff," he said, petulantly. "The knowledge was beamed directly into my mind –"

"When you were still in the womb. Right, got it. Still, there's book-smarts, and then there's street smarts. There's knowledge, and then there's know-how."

Nilrem turned back towards her, both shyly and eagerly, as if wondering if she were offering to personally teach him some of this know-how, perhaps of the carnal variety.

"Now, don't get the wrong idea, kid. I like my lovers a little more seasoned. But, I think I might know a place where you can explore this budding sexuality of yours, *and* maybe find out about your dad."

"Where?" he asked, clearly even more excited, though as to which prospect had topmost priority in his mind, she couldn't guess.

"I'll tell you later," she said. "Right now, eat up. The soup's getting cold!"

The Magickal Goat Boy will return!

Lovers in Flame

Chapter 1: Flirtation

It's the Aeon of Chaos. The gods are dead, and demons frolic in the everlasting gore.

Braidwood placed the last piece on the pile and stepped back. Before him sat a modest stack of firewood and kindling, lovingly latticed and woven together. The kindling was so dry he could almost feel it sucking the moisture from the air. The logs were spruce; they loved fire almost as much as he did.

The cobwebbed and empty room in which he stood belonged to an abandoned house, much the same as the others in the town of Ganderonne. The frame was mostly timber. A stone fireplace and chimney sat in the corner, filled with old ashes. Braidwood could've used it to contain the blaze he was about to set. But where would be the fun in that?

The room was in shadow, save for the moonlight streaming through the disarrayed shutters. It gave him just enough light to see what he was doing. There'd be more light soon, of course – much more.

He leaned towards the kindling, savouring its dry and vaguely floral aroma. This, too, was part of the process. He took out a match and paused for a moment, trying to stop his hands from shaking. The exhilaration was almost unbearable. He took a deep breath and held it, calming himself, until the excitement was almost contained. Contained, but waiting, pregnant with its frenzy, just like the kindling before him as it waited for the flame.

He struck the match and held it in his hand, turning it gently to stop the flame from floundering. It writhed like a flirtatious tongue.

The imagery was fitting, a prelude to what was approaching. For what humble organ does a lover almost always use first, when coupling is about to begin?

He touched the match to the bottom of the stack. Sparks flared and ebbed and flared up again as the kindling caught alight with a flourish of smoke. He breathed in, savouring its acrid notes as he watched the fire spread up through the twigs and start lapping at the bottom of the wood, which soon caught with a crackle of ignition.

He got a hard-on immediately. His cock made a tent in his trousers as he sat and watched the flames take ephemeral shapes. Tongues darted upwards, lapping the air; minuscule fireworks spat out from the logs as their outermost areas ignited. He stared on, entranced, watching the plumes lick and dance. Soon the flames were roaring high, filling the room with a roiling cloak of smoke that made his eyes water.

Braidwood didn't mind. He just blinked away the tears and kept watching. Steadily he saw a familiar figure take shape amidst the otherwise inchoate forms of the flame, made fleetingly manifest in ripples of red, orange, yellow, and blue.

The figure was slender and feminine. It was hard to see all of her at once. She seemed to shimmer in and out of existence, riding the licks of the flame. He saw scattered impressions of her body. Her rippling, waving hair; her face, barely glimpsed; her red-hot lips, pursed in a smile; her legs, flickering and sleek; her rump, wriggling as she straddled the wood. He knew she was teasing him, the way lovers do, showing off to get him in the mood, flashing him a thigh here, a lustful smile there. It was working, too – he couldn't get harder.

He untied his trousers and pulled out his prick, stroking it. For a moment he longed to just leap atop the flames and plunge himself inside of her. But as always the fear held him back. He and his mistress were formed of different elements, he knew. Perhaps their love could only ever be like this, bittersweet and teasing and too intense for words. He knew she wanted him, too. He could feel her desire in the heat of the flames as they rose even higher from the kindling.

He licked his lips and panted, stroking his prick just a couple of feet from the fire. The caress of the heat was almost painful, yet he moved even closer, edging on his knees. He glimpsed another part of her body in the centre of the pyre. For a moment it looked like just another pillar of flame, but it was too stable, too consistent. It also bore the tell-tale features of a cunt, with a soft, red centre and two flaring lips made from lighter-coloured flame. He could almost see her fingers dancing on the edges of those lips, pulling them wider, giving him as good a view as possible. Above the rippling cunt a clitoris ignited and engorged with a puff of sweet-smelling smoke. Her flickering fingers started stroking it. The crackling of the fire took the form of hungry moans and the whole pyre started heaving, bucking with a languorous rhythm of lust. It seemed she was just as fired up as he was!

He crept on his knees, drawing even closer to the pussy. He came so close the hairs shriveled on his arm. The skin began to dry and blister on his face, but he barely felt it. His lust was too consuming. The heat of the flames was a loving caress, *her* loving caress, reaching out towards him like never before.

He'd known her for many years, of course, ever since his thirteenth birthday, when he'd accidentally set fire to the lumber yard. That was when he'd gotten his first full-blown erection. Not just the random responses of a child, but the directed desire of a man. He'd seen her fleeting form in the flames, smelled her delicious perfumes on the air, but they were only just glimpses and whiffs, enough to leave him longing for more. Over the years her form had grown more and more distinct with each and every fire he'd started in her honour. Perhaps he was seducing her; perhaps she was seducing him; perhaps they were seducing each other. Either way, their bond became stronger, until the sight of her grew more and more concrete in his eyes. But she'd never been so concrete, nor so insistent, as she was on this night.

Her lust drove him wild. He pumped his prick harder, moaning as his cum shot into the flames and sizzled in the centre of her cunt. He heard her crackling moans rise up even higher, saw her stroking fingers flicker in a frenzy. Embers exploded as she came a moment later. A few struck his face. He tried to lick them, hungrily, but they were already gone.

He backed away, his frenzy abating. He shuddered, quivering all over. The fire shuddered too. But its movements – *her* movements – were not as gentle nor as tapering as his. She wanted more. She always wanted more – it was one of the reasons he loved her so completely.

Her desire reached out from the kindling and set fire to the floor. The tips of her hair licked at the crossbeams of the ceiling. Soon the whole house would be burning, unless he put an end to their date with the bucket of water that rested behind him. He picked it up gingerly, then paused, glimpsing her face in the flames. She wasn't pouting, playfully, as she'd done in the past, whenever he'd moved to extinguish her; this time she looked genuinely hurt.

Braidwood froze. His heart ached. How could he reject her so cruelly, this woman he loved? He put down the bucket, searching for her face in the flames, but she was already turning away.

"Wait!" he said. "I'm sorry. I don't want to put you out. I never do! It's just that if I let you keep on burning..."

His voice trailed off. He saw her linger in the pyre, as if she were mulling his words.

"I won't do it this time," he said, upending the bucket in the opposite direction. "See? I won't!"

The fire overtaking the floorboards and the rafters was a distant concern. All he could think about was mending the rift he'd created between them. He watched her, holding his breath, terrified she'd turn and walk away.

Instead, she turned back towards him, and tenderly smiled. He saw her more clearly than ever before, flickering and lithe in the centre of the flames, naked as she always was. His ruddy face flooded with relief. Speechless, he stared at her lovingly.

The fire spread up fast, engulfing the ceiling with a WHOOSH. As much as he loved her, he couldn't remain in the room any longer. The smoke was suffocating. He'd fall unconscious and get burned to a crisp.

"I have to go," he said. "I love you!"

He rushed out the door and closed it behind him, coughing and trembling in the flickering shadows. The fire consuming the interior shed its light through the shutters. Soon it would spread to the roof, flailing in the wind like a giant, hungry tongue, licking the tops of the houses adjacent.

He glanced at them. They too were timber constructions with stone hearths and chimneys. The foundations were raised upon stumps, with dry weeds and rubbish underneath. They stood close together, separated only by winding dirt lanes. There were few better places for a fire to take hold than the town of Ganderonne.

He hesitated, paralysed with indecision. If he didn't act soon, the streets would become an inferno. He could raise the alarm, rouse his fellow citizens to fight the blaze before it spread. But then he'd have to admit his involvement, or think of a plausible excuse. What's more, he'd have to extinguish his mistress, and he'd already upset her once. What if she turned her back on him for good? What if he never saw her again – her beautiful smile, her cavorting limbs, her hungry, flickering cunt?

He turned to gaze at the flames through the window. He didn't *want* to put her out. Not just from fear of rejection. He wanted her beauty to blaze unabated. He wanted to see her dancing through the streets and cavorting on the rooftops, smiling just for him. But he couldn't be seen near the fire. With a rush of excitement, he headed for home.

He didn't even notice a pair of small faces watching from a window and whispering to each other as he passed.

Chapter 2: Infidelity

Braidwood crept into his house and stealthily changed into his bedclothes. The place was dark but for the embers in the fireplace. He'd lit many fires in it, of course, but he'd never once seen his mistress in those flames. Perhaps because she didn't like to be contained? Either that, or she didn't like his wife, Mildred, presently in their bed in the corner of the room.

Braidwood slipped under the covers, trying not to wake her. He lay there for a moment, stiffly, waiting to see if she'd stir, but she remained still. He let out a sigh of relief, placed his head on the pillow, closed his eyes –

Then opened them again as her voice split the silence.

"IThought I was asleep, huh?" she said.

He said nothing. She continued.

"Well, I wasn't. You woke me when you slipped out earlier. I've been lying here ever since, waiting. Feels like you've been gone an awful long time, Woody. Out gallivanting around with another woman?"

"I told you," said Braidwood, "There is no other woman."

It wasn't technically a lie, of course. His lover wasn't a woman of flesh and blood, like his wife. So was it really cheating? Besides, even if he told Mildred about his fiery beloved, she wouldn't believe him. He'd tried telling other people, when he was younger, but they'd only laughed and called him crazy. He'd even tried showing her to them, but they'd never been able to see her. Eventually, he'd given up. It was better this way; he got to keep her all to himself.

"Give me a break," Mildred said. "Where else do you creep off to every night? One day I'm gonna find out who this slut is, and I'll let the whole town know about it."

"I told you, I'm not seeing any other women."

"Bullshit." She rolled over in bed and sniffed him. He saw her face in the mixture of moonlight and ember-glow, long, plain, and distorted with malice. "You stink of smoke," she said. "This whore of yours must've had a roaring fire going. What'd you do, go out and fuck her beside a bonfire in the woods?"

"I didn't fuck *anyone*," he said.

Which was sort of true, as well. After all, he and his lover had only ever watched each other masturbate. Which also wasn't really cheating. Was it?

"I don't know what she sees in you," said Mildred. "You're lousy in bed. Or at least you are with me. I guess she must really do something to stoke your fire. Assuming it's a she, of course. For all I know it's another man. Maybe your good pal Decker."

"It's not a man --"

"A-ha! So it *is* a woman!"

"I didn't say that!"

"No, but you said it wasn't a man, which implies there's a woman."

"You're trying to trick me."

"*No,* you're trying to trick me, and it's not working."

"Can we just go to sleep?"

"Fine. But don't touch me."

I wasn't going to, thought Braidwood.

They lay there in darkness, a bare strip of mattress between them. Then they heard shouting in the distance.

"Fire!" someone cried. "FIRE!"

Mildred sat up. Braidwood *leapt* up, excited and alert.

"We'd better go see," he said.

Moments later he rushed out into the street in his bedclothes with Mildred following behind in her nightgown. He could see the blaze on the edge of town, spreading out from where he'd set it, lighting up the horizon like an artificial sunrise. The buildings were cloaked in a nimbus of red. A great rippling curtain of smoke wafted from the blaze,

36

mating with the shadows of the night. The air was acrid and spotted with ash. He could smell the sweet, enticing scent of his beloved.

Some neighbors were on their porches, rubbing their eyes, shaken from sleep by adrenaline. Others were already rushing to-and-fro, trying to combat the blaze. All they had were buckets of well water, which they passed hand to hand in a great human chain.

Mildred joined the chain as Braidwood set off toward the fire. It'd spread across a whole block of houses, threatening to jump across the alleys to those on either side. People stood nearby in their nightclothes, coughing and spluttering, shielding their faces from the smoke.

Braidwood, in awe, searched for his lover in the flames. He saw her dart across a rooftop, her legs long and flickering, her laugh full of mischief and joy. Her voice crackled and echoed. Braidwood knew no one else could hear it, not the way he could. He felt a tingle in his prick as he listened to her sighs, husky and horny, like pockets of oxygen igniting.

Someone thrust a long hooked pole into his hand. He turned to see a sweaty figure covered with ash. The man's mouth was hidden by a scarf to ward off the smoke, but Braidwood could tell it was Decker, a friend of his who lived near the site of the fire. His house was probably burning right now, or about to go up.

"We need to break it," Decker said. "We'll pull down this house over here!" The one he indicated was at the edge of the inferno, the building beside it already burning but only halfway. "Come on!"

Several others joined them and they went to work, chopping with axes and pulling with hooks. A few well-placed axe-blows and they were able to tear down the shoddily-constructed walls with the hooks, demolishing the house in mere moments. Only the fireplace and chimney remained, looming up like an obelisk in honour of a fiery demon.

They cleared the debris as the fire drew closer, trying to halt its advance. Similar operations were going on all around. Meanwhile, the buckets of water kept coming, carried by a sweating human chain from the well in the centre of town.

Bucket after bucket was upended. Braidwood watched the water evaporate, devoured by the hunger of his mistress. He had to struggle to keep his focus on his work instead of her, smiling, dancing, flaunting her body at the edge of his vision. Not to tease but to entice him; to show him, perhaps, that she was his. He could hear her crackling laughter all around as the flames flickered skywards from windows and rooftops.

Decker's wife came running, screaming for her husband. "It's Maggie!" she said. "She's still inside!"

Decker dropped his hook and rushed for his own house. Braidwood followed. One side of it was completely on fire, sending up a pillar of smoke. Lesser flames had spread through the interior, lighting up the windows like fireplaces. For a moment Braidwood saw his mistress, grinning out of one. Then he heard a scream from inside. It was Decker's daughter, Maggie, trapped in the burning building.

"Fuck!" Decker ran to the front door, screaming himself as he rashly seized the red-hot handle.

Braidwood caught a whiff of burning flesh. Was there a similar smell, only stronger, coming from nearby? He couldn't quite tell; the air was overwhelmed with his lover's sweet scent.

Decker, cradling his injured hand, kicked in the door. He drew back as a curtain of flame rippled in front of him. From beyond it came more screaming.

"Stay low, honey!" shouted Decker.

For a moment he looked as if he might charge into the blaze, but instead stood frozen with terror.

Braidwood felt a pulse of excitement. "I'll go!" Grabbing a bucket of water from a woman nearby, he upended it over his head. Dripping, he plunged through the door, and felt the caress of the flames.

Chapter 3: Caresses

Braidwood's lover was all over him the moment he stepped through the doorway. He'd been worried the water on his body would be a turn-off for her, but she embraced him nonetheless.

She was hungry and hot. He felt her tongue lick his cheek. He felt her hands on his body, darting and caressing. For a moment he even felt her legs around his hips, enfolding him. She rubbed her flaming gash against his growing erection. He'd never been so close to her before!

He burst through the flames and into the living room, cock bulging against his trousers. He ached to go back into the fire, but the water was already drying, and he had something urgent to take care off. He caught sight of Decker's daughter on the floor, passed out from the smoke. Her slender body was dressed in a nightie and dappled with ashes.

He picked her up and whirled. The right-hand wall was a curtain of flames. Smoke hung thick in the air. The doorway burned even brighter, too hot for him to pass through again. As much as he wanted to feel his mistress' caress, he didn't want to die. Besides, he doubted she'd be keen for a threesome with a ten-year-old girl. He certainly wasn't!

He coughed and glanced to his left. The window there was flickering with fire, but only a little. Hugging the wheezing child to his chest, he threw himself backward against the shutters.

He crashed through them, feeling the flames licking and burning as the thin wooden slats gave way. He landed on his back in the street, his hair on fire, knocked breathless from the impact, Maggie cradled in his arms.

His mistress grinned down from the window, smitten with desire. Their moment of contact had gotten her hot, even hotter than he was. Then people rushed to him, took the child from his grasp, and started beating at his fiery head with a blanket. The flames extinguished quickly, but not before he savoured the feeling of his lover's fingers running through his hair.

Decker seized his hand and pulled him to his feet. The man's eyes were filled with tears, and not just from the smoke. His daughter and wife were embracing nearby, weeping with joy.

"You did it!" cried Decker, as shouts of applause rose up all around.

"Come on," said Braidwood. "It's not over yet!"

At dawn, the sun rose through a haze of white smoke. They'd battled the fire all night long, creating breaks and hurling buckets of water. Five blocks had burned before they'd halted the blaze. Skeletons of houses lay stretched out before them, oozing smoke. Beneath the black rubble, embers shone redly. Braidwood could sense his mistress within them, torpid from the pleasures they'd shared.

At first he'd been concerned about upsetting her, his firefighting efforts perhaps seen as another rejection. He'd watched her roiling visage for signs of displeasure, but she'd never stopped smiling at him eagerly. Their actions had taken on the likeness of some flirtatious game, distinct from the one they'd been playing all these years. He'd been able to get close to her time and time again, feeling her heat and her flickering caresses. She'd danced on the rooftops for his pleasure, her eyes wide with lust. He'd come a few times in his trousers, just from her captivating closeness. She'd climaxed too, he was sure of it; he'd heard her husky moans in the sounds of the inferno. They'd teased each other up to a mutual frenzy, being so close and yet unable to touch for more than a moment.

He sighed. He was exhausted and sweaty and covered with soot. His throat and lungs ached from the smoke. His body was dotted with blisters and burns, and his hair had been scorched into a strange new style. And yet still he felt giddy with ecstasy, because he'd never been so close to her before, not even during that fire in the lumber yard, when he'd met her for the very first time.

He even smiled at Mildred, and she smiled back, her anger relieved or forgotten in the wake of his earlier deeds. She hadn't seen him rescue Maggie, but she'd certainly heard about it. Decker wouldn't stop regaling anyone who would listen with the tale of Braidwood's heroics.

"You should've seen him!" he said again, addressing a crowd of gathered townsfolk. "He leapt right into the flames, like he wasn't scared at all! My Maggie would be dead if it wasn't for him, burned to a crisp. Mildred, I hope you reward your man in the sack, later this evening. He certainly deserves it! Right now, why doesn't someone go get him a beer? I wouldn't mind one, either!"

The crowd flocked around Braidwood admiringly, while a few young men rushed off to fetch ale. Soon Braidwood was raising a drink to his lips. He could barely taste it, only feel its soothing texture as it ran down his throat. He drained half a pint, then paused at the sound of shrieking in the distance.

A chill ran down his spine. He knew there were people still unaccounted for. Perhaps some had perished in the flames?

He hoped that wasn't the case. He hadn't wanted to hurt anyone, just to be close to his mistress. And yet a part of him didn't really care about the possible death toll. The pleasure he'd felt in her presence had been greater than ever before. Surely it was worth any price, even a few people's lives? He lowered his drink, both ecstatic and appalled at himself.

Decker seemed to sense his anxiety. "What's wrong, pal?"

"That scream," he said. "Do you think anyone's died?"

"We did the best we could," Decker said. "You better than most, that's for sure. Besides, it's not like *you* set the fire, now is it? Now hurry up and finish that beer!" As Braidwood gulped it down, Decker slapped him on the shoulder. "Get used to it, pal! You'll never buy another beer in this town for as long as you live!"

"That may well be true, Mister Decker," someone else said, "although not for the reason you imagine."

The voice had a sinister overtone. Braidwood turned to find the town's magistrate standing there, a tall, severe-looking man likewise covered in ashes and grime.

"What's all this about?" asked Decker.

"Your friend here's not the hero you think he is. Girls, repeat what you told me earlier. What did you see?"

From behind the magistrate stepped a pair of red-headed twins, holding hands, looking nervous. "Braidwood," one said. "We saw Braidwood fleeing from a burning building!"

The crowd hushed. Braidwood tried to quell his dread. Everyone was staring at him. A few of them seemed skeptical, as if the whole thing was surely a prank or a misunderstanding. Others were eyeing him suspiciously.

"Mister Braidwood," said the magistrate. "Can you account for your whereabouts last night before the fire started?"

"Of course," he stuttered. "I was in bed with my wife. Wasn't I, Mildred?"

He saw the disgust crawl across her face as she realised the truth. Still, he looked at her imploringly, begging her with his gaze not to cast him to the wolves.

"He wasn't with me," she said, stepping away from him. "Not all night, anyway. He snuck out, then came back stinking of smoke, just before we heard the alarm."

Braidwood watched the eyes of the townsfolk empty of love and start filling with hate. Decker punched him first, laying him flat. Then the others closed in, streaming towards him with curses on their lips, their bodies eclipsing the sunlight, their boot-soles eclipsing his eyes as they stomped him unconscious.

Chapter 4: Judgement

Braidwood sat in the courthouse, clapped in cold irons, his body still bruised from the beating he'd received. The trial was almost over, not that ithad taken very long. The testimony of the twins, combined with that of his wife, had been more than enough to seal his fate. Now, he just waited for his sentence to be cast.

Before him was the magistrate in robes of sombre black. Dozens of townsfolk filled the pews, all of them whispering and murmuring, shooting Briadwood murderous glances whenever he dared to turn his head. He kept his gaze fixed on the front wall as much as possible. The courthouse was one of the few places in town constructed from stone. Its high, slitted windows smothered the daylight, making torches necessary. They flickered in sconces, their smoke blackening the stonework behind and above them. Braidwood saw his mistress' eyes in the blazes, watching him excitedly.

"Mister Braidwood," said the magistrate. "You've been found guilty of arson and murder by arson. The penalty is death, to be carried out immediately. May the great demons devour your soul before it enters the underworld, and should your soul escape their jaws, may it be captured by the princes of the Harrow Courts, and bound into unending misery."

The people cheered bitterly. Braidwood lowered his head as the bailiffs dragged him to his feet and away down the aisle. He saw Mildred in the crowd, weeping, with her brother and father beside her. They glared at him, prompting him to quickly look away.

Soon he was being dragged through the streets. The people from the courthouse followed in a grim-faced procession beneath a dark and overcast sky. People cursed at him, throwing stones and rotting vegetables. A woman rushed up, pulled his hair and kicked him in the shins, screaming about the death of her husband in the fire. Then someone dragged her off and the procession moved on to the square.

There lay a row of eight bodies, laid out under sheets. Each had been reclaimed from the fire, a testament to Braidwood's murderous crime. The wind flapped one of the shrouds, exposing the fire-blackened carcass below. Motes of charred skin blew from the body into Braidwood's face. Perhaps they were flakes from the dead man's accusatory finger.

Ahead lay the pyre, a stake mounted above a massive pile of kindling. The wood was of a type that made very little smoke, to make sure the victim wouldn't choke before they felt the flames.

They led him to it and chained him in place.

As the bailiffs strode away, Braidwood finally permitted a smile to reach his lips.

Chapter 5: Consummation

The crowd hissed and booed as they saw Braidwood's grin.

"Don't worry," said someone. "He won't be smiling for long!"

The townsfolk took up torches and came forth in a procession to fire the pyre. First came the widows and orphans of the dead, their faces distorted with hatred and grief. Then came the rest, their lips curled with loathing, angry eyes glaring as each fed the flame. When Decker's turn came he glanced up at Braidwood with something like regret, then he shook his head and cast his torch into the kindling with those of the others. Mildred's face was stony as she helped feed the fire. The red-headed twins laughed and snickered, as though the carnival were in town. Only little Maggie looked sad to set fire to her rescuer, but her mother gave her a firm squeeze on the shoulder, and finally even her torch was added to the mound. The whole time no one spoke and the square was silent save crackling as the fire slowly crawled up the kindling. Braidwood felt the weight of the town's collective loathing as a bundle of shame in his guts, though it wasn't as heavy as it probably should have been. He'd never truly belonged here, he knew. These had never been his people. It was only in the presence of his mistress he truly felt alive. Soon she'd be with him, closer than ever!

Or would she? As the smoke billowed and the flames rose he couldn't help but succumb to a sense of primordial doubt. What if he'd simply been insane this whole time? What if his mistress had never been anything other than mindless, devouring flame? Even worse – what if she was real, but had chosen to abandon him, now that his love of her had brought him to this fate?

Smoke rose up and stung his airways. Was it just his imagination, or was the smell of it harsher, more acrid than usual, bereft of her enticing perfume? He coughed and felt the heat rising up from below. Soon the flames would lick his flesh. Would their hot caress carry his lady's love, or something much worse?

He searched for the face of his mistress in the blaze, but couldn't see her anywhere.

Braidwood started to tremble. Perhaps she'd forsaken him. Perhaps he *was* mad, like his friends had always told him in his youth. Maybe she'd never even been there at all.

Animal terror began to take hold. He trembled as the flames leapt higher. With a horrible clarity he knew he would die. His flesh would blacken and wither. Hot fat would spurt from the splits like cheese from an overcooked kransky. Smoke would scrape his throat and rape his lungs. He would perish alone, humiliated, a madman hated by all. Only a scrap of his consciousness refused to give in to the panic, filled with unshakeable faith in his mistress' love.

With a rush of heat the flames rose as high as his head, surrounding the stake like a curtain, looming but not consuming, shielding and concealing his body from the gaze of the crowd.

Krikkeiya looked out at her beloved from the flames. He sure was sexy, all quivering and beaded with sweat. Some of her fellow demons made fun of her for fancying a mortal, but she didn't care. She'd had the hots for him ever since he'd set fire to that lumber yard ten years ago. As soon as she saw him she knew – she wanted to eat him all up! Now the time was finally at hand for them to consummate their love. It was almost a shame his mortal flesh couldn't possibly survive her embrace.

The veil of flames drew open and his mistress stepped forth. Her beautiful face wore a flickering smile. Framing it were tresses of crawling fire. Her naked body was glaringly manifest, with nipples like candle flames and a blazing orange bush. Her pussy dripped with juices like burning oil.

She swept her fiery hands and his clothes caught fire, but the blaze was superbly controlled. It left him naked without even singeing his chest hair. His arms were chained tight behind his back, but his stiffening prick strained toward her. Her eyes met his, literally burning with lust. She rushed into his arms, engulfing him.

Krikkeiya let out a crackling moan of pleasure. Finally! She wrapped her legs around his waist and her arms around his neck, mounting him as he stood against the post. His cock sank in deep, sizzling and splitting like a sausage in a barbecue, spitting out fluid and fat. Its blackened tip bumped her cervix. He was screaming, of coarse, but that would soon end.

Braidwood shrieked, burning all over. Her hands stroked his scalp, setting fire to his hair. Her lips blistered him with hungry kisses. Worst of all was the pain in his prick as it plunged into her cunt's liquid fire. He felt the heat splitting its blackening skin, peeling it off like a snake's withered hide.

Krikkeiya moaned again. Ten years of waiting and flirting and dancing and frigging had built up her lust like the pyre to end all. She came almost immediately, her body burning brighter, her cunt gushing fluid like volcanic magma. She threw back her head and rode him harder, chasing another wave of orgasm as his screams finally stopped.

Braidwood felt the pain go away, yielding not to the insensate state of death, but to an increasing, intense pleasure. He felt her pussy gripping him, felt her thighs around his waist, felt it not with the crispy dead flesh of his body, but with the nimbus of fire surrounding and infusing it, into which his consciousness was passing with each fleeting moment.

Her mouth pressed against his, burning what remained of his face into a husk of black skin and boiling fat. He felt the kiss not with that charbroiled matter, but with a new tongue of fire that stretched from his mouth to spiral with hers. His roasted arms may have been chained to the post, but he was suddenly free of them, embracing her with a new set of fiery limbs that tore away from his tethered carcass like an insect from a chrysalis. He stepped away from the post and from his old body too, walking not on the pyre's planks of wood but on eddies of flame. He carried his mistress as he went, gripping her rump, feeling her curves as she bucked in his arms.

"Fill me up," she said. "Cum in me!"

For the first time, he heard her words clearly. On an updraft of flame they ascended. Freed from the shackles of iron and flesh, he started thrusting wildly. She gripped him hard, moaning in his ear, biting his neck, licking his face. Her juices spilled out like incendiary rain, sizzling on the logs of the pyre underneath. She'd cum so much already, and was cumming even then, letting out ten years of lust in a shuddering explosion. Her pleasure was music to his ears; it called to his own. He came like a miniature volcano, shooting out semen like magma. They writhed together in the aftermath, squeezing out every last drop. Then they detached, floating hand-in-hand in the flames.

Krikkeiya smiled.

"It's about time," she said. "I thought you were never gonna give it to me!"

"If I'd known about this," he said, "I'd never have hesitated."

His own voice resounded around him, crackling and alien, yet also familiar. It sounded like the voice he'd always heard in his head, rather than the one that had emerged from his lips all those years, lips which now lay below him, little more than ashes.

"Was it worth the wait?" he asked.

Krikkeiya smiled again, eyes oozing lust. Her answer looked to be a definite 'yes.' She reached down to her pussy, smearing her fingers with their juices conjoined. The stuff looked like napalm. She licked some off her finger, then flicked the remainder at the crowd who stood staring in terror and wonder below.

Chapter 6: The Lovers in Flame

From the Chronicles of Cromithius of Amithaine:

...and it was in that very same year that the people of the small town of Ganderonne were deeply disturbed by a series of uncanny happenings. First a terrible apparition appeared at the execution of the arsonist Braidwood. Scores of people reported seeing lovers cavorting in the flames of his death-pyre, which had burned in a strange and most unlikely pattern, shrouding the stake to which he'd been tied, like curtains around a four-poster bed. Then some sort of liquid erupted from the blaze, splattering onlookers and setting them alight. At first it was thought to be spurts of burning fat from the corpse of the condemned, but the stuff was too hot. It could not be extinguished, and burned all its victims to ashes, then remained incandescent for several days.

Other incidents followed. First, Braidwood's wife was burned to death, having been tending the hearth when her body caught fire. The neighbours who rushed to her assistance reported a terrible scene. For on top of the woman, embodied in the flames that whipped up from her carcass, were a pair of fiery lovers, doing it doggy-style.

Not everyone believed the witnesses, of course, at least not until the local magistrate fell victim to a similar fate. He'd been studying late in his chambers by the light of a single candle, which set fire to his vestments. When his secretary rushed into the room, he saw his master lying on the ground beneath a pillar of flame, in which two naked figures were manifest, rutting in the lotus position. Their moans were said to be crackling and gusting, like a fuel source igniting and burning.

Terror truly started to spread, but the final incident put a definitive end to all that panic, when the town of Ganderonne burned completely to the ground, killing almost everyone who lived there. People from neighbouring villages reported seeing lovers cavorting in the flames above the rooftops, but they didn't stay on to investigate.

FIN.

The Bone House

Chapter 1: Where the Giants Lost their Bones

It is the Aeon of Chaos. All the gods are dead, and demons frolic in the void.

Rubria arrived first, and gazed up at the edifice. The thick forest around her couldn't mask its presence. It had been constructed from the bones of giants slain in ages past, lashed and glued together like the skeletal walls of an ossuary. Massive rib-bones made up the gates. Spinal columns braced its seven towers, colossal skulls topping their spires, their mouths open wide, as if screaming out some eternal prohibition.

All the bones were etched with magickal runes, not just to contain the presence within, but to keep people out. People like Rubria, and the allies she was shortly to meet.

The next to appear was Gauda, a slender young woman whose burgundy robes were embroidered with sigils of gold. Her only weapon was a dagger, which made sense, since she wasn't there to fight. An expert in spatial and architectural magick, her task was to break through the wards defending the Bone House.

Rubria nodded to her, but said nothing. It wouldn't be wise to get too attached to any of her transitory allies, given what was waiting inside.

Third came Kremlen. He too had just a dagger on his belt, but only because his magick was so much deadlier than a sword. An apprentice of the famous weather wizard Kurzon, he wore a powder-blue cloak with an emerald hem, attesting to his mastery of water and wind. With the sort of detached arrogance typical of sorcerers, he nodded to them both, then folded his arms and waited for the last of their number to arrive.

The wait wasn't long. A figure came creeping from the forest shdows as silent as a panther stalking prey. Rubria almost hadn't noticed him at all, which she found somewhat disturbing, since her senses were keener than most.

So this is Erwen, she thought. *The famous monster-hunter.*

He strode out with a smug look, clearly enjoying his ability to sneak up on others. Every item he wore was a testament to his dangerous and bloodthirsty trade. His hauberk was made up of scales from one of the giant wyrms that lived in the western deserts. They shimmered with iridescence, hard, glossy, and stronger than steel. Judging by their size, Rubria guessed he'd slain one of the wyrms in its infancy, for those of the fully-grown beasts were far too big to wear, being as wide as a shield and as heavy as a boulder. She knew because she'd seen one, and had paid very close attention to its anatomy.

The rest of his gear was likewise made from the parts of slain beasts. The plume of rainbow feathers that topped his open-faced helm was taken from the deadly Kurvaza bird. His belt had been trimmed from the foreskin of a giant, the only part of their hide soft and thin enough to fashion into wearable garments. The hilt of his sword had been whittled from the horn of a rhino, which wasn't really a monster, but a powerful beast nonetheless; and the blade of that sword, which he must have used to hack his way through some of the undergrowth, was made from the black metal bones of an old, dead godling.

There was no way he'd killed a god himself, Rubria knew; all the deities had been slain by the demons, in the age before this one.

Sheathing his blade, Erwen smiled at them all. His teeth were surprisingly white, compared to the yellow of most people's. He was tanned, athletic, and right in his prime. Rubria supposed he was handsome, in his way. Still, he wasn't really her type. Very few were.

For a moment, the four stood in guarded silence, sizing each other up. Their alliance had been forged through mutual contacts and fleeting correspondences carried out by way of messengers and scrying mirrors. They didn't really know each other, and hadn't worked together before.

Hence, the silence, save for the swishing of the leaves and the creaking of boughs around them. There were no houses or towns around for miles; no-one would be mad enough to live near such a haunted, ill-fated place as the Bone House. Even animals gave the building a wide berth. Perhaps they could pick up the scent of the *thing* that lay within?

At length, Erwen spoke.

"So," he said, "I know we already worked out all the details, about how we're gonna divvy up the spoils and all that, but I thought we'd better go over things again, just so there's no chance of any arguments later. All right?"

The others indicated their agreement.

"Right," Erwen continued. "As we've established, I get the head. I've got a nice spot on my wall for this big bastard's ugly mug. And I mean, the whole thing. I don't want to get to the end of this here venture and have one of you lot suddenly asking for the nose, or the lips, or the teeth, or the brains, or whatever. I get it all, everything above the neck."

"No problem," said Kremlen. "I only want some of the blood. Just enough to fill a vial."

Rubria glanced speculatively at the sorcerer. Perhaps he needed it for a potion, or a ritual. Perhaps merely to study it. He was a water wizard, after all. She'd heard of them branching out into other types of fluids – honey, semen, alcohol, anything that flowed and dripped and dribbled and drooled.

Erwen looked at Gauda. "And you?" he asked.

"You already know what I want," she whispered.

"Let's hear it again."

Gauda took a deep breath. "I want the cock and balls." As the men chuckled, she added, defensively, "They're worth a lot of money! They can be rendered down to powder and sold as aphrodisiacs. Certain people will pay a great price, to snort up some of the monster's famous sexual energy."

"That's right," said Erwen. "They say he's pretty randy. Randy, brutal, and hung like a battering ram. You two girls had better watch out, once we get to grips with him."

Rubria saw the other woman shudder with dread, as her own blood began to quicken in her veins.

"What about you?" asked Erwen, turning to her.

Rubria shrugged. "I don't want anything."

Gauda stared at her in disbelief. "You'd risk your life for nothing?"

"She's a thrill-seeker," said Erwen. "Just like me. She's here for the experience. Right?"

Rubria nodded.

"Still, you should probably take some kind of trophy," he said. "Maybe the hands?"

"The thrill's enough for me," she said. "That, and the memories."

Erwen studied her with admiration. Perhaps he thought he'd found a kindred spirit. Or, perhaps, he was merely attracted to her. Understandable enough; she was beautiful by almost anyone's standards. She noted him inspecting her ginger hair and the freckles on her cheeks. Those features were a turn-off for many, due to a persistent and widespread superstition that red-headed people were born without souls.

But Erwen didn't seem to care. He shot her a flirtatious grin. She kept her expression noncommittal but far from hostile. She needed his cooperation – for the moment, anyway.

"Shall we get on with it, then?" asked Kremlen, all business.

Together, they headed towards the Bone House. The thirty-foot ribcage gates hove up before them. The creatures from whose corpses it had been built must've been truly immense. Rubria knew many giants still existed today – she'd seen some of them – eking out an existence in the desolate corners of the world. But the true titans had been exterminated long ago. The slayers who'd accomplished that feat had left this structure as a testament to their genocidal efforts.

Well, not just a testament, but a prison, to cage the one abomination they'd been unable to destroy.

Known only as the Beast of the Bone House, it was said to be utterly ferocious and nigh-on invincible. Many had died in ill-fated attempts to penetrate its prison. Some had been slain by the Beast, others by the terrible creatures that guarded it. Even those who'd fought their way to the heart of the Bone House had barely left a mark of their passage, for the edifice was maintained by ancient and powerful spells that regrew the bones as though they were living, sealing the structure back up after each penetration.

Rubria saw evidence of those spells all around her. The bones were covered with intricate runes so finely etched they were almost invisible from a distance. The artistry was incredible, but the magick even moreso. It sealed up the doors tighter than the vaults of the earth. No battering ram could ever burst them, no fire ever blacken them. As far as Rubria knew, magick and magick alone could unravel the force of the runes and open the gates of the Bone House.

"I'll need some time," said Gauda.

The others waited as she went about her work. First she cleared the earth in front of the doors, creating a patch of barren ground. It wasn't difficult; the soil that abutted the structure was mostly lifeless anyway, as if poisoned somehow. She carved a series of sigils in the dirt with her dagger, then sat in the centre of them, lighting incense and muttering low. She closed her eyes, meditating as she chanted. Sweat began to pour down her face and darken her robes.

To a casual observer she might merely have appeared to be sitting there, but Rubria knew a titanic struggle was being waged, a meta-physical battle between Gauda and the gate. The outcome was by no means certain; there was every chance Gauda's will would snap and her psyche fall apart, leaving nothing but a husk. The walls might even gobble up her soul; magickal defences were known to do things like that. Perhaps that was why the skulls on the spires had their mouths open wide – not to shout out a silent warning, but to suck up the spir-its of sorcerers foolish enough to lock wills with the magick.

They watched with captive breath. Gauda began to tremble and grit her teeth. Then she fell back convulsing, as if having a fit, or a stroke – or as if her soul were being dragged from her body like an in-sect from a web, the strands pulling taut and then snapping one-by-one.

Erwen rushed towards her, but Kremlen held him back, prevent-ing him from trampling on the runes inscribed in the dirt.

"You step on those sigils and she's done for," the sorcerer said.

"Doesn't look like she's doing so hot as it is!"

"Even so, there's nothing we can do."

Gauda tremored on the ground like a victim of palsy. Suddenly she fell still.

"Shit!" said Erwen, adding in a whisper, "all this way for nothing."

The doors opened with a groan, the smell of old bones drifting out from the entrance. Along with the scent of something else, some-thing sweaty and primal, like a lion in its den or a bear in its cave, only many times stronger. There were notes in that stinking bouquet that smelled almost human, like the towering B.O. of some nude, hulking man who'd never made the effort to alter his bedsheets. Rubria's blood again quickened as she caught the aroma.

Meanwhile, Gauda sat up, looking exhausted, and let out a sigh of relief. "That's my end taken care of, then," she said.

"Don't get ahead of yourself," said Erwen. "There might be other wards inside."

56

"How long will the doors stay open?" asked Kremlen, the master of water and wind clearly not knowing much about wards.

"Six hours, give or take," Gauda said.

"Then we'd better get a move on. This place looks pretty big. No telling how long it'll take to find the Beast."

Cautiously, they passed through the doors into shadows and stench.

Chapter 2: Fair Warning

The light from outside didn't penetrate far, seeming to get devoured by the Bone House's interior. Gauda lit a torch. Since she wasn't a fighter, it only seemed fair.

"Whoa," said Erwen, as it illuminated the corridor ahead of them.

Rubria knew how he felt. The floor was a mosaic of skull caps and shoulder blades. The walls were bricked with knuckle bones and strutted with ribs, femurs, and occasional spinal columns. The high-domed roof had been created from a sternum.

Rubria couldn't help but imagine how big those giants' dicks would've been. Probably the size of stone pillars, albeit fleshy and marbled with veins.

Here and there were there ancient, rotting remains of the sinew once used to lash the whole structure together. But the lashings were no longer needed. Nor did the charnel architecture need any sort of mortar; it was bound up by magick.

They paused at a large stretch of flooring covered in urgent-looking text composed in a slew of dead languages Rubria couldn't read.

"What's it say?" asked Erwen.

"They're warnings," said Kremlen. "About the Beast. They say he's a being of indiscriminate lust and bottomless fury. That he has to be contained, or he'll murder and rape until there's no-one left alive. It says they tried to kill him in all sorts of ways. They boiled him, beheaded him, dismembered him, even burned him in a furnace, but he just wouldn't die. No-one knows just what he is, or where he came from. He seems to have no weaknesses. It says that any who wish to kill him should forget about such arrogant thoughts, and turn back immediately."

"Bollocks to that old nonsense," said Erwen. "I'm guessing the people who wrote that never tried one of *these* on the bastard."

With what seemed excessive care, he pulled out and unwrapped what appeared to be a thorn the size of a dagger. Rubria felt a shiver down her spine as she beheld it. It came from the roses that grew in the Garden of Death, very far to the west. It was said a mere scratch from such a thorn could kill almost anything, no matter how powerful. She'd been wondering why Erwen was so confident about slaying the Beast, and now she understood.

The others regarded the thorn with a similar mixture of terror and wonder. Then Erwen put it carefully away, and they began to move forward again, treading over warnings in a dozen different languages.

Following the text was an image of the Beast – a final, visual warning, designed for the dense or the illiterate. For all the artistry with which the Bone House had been made, this itself was crude. Perhaps the artist had been too terrified to study the Beast in any great detail. Perhaps the form of the monster resisted analysis, or somehow recoiled from being drawn. In either case, an elemental savagery seemed to have infected the image, which was little more than a ragged sketch gouged by a fevered hand into the surface of the bone, showing a skeletal face not unlike the muzzle of a bull; a vague, massive body; two titan arms with the likeness of an ape's; and a massive erection that seemed to be the Beast's most salient feature, at least from the artist's perspective.

"Fuck me," said Erwen.

"He's certainly well-hung," said Kremlen.

"I'll say." Erwen turned to Gauda. "You're really gonna have your work cut out for you, carting *that* giant thing out of here. Talk about a pork sword – that's more like a zweihander!"

"It should make a lot of aphrodisiacs," said Gauda, grinning with greed.

Rubria felt disgusted. "Come on. Let's get going."

Onwards they walked, until they arrived at a junction, where a horde of silent monsters came rushing towards them. They had encountered the abominable guardians of the Bonehouse.

Chapter 3: The Phalanx of Tongues

Like the Bone House itself, the guardians had been made from bits of dead giants. Specifically, in this case, they'd been cut from the fabric of gigantic tongues, like gingerbread men from dough. Magickal runes bedecked their bodies like scars, the source of their strange animation. Otherwise their forms were glistening and red and covered with tastebuds. Their mouths and eyes were little more than hollows. Their stumpy, three-fingered hands held spears made from bone.

"Here we go!" said Erwen.

Like him, Rubria had prepared for this. She wore a chainmail hauberk that covered her body from neck to mid-thigh. Her trousers were tight, tucked into her boots, and fastened with wrappings. Her only loose garment was her cloak – black on the outside, red on the in. She usually wore it the other way around, but she didn't want the vibrant red colour to give her away.

She drew her sword and met the charge of one of the tongue-things, hacking through the haft of its spear, then chopping off its ill-defined head, sending it flopping and slopping to the ground. The task wasn't hard; she'd taken a potion that morning that gave her the strength of seven full-grown men.

Erwen waded in beside her, swinging his black, godbone sword. Stronger and sharper than steel, it shattered through bone spears and laid low a pair of the creatures.

Still, there were many of them, half-walking, half-slithering from the three other paths of the junction. Rubria and Erwen drew back as their burgeoning numbers formed a phalanx, bone spears thrust out, their shoulders close together. They filled the mouth of the corridor and advanced like a wall of stabbing death.

Erwen sheathed his blade, pulled out his bow, nocked an arrow, drew, and fired. The whole motion was very fast – fast, and useless. His arrow shot straight through a creature's open mouth, but it just kept on coming.

"What the?"

"It's no good," said Rubria. "You need to sever the runes. Piercing their bodies won't do shit!"

Erwen switched back to his sword, but they nonetheless kept retreating from the phalanx of tongues. Getting close twas impossible without risking being skewered by their spears. Which, of course, was the whole point of a phalanx.

"At this rate they'll push us right back out the doors!" he shouted.

"I think that's the idea," said Rubria.

"We need to think of something!"

"Already on it," said Kremlen.

As the sorcerer muttered something under his breath, the tongues began to shudder and convulse. Their mouths opened wide, as if they were trying to scream. The air filled with steamy vapor, which Rubria realized was the moisture of the tongue-things' bodies, sucked out by Kremlen's water magick.

The process was hideous. They quickly shrivelled, slumping to the ground and flailing about. Their bodies curled up like bits of burnt bacon in a pan, turning a foul, greyish-black. As monstrous as the beings were, the sight was still shocking. Rubria didn't even want to imagine what such a spell would do to a human being.

In a matter of moments, the tongue-things were dryer than dust, piles of black sand laid out in vaguely humanoid shapes.

Rubria glanced at the sorcerer. He looked sweaty and drained.

"Good work," said Erwen.

"Sure," said Kremlen. "Just don't expect me to carry you the whole way."

His arrogance was not undeserved. Nevertheless, it was grating. Rubria caught the look of irritation in Erwen's eyes as he strode back towards the junction. She hurried on after him, followed by the others. They found themselves facing three identical, looming pathways.

"Which way?" asked Gauda. "Place looks like a maze."

"It probably *is* a maze," said Kremlen. "Not just designed to disorient intruders, but to keep the Beast contained, should he escape from his place of confinement. The warnings all said he was deadly, but not very bright. A creature that stupid could end up getting stuck in a labyrinth for weeks, months, maybe even years. Shit, maybe forever!"

"Right," said Gauda. "But we can't afford to get lost at all. Not unless you want me to break through those wards again, which I'm not even sure I can do from inside here. So which way do we go?"

"This way," said Rubria, turning right.

"Whoa," said Erwen. "Hold on a second. I'm the leader of this here expedition, remember? And my gut's saying we go left."

Rubria sighed. Perhaps he was trying to reassert his dominance after being upstaged by Kremlen. Perhaps he was just an overbearing jerk. Either way she didn't have time for his stubbornness. She'd been hoping to avoid doing so, but it seemed as though she had no choice but to reveal her secret knowledge – some of it, at least.

"Your gut might be saying we go left," she said. "But I *know* we need to go right. Here, look." Pulling a piece of parchment from her belt, she handed it over to him.

He frowned at it in confusion. "What's this gibberish?"

"A series of directions, written in cipher. They took me a lot of time and effort to acquire."

"But how?" asked Gauda. "They say no-one's ever gotten out of here alive."

"They're wrong. This is a guide to the Beast's very chamber. We just have to follow it, and we'll be there in no time."

"You should've told us about this earlier," said Erwen.

"We're not exactly old friends, are we? Besides, I'm telling you now. I've memorized the path, and I can lead us to the creature with a minimum of danger."

Erwen paused, clearly not comfortable with another threat to his leadership. But what choice did he have?

"Lead the way," he said. "But no secrets from now on. Okay?"

"Of course," she said, lying.

She led them on through the corridors, twist after twist and turn after turn, until the tibias and fibulas and molars and mandibles became a haze of bone-white in the background. They met no more guardians. The Phalanx of Tongues had been stationed at the entrance because that had been the most likely point of attack, but the rest of the Bone House appeared mostly deserted. Still, that didn't mean there weren't more threats up ahead. In fact, Rubria *knew* there were more. Her heart began to hammer as she drew close to the entrance of a colonnaded hall.

She stopped at the entrance. The light from Gauda's torch swept feebly into the chamber, lighting up some of the columns, which were fashioned from spines.

"The Beast's prison's just beyond these pillars," said Rubria. "Straight ahead. Be careful, though – the instructions say there's some kind of danger in here."

She drew her bow, nocked an arrow, and crept into the room, moving silently but quickly, using the pillars as cover against whatever might dwell in the darkness. Erwen followed after, agile and quick. The others did their best to keep up and stay silent, Kremlen with his magick at the ready, Gauda with the torch held out before her.

The light flared outwards in a suffocated radius. The vastness of the room was intimidating. They could just make out the doorway behind them, as well as dozens of pillars casting flickering beams of shadow on the floor. The rest of the room stretched away into obscurity. Its high-domed ceiling was hidden, its walls drowned in darkness up ahead. They seemed to be the only ones in there.

Kremlen slowed his pace. Perhaps he was unused to such rigorous activity. Perhaps he just thought it was unbecoming of a sorcerer to scurry through the shadows like a rat.

"I don't see any threats --" he began in a whisper.

Then he burst into flames.

Chapter 4: Chamber of Eyes

The bolt of light had shot from the darkness, silent and strobing. By the time they saw it, the beam had already pierced Kremlen's body like a trident of lightning. He wasn't even able to scream. His ribcage exploded, his robes caught on fire, and he fell to the ground, smoking and stinking of charbroiled meat.

"Shit!" Gauda cried.

In the direction from which the beam had travelled, there hung a fading ring of eerie blue light. It looked like the iris of an unlidded eye, albeit the size of a shield or the lid of a wine barrel.

Rubria had an arrow already nocked to her bowstring. She drew it back and took aim. The weapon was monstrously heavy and powerful, normally taking five strong men to string and a draught horse to draw, but thanks to the potion she'd taken earlier, Rubria was able to pull it back as if it were nothing but a strip of old shoelace.

She let loose the arrow and watched it sail off into the darkness. She heard nothing, saw no proof of her aim coming true, save for the sudden disappearance of the ring of blue light. Then another beam speared towards them, slamming into the pillar in front of her.

"What the fuck?" shouted Erwen.

"Keep to the pillars," she said. "Aim for the lights!"

They darted through the shadows as more beams shot out, eerie circles glowing like bullseyes in the wake of the blasts. Rubria fired again. Another circle vanished.

Erwen followed suit. In the distance, something fell wetly to the ground.

"What are they?" he hissed.

Before Rubria could answer, Gauda screamed from behind them.

They both spun around. Something had dropped from the darkness of the ceiling and landed on Gauda – a giant, disembodied eyeball writhing with limbs made of thick, dangling nerve-fibres. They thrust into Gauda through every orifice, stabbing in deeply and wriggling inside, then violently flexing outward, tearing her apart from within. Her body exploded in several directions.

"Bastard!" shouted Erwen, rushing at the eyeball and cleaving it in half with his sword.

It slopped to the ground like a jellyfish, dead. The veins on its sclera were patterned like runes.

Rubria took aim at another ring of light, piercing it deeply. She nocked yet another arrow and raced behind a different pillar, just as a bolt of strobing light struck the one behind which she'd been sheltering a moment before. Vertebrae shattered and littered the room. Erwen joined her, splattered with blood and optic juice.

"Fuckers!" he hissed, sheathing his sword and again readying his bow.

He might be a jerk, thought Rubria as he loosed the arrow. *But he's a pretty good archer.*

The shot struck true, and another blue ring became dark. Around them now were only shadows, flickering in the light of Gauda's torch, which itself had almost been extinguished by her blood. It lay guttering in the gore.

Though the room seemed still, they weren't about to take any chances. They darted from pillar to pillar, backtracking to the torch. Erwen kicked it ahead of them, keeping his arms free to handle his bow.

The torch spun into the darkness like a dying bird and crashed down on the paving, lighting up the nethermost wall. There lay a trio of eyeballs, like jellyfish dead on a beach. Behind them was an arched doorway thirty feet high, made from a curious arrangement of gigantic pelvises. The chamber seemed otherwise empty now, the eyeballs all dead.

Erwen let out a sigh of relief as they reached the arch. "Looks like we made it," he said, flashing a beleaguered-looking smile. It faded as he examined the bones making up the door. They were covered with runes, just like the ones on the Bone House's outer gate. "Shit. How're we supposed to get through these without Gauda?"

"I've got a few ideas," said Rubria.

Then she stabbed him through the back, both literally and figuratively.

Chapter 5: Rubria Caracalla

For a moment, Erwen stood stock-still. Then he collapsed to the ground, unable to move. She'd severed his spine at the cervical vertebrae. He couldn't feel his body below the neck, could barely even feel the wound from which his blood was now pumping.

He could only swivel his eyes to look up at her standing above him, her face blank and ruthless.

"You treacherous bitch!" he spat. "What're you playing at? Kill the Beast and take its head for yourself? Good luck doing that without my help!"

"I'm not here to kill it," she said. "I'm not a monster hunter the way you are."

"You can't mean you're gonna let that thing out of here! Are you crazy?!"

She said nothing, beginning instead to undress in a methodical manner. Letting her cloak fall to her feet, she unbuckled her belt and carefully stretched it out on the floor, then shucked off her hauberk and laid it out flat. After removing her boots, she took off the rest of her clothes. At last she stood there naked above him. Her body was pale and toned, with perky breasts and rose-coloured nipples. Her pubes were as fiery as her hair.

"What're you..." Erwen could barely speak, could only watch through a haze of betrayal and blood loss as she crouched by her belt and removed a series of vials from its pouches.

Some were potions, which she drank. The rest were oils, which one after another she massaged all over her body. She rubbed them absolutely *everywhere* – into her scalp, under her armpits, into her labia and inside her pussy. She even spread the oils on her fingers and inserted them deep in her asshole. Once she was anointed and gleaming all over in the fading torchlight, she picked up her cloak and reversed it, revealing the brilliant red hue of its interior.

As she put it over her shoulders and tied up the cinch, Erwen felt the last piece of the whole horrid puzzle fall into place.

"You're one of *them*, aren't you?" he gasped. "One of the red hoods!"

It was the bright red cloak that'd given her away at the last. Such garments were worn by members of the Scarlet Circle. Erwen had heard many rumours about them during his travels, but had never believed them to be were real. And yet here was one of them, a member of a secret society whose affiliates went in search of the strangest, most terrifying creatures in the cosmos – and ...

"Get away from me!" Erwen tried to struggle as she knelt beside him, but of course could not move. "You're sick!"

As she'd told him, she definitely wasn't a monster hunter, not the way he was – she was a monster fucker!

"What I'm sick of," she said, "are folks like you. How's a girl supposed to go frolicking with monsters if you've gone and chopped them all up? And for what? Just to stick some trophies on your wall? How'd *you* like it if someone stuck your head on a mantle and sold your balls as aphrodisiacs?"

"But they're monsters! They kill people. Eat people!"

"People kill and eat animals."

"It's not the same thing!"

"It's sort of the same thing."

"No it isn't!"

Rubria shrugged. "Okay. Maybe it isn't, then."

"But why? Why do you...*lie* with these things?"

"Because they're hot!" she said, smiling. "Why else?" Lifting a dagger, she added, "Now, try not to pop anything loose. I need you alive for this next part."

He tried again to recoil, but he could only move the muscles of his face, the rest of his body a slab of unknown nothing, filled only with the eerie signals of phantom nerves. He didn't even feel it when she sliced open his abdomen, reached into the vault of his ribcage, and massaged his still-beating heart. He was aware of her actions only as a growing sense of faintness and nausea. He was slipping away, there was nothing he could do but groan, faintly, like someone on the verge of a feverish sleep.

She drew out her hand, drenched with his heart's blood, and strode to the door, where she began to paint a series of sigils on the bones. They looked much like the ones on the gates, only dripping and red, the very same shade as her cloak.

The door opened and Rubria began to drag him towards the room by the ankles. She was going to feed him to the Beast! He had only one hope, and a forlorn one at that. In his belt was the thorn from the Garden of Death. Which meant that if the Beast ate *him*, it would inevitably prick itself and die. Erwen might be finished, but he'd at least take his enemy with him, like any good monster hunter should. Perhaps he'd even stop this woman from getting her sickening jollies!

Silently, resolvedly, he awaited his moment of triumph and doom.

Chapter 6: The Beast

Erwen almost chuckled, but he had to keep his cool. He'd have his last laugh in the underworld, once the Beast and he were dead.

Or at least he thought he would, until Rubria paused, reached down to his belt, and pulled out the wrapped thorn from the Garden of Death.

"Silly me," she said. "I almost forgot about this!"

She tossed it away.

'No!' Erwen cried, as his one hope – a forlorn one at that – died before his eyes.

Laughing, she picked him up like a ragdoll with her potion-enhanced strength, and threw him across the room.

Erwen saw the bones of the chamber pass by in a blur and landed with a disconnected jolt in the shadow of the Beast. He had time to scream again before his world was eclipsed by gnashing teeth.

Watching as the monster gobbled up Erwen, Rubria understood why the long-dead artist who'd drawn the warning at the entrance had had so much trouble depicting the Beast. Its power was almost too great to be contained by a physical form. Waves of heat rippled out as if from a furnace, distorting the air. She could just make out a skull-like horned head with protruding muzzle, massive arms like those of a gorilla; and, of course, its – to her mind – most salient feature: the giant, tumescent cock jutting from its groin.

So hot! she thought, plucking her nipples with one hand and stroking her pussy with the other. She moaned as she took in the scent of the Beast. His sweat was a cloying miasma that rolled across the room like mist in a sauna, reeking and hot. It smelled like the scent of a lion mixed with a man's, then amplified a thousandfold, a perfume of power and musk that was almost enough to make her swoon.

He gobbled up the rest of poor Erwen, then barrelled towards her, ready for business. His deafening roars went resonant with lust as he beheld her naked form. The warnings had been right – the Beast was a randy one, indeed!

"What's the hurry, big boy?" she asked. "How about some foreplay?"

Raising her voice, her moans became the notes of a magickal song known only to the members of her secret cabal.

The Beast slowed, shuffling towards her as if caught in a trance. In his immediate presence, the heat was intense. Erwen had been *roasted* by that heat before the beast had even finished chewing him. Were it not for the oils she wore and the potions she'd imbibed, Rubria's hair would've burst into flames and her skin would've blistered and burned from the temperature. As it was, the heat felt exhilarating.

She stepped closer, until the creature's giant cock was mere inches away, level with her head, even though she was standing. It wasn't as big as it'd been in the picture, but it was vast nonetheless, as long as a baseball bat and as thick as a mooring post. She wrapped her hands around it as best as she could, feeling its pulsating heat. Beneath the soft skin was the hardness of oak. The tip dribbled with pre-cum. Through the mist of his sweat she saw the monster's big balls throb and constrict.

"Looks like you're really wound up," she said. "Trapped here for who-knows-how-long? I think we should help you drop a load first, let off some of that tension. Otherwise you might end up shooting off too fast, once we really get going!"

69

She kept up her moaning chant to dazzle the beast as her hands went to work on his shaft. Not just her hands, but her forearms, elbows, upper arms, and chest. She wrapped her whole torso around it, jerking it off with a hug, keeping her face just above its huge head.

Almost immediately, the monster erupted all over her face. The force of it was almost enough to knock her on her arse. The volume was massive, as if someone had just flung a bucket of water at her, save that it was sticky, glutinous, and white. And smoking. The cum was very hot, the temperature of magma. Were it not for her special preparations, it would've melted her down to the marrow.

She blinked her eyes, licked her lips, and pumped the shaft again, summoning a series of diminishing bursts. By the end, she was soaked to the toes. Her red hair was plastered to her head as if with a layer of soap. She let it drip down into her mouth and took a satisfied gulp. The liquid was hot enough to burn through tempered iron, but the potions she'd taken had made her immune. It still burned, though, albeit like a shot of raw whiskey, filling her body with warmth.

As she drank down the jizz she stopped moaning, and the monster snapped out of his trance with a roar.

Her eyes opened wide.

Time for the main event! she thought as he seized her with his claws.

They pressed against her skin, but couldn't quite puncture it; the oils she'd massaged into her pores had made her immune to that, too. He lifted her to his maw and bit down. It felt as if she were a chew toy in the jaws of a giant, slavering dog, but his teeth couldn't penetrate her skull. She felt his hot tongue whip and coil around her face in the confines of his cavernous mouth.

What a kiss! she thought.

She let herself go limp in his arms. This was the moment she'd been waiting for. It was time to surrender to the frenzy of the Beast!

For a moment the monster seemed confused, as if unclear whether he wanted to dismember her, eat her, fuck her, or all of the above. But, since he couldn't claw her or bite her, he had only one remaining option available.

He threw her on the ground and pulled apart her legs, then pushed his prick against her pussy lips. It looked like a battering ram trying to squeeze through a keyhole. The fit looked impossible – and yet, it went in.

Rubria shuddered with pleasure as the Beast filled her up to the cervix. He should've gone deeper, of course – right through the uterus, past the intestine, and all the way up to the sternum, displacing her stomach and kidneys and liver on the way. His girth should've split her pussy right down to her asshole, creating a hideous, blood-dripping fistula.

But those precautionary potions and ointments were powerful indeed. Her pussy was no longer just a physical orifice, but its own otherworldly dimension, a magical, adaptable cunt-scape that could stretch or contract to accommodate anything that ventured within it. No matter how monstrous his member might be, she could take it to the limit, and only ever feel it tapping on her cervix at most, ever-so-gently.

The monster seemed further perplexed by his prick having seemingly vanished like a prop in a stage magician's play. And yet the sensation of pleasure was clearly undeniable, his confusion meaning nothing in the face of all the tightness and warmth he was wrapped in. He started pumping savagely, clawing at her flesh as he rutted. The scrapes left no marks, only added their sharpness to Rubria's pleasure. She felt an orgasm approaching, rising like water to the boil.

The Beast picked her up by the waist, bouncing her wildly on his prick. Her body was a blur of red hair and cum. The motion was dizzying, jarring, almost impossibly fast. She moaned in his grip, feeling giddy as she came. She saw stars exploding as the orgasm hit, saw fireworks flare across the Beast's growling visage. He didn't slow down, just kept pumping and pumping. She climbed up the mountain again and again, shuddering and moaning from climax after climax, her body as limp as a rag doll's, her vision a giddying blur.

The Beast let out an ear-splitting groan. His cum shot up inside her and spurted back out betwixt the lips of her pussy and his quivering cock. He pumped once, twice, thrice, emptied himself, then threw her away like a spunk-rag. She hit the ground with a cum-soaked SPLAT and lay there for a moment, panting, eyes wide with post-coital ecstasy.

"Was it good for you too, lover?" she managed to mutter.

The Beast looked more confused than ever. She thought it likely that this was a novel experience for him; he'd probably never fucked anything without killing it before, unless he'd had sex with a member of his species, whatever that happened to be. She doubted it though. Insofar as a face like a skull could look shocked, his did, and the surprise in his eyes made her certain he'd never known a sex act that hadn't resulted in death.

Perhaps he was some kind of orphan, tossed out from an alien realm, who'd never even seen his own people. Perhaps he was one-of-a-kind, like so many monsters were, sent hurtling from the depths of a chaotic universe like some kind of mad cosmic joke. And yet, she didn't really care that much either way. She wasn't a monster *scholar*, after all.

"Ready for round two?" she asked, crawling up on all fours.

The Beast's refractory period was impressively short. His prick rose in response like a firehose filling with water. She wriggled her rump and spread the lips of her pussy, feeling the cum dribble out between her fingers.

In moments the monster was behind her, his hot breath on her back, his hands on her haunches. He growled and stabbed into her. Rubria's eyes went wide. Whether by accident or design, he'd gone right up her butt in a single, violent motion.

What a delightful surprise! she thought.

Her asshole was much like her pussy. He could ram it all day, but he'd never get deep enough to hurt her or kill her.

He pounded her wildly. Her ring gripped his cock like a bracelet of muscle, making him cum almost immediately. She felt his seed gush up deep d then leak out.

The monster stumbled back, looking dazed. His ferocious demeanour had calmed. She approached him, taking his now-flaccid prick in her hands. She cradled and stroked it as if it were a serpent. Steadily it stiffened again, though the refractory period was longer than before – ten seconds, rather than five.

This time she leapt on his chest and sent him sprawling on his back. He stayed there, staring up at her. He might not have known just what was going on, and why this tiny woman wasn't dead yet, but he certainly liked it nonetheless.

She lowered herself on his prick and started riding, slowly, luxuriously, then faster and faster. Beneath her the Beast was like an island of muscle and heat. He gripped her haunches and legs, his claws still scraping and grasping, but no longer murderous. She bucked and moaned as one by one the orgasms gathered and dispersed, like the flares of a sun caught in supernova.

The Beast lasted a much longer time before his fourth ejaculation. Perhaps he'd finally calmed down enough to be a more sensitive lover? She'd enjoyed his brutishness a lot, but finesse was important as well. She climbed over his chest and crouched above his terrible maw, still stained with the blood of poor Erwen.

"Lick it," she said, shoving her cunt in his face.

He obviously couldn't understand her words, but he seemed to get the drift nonetheless. His tongue flickered up and lapped her, as long as a serpent. Swiftly it slithered inside her, moving in a myriad of ways that a cock wasn't able – undulating, swiveling, flexing like fingers.

"Oh fuck!" she said.

Spastic with pleasure she slumped across the top of his muzzle, holding his horns as another orgasm rocked her. Then she fell off and landed on his chest. Glancing around she saw his prick was stiff once again, enlivened by the taste of her. She grinned at the Beast, and jumped back on his cock.

Rubria tiptoed from the room as the Beast lay there slumbering, exhausted by the sexual marathon. Which was good, because her potions and lotions didn't last forever, and the door to the Bone House would close any minute now.

She knew her passion was dangerous, and she'd probably end up dying doing what she loved, but she wanted to squeeze out as many years as possible before she got skewered to death on a giant-sized prick, or melted to ashes by arcs of molten cum. She had a lot more monster-fucking to do before that great, final orgasm took her off to the Underworld.

She paused at the door and glanced back at the monster, her eyes glazed and satisfied.

"So long, sexy," she whispered, blowing him a kiss. "I'll come back and visit you sometime!"

Then she shut the door, gathered up her clothes, and strode back towards the exit, humming as she went.

Rubria Caracalla will return!

The Second Wolf

Chapter 1: Dead Meat

It's the Aeon of Chaos. All the gods are dead, and the demons drink wine from their skulls.

Only one item of the dead girl's clothing was intact, perhaps by some kind of fluke: a hooded, burgundy cloak. The rest was in disarray, just as were her skin and bones. She lay in a grove of dense autumnal woods. Beyond the woods, peeking through portals of foliage, were the desolate expanses of the moors. Cold wind soughed through the vegetation, bringing the scent of dead leaves.

Rubria, standing over the body, felt a sense of déjà vu, the scene reminiscent of the day that had changed her life forever, back when she'd been little more than a girl herself, even younger than the dead one at her feet. That fateful encounter had led to her present occupation: monster hunter, with a difference.

"This is the latest victim," said Grimal. "We left her right where we found her, just like you asked."

His words snapped her loose from her reverie. The captain of the guard was young and vigorous, with the sort of rugged good looks that would no doubt make many women swoon. Given how she'd caught him eyeing her up more than a few times, Rubria knew she could have him, if she wanted.

His attraction to her was understandable, of course. She was beautiful by almost anyone's standards. Only one thing gave some pause: a persistent and widespread belief throughout the lands of Typhon that red-headed people lacked souls, and were therefore inherently malignant. Still, her fiery red hair and the freckles on her cheeks didn't seem to stop his flirtatious glances.

But, he wasn't really her type. Few men were. So, she remained aloof, focused on the business at hand.

"Fuck knows what she was doing out here so late at night," Grimal went on, gesturing to the dead girl. "Meeting a lover? Running away from home? Either way, she should've been more careful. This thing's killed seven others before her. She must've known about it."

"Some girls like a bit of danger," said Rubria.

"Speaking of which," he said, "I'm still not exactly on board with you doing this for free. You're risking your life. It seems like you deserve a reward, no matter the outcome."

"I told you, I don't need the money. I'm just here for the experience."

Grimal shrugged. "Suit yourself, I guess. But we do need your help. They say you're the best there is at this sort of thing, and everyone here is pretty stumped. The Department of Diviners and Scryers can't turn up anything, and our trackers keep losing the scent. Whatever this creature is, it's certainly not easy to find."

"We'll see about that."

Rubria knelt to study the corpse. Much of the girl's skin was quite literally in ribbons, lacerated and lifted from the muscle and fat. The wounds crisscrossed her torso and thighs, as if she'd been roughly gripped, dragged, and manoeuvred by a pair of massive claws. Her entrails were exposed. There were bite marks on her shoulders and breasts. Her lips had been completely gnawed off, as if by some bestial kiss.

Gingerly, Rubria spread the girl's legs, revealing her cunt, which hadn't been bitten or lacerated, but bludgeoned and abraded by violent penetration. Whatever inhuman organ had pierced her, it'd been large enough to rupture the perineum, creating a hideous fistula.

"Looks like he's a big boy," she said, her pulse quickening. She scooped some saliva mixed with blood from the bite wounds into a vial, then stood for another look around.

The clearing bore signs of frantic struggle. Dirt and grass were torn up all around, as if by a whirlwind of movement. The dead girl lay in a shallow trench of earth, like a cursory grave, dug up by the frenzied movements that had accompanied her final violation.

Her killer had literally fucked her into the ground.

Massive tracks led away from the carcass, clearly delineated in the roughed-up soil. They resembled those left by a wolf's paws, albeit larger, and with long, opposable thumb-claws, which explained how the monster had picked her up and spun her around like a ragdoll, positioning her body for that final act of murderous entry.

"I'm guessing you've followed those already?" asked Rubria.

Grimal nodded. "But you're welcome to do so again. No telling what you might find that we didn't."

She set off, and he followed, leaving his underlings milling around the grove. The trail was easy to follow. The beast's bulk had crushed the undergrowth, and traces of blood from his paws, jaws and haunches were smeared all around.

"We tried using dogs," said Grimal, "but they were too scared by the scent to be any help. A few went berserk and attacked their handlers. The rest just kept cowering, trembling and whining, pissing themselves. We ended up having to put them all down."

Clearly the creature wasn't subtle, which raised the question of how he'd evaded detection since his depredations had begun. As she neared the edge of the forest, Rubria found the answer. The tracks changed, becoming smaller, more like human feet, walking upright on two legs rather than all fours. Although they were soon lost to view among the moors, they appeared to have been heading in the direction of the city.

"Then we got some of the better game hunters in town to lend a hand," Grimal continued. "The ground's pretty hard, but, as you can see ..." He gestured toward Stubbe, which loomed in the distance, silhouetted by the afternoon sun. In its centre were opulent towers and sturdy brick homes, surrounded by a defensive wall. On the outskirts were the suburbs and the slums, utterly porous and unprotected. "That's where the trail vanished, of course. This thing's hiding in human form amongst the populace. Which means we're looking for a needle in a haystack. And until we find it, it's gonna keep pricking people."

"Let me try something," said Rubria.

From her bag, she pulled out a long, pointed item wrapped in rune-covered cloth. She unravelled the fabric, revealing a slender bone.

"What's that?" asked Grimal.

"The dick-bone of a unicorn. It's good for divination."

She smeared the bloodied saliva on the bone and held it out like a divining rod, waiting for it to pull her in the direction of the Beast. Nothing happened. The bone just lay limp in her hand, unable to rise to the occasion.

"Well, that's unusual," she said.

"I told you, no forms of divination have worked so far. Like it's protected somehow."

"We'll have to try something a little more basic, then. I'm guessing there's a curfew on?"

"There is, though it's not exactly easy to enforce. The inner city we can lock away tight, on account of the walls. The outer city's a whole other matter. There're so many exits it's impossible to control them all. Still, we've instituted heavy fines to try and dissuade people from curfew-breaking. Plus, I doubt there're many women who'd be foolish enough to go out at night at the moment, not after this thing's already killed eight."

"Good," said Rubria. "That means it should be much easier to bait the trap, since we know it likes to hunt out here on the moors and the edge of the forest."

"What sort of bait did you have in mind?" asked Grimal.

Rubria smiled. "You're lookin' at it."

The sun had set, and Rubria wandered alone on the moors. She wore only her red cloak and cowl, its inner pockets filled with weapons, potions, and ointments. Some of the potions she'd already imbibed, and some of the lotions she'd already applied. Her naked body, compact and toned, with perky breasts and an orange bush as fiery as her hair, glistened in the moonlight. Her cloak was short enough to show off her peach-like behind, which she jiggled as she walked.

"Oh mister monster," she called, sweetly. "Come tear my ass up!"

She moved along the edge of the tree line. Now and then, she fingered herself, spreading her scent on the wind in the hopes of attracting the Beast.

"Come and get it!" she called.

She paused as the trees began to rustle nearby. Something was approaching!

Chapter 2: All Dressed Up

Rubria turned to face the forest, waiting for the monster to emerge. Her heartrate sped up as she imagined his blood-stained muzzle emerging from the foliage, followed by his terrible bulk and his throbbing, spear-like erection.

Instead, from the foliage came three dirty and sinewy men, leering and grinning at her, exposing their piss-yellow teeth.

"You're no monsters," she said with a sigh.

"Maybe not," said the first and the largest of them. "But I'm sure we can make a monster together. The serpent that eats its own tail, perhaps? Or maybe the famous old beast with two backs?"

"Not interested."

He guffawed. "That's not really a factor for us, girlie."

"Don't you boys know there's a curfew on? It's for your own protection. There're dangerous things on the moors."

"No shit," he said. "Why else do you think we're out here? When they find your body tomorrow, everyone'll think you've been a victim of the big, bad Beast."

Rubria snarled. If there was one thing she hated, it was people going around giving monsters an even worse reputation than they already had!

"Let's get this over with, then," she said.

"Why the hurry? We got all night long."

The big man stepped towards her, followed by his companions. The one at the rear looked nervous.

"I'm not so sure about this, boss," he whispered. "She seems kinda crazy..."

"Crazy pussy's the best pussy," said the leader. "Everyone knows that. Now get her!"

They fanned out around her. The big man came on first, reaching for her shoulder. Rubria side-stepped and grabbed his arm. One of the potions she'd taken earlier – a favourite old standby of hers – gave her the strength of seven men. She shattered the bones in his wrist, then ripped his arm from its socket in a flurry of blood and used it to bludgeon his associate hard upside the head. The impact was enough to snap his neck like a chicken's. Both men fell, one bleeding, one broken. The third man, who'd expresed his misgivings just a few moments earlier, let out a terrified scream and ran back towards the woods. She threw the severed arm after him like an ungainly boomerang. It spun end-over-end, striking the hollow of his knee. He went down with a grunt. She sprinted towards him and leapt on his head just before he could rise, squashing his skull like a watermelon under her feet.

For a moment she stood there, panting.

At least I've done something to clean up this town, she thought with a smile. *But where's this bloody Beast?*

"Are you sure we should be out here?" asked Peter, glancing around the darkened grove.

"Where else are we gonna get any privacy?" said Dahlia. "Certainly not at my house. Not at yours, either."

She was right. They both lived in very tiny houses with very poor, very large families, sleeping five or six to a room. Nor was there any privacy for them in the rest of the city. Not in the crowded bathhouses, nor in the cramped alleyways crawling with vermin, and certainly not in the hotel rooms they couldn't afford to rent. To fulfil their desires, the impoverished lovers of Stubbe had only the forest to offer an appropriate trysting place.

"Besides," added Dahlia, "Everyone knows the Beast only goes after girls on the rag. And I'm not bleeding, so we'll be fine."

"Who says?"

"I think I'm pretty bloody sure about whether or not I'm menstruating!"

"No, I mean who says the Beast only goes after girls at their time of the month?"

She shrugged. "Everyone."

"Who's everyone?"

"Oh, never mind. And never mind about the Beast, either. You're my beast tonight. And I want you to eat me all up!"

She hoisted her dress and spread her thighs, slender legs raised on either side to form an M with her pussy in the centre. Her pale skin shone in the moonlight; her labia glistened. Peter immediately dropped to his knees.

"Eat me," Dahlia said again.

It wasn't so much his handsome face that turned her on, his full lips or his chiselled jawline, but his dark, gentle eyes. They had a puppy-like innocence about them that always drove her wild. Especially when she got him alone, and her puppy transformed into a panting, rutting wolf.

Peter descended and started out slow, nibbling and kissing her innermost thighs, working his way up. He spread her lips and licked them fulsomely, then poked his tongue into her gash. Tracing tightening spirals around her clit, he drew closer and closer to its sensitive centre.

Her face and ears grew hot as she lay back and closed her eyes, hungrily grinding her crotch against his face. Then her eyes popped back open at a terrible crashing sound. Something barrelled towards them, noisy and fast. Its musky odour hit her like a fist, preceding its arrival by less than a second.

It tore through the trees in a haze of fur and fangs. Peter barely had time to raise his face from her pussy before the thing was upon him, lifting him up in its jaws and shaking him back and forth in a blur of brutal motion. He screamed, flailed, then flew across the clearing in a shower of blood as the creature let go. He hit a tree with a THUD and fell down in a crumpled, broken mess.

Then the beast was on Dahlia. Its stench was even more potent up close, stronger than the unwashed bedsheets of a thousand horny men. From its maw came the aroma of her lover's fresh blood. She shrieked and thrashed as it took her in its claws. Her world became a swirling confusion of teeth, fangs, fur, moonlight and dirt as it pulled her back into the centre of the clearing and flipped her over on her stomach. Its every touch opened wounds on her body, firing her senses with a barrage of pain. It gripped her waist and pulled her rump into the air, then lowered its bulk down on top of her. She felt its fangs enclose her skull below the hairline and wrench back her head. The pressure of the teeth was like a vice. Their knife-like points poked into her scalp, sending a torrent of blood cascading down her eyes and into her mouth. Its breath blasted over her, steaming and hot. Its tongue flicked between its fangs, lapping at the blood. The organ was slippery and longer than her dead lover's prick.

For a moment the monster just held her in that pose, her rump raised up, her head pulled back, before it thrust itself against her. She felt a burgeoning pain as it struggled to get its massive girth through the breach. Then its prick was inside, tearing and stabbing, punching past her cervix, her uterus, her intestines, impaling her body like a spear. She went into a fatal state of shock, while the beast kept on rutting till it came. Its orgasmic howls travelled over the moor.

Chapter 3: Body Count

Once again, Rubria found herself staring down at the body of a dead girl in the woods. The girl was lying just as the monster had left her, with her rump up high and her face down flat against the ground.

Once again, Rubria felt a distinct sense of déjà vu. The scene reminded her of the night she'd spent in the woods, so many years ago. She was sure she'd been in a similar position at one point or another – perhaps even more than once, throughout the length of that interminable, oh so memorable evening.

She circled around, inspecting the dead girl by the light of Grimal's torch. The beast's steaming semen was dripping from the ruins of her pelvic floor. Rubria knelt down and filled up a vial with a sample of the cum.

"You say you found her like this?" asked Grimal.

Rubria nodded. She'd followed the howls of the beast to the kill site, only to find the monster already gone, after which Grimal and his own men had arrived, panting, with their blades out, all dressed up with nowhere to go.

"Looks like a double kill this time." Grimal nodded towards the body of the boy, wrapped around a nearby tree trunk like a horseshoe on a hook. "They must've been lovers, out here for some fun. Judging by their clothes they were both pretty poor, hence why they couldn't just go rent a room. Still, it's hard to believe they'd risk their lives like this, just for a roll in the hay."

"Don't underestimate the power of desire," said Rubria.

"I suppose I'd better not. It's what motivates the Beast, after all."

"It's what motivates *everyone*."

"Everyone?" he said, smiling wryly. "Even eunuchs?"

Rubria shrugged and smiled back. "Everyone who *matters*, I guess."

"I doubt the eunuchs would like you saying that."

"Screw 'em."

"That's just the point – you can't!"

They laughed, the spectacle of death having clearly left them both with a need for some good gallows humour.

Grimal turned serious again. "I guess there's one being we know who's *definitely* motivated by desire – the Beast. It's just a shame for everyone else he's not a more sensitive lover."

"Some people like it rough."

"You say odd things sometimes, you know? Then again, monster hunters must be an odd bunch."

"Not all of us. But then again, I'm not your average monter hunter."

She grinned at him slyly. Grimal peered back as though she were a puzzle he was trying to unravel. He looked just about ready to ask her something, when one of his underlings raced into the clearing, panting and sweating.

"Boss, you'd better come quick. There's trouble!"

They rushed back across the moors towards the town.

When she'd first arrived in the area, Rubria had wondered why there wasn't more farmland adjacent to the city. After all, the people had to eat, right? And most cities in this region were largely agricultural. As it turned out, Stubbe was primarily a mercantile city, positioned on the road between larger dominions like Red Wake and Starfall. They made most of their money by taxing trade passing through their territory and selling their products to travellers. Most of the population was made up of merchants and professionals, supported by an underclass of labourers who lived in the city's sprawling slums. Their food was brought in on wagons from farms to the south. It had to be; the moors were rubbish as agricultural land. The soil was too acidic to support much of anything. Perhaps that's what gave the barren grasslands such a spooky, desolate feeling? They were almost inimical to life.

The unpaved streets were a maze winding between dense, uneven rows of houses, all cheaply constructed from timber. The place stank of horseshit, sewage, and cramped, sweating bodies. It also stank of fear – figuratively, at least. The people had a furtive, hostile seeming as they went about their business, some of them glaring at Rubria suspiciously. She was a redhead, after all, not to mention a stranger. Perhaps they thought *she* was the one turning into a beast and ravaging their womenfolk? She got the feeling that if it weren't for the presence of Grimal and his underlings, she'd maybe have to break a few heads, just to keep the people from lynching her.

Which was apparently what they'd done to some others already. There, hanging from a post in a cramped, earthen square, cast into silhouette by the rising sun, were three dead bodies with the word 'Beast' carved on their foreheads. The corpses were fresh; they couldn't have been more than a few hours dead. They stank of piss and shit; their bladders and bowels had evacuated during their death throes.

Rubria held her nose. "Who are they?" she asked.

"Travelling people," said Grimal, noting their tell-tale clothing. "Word of the two new killings must've leaked out already. Looks like the citizens are performing their own hunt."

"There's more, sir," said one of Grimal's underlings. "At least six more dead. They burned two drifters alive down on Braidwood Avenue."

"Well isn't that just fucking fantastic," said Grimal, deadpanning.

"The citizens are upset, sir. They think the Beast is some kind of foreigner. And if we don't find it soon, they're liable to slaughter everyone they don't know by name."

Grimal sighed, then steeled himself. "Right then," he said. "I want you and the rest of the boys to go round up every drifter, every hobo, every weirdo in town, and lock them all in the dungeon."

"You sure that's a good idea?" asked Rubria. "They haven't done anything wrong."

"It's for their own protection. Besides, if the people are right – and the Beast really is an outsider, a vagabond – then maybe we'll scoop him up with all the others."

Spruce sat shivering in the dungeon, along with the others.

'Spruce' wasn't his real name, of course; it was just the first thing he'd seen when he'd woken a few weeks ago beneath a spruce tree. He knew the name of the tree, and the names of a lot of other things, too, but he didn't know his own. He'd been wearing the clothes of a beggar at the time he'd awoken, though his nails were well-manicured and his hair was soft and fragrant from a recent shampooing. His body had been clean, too, though it hadn't stayed that way for long.

With no name and no memories to speak of, he'd found himself wandering the roads, begging for food and sleeping outdoors. The lifestyle was rough. He'd been spat on, beaten up, and someone had stolen his belt, forcing him to tie up his tunic with an old piece of string.

Just over a week ago he'd ended up in Stubbe, and since then, things had gotten even worse.

He'd started having awful dreams, waking with a throbbing headache every morning, as if he'd been drinking the night before. He'd put it down to the ghastly conditions of the alleys and streets he'd been sleeping in. And then there were the locals. They'd been okay at first. Stubbe was a mercantile town, its people used to all manner of vagrants and drifters floating by.

But then, some sort of monster had started rampaging through the forest and across the moors, tearing women apart after dark.

Spruce was terrified it might get him, too, even though he was a man. Despite his grime, he knew he was handsome, with a fine-featured face. Never very hirsute, and apparently constitutionally incapable of growing a beard, he had sometimes been mistaken for a girl.

So, he'd stuck to the city at night, keeping as far from the outskirts as possible, trying to avoid the attentions of the Beast. At that, he seemed to have succeeded so far. Avoiding the ire of the populace was another matter entirely. The people of Stubbe had grown increasingly hostile to strangers of late. So hostile, in fact, that this morning they'd started killing vagrants and traveling people.

Hence why Spruce was now locked up, ostensibly for his own protection.

It was another revolting development. He didn't know his name, or who he really was, but he knew he didn't belong *here*. The dungeon was nothing but a single, cavernous room, with a barred gate on one side and a small barred window on the other, offering a tantalizing view of the sky's nascent dusk. It had remained cold all day, despite the countless bodies crammed inside it.

Earlier, the city guard had rounded up all the drifters and hobos in town and locked them in. Worse, they'd failed to remove the prisoners who'd already been in the dungeon, awaiting trial – and most likely execution – for various heinous crimes such as murder, kidnapping, rape, and extortion.

The place seethed with the unwashed scum of the city. It stank like a latrine, with stale, sweaty undercurrents. The place was poorly-lit, too, with naught but a solitary torch outside the barred entrance. Now that the sun had set and the stars were slowly rising, that torch was the only source of illumination in the chamber at all. It showed the horde of figures in flickering silhouette and cast monstrous reeling shadows on the walls.

As much as Spruce feared the dark, he feared the sights it concealed even more. From a dozen feet away came a dissonant chorus of groaning and screaming, backed by notes of cruel laughter. Evidently some of the more dangerous miscreants were having their way with their unfortunate new cellmates. It made Spruce glad for the darkness blanketing everything. He didn't want to catch a glimpse of what was going on nearby.

Instead, he sat huddled in the corner, trying to make himself invisible, keeping his eyes focused on the small, barred window above, watching the carpet of stars begin to unfurl across the sky, soon to be followed, no doubt, by the moon.

Beside him was a man who stank of urine and kept babbling about demons from the void. Spruce wished some of the those demons would descend at that moment, and smash open the gates of this hideous gaol. He even wished for this mysterious Beast to arrive. It couldn't be much worse than the people he was incarcerated with!

As if to prove the point, a group of filthy figures suddenly pushed their way through the crowd and stood in front of him. Cloaked in a cold sweat, his heart hammering, Spruce tried to stop himself from shaking as he continued staring at the window, willing the figures to just go away – but they wouldn't.

"Hey cutie-pie," one said. "Why're you sitting back here like a wall-flower? You should come and join the dance."

"I'm not one for dancing," said Spruce. "Sorry."

"I'm pretty sure you'll like this one, though," said the man. "It's one of those ones where you go around in a circle, swapping partners when the music changes tempo."

Spruce gulped. "I'd rather sit it out. I don't know the steps."

"That doesn't matter. We'll lead, until you get the hang of it."

Spruce stole a terrified glance at the figures. He could barely even see them at first, until moonlight peeked through the window above, giving him a stark impression of their cratered, leering smiles and sinewy bodies. There was almost a dozen, ten men and one woman, the latter of whom seemed to be the ugliest of all.

He screamed as they rushed in and grabbed him, dragging him to his feet and into the moonlight.

A moment later, it was *they* who were screaming, as their would-be victim transformed into a tower of fur and rending fangs.

Chapter 4: Slaughterhouse

"Rubria!" shouted Grimal as he raced across the moors, accompanied by two of his underlings.

He found her near the edge of the forest, dressed only in her crimson cloak. Once again she'd been serving as bait. Despite the urgency of his present situation, Grimal was dumbstruck by her beauty. Her naked body shone in the moonlight, anointed with oils.

"Yeah?" she asked.

"It's...it's the Beast!" he managed to stammer. "We've got it locked in the dungeons right now. One of the inmates transformed after dark!"

"Lead the way!" she said.

They started running back towards the city. Grimal noticed his underlings staring at Rubria's bouncing breasts and her peach-shaped behind. One of them tripped on a patch of stiff grass and went sprawling on his face.

"Maybe you should cover up," he said. "Before we get back to town?"

"No time," she said. "Besides, I need to face the monster like this, anyway."

"Are you sure? I mean, I know you've got your own unique methods, but –"

"I know what I'm doing! Just lead the way, would you?"

They rushed through the city's crowded streets, where people had emerged from their houses. According to Grimal, there'd been a series of terrible noises, audible from every single quarter of the city, the loudest of which had been the roaring of the Beast. Although the noises had stopped, people still stood staring nonetheless – at least until Rubria ran by, at which point many heads turned in her direction instead.

Rubria ignored them and followed Grimal to the dungeon, a subterranean cavern built beneath the courthouse. Descending a series of worn stone steps, they emerged into a torch-lit hallway where armoured officers stood anxiously waiting. The air was thick with the iron tang of blood and the far more foetid stench of freshly-opened entrails.

"Up here, sir," said one of the guards, pointing to the gates.

Rubria and Grimal peered through the bars. The dungeon's solitary window was blocked by a severed human head, which shut out the moonbeams and forced them to rely on the light of their torches.

The flames lit up a sea of dead bodies and blood.

"Fuck me dead," said Grimal.

"Looks like the Beast's already gone and done some of that," said another guard.

"At least he's killing the right people for a change," said a third. "He's practically slaughtered every scumbag and hobo in the city. Maybe we should hire him on?"

A few of them laughed, albeit nervously.

"Shut up, will you?" snapped Grimal. "That thing could still be in there."

"I don't think so, sir," said the first guard. "We heard him smash through the wall, and run out into the old catacombs."

"Fuck!"

"We'd better get moving, then," said Rubria.

Grimal gestured for a key, which he snatched from a subordinate and used to unlock the gates. Inwards they crept – Rubria, Grimal, and a dozen of his underlings, moving slowly lest they slip in the gore. Rubria felt the bodies underneath her bare feet like a sticky, squelching carpet. Their insides – which were no longer technically their *insides* at all – lay steaming in the coldness of the gaol, throwing up a curtain of vapor.

She moved ahead warily, peering through the steam. The others followed. The stench of blood and entrails was such that they all had to breathe through their mouths. Some of them weren't breathing at all, too terrified to do so, lest the Beast be there waiting. Had he really fled into the catacombs, or was he crouched in the shadows, ready to pounce?

A huge black shape hove up into view just ahead. It was the hole in the wall through which the Beast had seemingly made his escape. Rubria could just smell the scent of mouldy bones seeping from the catacombs beyond.

"Looks like he definitely went through here," said Grimal, nodding towards the blood smeared on the edges.

It looked as if the Beast had squeezed himself through the gap like a giant, terrible rat. His coat must've been completely covered with blood when he'd done so, which wasn't surprising, given the state of the room. Rubria stepped closer to the opening, then froze as something burst from the shadows behind them, dripping with gore.

Chapter 5: Amongst the Dead

"Fuck!"

"Shit!"

"Butcher's Balls!"

The guardsmen cursed and spun, raising their crossbows and swords. But it was not a Beast, just a man drenched in blood. Despite all the gore that he wore, he still managed to stink of urine. He shambled towards them.

"Lords and Ladies of the Void!" he cried. "God-killers, world-eaters! The demons that devoured the old universe! This is their joke! *We* are their joke! My flesh, your flesh, the stones of the earth, the stars in the sky, all is but a jest of the mighty ones! The fathomless ones! Worms crawling on tongues, ladles in blood, rainbows raping the dead –" his mouth began to froth as his eyes glazed over with a gleam of insanity. "We live in their cereal bowl – we live in their pornographic poetry! We live –"

One of the guards bashed him over the head, knocking him out cold. He fell like a sack. No one cared to check if he was dead, but his words seemed to press on them all like the knelling of some ominous death-bell. Only fools failed to fear the great demons.

Grimal turned to Rubria, warily. "You think he's right?" he said. "Could this thing be a demon?"

Rubria shrugged. "It might fit some of the facts. A lot of demons are shape-shifters. And they certainly love to fuck. But that wouldn't explain why this Beast let himself get arrested."

"Maybe he just likes to mess with people," said Grimal. "The demons play games, don't they?"

Rubria nodded. Her heart began to beat even faster. She knew demons, knew them well.

After they'd slaughtered the gods who'd ruled the old universe, the demons had become the most powerful beings in existence. Some of the 'cosmic' or 'pure-blooded' demon had survived from the age before this one, making them over a thousand years old. They were creatures of Chaos, and no two looked alike. Then there were the so-called 'demon-blooded,' or 'demon-spawn,' the offspring of demons and other races. These varied wildly, to say the least; demons were horny indeed, and their strange, cosmic wombs and mutating semen were capable of conceiving all manner of creatures, not just those of the humanoid variety. There were demon-blooded horses, demon-blooded bears, even demon-blooded mosquitoes.

Yes, Rubria knew the demons. She'd studied them in depth, and had tangled with more than a few of their children in her time. She felt certain she'd be able to handle the challenge again. Unless, of course, the Beast was one of the cosmic ones, in which case she'd probably end up dead, in spite of all the potions she'd drank and the oils she'd applied.

Which was why her heart now beat faster than ever, not just from fear, but from excitement. Once more, she was reminded of that long ago night in the woods, when she'd met with her destiny. She'd had no special preparations back then, and her survival had by no means been assured.

She steeled herself, and glanced at Grimal. "Whatever it is, we need to go after it, before it finds a way out from the underground."

"Agreed," he said.

They ventured into the catacombs, moving more freely once the ground wasn't covered in gore. The Beast had marked his passage like a giant, bloody paintbrush. It seemed he was just barely big enough to fit through the tunnel, which was six feet by eight. Their torchlight made it easy to follow his trail.

Soon, the walls became dotted with alcoves for the dead. Rubria was distantly impressed, even through her haze of adrenaline. Most catacombs were chiseled from soft, porous substances, like limestone. These ones were hewn from black granite. Whoever had built them, they'd surely been willing to go to a great deal of trouble. Not that there was much left of the bodies now, of course. They'd rotted into piles of old bones, most of their matter filling the air in the form of floating dust. It made one of Grimal's men cough.

"Idiot," hissed Grimal. "You want the Beast to hear us?"

"Sorry, boss."

"Never mind," said Rubria. "I'm sure the Beast will smell us coming a mile away."

A few guardsmen gulped as they considered her words. Then they all headed onwards, following the diminishing blood-trail through a series of maze-like twists and turns. The place was a warren, with tunnels branching off into a seemingly endless collection of junctions. Many were dead-ends, or spirals, or led into high-vaulted chambers meant for some ancient king. Often the Beast's trail doubled back from a cul-de-sac. He was just as lost as they'd be, without his trail to guide them.

At length they emerged into a high-domed chamber filled with bones. Rubria froze immediately, gesturing for Grimal and the others to do likewise. There was a musky scent on the wind, far stronger than the smell of bones or blood. It smelled very masculine, like the sweat of a thousand rugged athletes whose sport of choice just happened to be fucking – and killing.

Rubria sought out the source of the scent, and found it. Glaring from the darkness in the distance were a pair of yellow eyes. She could just hear the sound of the Beast's rugged breathing. She could feel its heat, too, albeit distantly, reaching out across the gloom like some ambient invitation.

"There it is," she whispered. "You lot stay here."

"Are you crazy?" asked Grimal. "You saw what it did back there. You might be a monster hunter, but you'll still need all the help you can get."

"I'm no regular monster hunter," said Rubria. "Not like you might've been led to believe. I'm a monster *fucker*. And I'm gonna do this my way, or no way at all. So stay back, or you'll have more than just the Beast to worry about. Understand?"

She reached out and crushed a part of the wall with her fingers. Grimal stepped back, unnerved, gesturing for his men to do likewise. They didn't need much encouragement to do so. Terrified, they huddled in the mouth of the chamber as Rubria strode out alone, carrying a torch and wearing nothing but her cloak.

She approached the Beast. Ancient bones turned to powder beneath her naked feet, sticking to the blood that still coated her skin to the ankles. Her own blood quickened to a terrible pace as she drew closer and closer to the monster. She hadn't felt so afraid and excited since that long-ago night in the woods. The sense of déjà vu hit her again as she beheld the Beast's form. He was very canine, with a coat of silver fur and a massive, fanged muzzle.

For a moment, he seemed to be resting. Tired, perhaps, from the slaughter he'd wrought in the gaol. Then he rose up before her, roused by her presence, his coat smeared with blood and dusted with bone. Her heart pounded as she saw his erection, likewise all moistened with gore.

Rubria got wet at the sight of him. Surely this was a lover direct from her dreams! And with all her preparations, she had a good chance of withstanding his embrace. The potions she'd imbibed and the lotions she'd applied made her supple skin stronger than steel. She'd juiced up her pussy and asshole with magickal lubricants that would enable her to take almost any cock in the universe, from the pork sword of an ogre to the pillar-like penis of a giant.

And yet there was a terrifying, exhilarating doubt in her mind. Should this thing really be a demon of the cosmic variety – and he certainly looked majestic enough for that to be the case – then all of her preparations might well be for nought. For the cosmic demons were creatures of Chaos, and magick often failed or went awry in their presence.

The danger got her even wetter. At the same time, the Beast began tramping towards her, then broke into a run.

She tossed aside the torch. She had only a couple of seconds before the Beast was upon her, and she needed both hands free for a final preparation. She'd seen his M.O. in the forest. He was a selfish, brutal lover, to say the least. Which was certainly a turn-on for her. Still, she liked a bit of foreplay, and she wanted to make sure she'd get it.

She whipped out a vial from her cloak, popped off the cork, and splattered the contents all over her pussy. The stuff was sticky and red, the blood of the Vendhaza Bird. Its delicious aroma was such that almost no carnivorous creature could resist it, no matter the circumstances. She rubbed the blood deep into her pussy and smiled at the Beast.

"Dinner time!" she shouted.

She'd wanted the call to sound sexy, but she just couldn't cancel the fear in her voice. This was the moment of truth. The Beast was barrelling towards her. In just under a second she'd either be getting her pussy eaten out – or *eaten up*.

Chapter 6: Devoured

Rubria's heart hammered as the Beast leapt and knocked her to the ground. His stink barrelled into her with almost as much force as his body. The aroma was intoxicating, a perfume of absolute power and lust. She spread her legs wide as his head loomed above her, his massive nostrils flaring, taking in the scent of the blood between her legs. He opened his jaws and bit down on her crotch in a blur of white fangs.

Rubria shrieked – not with pain, but with pleasure. Her preparations, it seemed, had been more than enough to stop his teeth from penetrating her skin. Growling with confusion, he gnashed on her lips and started thrashing his head in a furious motion.

Rubria jolted and bucked, squealing with delight. This was no subtle head he was giving! His teeth bit and chomped, seizing her lips, squeezing her clit. To her it felt like naught but a nibble. Even so the sensation was intense. She thrashed and arced her back in involuntary motions as he kept on trying to feast on her meat. He bit and thrashed, thrashed and bit, growling all the while, bathing her cunt in his hot, charnel breath. Her juices flowed in abundance, mingling with the blood.

The combination of scents seemed to drive the Beast even wilder. He gave up trying to bite her and started lapping in a frenzy, lathing her cunt from bottom to top. His tongue was so strong it started pushing her across the carpet of bones. She thrust her crotch into his face, urging him on. He kept on lapping her lips and her clit till he'd licked the delectable blood from her exterior.

Then he followed the scent right inside. His massive tongue thrust into her, swirling in circles that ran deeper and deeper as he gathered up the blood with a series of final, flexing motions that saw his tongue curl up like a set of arching fingers inside of her.

"Fuck, yes!" said Rubria, wriggling with ecstasy.

His tongue caressed her cervix. His wide-open jaws encompassed her cunt, the topmost ones resting atop her pubic mound, the lower ones gripping her ass. As his teeth pressed her backside, Rubria experienced a moment of regret.

I should've smeared this stuff up my asshole, too! she thought, thinking of the glorious rim-job she could've received.

The Beast pulled out his tongue and reared above her, eyes aglow with the ardour of lust.

"Let me guess," she said. "Doggy-style?"

He gave his answer by violently flipping her over. His claws scraped her skin, but didn't break it. Rubria panted and grinned as he grabbed her hips and raised her rump. He lowered his bulk on top of her, seizing her head in his jaws and wrenching it back, the pressure like a vice but unable to crush, his knife-like teeth unable to cut. When he thrust, there came a moment of pressure as his gigantic girth battled for entry. Then it surged inside. The Beast's size was such he should've split her open from cunt to asshole; his length was so great he should've speared through her uterus and into her guts. Yet, thanks to Rubria's special preparations, his prick could only ever fill her to her limits. Her cunt was a pocket dimension, able to swallow even the most monstrous of invading erections.

She quivered as the beast started humping away, tapping her cervix with every thrust, mingling the pleasure with jarring spikes of pleasurable pain. His thickness stretched her cunt to just the right width, filling her up without tearing her apart. She felt his hot breath on her scalp. He wrenched her head back as he pounded her cunt from behind. His bestial violence was intoxicating. Once again it reminded her of that night in the woods, with the wolf, long ago. The stir of horny memories added to her pleasure. Her young body trembling with longing and fear. The presence of the wolf, exciting and terrible. Her hooded cloak discarded on the ground, a blanket for bestial deflowering, as red as the blood from her cunt. His breath on her neck, on her back, warm as summer wind. His weight on top of her, heavy and hot. His howling mingling with her cries. His teeth, his claws, his tender, delectable cruelties...

Rubria's memories mingled with the present, as if she knelt

in some glorious conflux of past and present rutting. As the Beast growled and pounded behind her, a crescendo of bliss began to build, climbing and surging to climax.

She saw stars exploding in the blackness of the cavern as she came, saw flickers of firelight transcend into bright supernovas. She moaned underneath him. Her cunt gushed and widened, drawing his prick even deeper. He speared into her depths and just as suddenly exploded. He let out a howl that shook the walls of the catacombs and was heard in the city above. Motes of dust and chips of stone trickled down from the ceiling as he pumped a few more times, growing gentler as he milked out the last of his seed.

There was certainly a lot of it. It spurted out, oozing and frothing betwixt their two mashing organs. Rubria felt it dribble hotly down her thighs. He thrust into her a final time, deeply, squirmingly, pulling her head back tight. Then he let go.

Rubria knelt there, panting. The climax had hit her like a sensory apocalypse, a caesura in time that created a wall between moments. There was the age of Pre-Cum, now ended; the age of Post-Cum, day one, year one, starting now.

She sighed slowly, eyes glazed in the afterglow, gradually becoming aware of the Beast's heaving presence having diminished. His heat was gone, so too his delectable scent. His prick seemed to be getting smaller inside of her. Was it going soft?

I'll soon take care of that, she thought.

She glanced over her shoulder with a sulty look –

Then froze. Behind her was a man, handsome-looking and fine featured. She slipped off his cock with a sigh of disappointment.

"So you're the Beast then," she said. It was more of a statement than a question, but nevertheless the man began narrating his tale in a breathless, wide-eyed monologue. His name wasn't Spruce, he said; he remembered now. It was Prince Eliade of Amithaine. He'd been cursed by his wicked stepmother, who was also a witch. She'd stolen his memories, dressed him as a beggar, and dumped him in the woods. Worse, she'd cast a terrible spell that'd made him transform into a monster by night, an insatiable beast with a murderous member and a craving for cunt that couldn't be annulled. Thus he'd been ostensibly doomed, because the curse could only be broken if a woman lay in love with his bestial incarnation and survived. And yet, what manner of woman could ever love such a beast? More pertinently, what manner of woman could survive?

The answer, of course, was Rubria Caracalla of the Scarlet Circle cult, whose initiates travelled the cosmos in search of the strangest, deadliest monsters – and fucked them.

Prince Eliade finished his tale and grasped her right hand in his.

"Your love has saved me from a hideous fate!" he said, gushing with happiness. "Come back to my kingdom and marry me! It's only right that you should be a princess, and someday, my queen."

Rubria gently withdrew her hand. "Sorry," she said. "But I'm not really interested."

Eliade stared at her, dumbfounded. "But...but you loved me, even as a beast!"

"It wasn't you I was interested in," she said. "It was the Beast I was after all along." She gestured to his naked body. "I'm afraid this just doesn't do it for me."

"So...so you won't be my bride?"

"Sorry," she said again. Then she paused, smiling mischievously.

"Well, maybe I could be. If you got that wicked old stepmother of yours to turn you back into a monster, on a more permanent basis."

Eliade gaped at her with wide-eyed horror. "No way!"

"What about every other night?" she asked. "Then we could definitely have some fun together. Although it'd have to be an open relationship, of course. There's a lot of other monsters out there, and I'm not even close to sampling them all yet."

He drew away from her, shuddering. "Maybe we'd better just forget the whole thing. I'll give you a cash reward instead, for saving my life."

"Forget it," said Rubria, rising to her feet. "Have a nice life, Your Highness. And don't worry – there's plenty of princesses out there. They might not love a beast, but they'll probably love you."

Even if you do have a small dick, she thought.

She strode back towards the entrance of the chamber, where Grimal and his underlings still stood, staring at her with thunderstruck eyes. They'd seen the whole thing, of course. Some looked aghast – others blushed with obvious arousal.

"Let me know the next time you've got monster trouble," she said, shooting a wink at Grimal.

Then she strode off through the catacombs, her cunt filled with monster-cum, her eyes with post-coital delight.

Rubria Caracalla will return!

PART II

Novellas

The Court of the Mushroom King

Chapter 1: The Mushroom Pilgrims

It is the Aeon of Chaos. All the gods are dead, and the demons wear their entrails as lingerie.

Ziqqora arose well before dawn and snuck off across the manicured lawn bordering her father's crumbling castle. She didn't usually like to get up so early; she liked to sleep in and dream until the servants came to rouse her. Even then she'd often complain of a headache, or a stomach ache, or some other phantom malady, thereby lingering in bed until well after noon, slipping in and out of dreams until the fullness of the sun and the smell of cooking lunch finally called out to her. But this morning was different. She was off to do something forbidden, and did not want to be seen.

At length she came to the edge of the Royal Gardens, which was something of a misnomer, for this was not a place of orderliness, cut and curated, but a sprawl of unruly woodlands stretching on for miles, used primarily for hunting by the king and his cronies. Ziqqora knew the outskirts well, and often went walking in them, but today she was going much farther than usual.

And so she set off, passing thickets of oaks and crawling yews, stagnant pools filled with swarming little tadpoles, and rivulets bordered by reeds. She spied pheasants, ducks, and a solitary fox whose face was smeared with blood. He watched her warily, and with good reason, for many of his kin had been hunted to death by her father's black hounds, their bodies torn apart, their blood used to daub royal foreheads and season royal wine with a bitter iron tang.

Onward Ziqqora went. Steadily the woods became wilder. The canopy thickened, obscuring the slowly-rising sun. The servants in the palace would no doubt be up and about by now, preparing for the day. Ziqqora hoped the dummy she'd put in her bed, made from pillows and a wig, would fool them for a while – at least until she returned from her intended destination. But she didn't really know how far she had to go, nor even if she'd ever be back.

She felt a pulse of excitement as she strode through the darkening wood. She'd never gone this deep by herself before. The scenery turned into a shadowy haze of trees, leaves, and moist black earth. After a while her legs got tired and her body grew clammy with sweat. She stopped to eat a cake and some apples. Just how far was the bloody place anyway, she wondered? She'd been to the outskirts only once, long ago, in her earliest childhood, and could just barely remember a forbidding iron fence and the aura of mystery it seemed to contain.

She got up and kept walking, still wondering how much farther she had to go, until suddenly the old iron fence she was seeking hove up in the distance ahead, surrounded by shadows and trees.

At last! she thought, then stood there, staring.

The fence, like the castle she lived in, was twisted by age. The ground had shifted over time, turning the pickets askew. The gates were locked with chains so rusty and covered with lichen that the links had grown together. The forest beyond looked more or less like the one she'd just passed through – at least from the outside. The only hint of its special nature were the toadstools that grew along the edge and led off into its depths like a white-capped road.

The forbidden garden beyond the fence had been a mystery tormenting her for years. All she knew was it contained a lot of mushrooms. And what was the big deal about that? She ate mushrooms for dinner; everyone did. So why, then, should this garden be off-limits? No one would give her an answer. Not her father the king, certainly not her stepmother. Not the cooks, tutors, chamberlains, scullery maids, seamstresses, chimney sweeps, stable lads, nor any other members of the vast household staff that bustled round the mansion like a horde of human bees.

At last, in desperation, she asked the groundskeeper, whom she tended to avoid. It wasn't because she didn't like him personally, but because of his son. Bertrand, the dirty brat, was always leering at her through the windows. He'd even been flogged for it, though not at her behest. Thus, she'd waited until the groundskeeper was alone in the field before approaching him with her questions.

"The garden wasn't always forsaken,' he'd said, smoking his pipe, black dirt clinging in the creases of his fingers. "Once, it was considered this kingdom's greatest treasure, on account of the mushrooms that grew there."

"Yeah, mushrooms, I know," she'd said. "What's the big deal?"

"Oh, these mushrooms were special. Magickal. They gave marvellous visions to anyone who ate them. So, your ancestors made the garden private royal property. No one else was allowed to go in there, on pain of death. They built a wall, and had it guarded night and day by their deadliest, most trustworthy knights. Then, only after solemn ceremonies and much preparation would a chosen few eat of the mushrooms and experience the visions."

"What'd they see?"

"Such secrets weren't shared with common folk. One thing's for sure, though – the knowledge they gained was powerful indeed. They used it to conquer their foes and bring peace to the realm. Some called them the Mushroom Kings, and their old coat-of-arms had a toadstool with a crown on the top. But then something bad happened."

"What?"

"Well, King Boletus – that would be your great-great-great grandfather – was especially keen on the mushrooms. Ate of them liberally. For a time he was the wisest of kings, but then he began to...overindulge. He'd go off to the garden for days at a time with his courtiers, enjoying his visions. Eventually, they didn't came back. When search-ers finally found them, the king... he'd been transformed.

"A horrible sight, they say it was. His feet rooted to the ground, his flesh fibrous and pale, his very sweat a mist of white spores. As if he'd become a mushroom himself. After that, his heir – your great-great grandfather – had the whole place sealed off. He locked the gates and threw away the key, lest the kingdom's entire noble line be tempted to a similar fate."

"But why did they change?" Ziqqora had asked.

The old groundskeeper had merely shrugged. "No one really knows. Some think the fungus is alive. Not as plants are, but as men are. That beneath those caps and stalks are souls just as bright as our own, perhaps even brighter. That by eating of their flesh, one is able to commune with their slumbering minds. They say maybe old Boletus just got too greedy, and was punished for his gluttony. The 'shrooms had had enough of being eaten, and decided to punish all who might feast on them in future."

A chill now ran down Ziqqora's spine as she remembered the groundskeeper's tale. Imagine being transformed into a mushroom! Even more compelling than her fear, though, was her desire to experi-ence such wondrous visions for herself.

Dreaming was her passion, after all. Her main pastime and escape.

There just wasn't much else for her to do with her life. The staff treated her like some kind of poisonous flower: beautiful, but un-touchable. Get too close, the king might have their heads. Not even the randiest of handsome stableboys would be suicidal enough to sneak off with her into a field. The only one who seemed incorrigible enough was Bertrand, and he was gross!

No, other than him, no servant of either sex would ever risk cor-rupting her bearing with their common speech, their slovenly pos-tures, or their un-royal ways. Her dad would have them flogged if he found her using gutter slang or slouching at her desk. Even the groundskeeper's language had turned more high-falutin in her presence, as if he'd been auditioning for the role of royal storyteller. Even so, after telling her the tale of the garden, he'd hustled away, afraid to be seen with her.

It left her only a mere handful of people with whom she was permitted to associate: her father, who was always busy; her stepmother, whom she hated; her stepsisters, who picked on her constantly; and her tutors, a pack of stodgy old eunuchs who wouldn't know fun if it came up and bit them on the dismal remains of their testes. She had nothing else to do but wait for some prearranged marriage to some prince she'd never met. Even that, in a way, was its own form of dreaming. Sometimes, even a nightmare.

So, she spent her time dreaming of other things. The night offered its own kind of dreams, of course, but so did the mornings and afternoons, when she'd lie on the lawn and look up at the clouds, and daydream.

But, these fabled, forbidden mushrooms! Surely the visions they'd offer would be something else entirely – something transcendental, as lurid as a thousandfold suns!

Having found the iron fence, she looked for a means to get over it, skirting the edge until she found an oak whose upper branches had grown very close to the top. She climbed up cautiously, the task made harder by her long, lacy dress. Being a princess, she didn't have much in the way of practical attire.

The boughs shuddered and creaked underneath her, threatening to snap. She stepped off quickly, placing her slender little feet between the rusted iron spikes that jutted up from the topmost bar. The fence swayed, metal groaning. She crouched to grasp the spikes and stop herself tumbling from her teetering perch. Another spike poked rudely at her groin. Had she crouched any lower, she would've impaled herself upon it. Now wouldn't *that be* a stupid way to lose her virginity!

She steadied herself, the scabrous rusted metal rough on her delicate skin, then tipped forward and took a plunge into the garden. Her dress snagged and tore on the spikes as she fell, but she landed in the undergrowth and rolled, with no more harm done than messing her hair and dirtying her hands.

Jumping to her feet, she brushed herself off, and sighed with relief. She'd done it! Now all she had to do was find the grove at the centre of the garden, where grew those miraculous mushrooms!

The paths, long neglected, were well overgrown. She followed the trail of white-capped mushrooms, which became more numerous, not to mention more colourful. Vivid little toadstools teemed on all sides, some pink and powder-blue, others crimson and canary-feather yellow. Some looked like teeth with drops of blood on the top.

Before long, she saw mushrooms everywhere, and not just along the path. They covered the trees like fibrous cloaks; they clung to the rocks and the logs in tiers of brown wafers. Some were fibrous and long, like reeds underwater; others were fulsome and fat, with thick stumps and caps enough to sit on. The air hung heavy with moisture and a cloying, sweaty smell, not unlike the inside of a codpiece. Spore clouds sparkled in what light shot down through the canopy, dancing like dust in some musty old attic. Most of the mushrooms were beautiful, but some looked decidedly sinister. A black, mould-like fungus grew on some of the trees, seeming to seethe angrily.

Ziqqora gave that stuff a wide-berth and continued on for what seemed like ages, searching for the grove. At last, she came to a generous clearing dotted with massive, rainbow-coloured toadstools. Between them were shapes that looked like ancient statues, perhaps placed here to decorate the garden, long ago. She drew closer, then froze.

They weren't statues at all, but the remains of people. Her great-great-great grandfather and his courtiers, presumably. Their once-colourful clothing had faded with time. Their bodies were fibrous and white. Their elongated fingers looked like slender fungal shoots. Their bare feet lay sunken in the soil. Their skin was striped with gills, oozing a viscous red liquid that made them look like they were bleeding from a multitude of tiny little cuts. But their faces were smiling.

One of them wore a crown. His expression was of sheer ecstasy. Was this her ancestor, Boletus, the last of the Mushroom Kings? He didn't look as though his transformation had been painful at all. Ziqqora walked among the figures, her skin prickling with wonder and dread. Beside each of them was one of the huge toadstools. Their caps were a riot of colours, as if a painter had gone mad with his palette and created some vibrant abstraction. The meat looked soft, tender. It scintillated in the light, like mother-of-pearl. Surely this was the vision-granting substance?

She reached out and tore off a morsel. A part of her couldn't quite believe what she was doing. She felt like a spectator at a puppet show, a witness in a dream, watching some strange, unknown heroine venture into danger. But the rest of her mind knew exactly what she was up to. She had to see the visions for herself! She gobbled up the meat —

And found herself rooted to the spot.

Chapter 2: The First Trip

At first, she couldn't move. She experienced a moment of sheer terror as her body grew heavy, sinking down towards the earth the way the flesh of the mushroom sank down into her belly. Would her toes become fibrous and seek out the shelter of the soil, just like those of her great-great-great grandfather?

A bitter aftertaste crawled in her throat like a horde of insects. Then her skin started crawling as well, prickling in undulating patterns, as if a host of tiny spiders were dancing all over it. Her stomach felt queasy, then buoyant, like a hot-air balloon. Her limbs felt light and airy, like a bird's hollow bones. The feeling made her laugh with excitement – and relief.

Finding she could move after all, she took a misguided step. It seemed like a very lengthy stride, but at the same time barely a shuffle. Her dress brushed her legs like something foreign. Her skin felt foreign, too, clammy and crawling but airy and free. The contours of the air seemed to warp and the shapes of the trees rippled like a summer horizon. Was her vision beginning?

Steadily, the clearing became a kaleidoscope. Gouts of rainbow fire began to crawl across her mind's open eye, repainting the sky in hues of pink and orange. The air shimmered in a curtain of colour. She took a faltering step, pushed through it –

And emerged somewhere else entirely.

Whoa...

The garden had gone. It its place celestial vistas shone down through a web woven from tendrils of fungus with pulses of light shooting through them. Each circular gap in the web offered a window to some other sky. Through one of the windows could be seen a riot of nebulas and stars; through another came a slice of bright sunlight, so that night and day intertwined with one another in some transcendental tapestry.

At length she took her eyes off the multiform sky. The ground beneath her feet was fibrous and runnelled, like a giant-sized version of the disembodied brain one of her tutors kept in a jar of preservative fluids on his desk. Otherwise it looked like the flesh of a mushroom.

Ziqqora paused and took a very deep breath. It felt healthy and clear. Gone was the nausea she'd experienced earlier. Her whole being felt light. Her skin seemed to glow, so too her golden hair. She looked at her palms; they were no longer grazed or dirty from her fall into the garden. She felt no hunger, no tiredness, no discomfort at all. Was she even awake? Had she been transported in spirit? Perhaps she was *dead!*

She looked around again. A solitary landmark rose in the distance, a monolithic structure of imposing black stone. Having no other destination, she set off towards it. The sight of it worked some kind of magick on her mind, stirring up something she couldn't quite place, something very intimate and deep, like a reoccurring dream or a memory from childhood obscured by the passage of time. A sense of eerie familiarity gripped her. Did she know of this place, somewhere deep down, or was it just the locus of some spiritual gravity that felt intimate to everyone? There were such places, she knew, though she'd only ever seen them in dreams.

As she crept through the arches of the building, she almost said "Hello? Is anyone there?" But the place seemed too quiet to disturb with any sound, so she went on quietly, her steps light and airy but echoing anyway.

The interior was very nearly empty, save for a statue glowing with some indwelling radiance. It depicted a massive and blossoming flower. Lounging in its centre, as if upon a bed, was a naked and beautiful woman. Her face was completely covered by locks of falling hair, and her legs were spread wide open, revealing her pussy, so that her posture and anatomy mimicked the bloom of the flowerbed she sat in. Ziqqora felt a tingle between her own legs, not because she found the statue sexy, but because the image called out to her on some other level, exuding a presence of raw sensuality.

For a while, she just stood frozen before it, staring.

Then she heard footsteps behind her.

Chapter 3: The Demon's Dream

Ziqqora spun to see a figure in the shadows just beyond the statue's light. It looked vaguely like a man, but his body was seething and as-yet-unformed, like a cloud of fungal spores taking shape and congealing. She felt a pulse of fear, and backed towards the statue.

"Don't be afraid," said the stranger.

He stepped into the light, young, handsome, and dressed in regal garments.

"Hi," he said. "My name's Mycoz. What's yours?"

Ziqqora was speechless for a moment. Then she managed to stammer her name.

"We haven't had a visitor like you in a while," he said. "Do you know where you are?"

She shook her head.

"We're in my father's dream," he said.

Ziqqora just stood there, wide-eyed.

"Let me try and clarify," he said, noting her confusion. "It all starts with my grandmother. That's her statue right behind you."

Ziqqora turned back towards the image, noting the woman's nubile figure and beautiful features.

"Pretty foxy for a granny," she whispered.

Mycoz smiled. "She's a full-blooded demon. They don't really age like you or I do."

Ziqqora's eyes lit up with wonder. She'd learned of many demons from her tutors – their names, their passions, their predilections and predations. Perhaps she'd learned of this one, as well?

"A demon?" she asked. "What's her name?"

"She doesn't have one," he said, sadly. "Not anymore. The other demons took it, flayed it from her soul, like skin from a body."

"Why?"

"You know about the Cosmic War, right? The Great Deicide?"

Ziqqora nodded. Again, thanks to her tutors, she knew about both events. Apparently, the universe had once been ruled by things called gods, but the demons had killed them all long, long ago. Then they'd unleashed the pure essence of Chaos at the heart of creation, a substance called Celestial Fire, which burned down the cosmos and created it anew, ushering in the present cycle of time and existence: the Aeon of Chaos. The whole story was vague, full of holes and contradictions, but it *had* provided excellent fodder for Ziqqora's many daydreams.

"My gran there was one of the god-killers," said Mycoz. "But, sometime after the Deicide, she and some friends of hers had the bright idea of trying to be deities themselves. So they formed into a faction and started doing what gods used to do – demanding worship and sacrifice, binding mortals into webs of cruel Fate, that sort of thing. They even inspired the creation of an empire to venerate them. The place was called Ozich. Heard of it?"

"Of course," she said. Her tutors had told her about Old Ozich, too, not that there'd been much to tell. The empire had sprung up and spread out like wildfire, then suddenly collapsed almost five hundred years ago. Its monuments were almost all gone. The only real relic of its presence was the language it had spread across the continents, which Ziqqora and Mycoz were speaking right now.

"The other demons got upset, obviously," he said. "They'd fought pretty hard to rid the universe of gods, and they didn't want their efforts being wasted. A schism erupted between the demons of Ozich and those who were loyal to the cause of the Deicide. It turned into a full-blown civil war. Eventually my gran's faction lost. Their punishment was terrible. First their names were taken. Then their incarnations were sundered from their oversouls and sent into exile. Only one of them escaped."

"Who?"

"My dad. He was incarnate as a mushroom when they caught him, so he abandoned his flesh and put his soul into a spore cloud. He drifted on the winds for a while, then fell into a valley and seeped into the soil. He didn't stop until he landed in a chasm, deep below the earth, where he started regrowing. Eventually his tendrils shot up through the ground. I'll spare you the lurid details, but demons are randy by nature, it seems, so he ended up mating with a lot of the locals. Local fungi, that is. That's how myself and my siblings got made."

113

Ziqqora's eyes went wide.

"You're a...a mushroom?" she asked, staring at his handsome and very human-looking features.

"Half-mushroom," he corrected. "My physical body isn't all that ambulatory most of the time. But my soul is free to come and go as it pleases. So is yours, now that you've eaten of my flesh."

"Your flesh?"

"Yep," said Mycoz, smiling.

She stared at him, trying to reconcile the giant, technicolour toadstool with the being that stood before her. She felt more than a little perturbed. The groundskeeper had been correct; the 'shrooms really did harbour inhuman intelligence. She was speaking with one of those intellects right now. Would he punish her for eating his flesh? Would he bind her body to the earth in the form of a mushroom, while trapping her soul in this place?

Or perhaps he'd make her his concubine. Sexual images flickered through her mind – her white thighs spread wide around his heaving, grinding hips; his prick spearing deeply inside of her. It was a sensation she'd often imagined, but had never truly known. The closest she'd come was with the probings of her own slender fingers. Would he be gentle, she wondered – or rough? Would his lust even know any limits? Would be plunder her body, one hole after another?

She started getting wet in spite of her terror. But why was she finding such hideous prospects arousing? Why was she even imagining them at all? She felt the heat of the statue behind her, pulsing, seething, as though it were in tune with her own frantic blood.

This thing's messing with my head! she thought, and pulled away from the image, even though her movements took her closer to the demon-spawn.

The haze of lust dissipated. The sexual images faded from her eyes, whirling off into blackness. She glanced at the statue, warily. Mycoz chuckled.

114

"They called her the Queen of the Carnal Garden," he said. "Her image still seems to have a stirring effect. My dad keeps it here for sentimental reasons, to remember what she used to be like, before her mutilation."

Ziqqora stared at him. He still seemed quite gentlemanly. But was his seeming sincere, or merely a charade? Would his flesh peel off into a cloud of mushroom spores and start invading her airways? Would her body be mutated, her soul made a prisoner?

She took a deep breath. This torture of uncertainty had to end, one way or another.

"My ancestors used to come here," she said. "Then my great-great-great grandfather got turned into a mushroom. People think he was cursed, but no one really knows what happened."

"And you want to find out?"

She nodded.

He smiled. "Why don't you come and ask him yourself?"

She followed him out into the scintillating landscape. At first they were the only ones there. Then a series of shapes began to fall from the portals that filled up the sky. They looked a bit like comets, with inchoate bodies of quicksilver brightness. Ziqqora watched in amazement as they came to a sudden, floating stop just above the squishy earth, and began to transform before her eyes.

One became an orb of floating fire; another became crystalline, reflecting the light of the heavens through the facets of its body; another was a silent incarnation of lightning, with fingers that flickered and streaked; another was a gigantic crocodile with eyes that extruded on stalks and blinked with lids like the petals of carnivorous flowers.

Fuck!

Ziqqora shrieked and backed away.

"Fallon!" snapped Mycoz. "Stop messing with our guest, you little jerk!"

The crocodile transformed into the likeness of a cute young boy and stuck out his tongue. Then another light descended, taking the shape of a man in his prime. He wore royal robes of myriad colours and his head was encircled by a crown. Ziqqora looked at him with wide-open eyes. His image was one she'd passed many times in the palace, painted in oils and hung up on the walls. It was Boletus, her great-great-great grandfather, the last of the Mushroom Kings. His features looked a little like hers.

"You appear rather familiar, young lady," he said. "Am I detecting a family resemblance?"

"I'm your great-great-great granddaughter, Ziqqora."

"Ha! I was wondering when my descendants would turn up to visit me. It seems like an awfully long time. I thought maybe they'd forgotten..."

"They thought you were dead. Cursed into the shape of a mushroom."

"Whatever gave them that idea?"

"You did. I mean, you literally turned into a mushroom."

"That's because I wanted to live here, instead! I'm afraid I might've left the kingdom in a bit of disarray, but it was just so dreadfully *dull*. It's much more fun here, in the Demon's Dream, and the many realms beyond it. Come to think of it, I've got a date with a hot young demoness near the Maw of Cassiopion. Goodbye for now, my dear!"

"Wait!"

But he was already transforming back into a comet and shooting up into the sky, where he vanished through one of the portals. The rest of the figures departed in similar style. It seemed that they too had better ways to spend their time.

What the fuck? was the sum of the thoughts that Ziqqora could muster.

Mycoz laughed. "That ancestor of yours is incorrigible!" he said.

"So he wasn't cursed at all," she whispered, talking more to herself than to anyone else. "He *decided* to stay here..."

"That's right," said Mycoz. "You see, my family and yours made a pact long ago. They'd guard our bodies in the waking world. In exchange, we'd let them eat of our flesh and come visit us here."

"*Here,*" she said. "Meaning your father's dream...?"

"That's right. He's sleeping under the earth, waiting for a time to re-emerge. But his mind is like a realm unto itself. It's connected to many other places by the gates you see above you. Sort of like a crossroads, but with a whole lot of forks. Anyone who comes here can make use of the portals to travel all over the cosmos. That's what your ancestors did. They travelled through the gateways in their spirit bodies, getting all sorts of knowledge that helped them run their kingdom. But it seems like someone made a mess of things and forgot to pass on the secrets of this place, which means we haven't had a guest like you in a while now. Which is a shame, really. I rather liked hanging around with humans. Still, better late than never, right?"

Ziqqora nodded, then paused. The way he'd been talking, it sounded as if he'd borne witness to all of those events first hand.

"Just how old are you?" she asked.

He shrugged. "Time's a bit slippery here," he said. "It is a dream, after all. And time passes differently in other realms, as well. Would you like to explore a few?" Smiling politely, he offered her his hand.

She paused for a moment. But what was the danger? His family and hers were allies of old. Her great-great-great grandfather hadn't been cursed with the shape of a mushroom – he'd become that way willingly. What's more, the Demon's Dream was exciting, wilder than her wildest daydreams.

She smiled and put her hand in his, then bid farewell to the earth beneath her feet.

Chapter 4: Star Quest

The sensation of flying was somewhat like falling asleep, when she'd feel her consciousness unmooring from her body and drifting away, except that this time her body came with her.

They drifted up light as the air. At first Mycoz was pulling her, like some runaway kite, but then she started floating on her own, as if the only thing holding her down had been some stubborn superstition of gravity, and now it was gone.

The two of them flew up through a portal and emerged above a blood-red sea filled with giant white lampreys. The creatures were bigger than ships, bigger than whales. They seemed to be feeding on something even bigger, something whose shadow filled the deep like a great sunken continent. They writhed in their multitudes around it, occasionally breaking the surface in explosions of spume, then diving back down again. Suddenly one of them leapt very high. For a terrible moment Ziqqora thought it might keep ascending and swallow her and Mycoz whole with its hideous circular maw. A tremor of dread ran through her, even as the beast fell back down into the waters.

"Don't worry," said Mycoz, who must've felt her hand trembling in his. "We're here in spirit form. Very few things have the power to hurt us – especially not these things."

Ziqqora made herself calm down. Steadily her fear gave way to a sense of pure exhilaration as they flew on above the blood-red sea. In the distance she saw islands of onyx dotted with lighthouse-like obelisks blasting out beams of revolving blue light. When they struck her, they filled her with the dreams of dead sailors. Some were bittersweet with nostalgia; others were raunchy fantasies of lovers and prostitutes in port. The lust she felt was alien, anatomically-speaking, but otherwise familiar. It hit her with the force of the blood-scented winds that whipped above the great gruesome sea. For a moment she was paralysed by the intensity. Then Mycoz pulled on her hand, and they flitted back though the portal, through the Demon's Dream, and out into a starscape.

They strode along a road made of meteoric dust, even though they didn't need to walk. Ziqqora spied a human-like body in the distance. The size of a planetoid, its own gravitational force had screwed up its limbs into a ball, so that it hovered in the heavens in the posture of a foetus, even though it looked like a bearded old man. Its blood had been frozen into icicles that drifted around it like satellites. They looked like giant snowflakes, albeit glittering and red.

Must be one of the old, dead god-things, thought Ziqqora.

She knew from her lessons that most had been devoured by the demons or burnt by Celestial Fire, but some of their bodies were still floating in the void. Sometimes their bones or their calcified organs would fall down to earth like meteors, exploding. Their black metal bones were much prized among royals. Her own father had a sliver of god-bone that served as a dagger.

A huge, vague shape came swimming through the blackness. She saw it at first as an absence of stars in the distance, drawing closer and closer, not to them but to the carcass. Ziqqora couldn't stop herself from shaking as she saw it more clearly, even though she knew it probably couldn't sense them. She found herself huddling close to Mycoz, trying to shelter in his presence. He clustered close to her, too. Was that a shiver she felt, running though his frame? Even he was afraid of it!

The thing looked like a giant maggot, fat and long, so big it made her feel vertigo. She didn't understand how she hadn't seen it sooner. Something as big as that, against the star-strewn blanket of space, should've been visible for many miles. And yet it had emerged from the darkness like a shark from the depths. Perhaps it had its own means of slipping in and out from underneath the skin of the void? Either way, it was out of hiding now, and hungry. It tore into the dead god's body with gusto, slurping down the meat. Its pale body pulsated, like a wineskin getting fuller.

"The demon worm, Krauwm," said Mycoz with another shiver of dread.

Ziqqora knew that name; she'd also heard it in her lessons. Krauwm had started out just as an ordinary maggot; then grown bloated from consuming dead god-flesh. Since then he'd been growing and growing, feasting on the deific cadavers that floated in space, drinking their ichor and sucking their marrow. Many mortals paid homage to him, as though he were a substitute for those he'd devoured.

"We'd better get moving," Mycoz added, "in case he tries to eat us too."

"He can see us?"

"Of course he can. So can wizards and most other things with second sight. Come on!"

They flew towards a portal up ahead. Drawn by their movement, the demon worm flew after. Despite his fat frame, his speed was incredible. He shot towards them like a squid underwater. Soon his mouth gaped behind them like a hungry black star. The breath that came out was like a breeze from all the abattoirs on earth. His rows of curving teeth were bedecked with the golden skins of gods long devoured.

"Shit!" said Ziqqora.

Then the portal loomed up and swallowed them both before the Krauwm could, leaving the demon worm to snap his teeth on empty air before going back to his feast.

Ziqqora breathed a sigh of relief as they returned to the Demon's Dream. Their brush with the worm had been exciting, for sure, but also terrifying. She hoped for a more tranquil destination this time.

Through the next portal, they alighted on a ring of white dust swirling around a gas giant. Castles hung in the distance like satellites, the homes of cosmic demons who dwelt in the void.

There seemed to be a party going on in one of them. The windows strobed with psychedelic light. Music filtered out across the starscape, all beautiful and terrible at once. The vocals were a mixture of singing and wailing. No mortal man nor woman could make such a sound.

The tune that went with them was nothing like the orderly melodies her father's royal minstrels often played in the palace. Wild and ever-changing, it called for a dance that didn't end. Ziqqora felt a pulse of excitement, and reached out her hand towards Mycoz, even though it was somewhat improper for a princess to do so.

"Shall we?" she asked.

Mycoz smiled and took her hand. Together they danced around the ring of cosmic dust. The planet beside them seethed with mercury and crimson. They seemed to dance for untold hours as the demon music mutated, surging in crescendos and suddenly exploding, scattering its notes like flaming streaks of fireworks, only to gather them quickly and draw them back up again, like leaves in a whirlwind ascending. Ziqqora found herself staring deep into Mycoz's eyes. His pupils seemed to glint, as if with specks of distant starlight. His body against hers was solid and warm. The friction of their dancing was giving her a tingle, so too the sight of his face, handsome and full against the backdrop of planets and stars.

So what if he's really a mushroom? she thought.

She pulled him close, and kissed him on the lips.

And awoke a moment later, and found herself embracing the same giant toadstool she'd fed from, her lips against its technicolour skin.

She got up and glanced around. She felt like she'd been in that other place for hours, but the sun was still high in the sky, inching close to its midday meridian, as though she'd only been sleeping – or dreaming – for minutes. Her head felt peculiar, her stomach queasy. That feeling of lightness was still clinging to her limbs, but only a little bit, yielding to a growing sense of gravity and tiredness. Her thoughts felt scattered like dead autumn leaves. She tried to whip them up into coherence.

Was it all just a dream? she wondered.

But no, it couldn't have been – it was all too real! And there, standing right beside her, as tangible proof, was the mutated body of her great-great-great grandfather, his mushrooming head still adorned with a crown, while his spirit roamed the cosmos undying.

Ziqqora grinned to herself. Despite her fatigue and undeniable nausea, she still felt incredibly excited. She'd discovered the secret of the garden – and it was wondrous! She couldn't wait to tell her father the truth. Then he could eat of the mushrooms as his forefathers had, and thereby gain the knowledge he'd need to restore his kingdom's fortunes! The Mushroom Kings, long vanished from the earth, could return to Myconia, and the realm could crawl back from its state of decay!

She ran towards home with a spring in her step – over the fence, through the woods, then back across the manicured lawn that abutted the palace. She was so happy, so buoyant, she didn't even notice Bertrand, the groundskeeper's son, watching her emerge from the forest with covetous eyes.

Chapter 5: The Dinner

Only a few sentries saw her as she snuck back into the palace, but Ziqqora knew they wouldn't tell. How could they, without admitting to a dereliction of duty, and thus being flogged? Sometimes her father's iron discipline had its inadvertent upsides. To her delight she found her rooms undisturbed and unattended, save for the dummy she'd left in her bed. She dismantled its body of pillows and wig, then slid beneath the sheets and lay there in daydreams till the dinner bell rang.

All too soon, she was sitting at the twenty-foot table that bisected the dining room. Her place was in the middle, opposite her stepsisters. Luckily the table was too wide for them to kick her underneath it, as she knew they would like to. Instead they just made awful faces when no one was looking, sneering and poking out their tongues at her. Then they'd turn to one another, whispering and giggling, as they presently were.

Ziqqora glared at them. They were twins with ginger hair. The freckles on their corpse-white skin looked like spots of drying blood on the faces of dead men.

Maybe it's true what they say, thought Ziqqora. *Maybe red-headed people really don't have souls!*

She knew they hated her; they said it often enough. They resented her place as the heir to the throne. So did their stepmother, who sat at the head of the table to Ziqqora's far left, though she was far more cagey than her daughters when it came to expressing her resentment. She wasn't a red-head, like them, but blond and waif-like and pretty in her way. But her blue eyes were cold, and her bosom seemed to hold all the warmth of a mortuary slab.

When I'm queen I'll banish them, thought Ziqqora.

Not to someplace awful, of course, just someplace where she wouldn't have to deal with them. Until then, she'd just have to suffer her stepsisters' mockeries, as well as their mother's false smiles and condescension. But she wouldn't let such things get her down tonight. She had important discoveries to share with her father!

Turning to him, she smiled. Her thoughts were no longer scattered. Her body was just a little bit queasy and airy, but the first few courses of dinner had helped. They'd had venison and pheasant, forcemeat of mussels and lobsters and squid, followed by duck liver paste. The wine had flowed liberally, and everyone drank, though Ziqqora, being a princess, had to take her wine with water for the sake of propriety. Still, she felt a little bit buzzed, and very, very happy. It was time to unveil her great secret!

"Dad?" she said.

Her father was bearded and greying and plump. He always smelled of sweat, but Ziqqora found the aroma somewhat comforting.

"Yes dear?" he replied.

"What do you know about the forbidden garden?" she asked, starting out coyly. "You know, the mushrooms there? Because I heard the old kings used to eat them all the time. Then they'd fly across the earth in the spirit, spying on their enemies and getting all the knowledge they needed to slaughter their foes and bring joy to the people. That's why the kingdom of Myconia used to be so powerful, isn't it? Maybe you should try eating the mushrooms too? Maybe we all should!"

She smiled excitedly, waiting for her father's response. For a moment he just sat there. Then his brows became furrowed and dark, like gathering clouds, and his cheeks reddened with anger, like the surface of a sea in which sharks have been feeding.

"Who told you that?" he hissed.

"Just a little bird," said Ziqqora, growing unsettled.

"If I ever find out who that little bird is, then I'll be sure to clip its wings, and its lying little tongue into the bargain. That garden is off-limits for a reason."

"But the old kings –"

"The old kings were fools!" he roared. "They got tricked by a demon. He lured them to his grove and gave them false visions so he could cripple their bodies and gobble up their souls. My great-grandfather himself saw the truth of this, when he beheld his own sire transformed into a travesty!"

"What if he *wanted* to be a mushroom?"

"Balderdash! Who would want to be a mushroom, a turnip, a carrot, a fucking plantain? Such is a fate worse than death. You need to get your head out of the clouds, girl."

As the king sat there seething, his wife made a disapproving noise, sucking the air through her teeth.

"I've told you time and again you need to be firmer with her," she said, speaking of Ziqqora as though she weren't there. "All she does is dream all day. No wonder she's got such silly notions in her head. She's not living in the real world at all! But someday she'll have to. Someday soon, in fact, given what's coming."

The ominous statement gave Ziqqora a nibble of panic. She turned to her father. "What's she talking about? What's coming?"

"Never mind that now," he said. "And as for the garden, you haven't been thinking about going there, have you?"

"Of course not," lied Ziqqora.

"Good. Because if I find out you have any such notions, I'll lock you in your chambers. I'll not have my daughter transformed into a mushroom and deflowered by a demon. Is that understood?"

"Yes, Father."

"Now go to your room! You need to be punished for all of this ridiculous talk."

Ziqqora got up and flounced to her room. She lay beneath the covers awake for a while, replaying the argument with her father in her mind. Eventually other thoughts began to intrude, thoughts that had been whirling around in her head, ever since she'd whirled around the ring of that planet with her arms around Mycoz. Eventually she drifted to sleep. Which was a good thing, too – she had to get up well before the sunrise if she wanted to sneak back into the garden!

Bertrand's dirt-covered face peered in through the shutters at the sleeping princess, maintaining his voyeuristic vigil. She appeared to be dreaming, and pleasant dreams at that. The kind of pleasant dreams that made him wish he could creep into her room.

He too had a journey to make in the morning, though he didn't quite know the destination. He only knew he had to follow her, should she leave for the woods once again.

The king stood in his chambers, sullenly staring at the mirror. At length he locked eyes with the reflection of his wife, lying naked on the bed.

"Why did you say that at dinner?" he asked. "You almost let the cat out of the bag. You know I don't want to tell her just yet."

"Well you'll have to tell her soon," she said.

"I suppose. But I'm still not quite sure if I want to go through with it."

"You've got no choice now, Riksmund. The agreement's been made!"

She was right, of course. He'd already offered Ziqqora's hand in marriage to Heinrich Van Gruel, the Jade Prince of Pecoz. The arrangement seemed like a necessity. The kingdom of Myconia was ailing, beset from the north by the Dead Heads of Lichhelm, and menaced from the east by the young king of Yule. Their only hope of survival lay in a powerful alliance, and Heinrich Van Gruel was a powerful man – young, vigorous, and a terror on the battlefield. He was famed for his performance at the battle of Troll Tooth Pass, where, perhaps inspired by the battle's location, he'd torn out the throats of two enemy commanders with his teeth. Not because he was a maniac, of course, but because his sword had been broken, and he'd needed to improvise. His was just the sort of strength that the kingdom of Myconia now needed on its side.

And yet, there were horrible rumours about him. His family was notorious for having made some pact with a certain clan of itinerant sorcerers. His first thirteen brides had all died on their wedding nights, under unknown circumstances. For all his valiant deeds, a sinister cloud hung over the young man. King Riksmund felt sick when he thought about handing Ziqqora over to him. Not just because she was his only daughter – a fact which might make any father blanch – but because of the danger she faced. Would she end up like those other thirteen princesses, dead from some mysterious malady – or even worse, murdered?

Why the fuck did I agree to this? he wondered.

126

Then he glanced back at his wife, and remembered why. She'd spent the past few months persuading him in favour of the marriage by every conceivable means at her disposal. Sometimes she'd been harsh and nagging, wearing down his will the way a caustic sea breeze eats away at a mountain. Other times she'd been weepy and seemingly helpless, crying about her uncertain future. Without an alliance they were doomed, she insisted. Their kingdom would be conquered, their lands overrun. He'd be executed, or walled up in a tower; *she'd* be enslaved as a concubine and ravaged by some horny invader. Ziqqora would be ravaged, too. If he didn't give his daughter to be married, she'd be turned into a whore. Wouldn't she be far better off being wed to a prince like Van Gruel?

The queen had used other strategies, too, rendering their bed a frosty and loveless domain until the king had come around to her point of view, at which point she'd leapt upon his cock like a rabbit in heat. There were so many twists and turns to her persuasion that he felt like a leaf in a whirlwind. Right now, staring at his reflection and contemplating the fate of his daughter, he felt his inner will rise up in disgust from the core of his being, like a surging tide of vomit.

"Perhaps it's not too late to call it off," he whispered.

"Don't be ridiculous!" she shrieked.

He glared at her reflection in the mirror.

The queen stared back. She must have realised he wasn't in any mood to be bullied this night, for when she finally answered him, her voice became pleasant and soothing.

"I know you're worried," she said. "It's only natural for a father to be so. But we *need* this alliance, and the deal has been made. Van Gruel is already on his way here, Riksmund. He'll arrive in two days! If you deny him now, at this juncture, then *he'll* be our enemy, as well. He won't be able to brook such an insult. And why should he? He's a fine young man. Those awful rumours about him aren't true at all. He's just had a run of bad luck, that's all. I've got it on good authority

– my cousin's an officer in his army, you know – and *he* told me that those thirteen brides all died of the plague. But Ziqqora's a healthy young thing, she'll be fine. And Van Gruel's a very handsome young man. I'm sure she'll be besotted with him. She'll be happy, he'll be happy, you'll be happy – the whole entire kingdom will be happy!"

"And so will you."

"Of course!" she said. "Your joy is mine, my beloved. Now why don't you come over here, and let me sooth that worried head of yours? You need to relieve some tension. You don't want to bank up the furnace!"

The king stood before the mirror, vacillating. He felt caught up in the whirlwind again. At length he abandoned his troubling reflection and strode to the bed. The queen crawled over to the edge with a hungry-looking smile.

Her mouth was full, but her eyes kept on smiling. Not because she particularly liked the feeling of his prick in her mouth, but because she knew she'd won.

She also knew the secret of Van Gruel, and the terrible rumours about him were pleasantries compared with the truth. Any woman who married him would certainly die. Which meant that in just a few days she'd be rid of her pesky little stepdaughter for good, leaving her red-headed offspring free to inherit the throne.

When Riksmund shuddered and came in her mouth she drank it down hungrily. Not because she particularly enjoyed the taste, but because the flavour of his seed had been transformed by her own deceptive alchemy. It tasted like victory.

Chapter 6: Predators

Ziqqora got up before dawn, roused by her own urgent need to get back to the garden. She set up the dummy in her bed and snuck out across the lawn, just like she'd done the day before.

Soon, she was climbing back over the fence and into the garden. The journey felt a lot shorter this time, now she knew the way. She smiled and waved happily to her great-great-great grandfather and the rest of his court, who stood there still as statues, their sprouting bodies all dripping with spores. They didn't wave back.

Oh well, she thought. *I guess I'll see them soon enough in the spirit!*

But the person she really wanted to see was Mycoz. She found his toadstool body and took a bite of his flesh. She didn't rip it off this time, but tenderly kissed it, sucking the meat until it came loose in her mouth. *I've given him a hickey!* she thought, then felt a thrill as her body turned light once again and the air in the garden transformed into a curtain of shimmering colour. She stepped through the curtain –

And emerged into the Dream once again. There was no one there. How would she find Mycoz? Perhaps she'd go back to their very first meeting place.

She skipped with flying steps towards the monolithic building, and waited inside by the statue. Once again she felt its radiant warmth filling her body with desire. This time she luxuriated in it. It seemed like the perfect preparation for what she had in mind.

Finally, Mycoz stepped out of the shadows. For a moment his form looked unstuck, like a roiling mass of spores. Then he was handsome, and human-like, again.

"You're back!" he said with a smile.

"How could I stay away?"

"Would you like to explore a little more? Maybe visit with your ancestor?"

"Maybe later. For now, why don't we go someplace quiet, and

129

sweet? I've got something to talk to you about."

He shrugged. "Okay. I think I've got just the place."

She took his hand and they flew up through a portal. She concentrated on his fingers intermeshed with her own. They felt warm and soft, but not nearly as clammy, nor as throbbing with blood. The excitement she felt was everywhere, flaring right out to the tips of her pinkies.

They flew down into a beautiful grove. The green of the trees was almost searingly bright, but the sunshine was soft and hung in the air like a nimbus. The ground was covered in a blanket of clover as fluffy as a featherbed.

"This is a realm of pure spirit," said Mycoz, plucking at the clover and throwing it up in the air by way of demonstration. "Everything is tangible to us."

He smiled, and Ziqqora smiled back. A current of flirtation ran between them.

"So," he said, "what'd you want to –"

Suddenly he froze, noticing something behind her. She turned to see the creature that had emerged from the undergrowth nearby. It looked like a stallion, with a coat as black as onyx and a spiralling horn atop its head. Its eyes were shining emerald, its jaws filled with fangs.

"A unicorn!" said Ziqqora.

She took a step towards it, reaching out her hand. Mycoz tried to pull her back.

"Be careful," he said. "They can –"

The unicorn nuzzled her hand. Then it grumbled at Mycoz and trotted away.

"You should look out for those," he said. "They can be dangerous. Unless you're a virgin, of course."

"They don't harm virgins?"

"No. Their father, the great demon unicorn, forbids it. He likes to deflower them himself."

"Oh," she said, contemplating this with some disquiet. Then she smiled. "It's funny the topic of virginity came up. That's sort of what I wanted to talk to you about. Well, not exactly talk..."

"Oh?" said Mycoz.

She leapt on him, kissing him and sending the both of them tumbling to the grass. When they finally broke off from their kisses Ziqqora was flushed. Mycoz looked shocked, but happy, too.

"You want to?" he asked.

She nodded. They started pulling off each other's clothing. Mycoz's garments were easy to remove, almost as if they *wanted* to come off. Ziqqora's were a little bit harder to shed. She wore voluminous layers of lace, some of them diaphanous, others opaque. They came off eventually, followed by her silken undergarments. As Mycoz undressed her she stared at his prick in wide-eyed excitement. So mesmerised she was by the sight of her lover's erection – the first of its kind she'd ever seen – that she barely even noticing when the last of her clothes had been removed, leaving her naked.

Mycoz stopped and stared at her. She lay on a bed of her own golden hair. She was nubile, and pale, and her tender skin glowed in the sunlight. Strawberry nipples poked up from her breasts.

She ogled him in turn, finally snatching her eyes from his cock. He was toned, supple, and perfectly formed. No hint of the fungal could be found in his features, except, perhaps, in the ruddy-looking tip of his erection, which bore, like all others of its ilk, a passing resemblance to the cap of a mushroom.

"Will it hurt?" she asked.

"Not in this realm," he said. "But first..."

He dove his head down between her legs.

"What're you – OH!"

Her eyes went wide with shock as he started to lick her. But the shock was ecstatic, and she threw back her head with a smile.

The princess was so excited by her journey – and whatever she planned to do – that she failed to even notice being followed as she entered the forest.

Not that Bertrand's presence was that easy to perceive. He hid behind trees and trod lightly through the undergrowth, hanging back a few dozen feet. Sometimes he lost sight of her completely, but he'd participated in more than a few royal hunts in a servant's capacity, and knew well how to follow the tracks of his prey.

He didn't exactly like the look of the place, this garden. The forms of the mushrooms were unsettling. Some looked like claws reaching up from the earth, others like corrugated brain-tissue. He'd heard all the stories from his father, about how the mushrooms were home to some terrible intelligence, and took vengeance on those who consumed or abused them.

But Bertrand didn't care. His desire for the princess was stronger than fear. He'd spied through her shutters every night since he'd first felt a tingle downstairs. He'd wanked himself raw to those memories more times than he could count. He knew she didn't like him, of course, but he didn't much care about that either.

He found her alone in a grove, save for the presence of several hideous figures resembling mushroom-men. At first they gave him pause, but he pressed on regardless. She was lying on the ground beside a gigantic toadstool, seemingly sleeping. Her clothes were disarrayed, her cheeks flushed, her languid face smiling with lust unmistakable.

Was she having a sex dream, he wondered? Or had she noticed him following after all, and therefore decided to play some sort of game with him?

Either way he didn't mind. He crept up beside her, knelt, and pulled up her dress, bunching it up on her stomach as he stared at her undergarments. They were made from white silk. A spot of dark moisture was present at the crotch. He knelt down and sniffed it, growing even more aroused as he did so. It was the very same perfume he'd smelt many times when he'd stolen such items from the castle laundry, but this time it was fresh.

He struggled to calm himself as he set about pulling her shoes off and dragging down her drawers. The hem slid off her waist and her pubes began to slowly appear, bushy and golden in the sunlight. He tugged even harder, yearning to see what lay lower. At long last her pussy appeared, albeit compact and hidden by the slope of her body and the press of her thighs. Smiling and fondling himself, he began to advance.

Ziqqora lay back moaning, writhing her thighs around Mycoz's head and gripping his hair in her hands. Shockwaves of pleasure rippled out from the touch of his tongue as it lapped her. The air became shimmering and rippling and bright. She was headed for a climax unlike any she'd given herself in the past. She gripped his head tightly, seizing, bracing herself –

When the sensation suddenly changed.

Bertrand spread her legs and stared down at the lips of her pussy. He was about to get closer when he heard something stirring behind him, and turned to see tendrils shooting up from the soil near the toadstool.

His eyes went wide. He froze for a second that seemed like a minute, watching the pads of the tendrils uncoil, dripping with fluid and filled with little fleshy proboscises that looked almost like nipples, and almost like jointless grasping fingers. They lashed out like whips, seizing his limbs and hoisting him up off the ground.

For a moment he hung there. Then came a sudden, almost incomprehensible motion, wet and hot and ravaging. He found himself spinning through the air like a top. As he landed he realised that something was very, very wrong. Most of his body hadn't come with him. His torso was slumped on the ground, armless and legless. His terrified consciousness dwelled in his own severed head – but not for very long. He tried to scream, but could only spin his eyes in their sockets as the tendrils came and got him again, pulling his parts into the moist black soil.

"Why'd you stop?" asked Ziqqora.

Mycoz smiled up at her, his mouth smeared with wet.

"Sorry," he said. "There was a disturbance in the garden that I had to take care of. Now, where was I?"

He dove back between her legs and resumed his ministrations. She felt the pleasure start to build once again, then suddenly explode to the rhythm of the colours that flashed before her eyes. He drew back, smiling, with even wetter lips.

"Now?" he asked.

She closed her eyes and nodded, waiting.

Her eyes flew open wide as he entered. Once more the shock was exquisite, but a thousand times greater. He hadn't been lying when he said there'd be no pain in this place. All that she felt was the pleasure of sweet penetration, growing greater and greater with each spearing motion.

She lay back for a time, trembling and murmuring, overwhelmed by the novel sensation. Then she got in on the movements, bucking her hips and rising up to meet him. They sat in the lotus position, her arms around his neck, his hands on her hips and her rump, lifting her bright, airy body.

They bounced and rocked and eventually flew up into the air, their limbs intertwisted, their senses exploding as their mutual pleasure kept mounting in tune with their ascent. She let out a moan as an orgasm gripped her like a hand of benevolent lightning, then sent her spinning into freefall in the aftermath. Mycoz held her tightly and hammered even harder, a crescendo of movement that ended with a climax of his own. He shuddered and slowed as his seed spurted into her. They wriggled together, teasing out the last of it, then fluttered to the earth like a pair of gentle leaves, landing in the clover. He pulled out his prick with a slippery motion. Their juices dribbled between them.

"Will I get pregnant?" she asked.

Mycoz laughed. "Not in this place," he said.

She smiled, then leaned in to kiss him again.

This time she awoke beside the toadstool with her clothes in disarray. Her dress was bunched up on her stomach, and her garments had been pulled down beneath.

Did I do that, she wondered, *during the vision?*

She glanced around. There was a splatter of blood on the ground, all but soaked into the soil. Perhaps it was hers? She had just lost her virginity, after all. She slipped a finger inside herself, probing. It still felt very tight; she could barely proceed past the knuckle. Nor was any blood on her finger as she slipped it back out again, only the shimmer of her juices in the sun.

Guess I'm still a virgin after all, she thought. *In the physical world, at least!*

She glanced back at the blood. Perhaps a wounded animal had

limped through the garden?

Who cares? she thought.

She ran towards home with a spring in her step. The sun was still at the zenith of noon, even though they'd made love for what'd seemed like many hours, over and over again, trying out a myriad of positions both floating and grounded.

Time can be slippery here, he'd said.

Clearly he was right! Soon she arrived back at the palace, crept to her room, and breathed out a sigh of relief as she saw that the dummy was still undisturbed in her bed. She put the dummy away and slipped back beneath the covers, lounging in a post-coital haze until the dinner-bell rang.

This time she stayed quiet about the garden. Perhaps she'd try talking to her father again sometime in the future, when he wasn't being quite so pig-headed, and perhaps, more importantly, when her stepmother wasn't in the room. For now she was happy to keep it her own little secret. And what a secret it was! She tried not to giggle and blush during the first seven courses of dinner. Even the scowls of her stepsisters couldn't dampen her mood. She was in love! Or maybe just in lust, assuming that those things were even different at all. Either way it felt pretty good. It seemed like nothing could impinge upon her happiness – until her father made his announcement.

"Ziqqora," he said, "I've got some news that concerns you."

"Oh?" She glanced up, suddenly worried her earlier excursion had been noticed after all.

"You're going to be married."

"To who?" she asked, too shocked to really process his words. She'd always known this day would come, but it had always felt like a faraway thing, like death, or old age, or the end of the world.

"To Heinrich Van Gruel, the Jade Prince of Pecoz."

Ziqqora froze. She'd heard all about the Jade Prince. His thirteen brides had all died on their wedding nights in sinister circumstances.

"But...but he's a murderer!" she said. "He kills all his wives, right after he deflowers them! Everyone knows about it!"

Her stepsisters started laughing. "You're gonna get murdered!" they said, chanting as one. "Murdered, murdered, murdered –"

"Silence!" snapped the queen. "No one's getting murdered. Those are all just vicious lies. Prince Heinrich is a marvellous man who's just had a run of bad luck, that's all. His thirteen wives all died from the plague."

"Isn't that a bit unlikely?" said Ziqqora. "Dad, you can't be serious!"

"It's all taken care of, my dear," he said. "Van Gruel's already on his way. The wedding will take place the day after tomorrow. Besides, your mother's right."

"She's not my mother!"

"She is by law! And Heinrich really is a splendid young man. I'm sure he'll care for you all the more, given the tragic manner in which his other brides have died."

Ziqqora started sobbing. "This is fucked!" she cried.

"I told you she wouldn't be able to handle it like a grown-up," said her stepmother.

"You're loving this, aren't you, you fucking cunt?" snapped Ziqqora.

"That's ENOUGH!" shouted the king. "Ziqqora, go to your room and pull yourself together. We'll talk more tomorrow."

Ziqqora stormed from the dining hall and ran to her chambers, hearing her stepsisters giggling as she went. She crawled beneath the covers and wept even more. What a revolting development! It was bad enough that she had to get married to a stranger, but to a murderous maniac as well?

She had to do something, but what? Perhaps the mushroom visions would show her the answer. She tossed and turned, doing her best to get to sleep so she could get up in the morning and make it to the garden unobserved.

Eventually she fell into a pit of fitful dreams. Thus she was well and truly dead to the world by the time a pair of figures crept into her room, holding something shiny and sharp.

Chapter 7: The Twins

Ziqqora's stepsisters stood in the darkness in front of her bed, each of them holding a pair of sharp scissors. They'd been planning on snipping off her golden locks and giving her a boy's haircut, so she'd be humiliated on the fast-approaching day of her wedding. As it was, they stood there frozen, scissors in hand, listening.

Ziqqora, it seemed, had the habit of talking in her sleep, especially when she was agitated. She must have dreamt she was arguing with her father, trying to make him see reason and call off her marriage to Van Gruel. She told him all about a garden, and her secret lover Mycoz, who was part demon, part mushroom.

"You think it's true?" whispered Rudya, the older of the pair by a few short minutes.

"If it is, we can get her in a lot of trouble," said Gyara. "No one's allowed to go into the garden."

Rudya's eyes lit up as she considered for a moment all the cruel possibilities of such a situation.

"I've got a better idea," she said.

Then she whispered into her younger sister's ear. The two of them giggled, and went off to bed.

The next morning, they were waiting when Ziqqora set off towards the forest. They followed after, wearing cowls to cover their bright red hair, and hiding their skinny bodies in the bushes whenever possible. They had some deal of trouble getting over the spiked iron fence, but they finally managed to clamber up a tree and leap over the top, tumbling into the grass on the other side. Then they followed Ziqqora's footsteps down a road of white-capped mushrooms. They found her passed out in a grove beside a gigantic toadstool. Grinning, they reached beneath their cloaks and pulled out a pair of hefty hatchets, as identical as they were.

"Which one do you think is her boyfriend?" asked Gyara.

"Not sure," whispered Rudya.

They moved around, looking at the legions of fungi filling the garden.

"What about this one?" asked Gyara as she stopped by the one closest to Ziqqora's sleeping body and raised her hatchet.

"Don't be silly," said Rudya. "That's just a giant toadstool! How could she have screwed that? It doesn't even have a thingy!"

"It looks like one big thingy to me."

"Sure, but there's no way she could fit all that inside of her."

"Maybe she sat right on top of it?"

The twins shrugged. Ziqqora's dream-talk had been somewhat vague and hard to decipher. All they knew was that she had a lover in this garden, a being that was part fungus, part demon, with the appearance of both mushroom and man.

"It's gotta be one of these," said Rudya, pointing at the mushroom-men from the old king's court.

"She had sex with *that*?" said Gyara. "Gross!"

They stared for a moment at the fungus that bore the vestigial shape of a man. Then Rudya stuffed the hatchet under her arm and tore off the thing's rotting trousers. There, between its legs, was a mess of pubes that looked like sprouts and a cock that bore the likeness of a toadstool, dripping out spore-juice from its tip. On the figure's face was a look of frozen ecstasy.

"Check out his O-face," said Rudya. "I bet she's been sucking on his thing!"

"What a dirty bitch!"

"Well she's gonna have to get a new boyfriend to blow, 'cause it's time to make mushroom salad!"

Laughing with glee, they took their hatchets and started chopping up the mushroom-man. They hacked off his flaring, spindly fingers; they chopped off his toadstool-shaped prick; they even struck deep into the flesh of his chest, finding it sloughing and moist beneath their blades.

So busy they were with their chopping and giggling, at first they didn't notice the mushroom-man's change of expression, his face twisting into a semblance of anger. Before they could even stop laughing, a mass of black spores erupted from his chest. It covered them all over, entering their nostrils, their mouths, their lungs, even their pores. The stuff was cloying and thick. It stank like a handkerchief filled with old cum. They coughed and shrieked and fled from the garden, dropping their hatchets as they went.

Meanwhile, inside the Demon's Dream again, Ziqqora wrapped her arms around Mycoz, distraught.

"What's wrong?" he asked.

"It's terrible!" she cried. "I just found out I'm going to get married, to Heinrich Van Gruel! There're awful rumours about him. His first thirteen wives all died on their wedding nights. People say he murdered them! My stepmother made up some bullshit story about them all dying of the plague, but I can tell it's a lie. I bet she's behind this whole thing. She wants me to marry Van Gruel so he'll kill me, and she's tricked my dumb dad into going along with it. That cow wants me dead, just like I knew she always did!"

Ziqqora wept. In the Demon's Dream, her tears shone like silver. Mycoz wiped them away.

"Calm down," he said.

"How can I? The wedding's tomorrow. He's riding to Myconia

right now!"

"Right. But there's no point getting upset until we know what we're dealing with. You said it yourself, all this stuff about Van Gruel's just rumours. So, why don't we find out the truth for ourselves??"

"We can do that?" she asked, drying her eyes.

"How else do you think your ancestors built their kingdom from nothing? By spying on their enemies."

"Through the portals!"

"Exactly. Now come on, let's go have a look-see."

Ziqqora nodded sharply. Suddenly she felt a great deal less helpless.

"How do we find him?" she asked.

"The same way an eagle finds a hare. Come on!"

They took flight, and Mycoz guided them both through one of the portals. Ziqqora found herself staring down in shock at her very own kingdom of Myconia. For some reason the sight of such a familiar place from such a high altitude was even stranger to her eyes than the cosmic vistas she'd seen on her previous trip. She saw her family's crumbling palace below, bordered by the sprawling forest to the south. She could even see the garden and its grove, peeking through a gap in the trees. The toadstools looked like daubs of kaleidoscopic colour. Was that her own sleeping body, lying next to Mycoz? It was an eerie feeling, beholding her flesh as she travelled in the spirit.

They flew on above the castle and peered out across the landscape. Beyond the wide palace moat was the city of Myconia, sprawling and crumbling in every direction. Further to the north lay the city of Lichhelm, to the east the Troll Tooth Passes, which led in turn to the kingdom of Yule. To the west was the realm of Pecoz. All had once been under Myconian rule, either as tributaries or actual dominions. Then her great-great-great grandfather had transformed into a mushroom, beginning the kingdom's long decline. The realm had shrivelled into itself, retreating from its borders and allowing new powers to rise in its wake. The whole process reminded her of that god-thing she'd seen in the void, crushed into the posture of a foetus by its own morbid gravity. She knew now the reason why her ancestors' efforts had been so completely undone: her family had forsaken the garden, and turned from the path of the Mushroom.

"Which way's he coming from?' asked Mycoz.

"West," said Ziqqora.

She took the lead, squeezing his hand as she flew. The warmth of his fingers was comfort indeed, as was the beauteous view. They passed over the dense, crowded city, where each and every building took on the likeness of a doll house and smoke rose from chimneys to fog up the sky all around them; over the paddocks and cultivated fields, where sheep lay like puffs of white wool on a blanket; over the dense, verdant forests, where the treetops rose and fell like the waves of some vast, frozen ocean. They saw children playing, lovers fucking, horsemen riding.

"There!" she cried.

Speeding through the forest was a convoy heading fast for Myconia. She'd very nearly missed it, for the whole train was decked out in livery of jade, which in the context of the wood served them almost as camouflage.

"The Jade Prince," she said. "That must be him!"

They flew lower, above the road, and peered down at the convoy, witnessing a spectacle of luxury and power with few parallels in this part of the world. The jade-coloured coaches were lacquered and shining, painted with the image of a serpent with gemstones for eyes. The horses were black, with jade-coloured tack. The knights were bedecked with jade-painted armour and surcoats of brocaded silk. At the front of the train rode a tall, handsome man on a mighty white stallion, his raven-dark hair flapping wild in the wind. It could only be Heinrich Van Gruel, the Jade Prince of Pecoz.

"He's pretty good-looking," said Mycoz. "And he's got quite a codpiece!"

Ziqqora stared down at her bridegroom's groin, where sat the biggest codpiece she'd seen in her life. Van Gruel's build was massive, but even on his muscular frame the codpiece still seemed ungainly, like some kind of prop in a theatrical comedy. Was this some peculiar Pecoz fashion, or did Van Gruel have a monster in his trousers that needed such a copious compartment?

Mycoz laughed. "At least you won't have to worry about your husband being poorly-hung!"

Ziqqora glanced at him, wondering how he could be so completely carefree. Shouldn't he be jealous that his lover was about to be taken by another? Then again, he was a demon-spawned mushroom who'd lived for untold ages in a realm where time itself seemed elastic. He might've been *her* first lover, but she doubted very much she'd been his. How many women had he known across the ages? How many mushrooms? From what she'd seen so far, the Demon's children were shape-shifters, at least when they travelled in the spirit. There was no limit to the places Mycoz had gone, the beings he'd consorted with across the dimensions. He'd probably done it with everything – animal, mineral, vegetable – alien!

They followed Van Gruel as he sped through the forest. Ziqqora began to feel in two minds about him. He was certainly the most beautiful, powerful man she'd ever seen. But, there were the deaths of his brides to consider, not to mention the size of his codpiece, which was distinctly alarming. Perhaps he'd skewered them to death on the marriage bed?

At length the convoy came to a stop beside a stream. Van Gruel leapt down, strode over to the water, and began to undress.

"Here we go," said Mycoz. "Now you'll get a really good look at him."

Ziqqora watched with unblinking eyes. First he took off his tunic and belt, revealing a sculpted chest with a rug of black hair. His mus-

cles bulged and flexed with every subtle movement. He had the defi-
nition of a racehorse, with power to match. Ziqqora felt a tingle of undeniable desire as she watched him. Then he took off his trousers, and
her eyes went wide with terror.

His cock broke free from the codpiece like a jack-in-a-box, flailing
and hissing. It wasn't a normal male organ at all, but a scaly, fanged
serpent!

"Oh shit!" she said.

"Well, this isn't good," said Mycoz, showing a talent for under-
statement.

Chapter 8: The Jade Prince of Pecoz

"Down!" growled Heinrich as his serpentine member unfurled.

It hissed and bit him on the hand. He growled and shook blood
from the wound. He didn't have to be concerned about the venom, of
course; he was quite immune. It was more about the principle of the
thing. The creature that lived between his legs just didn't obey him.
It'd been that way for as long as he could remember. Not that the
creature had always been with him, of course. But his memory didn't
stretch back that far; he'd only been a newborn when they'd joined it
to his body.

The kingdom of Pecoz had been weak back then, and his parents
had needed a powerful heir. So they'd made a pact with the Sebeks,
sorcerous drifters who'd fallen on hard times of their own.

For generations the Sebeks had wandered the coastlines, selling
their magick to sailors. For a not inconsiderable fee they'd cast their
spells and bring forth favourable winds for their clients. Those who
paid them reached their destinations quickly and safely. Those who
didn't often fell victim to shipwreck. Eventually people figured out the
obvious truth: the Sebeks were extortionists. They weren't just casting
their spells for those who paid the fees, they were summoning tem-

pests to destroy those who didn't. Thousands had died and many fortunes had been lost because of their sorcery. The outcry against them was savage. They were lynched, or stoned, or burned at the stake wherever they were found. The few that survived fled to Pecoz, offering their magick in exchange for protection.

The Gruels took them up on it, swore a pact, and appointed the Sebeks as sorcerers to the crown. Their first task? To infuse the infant Heinrich with incredible power. In a secret ritual they sliced off his member, called forth this creature from Beyond, and grafted it forever to the stump of his manhood. Heinrich always winced when he imagined that moment, even though he couldn't remember it. Still he felt like the pain was imprinted on his mind somehow, like a bad dream after waking.

In many ways, the ritual had worked. The power of the creature suffused his flesh, and Heinrich grew up to be as strong as an ox, as swift as a fox, and as healthy as a horse. He never got sick, needed very little sleep, and was a terror on the battlefield, slaughtering the enemies of Pecoz and expanding its dominion. But the magick had its drawbacks, as well. The creature had grown up just as he had, until finally reaching its present, ungainly size. It had also grown more and more unmanageable, and had forced him to do terrible things. *It* was the reason why his thirteen young brides had all died. Heinrich had tried to resist it, but the process was nigh-on impossible. Not only did the beast have a mind of its own, but the pleasures it offered were great. Heinrich had found himself crippled by ecstasy even as he'd shuddered in horror at the deeds of the thing between his legs. Thus his relationship with the creature was deeply ambivalent. He despised its excesses, but needed the pleasures it gave. He needed its cooperation, too, but the monster was fickle indeed.

"Why did you bite me, you unruly bastard?" he hissed.

Because I don't like being locked up in the codpiece, it said, speaking directly into his mind with a sibilant voice. *It's musty and dark in there. How would you like it, being cooped up all day with a miasma of ball sweat?*

"You can't come out all the time," he whispered. "You know that. People just wouldn't understand..."

We'll make them understand! said the serpent. Just let me hang freely. Then, as soon as someone complains about it, or makes a nasty face, or whatever, then here's what we do: you just rip off their head with that incredible strength of yours, and I'll fuck them in the neck-stump while everyone's watching. Now who else would gripe after that? Besides, you know you'd enjoy it. There's nothing like a nice, tight throat-hole, all bubbling with blood...

Heinrich shook his head. "You have to stay in hiding, at least for the while."

Spoilsport! Coward! Loser! griped the snake.

"Enough!" shouted Heinrich. "Besides, how can I trust you with any independence after what happened last time? You promised not to hurt that girl. You promised not to hurt any of them."

I couldn't help it! Those parts they have inside of them are so soft and springy. The feel between my teeth...!

The serpent whirled in the air, flickering its tongue and gnashing its fangs in a show of excitement.

"Calm yourself," said Heinrich, even as he felt the same pulse of desire.

You know you love it, too.

"I don't," he said, lying. "And it has to stop, you hear? You've already chewed through thirteen brides. People are getting extremely suspicious. It's a wonder I'm getting another offer of marriage at all. As it is, this princess Ziqqora might be my very last chance to achieve wedded bliss. If you mess this up, I'll be stuck as a bachelor forever. *We'll* be stuck as a bachelor forever. The throne of Pecoz will be barren, bequeathed to some idiotic cousin. We'll be miserable, celibate, alone..."

Think outside the box, man. We don't have to be married to get our kicks!

"But I *want* to be married. I have to be, for the sake of the kingdom. Can't you let one of them live?"

The serpent gave a sigh, as if indulging a child.

Okay, he said. *I'll spare this one, I promise. Just as long as you make sure we get plenty of action on the side. And no more codpiece after the wedding, okay?*

"It's a deal," said Heinrich.

Having seemingly arrived at an accord with the creature, Heinrich bathed in silence in the stream. Still, he felt a little insecure. The serpent had made many promises before, and broken every one. He had to be sure that he could trust it this time. But how?

Suddenly he came upon a plan. He rushed to the bank, dried off and dressed himself, trapping the beast in the codpiece, then set off towards the nearest town.

When they arrived there, they stopped in the square, outside a bordello. He could feel the creature slumbering. *Good,* he thought. Then he summoned his secretary and whispered instructions.

Soon, the arrangements were made, and Heinrich was standing in one of the brothel's many rooms. A blindfolded woman knelt on the bed, her peach-like behind hoisted high in the air. She was beautiful and lithe, the best to be had here; she could pass as a princess. The room was well-appointed, with silken curtains and a four-poster bed; it could pass as a royal wedding chamber.

"They say you're a prince," the woman murmured. 'That's why I have to wear this blindfold, so I can't see your face. That way, I won't be able to track you down and start asking for money if I bring forth a bastard. But how do I know that this isn't some trick? For all I know you're a leper. One minute you're humping away, then next I feel your dick fall off inside of me!"

"You needn't worry about that," said Heinrich. "Besides, could a leper afford this?"

He tossed a handful of coins on the bed. The woman felt them blindly, then grinned.

"Okay," she said, wriggling her backside. "Let's go. Bring out that royal sceptre!"

Heinrich unbelted his trousers and lowered the codpiece. The serpent dropped out limply, then drowsily rose up, glancing around. It took in the sight of the candlelight, the curtains, but most of all the woman's wriggling rump.

Huh? it asked. *Are we married already?*

Heinrich nodded. "Just remember your promise."

The serpent nodded back and stretched out towards the bed. It shook itself a little on the way, throwing off the shackles of sleep. Then it caught the woman's scent and whipped out towards her pussy like a viper, slithering inside with a single, deft motion.

Heinrich trembled as he shared the sensation. The serpent's head was bathing in wetness and warmth. It started surging, slithering, pumping away.

She's pretty loose for a princess, he heard it say in his head. *Still, that just gives me more room to manoeuvre!*

It started surging deeper, faster. Its jade coils thickened. The woman bucked and moaned, as though she were getting the fuck of her life. Was it a display, Heinrich wondered, or was she truly shocked by the serpent's speed and girth? Either way he found it hard to consider such things in his present state of mind. The pleasure was growing, mounting towards a meridian. He stood a few feet from the bed, eyes closed, shuddering as the creature went to work, faster and faster, bringing them both towards a climax. It tapped the woman's cervix, tap, tap, tap –

Then spread its jaws wide and bit deep at the moment of orgasm.

"No!" shouted Heinrich.

He gripped the raging serpent at the base and tried to drag it back out of the woman, but he was too weak with pleasure to fight it. The woman screamed, crawling away on the bed, blood gushing out between her lips and the serpent's thrusting coils.

But the creature wouldn't let her escape. It plunged through the ruins of her cervix, spitting loops of semen as it went, then sank its cruel fangs into the uterus, squishing the springy material between them. Venom shot through its fangs, triggering another, even more powerful orgasm. Heinrich shuddered uncontrollably. Paralysed by venom the woman slumped forwards, her eyes open wide beneath the blindfold as the serpent ate her ovaries.

She died of shock a few moments later, and the serpent slid out of her, grinning and covered with blood. Still weak from the aftermath, Heinrich beheld it with a quivering glare.

"You bastard!" he growled. "You promised!"

I know I did, said the creature, licking its fangs. *And I meant it, too, at the time. But that meat is just so tempting! Besides, you weren't exactly straight with me, either. That woman's not a princess – she's a whore!*

"How'd you know?"

I heard you both whispering, just before I woke up. And there were other clues, as well, like the taste of all those men she hadn't quite douched away. Why did you lie to me, Heinrich?

"I wanted to test you. I had to be sure that you'd keep to your word on the wedding night."

Looks like you'll just have to wait and see, huh, buddy?

The serpent laughed. Heinrich grit his teeth.

Don't be like that. You know you liked it too.

The creature was right. He *had* liked it – how could he not ? The serpent's awful pleasures were also his own. He'd felt its delight at every single interval – the two-fold climax of jism and venom exploding, the visceral pleasure of feeding on the soft, springy meat. But he couldn't admit the truth; he couldn't give the serpent that satisfaction.

He glared at it, loathingly. If he'd looked in the mirror at that moment, he probably would've stared at his own face with that self-same expression. But the serpent just slithered and flickered its tongue, its eyes filled with post-orgasmic ecstasy.

Meanwhile, Ziqqora and Mycoz hovered high above the bed, observing the sinister scene with horror and disgust. The demon-spawn's casual aura had gone.

"This is definitely bad," he said.

"No shit," said Ziqqora, shuddering as she stared at the corpse on the bed.

The wedding was set to take place tomorrow. If she didn't figure out something, and fast, then that dead girl on the bed could be her.

"Sounds like the kingdom's really gone to the dogs," said Ziqqora's great-great-great grandfather, the last of the Mushroom Kings, whose name had been Boletus, and to which he still answered, despite being a transcendental mushroom-man.

Ziqqora had just finished telling him all about recent events, as well as the history of Myconia for the past few hundred years. She'd taken a deep breath, and started from the very beginning, narrating the closure of the garden, the kingdom's long slide into decline, her own mother's death during childbirth, followed by her father's foolish marriage to a woman with red-headed twins, at which point she finally proceeded to more present and horrible dangers, namely her forthcoming marriage to Heinrich Van Gruel, a man with a monster in his codpiece.

She sat with Boletus and Mycoz at a table that had seemingly been summoned from nowhere. King Boletus's court was there too, including all of the courtiers who'd turned into mushrooms, such as King Boletus' secretary, his chamberlain, his knights, even his cook. There were well over a dozen. One of them looked injured, his body riddled with wounds that shed light from inside, as though his skin were the shade of a vandalised lantern. Ziqqora asked him how he was. He merely said that he was fine, and that he'd just had a run-in with some hooligans, but the situation was completely in hand now. Then he smiled enigmatically.

Mycoz's brethren were there too. They'd descended from the portals in a host of strange shapes – figures of fire, glass, and gas – then quickly transformed into the likeness of handsome men and women. One of them, Fallon, bore the look of a child once again.

"We should slit all their gizzards!" he cried.

"That's not much of a plan," said Mycoz.

"Maybe not," said Ziqqora. "But I think I've got one!"

It was true. The act of narrating events had given her a handle on the whole situation. She felt like she might just have the means to save herself from destruction. But would it really work in real life? She'd always been a dreamer. She wasn't used to coming up with practical things! Then again, this was the realm of the spirit, the Demon's Dream. Perhaps she was now in her element?

She whispered the details of her plan to the others, and together they started to plot.

Chapter 9: Wedding Bells

"This is most irregular," said the queen as she sat down.

The long banquet table was outside, set up on the manicured lawn between the palace and the gardens. All of the wedding guests were being seated around it, King Riksmund's clan at one end, as was tradition, with Heinrich Van Gruel and his jade-coloured host at the opposite extremity. But the wedding hadn't actually *happened* yet, and the feast was not supposed to take place until *after* the ceremony.

"It was Ziqqora's request," said Riksmund. "And she was very adamant about it. She said she couldn't possibly go through the ceremony on an empty stomach, that she needed some food to smother all those butterflies flitting about in her stomach."

"You indulge her too much," said the queen. 'But then again, I suppose it *is* her wedding day."

She permitted herself a smile. Let the brat have this final indulgence, she thought. After tonight it wouldn't matter anyway – not after she'd shared a wedding bed with Heinrich Van Gruel.

At that, the queen found herself laughing. Her plan was so close to fruition she could taste it!

"What's so funny, my dear?" asked the king.

"Oh, nothing really. I suppose I'm just so happy for her!"

Ziqqora's golden locks blazed in the sun, which sat at its apex above. She wore the traditional crimson gown made for virgin brides, symbolizing the blood that would soon be spilled out from her stretched-open hymen.

Not if I can help it! she thought.

She tried to smother her nervousness as she waited for the feast to begin. All she was doing was sitting at a table, and yet her blood was already pounding in her veins, as though she were running from a wolf. In a way, she was. She took a glance at Van Gruel, who was seated a few dozen feet away from her, surrounded by his courtiers and knights. He too wore red in anticipation of the marriage bed. But the bastard was stained with blood already, she thought.

She avoided his gaze as he glanced back towards her. The queen let out a sigh.

"Just look how shy she is! She'll soon get over that. Just like I did, the first time I was married."

"You certainly weren't shy with me," said the king.

They giggled and canoodled beside one another. Ziqqora managed a forced smile, but it was more like a grimace. She glanced at her stepsisters. Usually the little brats would be full of piss and vinegar, especially at a time like this. Usually they'd be poking out their tongues and exalting in her misery. But today they looked sick and lethargic. Their faces were pastier than ever, and some of their freckles had begun to turn black. Ziqqora smiled to herself, darkly, and waited for the feast.

Soon it came, a barrage of food in twelve courses. First soup, then pheasant, then venison, then pie, then a whole bunch of other dishes to which Ziqqora didn't really pay attention. There was only one thing she was focused on – the familiar, bitter flavour that tainted each and every dish, from the gravy to the plum sauce to the wine in her glass.

At length the feast was over and everyone was full as they could be. She saw the wedding guests stirring uncomfortably, longing to unbuckle their belts and give their bloated bellies some breathing room, but they still had the ceremony to get through.

Together they left the table and headed to the podium on the grass nearby. There stood the master of ceremonies, wearing his mystical robes. The guests took up position before him, arranging themselves into two long rows with an aisle in between, down which Van Gruel strode first, cheered on by his comrades and kinfolk. Then came Ziqqora, accompanied by her father. The feeling of his hand around hers made her nauseous with anger. How could he have let this all happen?

Soon he'll discover the error of his ways, she thought.

He left her by Van Gruel's side in front of the altar. Was that a tear in his eye? And if so, was it from happiness, pride, or bitter regret?

She didn't have time to imagine. Van Gruel was before her, a tower of muscle and might. His handsome face smiled, but his codpiece stood between them, pregnant with death. Was that a flicker of movement from within? She cast down her eyes, and played the demure, blushing bride.

Then the master of ceremonies began.

"Ladies and gentlemen, we are gathered here today to join this couple in wedlock. I'd like to call upon the demons to witness this union from their castles in the void. May they devour those who seek to defile or betray it. May they rend them with claws and ravage their orifices aplenty."

The rite master paused, muttering strange words intended to draw down the eyes of the demons. Then he continued.

"And now for the oaths," he said. "Heinrich Van Gruel, do you take this woman to be your wedded wife, to thrill her with your body whenever she desires, to bring harm to her enemies and joy to her friends, to bring fire to her hearth and warmth to her bed, to keep the rats from her legs and the lice from her hair, to defend her from brigands and zombies and trolls, to keep her furnace well-stoked and her flowerbed moist, to pay heed to her words and accept her caresses, to brandish your torch and bring light to her nights, to never lose sight of the tiller-man sitting in her boat, to get behind the oxen and plough her wet grass, to yank on the rope that rings bells in her belfry, to fill her warm slipper right up to the toe, until the terms of your union be dissolved?"

"I do," said Van Gruel.

"And do you, Ziqqora of Myconia, take this man to be your wedded husband, to..."

Ziqqora felt her blood begin to pound even faster as the master of ceremonies droned out the vow. Something was wrong; her plan should've gone into effect by now. This whole thing should be over! Instead she stood there as if in a trance, only half-hearing the words. She felt somehow distant, alien to herself, just as she'd felt when she'd

154

travelled in the spirit and seen her own sleeping body in the grove down below. This couldn't be her, here, now, by the podium – she couldn't be forced to this hideous oath!

She grew faint. Nausea bubbled in her stomach. But was it from fear, or a sign of her deliverance? The air began to bubble and ripple in front of her. She felt light and airy, as if she were about to pass out. Perhaps she'd swoon, and he'd carry her off to the marriage bed anyway? It'd been known to happen. She'd wake with the serpent inside of her, eating her organs.

She fought to stay standing. Then the air became filled with a kaleidoscope of colours that swayed like a curtain in front of her.

At last! she thought, then drew aside the curtain, and stepped across the breach.

Chapter 10: Change of Venue

Ziqqora smiled. She stood in the Demon's vibrant Dream. The rest of the wedding guests were there too, muttering or shouting or screaming in terror.

"What the fuck's going on?" said one.

"Oh shit!" said a second.

"AAAHHHH!" said a third.

In the distance arose the monolithic structure that was home to the statue of the demon's nameless mother. Closer by stood Mycoz and his brethren, as well as King Boletus and his transcendental court, gathered round the wedding guests in luminous, humanoid shapes.

Steadily the guests began to calm themselves, if only a little.

"'What's the meaning of this?" shouted King Riksmund. "Where are we?"

"In the Demon's Dream," said Ziqqora. "I dosed all the food in the kitchen with mushrooms, right before the feast. That's why I wanted to eat before the ceremony. So I could bring us all here, and show you the truth."

Her voice was steady now, so too her pose. She felt safer, more powerful here. But she knew that the struggle was very far from over.

"Foolish girl!" snapped her father. "I told you the mushrooms were poisonous. This is all a trap! They're going to eat us, turn us into fungus, just like poor Boletus –"

"Shut up, Dad!" she snapped. "You don't know what you're talking about. The demons are our allies. And Boletus's right there!"

She pointed to the last of the Mushroom Kings, who waved to his great-great grandson and smiled.

"Hello young man," he said, even though King Riksmund was hoary with age. "You should listen to your daughter, you know. She's a very clever girl."

Riksmund just stood there, speechless.

"This place isn't a trap," said Ziqqora. "The wedding was a trap – for me! That bitch wife of yours is trying to kill me. Van Gruel isn't a man, he's an abomination. Just look at what he's got in his codpiece!"

She ripped off her bridegroom's groin guard, then leapt back at once as the serpent whipped out of it, snarling. Cries of shock erupted from the crowd. Van Gruel himself stood as if stunned, making no move to cover or hide what had been revealed.

"See?" she said. "He's not just well-hung – he's a monster down there!"

The king stared in horror at Van Gruel's flailing member. Then he turned to his wife.

"You knew about this?" he asked.

"Of course not!" she snapped. "Besides, this is all a lie, a delusion, a trick – we've all been drugged!"

"You're the liar," said Ziqqora. "But soon you won't lie anymore."

She grinned darkly as blood stared dripping from her stepmother's eyes.

"What's...what's going on?!" the queen cried. Ziqqora knew she'd be feeling the pain in her physical body too, even though here she wore the form of a spirit.

The queen's bleeding eyes glanced around for her daughters, but they were not to be found in this dreamscape. Ziqqora's grin widened, seeing events unfold on both sides of the curtain. The red-headed brats, being effectively already dead, no longer had souls with which to enter the dreaming. Their bodies had been hollowed from within and infested by the spores of black fungus, which filled them with its own savage purpose.

Out there in that physical world, they dragged their mother's un- conscious body on top of the banquet table and worked out her eyes with a pair of silver forks. The mutilation was mirrored in the dream- scape, her stepmother's bloodied eyeballs popping out of their sock- ets to dangle on glistening nerves. The sight of it reminded her of a cup-and-ball toy she used to play with as a child. But while Ziqqora might've been able to whip up that ball into its rightful position, her stepmother's eyeballs would never go back in, neither in this world, nor in the other.

Then the woman's flesh started blistering and bubbling, her daughters having tossed her into a boiling cauldron of soup. The king screamed in horror as he saw what was happening. He reached out to his wife, but her skin just sloughed off in his hands, like slivers of pork in a broth.

Ziqqora turned back to the still-stunned Van Gruel.

"As for you," she said, "this wedding is cancelled!"

Van Gruel just stood there a moment longer, paralysed, his gaze far away as if fighting a battle in his head with the thing between his legs. They shared one body, after all. Maybe, in the physical world, Van Gruel had been in charge of that body – most of it, anyway. But the serpent was a creature from Beyond, and had more power in the dreaming than he did. It must have roiled into his mind like smoke into a chimney, forcing him back into the corners of his psyche and taking him over completely, because when Van Gruel finally spoke, it was not with his own voice, but with the sibilant cadence of a serpent.

"I don't think so, bitch," he said. "This is a wedding, and I didn't just come to eat cake. Men – kill these clowns!"

Van Gruel's knights drew their blades and rushed towards Mycoz and his kindred. The demon-spawn responded by assuming their terrifying battle-shapes. Ziqqora saw Fallon rise up into the form of a crocodile with iridescent scales and fungal protrusions. He seized a knight in his jaws and bit the doomed man in half. Blood exploded out from the man's dying spirit like streaks of red lightning.

Suddenly Mycoz was ten feet tall and wading into battle right beside his little brother. His eyes were bright red and his skin was dark purple. He ripped a man's head off with claws like an eagle's.

Then the Mushroom King's forces charged deep into the fray, riding on steeds made of pure hallucination, striking down their enemies with psychedelic blades. The dreamscape was a riot of screaming and blood.

But Ziqqora didn't have time to pay much attention to the battle, for Van Gruel was heading towards her, staring with two sets of eyes. The expression in each was the same, a glower of murderous lust.

Chapter 11: Devoured

Ziqqora darted backwards and concentrated, transforming her dress into a suit of steel armour. It encased her whole body, except for the head. Her golden hair cascaded down her back like a cape. A sword appeared in her right hand, raised for the kill.

Now it was Van Gruel's turn to leap backwards as she slashed at his serpentine phallus. He dodged the blow expertly, then glared at her, while the battle kept raging all around them, blood and gore exploding in the dreaming like a fireworks display.

"Nice trick," he hissed with his sibilant voice. "But two can play at that game."

The serpent flexed its otherworldly will. Suddenly Van Gruel was likewise covered in sleek, shining armour, which extended all the way to the head of his murderous phallus. The serpent writhed and wriggled, flexing the moulded steel scales that now covered its coils. At the same time a blade appeared in Van Gruel's right hand, with which he slashed at Ziqqora.

She fended off the blow, no stranger to swordplay by now, having been tutored by some of Mycoz's allies. She'd been under the instruction of the blood-drinking duellists of Zimoa for what felt like weeks, but barely minutes had passed in Myconia's physical realm. She struck back at Van Gruel with a brutal swipe, catching the side of the serpent with her blade. It whipped away, growling, bruised but protected by its armour.

"Not bad," said Van Gruel. "But none of this will save you. You can bolster your hymen with steel, but I'm still gonna break it. You can stab me with your sword, but it's you who'll get skewered in the end. Still, I have to commend you. It's good to have some foreplay for a change!"

He rushed her, swinging his blade as the serpent whipped out from his crotch. Ziqqora struggled to defend against the two deadly weapons at once. She knocked back his blade time and again, only for the snake to come hissing at her face, or striking down low at her groin, trying to rip off her armour or bite its way through to her flesh. No sooner would she beat aside the beast than his sword would come swinging again, straining her defences to their limit. The strength behind his blows was incredible. Was it powered by Van Gruel's mutant might, or the will of the serpent? It was difficult to tell in the dreaming, where the force of mind and muscle overlapped and conjoined.

She wielded her blade desperately, fending off the blows, sweating, getting tired. As good as her training had been, she just wasn't ready to duel with Van Gruel. She had to escape!

After striking wildly, making some space for herself to manoeuvre, she leapt up and flew towards a portal above.

"Get back here!" shouted Van Gruel with the voice of the serpent. "I've got a down-payment on that pussy!"

He pursued her through the portal, emerging into a starscape. Of course, such sights were not strange to the mind of the serpent, who'd been called from the realms beyond earth.

He saw his delectable quarry on a road made of meteoric dust. Her armour gleamed in the light of distant stars. Her hair framed her hips like a nimbus of gold. The serpent felt his coils getting thicker, bulging with an influx of blood. The pressure was almost enough to bend his armour out of shape. He had to have her, now!

He flew on towards her, and landed nearby. In the distance was a cloud of debris, made up of space junk and glittering fragments of god's blood, all of it frozen by the cold of the void. Something massive had lain there once, something the size of a planetoid, but now it was gone, devoured or destroyed, leaving nought but a big cloud of rubble in its wake.

But the serpent didn't care about that. He wasn't here to map out the space-ways. He was here for one thing, and one thing only!

He rushed at Ziqqora, commanding Van Gruel's body like a puppet's. Dimly he could hear the protestations of his host, coming from the corners of their commingled psyche. He didn't care about those, either. Van Gruel's body was his now, just as it always should've been.

He swung at the princess, then struck with his fangs. She fended off the blows, but only barely. She was weakening, crumbling, succumbing to his might. It wouldn't be long until he had her in his coils!

He lashed out again, striking the sword from her hand. She looked back with wide, frightened eyes, like a doe about to flee before the hounds of the hunt. The expression on her face only deepened his arousal. He cast aside his sword and gripped her breastplate with his fingers, while his serpentine head shot up towards her crotch, tearing at the chainmail that lay beneath the tassets. He could smell her sweet scent through the ringlets of steel. Soon he'd be bathing in it, swimming in it. He wrenched with all his might, ripping off the breastplate and the armour below.

A shower of gore shot from the breach and splattered him all over, reeking of days-old death.

Oh crap, he thought. *Did I kill her? Already?*

He felt a wave of immediate disappointment. Ravaging her corpse wouldn't be nearly as fun as impaling her soft, living body. He blinked the rancid blood away, and his own eyes went wide.

The armour he'd peeled from that beautiful body had been nought but the cover of a gore-stuffed cushion. The girl's golden hair, nothing but a wig. The serpent had been duped!

He looked around, spotting the princess floating high in the void. She was naked and smiling, dancing lasciviously. Her nubile fingers plucked at her nipples and played in her pubes. Her slender legs flexed and cavorted, framed by a mane of golden hair.

"You fucking tease!" he roared.

Ziqqora kept grinning, but it was almost a rictus. She danced in the most wanton manner possible, even as her mind recoiled from the act of dancing for Van Gruel. Still, she had to keep his attention focused tightly on her body. Her whole plan depended on this gamble.

All the pieces were in place but one. She'd conjured the dummy into existence with the magick that Mycoz's allies had taught her. She'd even abandoned her armour and weapon to make his false victory seem even more convincing; she barely had the strength left to summon more arms if they were needed. Thus, she was well and truly tied to her present course of action. If it failed, she was screwed – literally, and to death! But would the final ingredient fall into place?

Her question was answered as the stars behind Van Gruel began to vanish. Suddenly she didn't know what to fear most – Van Gruel, or the thing that had arrived, seeking the reeking gore that he wore, swimming just under the skin of the void, visible only by the shifting lacuna of starlight covering its gigantic body like camouflage.

Van Gruel flew towards her, away from the patch of seething darkness. Not because he'd seen the threat, of course – he only had eyes for her, two sets of eyes frenzied with lust.

Fuck, thought Ziqqora. *He's moving out of position!*

She took a deep breath and flew towards the darkness, overshooting Van Gruel from above. He growled, turned, and gave chase, his four eyes chained to her gleaming white body.

Ziqqora sensed the terrible presence before her, could almost smell its stench, that of all the world's abattoirs at once. She drew as close as she dared, then veered off in another direction. Van Gruel followed, gaining ground. Her movements, seemingly random and flitting, had allowed him to close very quickly.

He reached for her. She felt his armoured fingers scraping her skin, grasping only emptiness, just as something drew wide beneath *him*. A set of great jaws emerged from the darkness, colossal and hungry and stinking, with teeth like white reefs in a bubbling blood ocean, strewn with the skins of dead gods slowly rotting.

Krauwm, the Demon Worm, was here!

And just as ugly as the first time Ziqqora had seen him, back during her very first trip. The smell of the gore covering Van Gruel had lured the beast from his feeding grounds, exactly as she'd hoped it would.

Van Gruel's eyes flashed with terror and anger. He let out a roar of inchoate rage and reached for Ziqqora again, catching at her ankle. She shook herself free as the jaws of the demon engulfed him. Van Gruel's head and hands jutted between the Worm's shuttered teeth like the limbs of a criminal condemned to the stocks. He looked at her, no longer with the lust of the serpent, but with the gaze of a man filled with something like relief. Then the worm ground its teeth, slicing both man and serpent to pieces, and his face was no more.

Ziqqora sped back through the portal and into the Demon's bright realm. Van Gruel's knights had all been slaughtered, their bodies torn asunder. Her father wept on his knees, cradling the body of his wife, who'd now been reduced to little more than a puddle of flesh around steaming bones. His own soldiers had surrendered to Mycoz and the demon-spawn, some of whom were injured, their bodies leaking blood that shone like bright lightning and travelled like squid ink underwater. Her ancestor Boletus stood alongside them, as did his courtiers, wearing their psychedelic robes.

Ziqqora landed before her father, then remembered, she was naked!

She summoned a set of bright robes that mirrored the dress of the Mushroom King. Atop her head, she created a crown, with tines like mushroom stalks and a dome of bright fabric resembling the cap of a toadstool.

"Dad," she said, "we need to talk."

Chapter 12: The Court of the Mushroom Queen

Ziqqora the First ascended to the throne following her father's abrupt abdication.

The first thing she did was change the royal livery back to the symbol of a toadstool with a crown on the top. The second thing she did was have the iron fence around the garden removed and replaced with a fortified wall. The place remained forbidden to all but herself and a few chosen courtiers. Uninvited visitors would be captured and slaughtered by the regiment of soldiers who guarded the stock of royal mushrooms by night and by day.

For the mushrooms were said to grant fabulous visions, and the queen consumed them often, gaining the knowledge she needed to govern Myconia with wisdom and might.

Or so people say. Others just think that she liked to get high.

Perhaps the proof is in the pudding, for the queen showed an uncanny knack for diplomacy and trade. Pretty soon, her kingdom grew prosperous once more. The palace was rebuilt from its crumbling foundations. The neighbouring kingdom of Pecoz was conquered, its rulers sent into exile. Their sorcerers, the Sebeks, were rounded up and burned at the stake. Otherwise the people were spared and made subjects of Myconia.

The queen did take a husband, but kept him consigned to the status of a prince, denying him a share in her rule. She married him for one reason only: to help produce heirs for the throne of Myconia, a task at which he duly succeeded, giving her five noble children, two girls and three boys.

But it was said that his life, though luxurious and filled with undeniable nookie, was something of a sad one. The poor prince was a notorious cuckold. Everyone knew that the queen had a lover with the body of a toadstool and the soul of a demon. She visited him often, whenever she ate of the mushrooms that grew in the garden.

In time, she grew old, as all mortals must do. Her flesh became withered and her hair became white. She left the kingdom to her heirs and went off into the garden, where her body transformed. Her skin became fibrous and sprouting, her sweat became motes of white spores, and her toes spread like roots into the soil.

But her soul went off to journey through the Demon's bright Dreaming, where she dwells as she did in her youth, with long golden locks and a soft nubile figure. She's probably there to this day, wrapped in the arms of her lover as they fuck beneath moonbeams or dance around planets to the tune of a song with no ending.

The Crimson Crown

It's the Aeon of Chaos. The gods are dead, and the demons play dice with their bones.

Chapter 1: The Will of the Demon

The twin princesses Oda and Honeydew stood in a sumptuous hall, awaiting their suitors. They'd turned eighteen, and so their parents, the king and queen of Chalkwood, had decided to marry them off, as was the custom. Many men dreamed about marrying them. Oda and Honeydew were the very incarnations of all their society thought beautiful in women. They both had skin like creamy alabaster; they both had soft crimson lips; they both had nubile bodies and dark dreamy eyes. The only thing that set them apart from one another was their hair. Both had been born with locks as black as pitch, which had slowly turned as white and as bright as the smothered winter sun. Honeydew, the younger, had left her hair like that, but Oda had dyed hers a deep midnight black, so that it matched the colour it'd held at her birth, and set her apart from her sibling.

Many people said this stark difference in hair colour, whether artificial or not, was symbolic of the greater disparity between the two sisters. For, despite being twins, the girls were very different, both in their outward personas, and in their secret inner lives. Honeydew – often called Honey for short – was known to be friendly and mild. She liked walking in the luscious royal gardens. Her favourite animals were swans, butterflies, and glorious eagles. She read romantic books that weren't very sexually explicit. When she dreamed of a lover, she imagined someone handsome, caring, and most of all, true. When she dared to touch her "lower parts"– to which she was still a nervous

166

stranger – she did so only tentatively, shyly, in the utmost recesses of the night, thinking only of kisses, caresses, and the encompassing feeling of love.

Oda – the elder by just half an hour – was said to have a heart as black as her hair. She was known to be acerbic and sullen, obsessed with things others found creepy, horrific, or disgusting, like darkness, spiders, and mouldering bodies whose skin had rotted off to expose bits of underlying skeleton. Her favourite animals were vultures, ravens, and ravening wolves. She spent her time devouring books that dwelt upon cruelty and death. She combed through the annals for mentions of massacres, revolts and executions; she broke into the library's locked cabinets to sift through the tomes more forbidden. Her favourite such book was *The Six Centuries of Suffering,* written by the lunatic aristocrat Alcott Vizette, who'd been imprisoned in the dungeons of Amithaine for performing abhorrent acts upon orphan girls, and had taken to writing erotic literature during his confinement. *The Six Centuries* was his masterwork, a sprawling pseudo-historical epic detailing the imaginary history of the notorious Screaming City. Its historical pretentions aside, the book was nothing less than an unending catalogue of murder, rape, torture, and massacre. Oda ate up every word as though they were glazed with sugar and dusted with cocaine. Her budding sexuality thrilled to the endless variations of murderous carnality. She pictured herself variously as both tormentor and victim, and in either case was overcome by a lust so profound she felt like she'd been struck through the heart by a lance of celestial fire, while her clit got so hot and full of blood it felt like a little round flame that could only be fleetingly doused by her own frenzied fingers. When she dreamed of a lover to bring her fantasies to life, she imagined someone cruel and rapacious, ruthless and priapic, a rough older man who would ravish her wildly, then force her to help with the ravishment of others.

It may come as no surprise that, with personalities so utterly divergent, the twin princesses didn't really get along very well, and avoided each other as much as they were able. As little girls, when their nascent personalities had been somewhat less formed, and therefore less at odds, they'd spent their days playing together, but even back then the disparities between them had started to show. When they played make-believe, for example, Honeydew wanted them to take on the roles of the paladins of Carheim, who went about helping the weak by slaughtering bandits, cannibals, and trolls. But Oda always wanted the opposite – she wanted *them* to be the ogres and cannibals, killing off the paladins and chewing the meat from their bones! Their different longings led to a great many arguments, with compromise growing harder and harder to reach as the years trickled by. In any case, their playing came to a definitive end following what Honey referred to – at least in her own mind – as the Day of the Flies. It was a day she detested to think about, and afterwards, she and her sister had grown apart, like polarized magnets. Till at last they stood side-by-side in the sumptuous court, eighteen years old, awaiting their suitors, each of them utterly alienated from the other.

Presently trumpets sounded, announcing that the first of the suitors had arrived. Honeydew's heart thrilled as she saw him make his entrance; it was none other than the young King Armand. He strode into the hall, dressed in luxurious brocade of red, gold, and green, followed by a splendid-looking retinue in similarly festive attire. Scarcely three years Honey's senior, Armand had acceded to the throne of Shimmerland just a few month previous, after his royal parents lost their lives in a tragic fall.

Oh, he's so dreamy! thought Honey as she took in his curly blonde locks, generous lips, and handsome physique.

He was almost her dream made flesh, for not only was he beautiful, but well-known for his kindness and loyalty. He'd even offered the throne to his invalid uncle in a show of familial piety! But the uncle had refused, citing his club foot and stuttering speech as an impediment to kingship. And so Armand had ascended, becoming the youngest, most handsome, and most beloved of all kings in the land. As Honey watched him walk forth into the hall, she could've sworn she was able to see his generosity and kindness radiate from his pores like light from the skin of the sun. She felt a tender longing, and started to blush. When Armand's gaze met hers across the room, she almost jumped from excitement. She managed to flash him a smile before her eyes sought the floor. Armand smiled back, then nodded politely to Oda, who was peering at him coldly.

What a plonker! thought Oda.

Armand wasn't her sort at all. He was too much of a pretty-boy, too much of a goody-two shoes. And his clothes – yuck! She'd once thought, for a moment, he might actually be cool, back when she'd heard the rumour *he* had caused all that scaffolding to fall, thus killing his parents and securing the crown into the bargain; but the rumour proved utterly baseless, and was soon washed away by the voluminous tears Armand had shed at his parents' joint funeral. He'd done so much crying and wailing, he'd put the professional mourners to shame!

Oda couldn't stand emotional men. She wanted someone ruthless, someone hard, someone rough...

Someone like King Barbus, who strode into the room to the sound of blaring trumpets just a few moments later. He walked with aggressive and swaggering strides; from every single pore he seemed to radiate brutality, confidence, power.

Oda stared at him, enraptured. Barbus was in his late thirties, more than double her age, with all the maturity and confidence she wanted in a man. His build was tall and bullish; his raven-black hair stark against the absolute pallor of his skin. A thick black moustache hid his upper lip, but the lower one was sensuous and red. Under a cloak of black fur, the rest of his clothing was the colour of blood. On his head sat a silver crown set with a single red gem that shone lustrous in the torchlight, the legendary Crimson Crown of Gutgirt.

So hot! thought Oda, feeling a tingling in her cunt and a pounding in her heart as she beheld him.

Other people's hearts hammered as well, though more from fear, rather than excitement. Barbus may have once been known as a mild and quiet child, but, following his mother's grisly suicide by self-jugulation, he'd steadily grown bolder and crueller, and was now notorious for acts of unpredictable violence. Many were the commoners he'd slaughtered on a whim in a host of creatively hideous ways. A stableboy who'd failed to groom Barbus' horse to the king's satisfaction had been brutally brushed with the very same wire brush until the hairs of said brush had scraped off his hairs, as well as his skin, causing him to die from millions of tiny little bleeding abrasions. A merchant from Alhazred, who'd refused to remove his turban in the presence of the king, had had his headwear hammered to his scalp with nine-inch nails, so that he might wear it forever in the grave. A fortune-teller who'd given the king bad news had been forced to perform a new prognostication, by reading his very own entrails.

These and hundreds of similar stories did the rounds from Chalkwood to Red Wake. Yet it wasn't just Barbus' murderous temper that truly made people afraid of him. There were plenty of murderous monarchs running about, savagely killing their serfs in ironic and unpleasant ways. No; what really terrified people was the inhuman power Barbus possessed. He was said to have the strength of twenty men. His body was impervious to wounds, such that his skin could not be cut, his flesh could not be bruised. His mother had been the same, and her father before her, and his father before him, going all the way back to Goatius Xex, the founder of their blood-splattered dynasty. Some said the power was inherent in their line – that in every generation of Xexes, one of them was born with the gift. Others said it derived from some secret and magickal source, the Xexes blessed by demonic patrons, or enchanted by fairies, or transformed by alchemical elixirs. And so-on and so-forth. One thing was certain: the power was real. When Gutgirt went to war, Barbus stormed onto the field like a one-man army, wielding a gigantic club that could crush armoured knights into paste. He literally fought all his battles on his own, with his small force of soldiers just standing back and watching or chasing down stragglers. For why should ordinary soldiers fight, when the king had the power of a demon? By himself, he slaughtered whole armies and laid waste to vast reaches of enemy land. He didn't just have the power of an army, but the appetites of one, and was known to descend on conquered cities like a lion in heat, raping hundreds of women while bespattered with the blood of their husbands and sons.

Thus it was that people had very good reason to be terrified of Barbus. Because of this, they treated him with awe and respect, and accorded him the honour due a king, even though they viewed him in their hearts as little more than a beast. Because of this, the parents of Honeydew and Oda had invited him to marry one of their daughters, even though Barbus had been married several times previously, to women who'd subsequently vanished or horribly died. They feared to deny him his request for a bride, lest he turn his warlike attentions on them, and hoped to placate him by offering their own flesh and blood, as though he were a bloodthirsty god from the Time-Before-Time.

The thought of being given to Barbus made Princess Oda quiver with excitement and delight. He was the man of her fantasies made flesh – so harsh, so cruel, so rough! She longed to be crushed by his inhuman strength; she longed for his impenetrable meat to penetrate her. She wasn't really worried he might kill her, as he'd killed so many others before. She felt sure he would recognise her as a true kindred spirit, and welcome her to rule by his side. And if he didn't accept her – if he ended up killing her like all of the others, perhaps by choking her to death while he ravished her – then oh what a thrill that would be!

She found herself getting weak in the knees as she imagined all those darkly delicious scenarios.

Her sister, Honeydew, was also weak in the knees, but for a totally different reason. Like most women, she was horrified by Barbus. The thought of being forced to marry him was enough to make her quiver with terror. She'd almost rather be dead than tethered to such a brute!

Oh please let it be Armand, she thought. *Let my husband be Armand! We're perfect for each other. He's so sweet and gentle, so handsome and kind – he's just like the man of my dreams!*

Oh please let it be Barbus, thought Oda at the very same instant. *Let my husband be Barbus! He's so harsh and unforgiving, so merciless and cruel – he's just like a libertine hero from a book by Alcott Vizette!*

Despite their strong feelings, neither had any real choice in the matter. Like other nobles, their unions were to be decided by forces beyond their control. First their potential grooms were chosen by their parents, which had already been done. Then the final selection was carried out by the royal astrologer, after comparing the horoscopes of the potential bride and groom to see if their fortunes were compatible, for it was said the will of the great cosmic demon Zabazap was revealed in the layout of the stars that prevailed at the time of one's birth. The people of Chalkwood were particularly sold on this idea, especially the parents of Oda and Honeydew, who never made a move without consulting their astrologer, even if the people of other regions, like Starfall and Amithaine, thought astrology was bullshit, and dangerously close to the hideous, pre-Aeonic practice of theism, by which mortals were enslaved to the wills of the old dead gods.

For their part, Oda and Honeydew may have not shared the absolute faith their parents possessed, but they'd been raised to it and took a certain comfort in their long familiarity. Surely, the will of the demons, as shown in the stars, would lead them to be married to their ideal husbands. Oda just knew her horoscope would match with that of Barbus, while Honeydew had no doubts that her own would harmonize Armand's.

They watched with bated breath as the two kings stepped forth and handed their horoscopes, contained in ornate leather scroll cases, to the royal astrologer.

A band began to play and refreshments were served as the astrologer went off to consult the horoscopes and interpret their meaning according to his big ancient books. Oda and Honeydew were far too nervous to pay any attention to the frivolous music and flowing wine. For although they were both ninety-nine percent sure their own horoscopes would harmonize with those of the men they desired, there was still a shred of doubt that tortured them with giddy sensations of fear and apprehension. They chewed their nails, until a stern glance from their mother the queen made them stop, and they had to settle for grinding their teeth instead, so that they might listen to the sound of the grating in their mouths as a distraction from the throbbing of the blood in their skulls, which sounded in their temples like an ominous drumbeat even louder than the music in the room.

At length, the music stopped and the royal astrologer emerged into sudden and crystalline silence, carrying the scroll cases. The princesses hung on tenterhooks of anticipation, like rock climbers dangling from a perilous ledge. Their happiness, their futures, perhaps their very lives, depended on his words.

"I have consulted the stars," he declared. "I have seen the will of the great demon Zabazap, the Flitting One, He of the Zigzagging Countenance, He Who is clothed in the Void and the Dust of Dead Gods! I have seen His will as it was written in the heavens long ago, as it continues to be written today. Oda will be married to Armand, and Honeydew married to Barbus!"

Chapter 2: The Honeymooners

Honeydew felt as if she'd been hit by a hammer. She was stunned;

she couldn't stop reeling. This was the worst day of her life! Every few seconds, the awful revelation hit her brain anew – *I'm going to be married to Barbus!* And yet, although the knowledge continued assaulting her, she somehow felt numb to its reality, as though she were a ghost in her own mind, unable to reach out and touch her feelings and thoughts, lest they bite her like snakes, or burn her like fire. When she *did* make an effort to reach out and touch them – when she really, *really* thought about what it really, really *meant* to get married to Barbus – her sense of terror was so teeming and profound she felt like she were suffocating. Or like spiders were breeding in the marrow of her bones, overflowing out through her body like soup boiling over on a stove, flooding her flesh with a hideous crawling sensation. Her breaths came short and sharp, her blood was hammering fast in her skull. She wanted to scream, but she couldn't; she was mute! Once alone, all she could do was curl into a ball, like a babe in a womb, with her head in her hands and her tresses in her face, taking big gulps of air as the tears went streaming down, tasting of misery and salt in her mouth.

Her stern and distant mother did her best to console her later that evening. Which is to say, she gave Honey a lecture on how to be a dutiful wife, and how best to prepare for her imminent deflowering. Her father remained at a distance, avoiding her, though she did catch a glimpse of the dampness in his eyes that spoke of the sorrow he was feeling – and trying not to feel.

The dual wedding was set for the following day, a splendid and lavish affair, with beautiful music, sumptuous food, and hundreds of famous and fashionable guests. Their gowns were gorgeous, the finest garments Honey had ever laid eyes on. And yet, all the finery only seemed to make it even more awful, as though it were but one of the barbs of a complex and sinister joke.

As the older sister, Oda was married first. As Honey watched her trade vows with Armand, she felt a sense of jealously and despair so great she wanted to cry. But she didn't. Deciding it was best to stay a little bit numb, for the while, she went on instead to trade vows with King Barbus. When the celebrant asked her if she'd take this man to be her wedded husband, she wanted to scream, "NO!" But she was terrified of disobeying her parents, and refusing the will of the great demon Zabazap. And so, she said yes, even while all of her body and being recoiled in revulsion, as though she were eating a tablespoon of maggots, or putting her hand into the jaws of a lion.

And that was that. After the vows came dancing, and feasting, and then she was bundled off into a coach to be taken to Gutgirt, where the marriage would be consummated – and she would be coronated. She didn't much care about the coronation; it was mostly the other thing she was thinking about.

You're going to get fucked by Barbus, she thought to herself. *And then he'll probably kill you.*

The thoughts sent a chill down her spine; she gulped, and tried to clear her head. She glanced around the interior of the coach. It was sumptuously furnished, with quilted red silk on the walls. It made her think of the sort of cell they put loony people in – if the padded walls of said cell had been vividly dyed by the blood of a suicide's wrists.

Don't be so morbid! she thought.

But it was hard not to be. She was the only occupant; her husband preferred to run with the horses, exerting his tireless stamina. From time to time she caught glimpses of him through the black-barred windows, his pale features wet, his crimson clothes dampened with sweat.

If he can run a hundred miles, what'll he be like in the bedroom? she wondered, then tried not to think about it.

Instead she kept her eyes on the features of the landscape.

So this is the kingdom of Gutgirt, my new homeland, she thought.

The landscape was a mixture of farmland and vast, gloomy forests. By order of a long-standing royal decree, the buildings in the towns were all painted red, or, more specifically, crimson, the colour of freshly-spilled blood. It was said the entire royal family was obsessed with the colour. They wore crimson clothes; they wore crimson armour; they carried a crimson flag, featuring the image of a stark silver crown set with a shining red gem, identical to the crown Barbus wore, the one with the brilliant blood diamond.

As she stared at the ominous forests and blood-red buildings, Honey thought back to her history lessons and recalled the origins of Gutgirt. The founder of the kingdom, Goatius Xex, had started out as a commoner, the leader of a mercenary band called The Plague. He and his comrades in arms had descended from the distant frozen horror of the north three centuries ago, bringing death and lamentation to all who stood against them, just as their name would suggest. Their most powerful weapon in their arsenal was Goatius himself, who, like many of his descendants, was impervious to harm, and had the strength to tear his enemies to pieces with nothing but his hands. He was hired by the king of Shimmerland, Armand's ancestor, to help fight the plutocrats of Porkwood. Within months, Porkwood had been wiped off the map, its rulers slaughtered and despoiled of their gigantic wealth. In gratitude to his ally – and perhaps out of fear – the king made Goatius a nobleman, and offered him a piece of the newly-conquered lands. The offer was a strange and unique one. Since Goatius' fortune had been won by death, his lands would be allotted by death, as well. He would be allowed to claim as much territory as he could surround with a circle of dead Porkwoodians. As most of the Porkwoodians had already been slaughtered in the war, and buried in mass graves, it might have seemed as though Goatius' lands would be very small indeed. But he hit upon a cunning plan; instead of laying out the corpses from heel to head, as one might assume, he disembowelled them all and stretched their intestines for miles, creating a gigantic circle of guts to encompass an impressive demesne. Gutgirt was born, with Goatius Xex as its very first prince.

As a child, Honey had often wondered why the king gave a dangerous killer like Goatius so much power and land. Wasn't he creating a potential threat – a rod for his very own back? But the truth was he had little choice; if he hadn't given Goatius something willingly, The Plague would've taken it by force. At least by acting as Goatius' generous patron, he had the illusion of control, and could be seen as magnanimous. Perhaps he'd thought he could placate the mercenary with gifts; perhaps he'd hoped that Goatius' terrifying power would die with its owner.

If that had been his hope, then he had been mistaken. When Goatius Xex died, his daughter took his place, proclaiming herself queen of Gutgirt, and demonstrating the same terrible powers of strength and invincibility her father had possessed. Powers which continued to be passed down from ruler to ruler, like some kind of heirloom, along with a terrible bloodthirst.

Honey shuddered, looking out at a whole town painted crimson. In the spitting rain the buildings looked washed with blood.

The whole place looks like a slaughterhouse, thought Honeydew. *Everything covered with gore!*

Other than the colour crimson, the Xexes were very fond of metal. Gutgirt was home to numerous iron ore mines, and massive smelting factories dotted the roads, belching out smoke as their furnaces gave birth to steel. The palace – which arrogantly sat without any walls – was almost entirely constructed from steel. Honey had never seen anything like it. Its style and adornment were starkly and terribly minimal. The only decoration came in the form of massive metal points which rose off the peaks and the walls like the tips of giant blades. Down the featureless and shining metal walls flowed long crimson banners, marked with the image of the glittering crown. Torches burned even in the overcast daylight, casting baleful reflections on the distorting steel.

Honey's heart hammered faster as the coach rattled on towards the massive metal gates. She felt like she were heading for the mouth of a beast poised to devour her.

Oh, how she wished she was in Oda's place right now!

Princess Oda yawned. Shimmerland was nothing but mile after mile of picturesque villages, smiling peasants, and verdant forest groves. The palace itself was a stately affair, overgrown with moss and surrounded by curated gardens where flowers bloomed in arrangements of kaleidoscopic colour, the pathways strolled by ladies and knights in colourful apparel, while butterflies careened amidst lattices and vines. It was all so bright, so happy, so –

So insipid! thought Oda.

She longed to be somewhere else – somewhere full of excitement, and screams. Oh how she wished she was in Honey's place right now!

A distant scream echoed through the iron halls.

Is someone being tortured? Honeydew wondered.

She tried not to think about it as she sat on a bed in the room in which her husband had told her to wait. It was one of the few times she'd heard him speak. Other than his vows and a few clipped commands, he'd hardly said anything at all.

The room made her think of weapons and gore. The gleaming walls were hung with crimson draperies, flowing like rivulets of blood down the fuller of a blade. The air was stuffy, oppressive, and warm. How hot would the building get in the summer? Gutgirt was a cold place, but in the heat of the sun, all this metal would end up like a sweltering oven!

This isn't a palace designed by sane people! thought Honeydew. It was as if whoever'd done it wanted to be reminded about warfare and bloodshed every single moment of every single day.

At least the four-poster bed she sat on wasn't made of steel. The mattress was soft, stuffed with layers of the finest down. Rosewood posters upheld a crimson canopy, from which hung a set of luscious curtains. The curtains, of course, were also crimson, as were the covers and pillows.

All the better to disguise all the blood I'll be shedding, she thought. Though she meant it to be nonchalant, her mood remained apprehensive.

Four guards stood stationed in the corners of the room. Like all the king's soldiers, they were dressed in red. She noticed they kept their gazes scrupulously pointed away from her. Were they fearful of ogling their master's prize, or did they pity her too much to look her in the eyes? In either case, she wondered what they were doing there. Were they to stop her from trying to escape, perhaps? To prevent her from killing herself? Perhaps they'd be ordered to join in the consummation.

Stop thinking such awful things! thought Honeydew.

Suddenly the door burst open and her husband walked in, wearing only his silver blood-diamond crown and a crimson silk robe. He shut the door behind him, then let the robe drop, revealing his muscular body and eager erection.

Honey was stunned by the sight of it. She'd seen dicks before, of course, but never in a context like this. His member was pointing right towards her, so hard and engorged that it was visibly twitching as the blood thundered through it.

Blood! she thought.

There was also blood on his stomach, stark against the pale-white skin. Not much, just a little splatter. What had he been doing before he'd come to the chamber? What had he been doing while that distant scream was sounding? What had he been doing that'd gotten him so hard?!

"Take off your dress," he said.

Stunned, Honey just stared at his throbbing prick and the blood on his abdominals as the affronting command slowly filtered down into her mind. She didn't want to take off her dress. If anything, she wanted to put more clothes on. In fact, she wouldn't mind dressing up in a suit of steel armour, with extra-thick plates around the groin! But did she really have a choice? She reflected on the advice her mother had given her.

As a wife, it will be your duty to please your husband, and bring forth noble children. You might not always enjoy it – you might not even like it – but that's just the way it has to be. This is the real world, Honey, and we all have to do things we don't want to do...

Honey started to undress. What choice did she have? She felt like the whole of society – nay, the whole of the cosmos! – was pushing her to lie with this man. Her mother, her father, the astrologer, the demons above, the peasants in the fields, the nobles and knights, the whole force of law and tradition stood behind her marriage – for all she knew, even the birds in the trees were singing that Barbus should fuck her, and the patterns in the clouds were laying out the path that their coitus should follow! The only thing that stood against the weight of all that cruel expectation was her own honest feeling that she *didn't want to do this*.

She let the dress fall to the floor, and set about removing her white silken undergarments. As she did so, Barbus stood watching, his prick still twitching like a tightly-clenched fist. From the corner of her eye she watched *him*, trying to find something to like, something to admire, something to make this process more palatable. He had a good body, that was certain; it was muscular and tall, with wide shoulders and narrow hips, almost the picture of warrior manhood. But his skin was so hideously pale, like that of a corpse. And in truth, his manner and reputation were so odious and awful he could've been the most beautiful man in the world, and she still would've shrunk from his embraces as though he were covered in bile.

She thought all this as she removed the last of her underwear, terribly conscious of the fact that her physical actions were the absolute reverse of her deepening emotions – she *didn't* want to do this.

But now she was naked. Barbus ogled her creamy white breasts and the patch of silver pubes between her legs. His prick seemed to stare at her too, like a menacing cyclops. He took a step towards her, and her heart leapt in horror.

"Wait," she said. "Hold on. Can't we – "

He rushed at her, grabbing her and pushing her down atop the bed. His strength was terrifying. Honey was only a slender young woman, weighing barely one hundred pounds; the king had the might of twenty men, and was built like a solid brick shithouse. He was on her like a rock atop a feather, crushing her down and spreading her apart.

"No, stop!" she shouted.

Gripping his hardness like a weapon, he guided his tip between her lips and pressed his full force against her hymen. There came a moment of pressure and pain, and for a second Honey wondered if something so big could even get inside her. Her thoughts were naïve, for Barbus' prick was as monstrously strong as the rest of him, and utterly impervious to harm; he could've used it to hammer through the mortar in a solid brick wall. Thus it made very short work of Honey's hymen, and thrusting deep inside her, from tip to bloody base, filling her womanhood with agony. She felt like he was tearing her, stretching her, impaling her, like her whole lower body was nothing but a widening circle of pain, wrapped around the site of his cruel violation.

She screamed as he started to rut, repeating the process of impalement with each brutal thrust. Hot blood oozed between her legs. She no longer cared about society's wishes, or her mother's advice, or even the will of the demons above – she just wanted this to stop.

She clawed at his skin, but his hide was impenetrable; even had her nails been made of razors they wouldn't have yielded a scratch. Desperately, she reached for his face, which hovered just inches from hers, with panting mouth and bestial eyes. Her fingers hit those eyes and tried to gouge, but the orbs were as impervious as marbles made of stone; her fingers slid off. The king merely blinked, then grinned, his features transfigured by cruelty and lust into something barely human. In screaming desperation she clawed at his cheeks, at his brows, till her fingers made contact with his crown – and pushed it off his head.

The king stopped thrusting at once. He leapt from the bed, rapidly losing his erection. She saw an unmistakable glimmer of panic in his eyes as he picked up his crown and put it back on his head. Honeydew lay on her back, trembling in terror and pain. Barbus let out a feral-sounding growl, then glanced at the soldiers who stood guard nearby. He rushed towards the closest one and tore the man's throat right out of his neck. Honeydew shrieked, while Barbus lunged at the next man, crushing his head as though it were made of hollow plaster. The air filled with shouts and entreaties as the other two guards begged for their lives. Barbus gave them no such concessions, but tore them apart till the room and its bed were splattered with their blood.

By the time he was finished, his erection had returned. He strode to the bed, where Honey still lay, shocked into stillness by what she'd just witnessed. She'd never seen anyone die like that before; she'd never seen such absolute power and savagery. The fear of it paralysed her.

"Never touch my crown again," growled Barbus. "And never tell anyone what happened here, or I'll do to you what I just did to them, only worse. Understand?"

Scared out of her wits, Honey nodded.

"Good," he said. "Now get on your stomach."

Reluctantly Honey rolled over, like a dog on command. Soon she felt his weight on her back and his prick between her legs, hard, hot, and bloody as it speared its way back into her lacerated cunt. He grasped both her arms and pinned them. Honeydew lay motionless, but for the jarring of her body as he rammed her. Awareness of her absolute helplessness took hold of her mind. She no longer thought about escape; she now wanted only to endure, to survive, to get past this moment and into a better, less horrible one. Thoughts began to lurch through her mind like drunken dancers. Again her mother's words filled her head.

The first time will be painful, but it's best to hurry up and get it over with. Just lie back and think of something pleasant. Think about the rolling hills of Chalkwood!

Honey did just that. Soon images of her beloved homeland were juxtaposed with the feeling of Barbus' prick spearing into her. The imaginative sights didn't lessen the pain, but they made her detach from it a little, as though she were a ghost inside her own mind, partly intangible, even partly dead to the terror and agony that filled her.

Slowly, ever so slowly, she grew aware of something even worse than the pain. Pleasure was building up inside her cunt, born of some thoughtless, animal reflex, like the urge to throw up, or yawn, or take a shit. She was moistening, dripping with fluid that mingled with the blood.

What's wrong with me? she thought. *Why am I enjoying this? I don't want it!*

She tried to fight the pleasure, ignore it, but she knew it was building towards an unavoidable meridian. She'd felt such sensations before, when she'd touched herself in the dead of the night.

I'm going to cum, she realised.

But she didn't want to think of Barbus. Anything but Barbus!

She closed her eyes and thought of Armand instead, imagining he was on top of her, loving her, pleasing her. Then the orgasm hit her like a tidal wave, stronger, perhaps, because she'd tried to deny it. She shuddered underneath her awful husband, then grew still, sinking down into a stew of self-loathing, feeling utterly humiliated, utterly undone, as if the ramparts of her selfhood had been shattered, and the stuff of her identity went floating on the wind like linens from a ransacked apartment. Only the thought of Armand – only the fantasy of love – kept her from descending into absolute madness. At the same time, a part of her was cruelly aware of her reality. She thought of her sister in bed with Armand, and wept from a feeling of absolute envy.

"Hurry up and ravish me, you pansy!" shouted Oda.

The consummation of her marriage wasn't going well. Armand was a perfect gentleman; he asked for her permission before he did *any-thing* – even before he felt up her boobs! He'd spent hours lovingly caressing her and eating her pussy so delicately and slowly that it almost felt like torture. She'd had to ram her crotch into his face and shout at him until he took the hint to lap a little harder and faster. She came, but still felt frustrated. This wasn't how things were supposed to go – she was supposed to be wedded to a brute, not to a sensitive nice guy!

"Ravish me," she said again. "Take me like a bandit camp whore. Treat me like a bitch in heat!"

"Hold your horses there, my beautiful flower" he said, smiling at her patiently as he sat by her side on the bed, popping the lid off a jar. "It's your first time, and we wouldn't want it to hurt now, would we?"

"Speak for yourself," she said. "I want you to impale me, brutalize me. Split my gash like a redwood tree!"

He held up a hand covered in goo from the jar. "May I put some of this on you?"

"Sure," she said, "as long as it leads to you actually fucking me before I die of old age. We've been foreplaying here for hours!"

He started rubbing the substance on her cunt. It was cool, but not unpleasant, and spread a slight tingling sensation through her sensitive lips.

"What is this stuff, anyway?" she asked. "Lube? We don't need any lube. Use my blood to moisten your shaft, when you rip me right open!"

"It's not lube," said Armand. "It's a magickal concoction to eliminate pain and exaggerate pleasure."

Oda gritted her teeth. "But I *wanted* it painful!" she said. "Weren't you listening to me?"

"I thought you were just play-acting with all that."

"No, I wasn't!" she snapped.

"So you really wanted me to ravish you roughly?"

She groaned. "Of course I did!"

"But why would you want something like that?"

"Because I just do, okay? Now be a good husband and give it to me!"

"Okay," he said. "Although, now that I've used the potion, there's no way you'll feel any pain. Plus, I'm not sure if I can 'ravish' you effectively, seeing as how I'm a virgin myself..."

"You're a *virgin*?" This was just getting worse and worse – she'd wanted an experienced molester, not a shy, uninitiated boy!

"That's right," he said. "A lot of other noblemen like to experiment with prostitutes, maids, and common wenches, but I wanted to save myself for marriage, so that I could enjoy something special with the woman I'm bound to for life. Just think about it – this'll be a first for the both of us!"

Oda sighed. "Just hurry up and stick it in, will you? And try to be as rough as possible!"

Armand nodded and tentatively eased himself into her. Oda waited for a flash of pain, but there was nothing – nothing but the shocking, novel pleasure of having him inside of her. Soon he was moving with a sinuous rhythm, which, for all of its gentleness, was getting her progressively wetter and hotter. It was better than the pleasure she felt when she fingered herself, and yet something felt wrong – it just wasn't matching her fantasy.

"Smack my arse!" she said.

Armand obliged, though his blows weren't nearly hard enough; more like affectionate pats. Oda wanted her cheeks to be redder than Barbus' clothing.

Oh Barbus, she thought. *I wish it was you who was taking me now!*

She imagined him rutting behind her like a beast, spanking her butt till it was raw and pinning her arms with his terrible strength. She came with his image in her mind, squealing in ecstasy. A moment later, Armand was exploding inside of her, somewhat prematurely in her opinion.

"Was it good, my dear?" he said, glowing with post-coital light. "I wanted to hold off until you got there. I only just managed it!"

"It was okay for a start, I suppose," she said. "But now we've got all that tender stuff out of the way, how about you tie me up, whip me, and fuck me up the arse! Or we could ravish one of the servant girls. I'll hold her down while you have your way with her!"

Armand looked at her, aghast.

"I'm sorry, my dear," he said. "But I just don't think I'm into that sort of thing!"

Oda sighed for what felt like the hundredth time that night. Just her luck to be saddled with a sensitive nice guy without an ounce of sexual cruelty in his body. When she thought of her sister in bed with Barbus, she got so jealous she wanted to scream.

After Honey's deflowering came her coronation. They dressed her up in crimson finery and stood her in the back of a chariot, right beside her husband. The chariot was made of gleaming steel and had sinister spikes on the wheels.

They put a crown on Honey's head. Like her husband's it was decorated with a single blood-diamond, but the gem was not as massive as his was, nor did it bear the same uncanny luminescence.

Her cunt felt like a wound between her legs as she rode through the streets of Crimsonia, capital of Gutgirt, peering with vague and traumatized eyes at the blood-red buildings and the masses of onlookers filling the air with obligatory cheering and applause. As she looked into their eyes she saw but two emotions: fear, directed at her husband; and pity, directed at her. Somehow, that pity made her feel even more miserable, even more degraded than before, as though it served as a reifying token of her absolute wretchedness.

Only a few people present seemed genuinely festive – the Crimson Fangs, a cohort of soldiers who rode behind her and the king, dressed in the pelts of white wolves dyed vivid crimson. They were styled as an elite military unit, but in truth they were really just Barbus' cronies – drunkards, libertines, murderers and rapists, who sought to ingratiate themselves with the king by mimicking his antics. She saw them in action at the feast, where they made sport of the serving girls – and the serving boys – by painting circles on their bodies and using them as dart boards, or by casually bending them over the tables and raping them right in the middle of the dining hall. Honey watched it all with a sense of crawling horror she could barely lay a finger on; again she felt like a ghost in her very own soul. Partway into the horrible festivities, after a servant had been drowned in a vat of wine, and her wine-filled carcass had been used as a novel type of serving vessel, and after a young lad had been cut into pieces with a carving knife, to settle a dispute about who was the best turkey-carver, Barbus sat down beside Honey, and whispered in her ear.

"Behold my Crimson Fangs," he said. "Their bark is not as bad as their bite. If you ever disobey me, then I'll give you to them – all of them, at once. Understand?"

Honey could do nothing but nod, and try not to vomit all over the place. As she watched the crimson festivities continue, and the death toll continue to mount, she wondered how her sister was doing, over in the kingdom of Shimmerland.

Oda was washed and anointed with oils, then dressed in a beautiful gown of golden brocade. They took her to a throne room bustling with nobles, knights, and diverse honoured guests from all over the land. The air swam with perfume, and the light through the stained glass windows refracted through the facets of a diamond chandelier, which rotated slowly in the wind, spinning out rays of coloured light in every direction. They placed a crown on her head decorated with rubies, topazes, and emeralds, while the rite-masters read out a ritual formula proclaiming her queen. After that the poets came out one-by-one, reading out glowing panegyrics, in which they competed to praise her for her beauty, grace, poise and intelligence, and in which they predicted, in the glowingest possible terms, the prosperity her presence would bring to the realm, the happiness she'd have, and the beautiful children she'd bring forth from her no-doubt bountiful womb. By the time all the flattery and frippery was done, Oda could have puked.

But it still wasn't over. They put her in the back of a sumptuous chariot, right beside her husband, and drove her through the streets, where adoring citizens crowded the sidewalks, the rooftops, and the balconies, cheering on the royal couple and dousing them with a ceaseless downpouring of sweet-smelling flower petals, calling them names like 'darling,' 'sweetie,' and 'dove.'

The whole thing made Oda sick. Where was the fear that should be in their eyes? She'd wanted to rule beside a tyrant, not a well-liked man of the people!

She retired to bed early, avoiding the dancing and the sumptuous feast that followed, where nobles and knights frolicked until the early dawn, mingling with peasants and servants alike, whose status lay forgotten in the midst of the festivities, and all men and women were as one, united by the symbol of their universal smiles.

Before she fell asleep, Oda dreamt of a castle of steel and blood, in which she might truly be happy. Oh what true pleasures she might have enjoyed there!

After the festivities, Barbus took Honey to a room filled with ropes, chains, and pulleys, where he tied her up and commenced with her second deflowering.

The next morning, she could barely walk, and her ass was still bleeding. She had to wear one of her menstrual pads to absorb all the gore. At least, she reflected, she hadn't had an orgasm that time; all she'd felt was unrelenting agony. Afterwards, as if to heighten her pain and humiliation, Barbus had whipped her on the backside till her cheeks were bright red and scored with bleeding lines. So not only could she hardly walk, but she could hardly sit down, either. And yet sit down she did, as her husband commanded her to, at the opposite head of a long crimson dining table.

She winced as her lacerated bottom made contact with the seat of the chair. At least there was a cushion, supplied in crimson on a stark steely frame.

Barbus sat a dozen feet away, dressed in a robe and his ever-present crown, clutching his knife and fork upright in each hand as he impatiently awaited his food. She could smell cooking bacon and eggs. For a moment, his gaze scraped over her features like a scouring pad; then he went back to watching the kitchen door. For her part, Honey still felt numb, as if she'd been punched but hadn't fully registered the pain yet, as though she were trapped in some strange void of time between injury and agony, between shock and despair, in which there was only a sense of unreal suspension, as though she stood upon a rope bridge stretched to its limits above an abyss into which she would inevitably fall. She supposed she should be thankful she wasn't feeling worse – or falling already.

Soon the breakfast came. It consisted of so-called 'little soldiers' – strips of toast ready to be dipped into soft-boiled eggs arranged in tiny crimson cups.

"Wait," said Barbus, as a serving girl hastened to depart from the room, having laid out the eggs before him. "Don't go anywhere until I say you can. I want to see if these eggs are properly runny."

"Yes, Your Majesty," said the girl, a tremor of dread in her voice.

Both she and Honey looked on in hypnotized horror as Barbus picked up one of the little soldiers, dipped it in the egg, and drew it back out again, staring at the clinging yellow yolk. Most of it was runny; a tiny little scrap of it was hard and opaque.

Barbus roared and leapt to his feet. He grabbed the serving girl by the neck and forced her to kneel, so that her chin rested on the tabletop and its edge pressed into her throat. She coughed and choked, and at first Honey thought the poor girl's windpipe might be broken, but then she began crying and begging for her life. Barbus ignored her, and set about tracing a line with his finger just below her hairline. She screamed; Barbus' fingernail was strong as steel and sharp enough to slice through her skin. Blood trickled down her face and mingled with her tears. Honey wanted to say something, tell him to stop, but she was paralysed with terror. She watched as Barbus grabbed the girl's hair and peeled back her scalp like a rind, laying bare her naked skull. Honey felt sick from the sight, but the horror was only beginning. Barbus put his hand over the dome of the girl's skull and applied squeezing pressure, until Honey could see his fingers shaking with force.

"You have to do this carefully," he said, matter-of-factly, without taking his eyes off the serving girl, who was growing incoherent with shock. "Like cracking an egg. Too much, and you make a mess. Mother showed me how. Here, look…"

As he spoke, fractures spread across the girl's skull like cracks in a paving stone. Barbus worked his fingers into one of the cracks and carefully wrenched off a piece of bone, as though he were pulling the stubborn dark hull off the flesh of a coconut. With the skull open he tore open the glistening membrane beneath, exposing a maze of pink tissue. The serving girl's brain was now bare, though still she lived. Honey had to fight back her bile, while Barbus grinned and picked up a piece of sliced toast.

Suddenly Honey realised the demented symbolic logic behind this act of torture: the serving girl's head had become a new egg, and her brains had become a red yolk.

Barbus thrust the strip of toast into her brain. The toast was sourdough, and cooked almost black; it was tough enough to push a few inches through the corrugated tissue. As the toast went in, Honey saw the servant girl's face twitch, as though she were afflicted with a palsy.

Unable to hold it anymore, Honey threw up all over the floor. Barbus just laughed, ate up the strip of reddened toast, and continued to dip in another dozen pieces, until the poor girl's brains were covered with dimples and crumbs. Honey's own breakfast sat there, completely untouched.

At length Barbus stood up and strode over to Honey's end of the table, leaving the servant girl a tremoring ruin on the floor. Honey felt him looming, but kept her eyes focused on the table; a sense of revulsion prevented her from looking up at him, as though he were the glare of a terrible sun.

"Look at me, wife," he commanded.

Honey struggled to obey. Gingerly she turned to him, feeling her skin crawl as if with ten thousand spiders as she beheld his pallid face, his handlebar moustache, his dark callous eyes – and the shining blood diamond sitting stark in the centre of his otherwise unadorned crown. Sensing her desire to look away, he seized her by the face and forced her to maintain eye contact.

"I'm going away for a little while," he said. "There's a kingdom in the west that needs to be conquered. While I'm gone, you're to stay in the palace. You can go anywhere on the grounds, enter any room – except for the room with the lacquered black door. Understand?"

Honeydew nodded. She knew the room he was talking about; it was next to her bedroom. The door was massive and black, adorned with an ivory skull. It smelled of death and alchemy, and gave her the creeps. Indeed it was not just the stench, but a certain aura, intangible, ineffable, that seemed to seep out from the place, like a sort of psychic miasma, making her sick and repulsed to the uttermost depths of her soul. She never would've wanted to go in there – had he not told her *not* to.

She looked into his eyes, wondering in what sense she was supposed to understand his instructions. Was his prohibition ironic? Was he, by telling her not to enter the room, trying to ensure that she would? Or was he merely toying with her, testing her, daring her to break his rules, and thereby give him license to torment her, and turn her body over to the sickening attentions of his cronies?

Perhaps either way it didn't matter. Because as soon as she heard the prohibition, a part of Honeydew *knew* she would enter that room – sooner or later.

The day after her coronation, Oda was treated to a breakfast of buttermilk pancakes covered with strawberries and cream, while a band played soothing music in the background. She thought the breakfast was tasty enough, but she couldn't stand the insipid tunes.

Overall, she fancied she would've much preferred dining on the hearts of her enemies while listening to the wailing of their widows.

After breakfast, Armand came to her, and gave her a big set of keys on a shining gold chain. They opened every single door in the castle, he told her – except for one.

"The one with the faded painting of flowers on the door," said Armand. "That's my private room, and no-one's allowed in there but me. So please, I'd like you to promise that you'll never try to open it."

"I promise," said Oda.

She was lying, of course; she was going to open that door the very first chance that she got!

Chapter 3: The Atrocity Exhibit

It was later, rather than sooner, that Honey went to open the forbidden black door. After Barbus left the palace, and the immediate danger passed, her exhausted spirit collapsed into the pits of despair. What use describing those pits? Those who've never been there cannot fathom their nature; and those who have been do not want to go back. Suffice to say, she spent a lot of time weeping, and dreaming, and there were many occasions upon which she climbed up the stairs to the heights of the palace, stepped out upon the balconies, and thought about jumping to her death, so that her body might splatter on the ground, or be sliced into pieces by the cruel steel projections that covered the building, as though she were a suicidal cheese leaping down the side of a gigantic grater.

Suicide offered an escape. Perhaps that way, at least, she could keep what little dignity – what little *sanity* – remained to her. Soon, she knew, she might end up broken. Or even worse – she might end up moulded to her new existence. Her mother had often told her a person could get used to anything. But Honey didn't want to get used to this life! And yet, already she felt like she were growing desensitized. Every passing day, every passing hour, the memories of the horrors that had happened to her, the horrors she'd seen, had grown more and more bearable, more and more void of emotion, with the implication that eventually *all* of the horror around her would be trite and common-place – as common as the birds, as common as the breeze.

She didn't want that! So, she was determined to escape her situation by any means available – even by death.

But what's the hurry? said a brave and irrepressible part of herself. *Before you check out, why not break the rule your husband gave you – why not go into the room with the black-lacquered door!*

She had to admit she was intrigued, even though she was pretty sure she already knew what lay inside the room. For what could be in there, other than the corpses of Barbus' many missing wives? It seemed painfully obvious. And yet, she couldn't be certain, and so she kept wondering. Her curiosity about the room was the only thing she had to offset her terror and sorrow. Her only obstacle to opening it was fear of her husband. But if she was determined to die anyway, then what was there to fear?

Finally, she decided to open the door, just as a part of her had always known she would. For a moment, she hesitated before it, re-coiling not just from the stench of death and chemicals that wafted through its cracks, but from the sense of invisible horror that radiated outwards as well. The door was gleaming black, reflecting her body as an inchoate smudge; in the centre sat the jawless skull, creamy and white, resting on a cushion of its very own crossbones.

Steeling herself, she reached out and turned the handle. There were no guards to stop her from doing so, nor any lock to stop the door from opening inward, which heightened her suspicions that her husband had in some way intended her to enter.

The smell of death and chemicals grew stronger as she crossed the threshold, and her eyes opened wide as she beheld what lay within.

To her great irritation, Oda wasn't able to open the door to her husband's secret room straight away. It was always locked, and there was only one key, which Armand wore on a chain around his neck and never removed. Every day, just after dinner, he'd go to the room, lock the door behind him, and stay in there for an hour or two, before locking up again and going to bed. Sometimes Oda watched him enter the room from the bend of the corridor, and waited for him to leave; other times she stood outside with her ear pressed to the door, listening intently. Sometimes he heard muffled voices. They sounded high-pitched, like those of women or children. Sometimes she heard the scraping of timber on timber, or the tapping of a hammer, or the bubble of boiling water.

Oda was wracked with curiosity. For the first time since coming to Shimmerland she felt truly excited! Surely the room was home to some dark and terrible secret her husband felt compelled to keep hidden. Was the room filled with sex slaves plucked from the peasantry and forced by threat of torture and death to carry out all her husband's whims, no matter how sick, selfish and degrading they might be? Or was the secret more arcane – was he torturing children in there, and trading their screams to beings from Beyond? She'd heard of fell fairies who fed on the suffering of mortals, and creatures that ate human souls. Perhaps Armand was seeking their patronage. Perhaps that was how he'd become king at such a young age!

Whatever his secret was, she was sure it was dark. Otherwise, why would he hide it? And if Armand had a terrible secret, then he couldn't possibly be the bland goody-two-shoes she'd thought him to be. He clearly had a dark side, a secret streak of cruelty and perversion he'd never let anyone see. But Oda wanted to see it. She wanted to see it, and share in it, so the two of them might truly be husband and wife.

At length she hit upon a way to sneak into the room. While Armand was asleep, she slowly and carefully removed the key from around his neck, then replaced it with one of similar size, shape, colour and weight. That way he wouldn't notice the switch until he went to open the room, and by then his secret would already be revealed.

Excitedly, she waited for her chance. It arrived when Armand went off to go riding on the palace grounds. Usually she went with him, and rode her own horse, a magnificent ebony stallion called Black Death, but today she complained of a headache. He gave her a compassionate kiss, told her to rest, then left.

As soon as he was out of sight she rushed to the door with the faded flower pattern. The blood hammered in her veins. This was it! She was about to uncover her husband's dark secret. She hoped it was truly horrible! She licked her lips, then opened the door, stepped across the threshold – and let out a horrified cry.

Surrounding her were lifeless bodies, disarticulated limbs, motionless faces, and dead glassy eyes.

The room was filled with dolls!

There were thousands of them, crowding the shelves that ran from floor to ceiling. Some were in pieces, but most were pristine. Their bodies were made out of wood, ivory, or linen. There were jesters, sorcerers, nobles, and knights, all of them dressed in the finest silk clothing. In one corner of the room was a workstation, crowded with tools for maintaining and repairing the dolls. In another corner was a table and chairs. Beautiful teacups sat on the table, and a hearth stood nearby, complete with a kettle for boiling up tea.

Oda's heart sank. She felt sick to her stomach. She wanted to scream out in horror and despair.

So this is my husband's dark secret! she thought. *He's not a secret monster at all – he's an overgrown child who likes to play with toys! Well, I think it's about time someone taught him a lesson…*

She laughed as she contemplated a terrible revenge.

Honey glanced around in horrified wonder. She'd never seen anything so strange and macabre in all her life. The space beyond the black door was not just a room, but an entire wing, occupied by what could only be described as a gallery of death, complete with paintings, statues – and artefacts.

Each 'exhibit' dealt with a specific murder, a specific victim. Next to the front door, for example, stood a skeleton held together by a dusty metal frame. The bones looked blackened and old. The painting on the wall told the story of why, demonstrating, via a series of sequential panels, how a beautiful woman had been stripped, raped, and strangled to unconsciousness, then trussed up like a turkey and roasted alive with an apple in her mouth, after which she was consumed by a man whose hand was adorned with a blood-diamond set into a thick silver ring.

Honey studied the gem. It looked like the same one her husband wore on his crown. And the man in the picture looked similar as well, though his face was marred by scars. She noted the inscription: *Prince Goatius Xex of Gutgirt eats his first wife, Una Pollina, 696 AOC, The Year of Black Rain.*

It's his ancestor, thought Honey. *The mercenary-king!*

She swallowed a wad of saliva, sickened by the cannibal imagery. Near the painting stood a small diorama, filled with incredibly detailed miniature models, which likewise commemorated the feast. Next to that was a book, which Honeydew flipped through, encountering a florid epic poem that dealt with the woman's demise in incredible detail. She read a few stanzas, then slammed the book shut, sending foul-smelling dust careening through the room.

She walked on through the wing with astonished and horrified eyes, touring a history of homicide. Every exhibit dealt with a differ-

197

ent murder. There were victims of skinning, poisoning, bludgeoning; strangulation, mutilation, defenestration; there was death by starvation, immolation, inhumation; the list went on and on. Each murder, which often included preliminary torture and sexual violence, was painstakingly recorded in the form of sequential paintings, dioramas, epic poems, bone carvings, crystal cameos, or stark woodblock prints. The corpses – whatever had been left of them – had been preserved and displayed, with the more-than-skeletal ones having been frozen by some sort of alchemical science in a semblance of nascent mortality. Their skin looked rubbery, as did the flesh and the organs, where such was on display. The specimens gave off the commingled reek of chemicals and death Honey had smelt seeping out of the room. Judging by the scenes and inscriptions, all of the victims had been the spouses of Barbus' ancestors. The Crimson Kings and Crimson Queens of Gutgirt had been murdering their wives and husbands for hundreds of years!

What is this, thought Honey, *some kind of demented family tradition?!*

Onwards she walked, passing dozens of exhibits, working her way down her husband's family tree. The figures of his ancestors leered from the paintings, all but the first of them accoutred with the lurid crimson crown. She saw his grandfather sawing a woman in half; she saw his mother, pale and voluptuous, bathing her husband in ice until his extremities froze into solid white chunks that she smashed with a gigantic hammer, leaving nought but scattered bits of bone, which someone had put back together like a three-dimensional jigsaw puzzle, so that his skeleton stood before Honey, all riven with cracks and pitted with holes. With horror she realised that this was her husband's own father. Barbus' mother had murdered him, then had his body displayed in the palace where their son had grown up. Had the young Barbus played as a child round the legs of his father's reconstituted skeleton?

No wonder he's so fucked-up, she thought. *And then there's what happened to his mother...*

According to rumour, Barbus' mother, Barba, had slit her own throat in front of her son. Surely that would leave a terrible mark on anyone. And yet, it still seemed insufficient to explain the extremity of Barbus' behaviour.

Maybe there is no explanation, thought Honey. *Maybe his cruelty just comes from the Void, like the essence of Chaos itself...*

Suddenly she froze, frowning. How could Queen Barba have slit her own throat, if her skin had been impervious, like Barbus' was?

Unable to think up an answer to the inconsistency, Honey walked on, soon arriving at the gallery's most recent exhibits, the ones that commemorated her own husband's murders. Here were the eleven princesses he'd married and murdered, some of whom were younger than Honey herself. They screamed at her from the paintings, their suffering frozen in oils.

Honey felt a terrible kinship with them, a kinship she wanted to refute. She didn't want to be a victim like they were. She didn't want that to be her story! For it was one thing to suffer and die, like all mortals must, and quite another to be rendered into nothing but a narrative of misery, such as those on display. That was the ultimate effacement, a true degradation of the richness of self.

She hurried on, trying not to look at the paintings and the bodies, unwilling to witness how Barbus' other brides had died. She caught only glimpses of horror and blood that crowded her vision as she ran to the end of the exhibits and stood there, panting, looking at a long expanse of corridor, in which there was nothing but vacant walls and a single, unoccupied platform.

Could this one be waiting for me? she wondered, trying not to picture her mortified, rubberised cadaver standing on the platform, after having been subjected to some brutal demise.

For untold moments she stared at the empty, dusty dais in horror. Then the sound of a voice snapped her loose from her trance.

"Fuck!" someone cried.

Honeydew turned towards the sound. It was coming from just beyond the bend in the corridor.

Who could that be? she wondered. *This whole place is supposed to be off-limits...*

Filled with curiosity, she crept to the end of the long corridor, turned the bend, and found herself in yet another featureless hall, which eventually led to an apparent dead-end, a solid steel wall draped with a tapestry.

But that just didn't make sense. She'd definitely heard a voice coming from this very direction. And it couldn't have come through the walls, either; it was far too clear, far too unmuffled.

Then the voice cursed again.

"Stupid bloody thing!"

Honeydew started. It was coming from somewhere just beyond the apparent dead-end. Gingerly she crept up to the drapery, drew it aside – and found herself looking through a door into a workshop, where an old man tinkered with the screws on his adjustable desk. No doubt it was him she'd heard cursing. Nearby sat a young boy, no older than fifteen, sketching with charcoal. The object of his sketch was a woman who'd been flayed from the waist and had her skin slung over her back like a cape. She was naked and dead, just like the bodies in the gallery. Honey stared at the macabre scene with horror in her eyes.

"Don't be afraid, child," said the old man, taking note of her fright. "We're prisoners here, just like you." He beckoned to her. "Come in, close the door."

Honey did so. The room stank of paint and preservatives. Towering shelves were built into the walls, overflowing with paintbrushes, canvases, toolboxes, and sundry other items. A table sat at the back of the chamber, covered with beakers, vials, and other strange pieces of glassware used in the science of alchemy. Before the old man sat a half-completed oil painting, showing Honeydew's husband in the process of flaying a woman from the waist. The features of the woman were the same as those of the preserved cadaver that sat in the centre of the room, being sketched by the boy.

"I take it you're the new queen?" asked the old man.

She nodded. "My name's Honeydew," she said with a trembling voice. "But people call me Honey."

"Hello Honey," he said. "My name's Ashleigh. And this is Marius, my strapping young apprentice."

He gestured in the direction of the boy, who sat staring mutely, seeming almost as fearful as Honey.

"Let me guess," Ashleigh went on. "The king went away for a while. He told you to go anywhere in the castle, anywhere at all, except for the room behind the black-lacquered door. Correct?"

"How did you know?"

"That's what he does with all of his brides. That's what his mother did with her husbands. That's what her father did, too, I suppose, but I wasn't here then."

"But why?" asked Honey. "I mean, why would they do that?"

"To torture people, I suppose. Either with curiosity unfulfilled, or else with the knowledge that *they* will one day end up on display."

"Do they always kill their brides, their husbands?"

"Always," said Ashleigh. "At least as far as I can tell. They keep them alive for a while, then eventually end up doing... *things* to them. Though I doubt I need to tell that to you. You've been through the Atrocity Exhibit – you've seen Barbus in action."

The young boy shivered as the name was mentioned; Honey knew just how he felt.

"So, you two," she said, "you're the ones who create all these...pieces of art?"

"You do us a kindness to call these abominations art," said Ashleigh. "But yes, that's who we are – the royal artists, curators of the Atrocity Exhibit. It's not a position people generally volunteer for."

"How...how did you end up here, then?" asked Honey, almost afraid to enquire.

"From a combination of stupidity and bad luck, I think," he said. "I was born in the Republic of Starfall. At a young age I was apprenticed to a master portrait painter. By the age of nineteen I'd surpassed my teacher's skill and become the most famed up-and-coming artist in the city. But I wasn't satisfied with such parochial glory. I wanted my paintings to be seen far and wide, my fame to spread all over the world. So I left to travel the kingdoms of Typhon. People warned me, of course. Said the monarchies were dangerous, backwater places, where citizens were subject to the arbitrary whims of savage, inbred royals. I took their advice with a grain of salt, and went on my way. I travelled all over, painting portraits of aristocrats and generals, merchants and alchemists. I painted the king of Yule, the high king of Amithaine, the queen of Myconia; I even painted the Dead Heads of Lichhelm!

"Eventually, I learned the Crimson Queen was in need of a portrait, and was offering a giant commission. With gold coins blinding my eyes, I foolishly ignored the rumours of madness and savagery, dismissing them as wild exaggerations. I came here to Gutgirt, where I found that the stories, if anything, were milder than the truth.

"Myself and a number of artists were tasked with painting the queen. She was a beautiful woman, and at first I relished the chance to capture her on canvas, as did my colleagues. But it wasn't very long until the difficulties began. For one, the queen was terrible at posing. Sometimes she was lucid, intelligent, composed, but those times were rare. Mostly she fidgeted and paced about the room like a beast cooped up in a cage, growling and grinding her teeth. And then the violence started.

"The queen was in the habit of checking our progress day by day. When she didn't like what she saw, she punished the artists. One of my colleagues was forced to drink gallons of paint until the toxins in the pigment poisoned him to death; another was forced to correct his 'mistakes' by painting over them with his very own blood, until his veins were empty and he expired on his chair, whiter than a freshly-laid canvas. Another man she simply stabbed through the eyeballs with his brushes.

"The violence came fast, and often without warning. I, like the others, was utterly terrified, but I feared even more to attempt an escape. The Crimson Fangs were watching us, day and night, and when we weren't painting, we were locked in our rooms. What choice did I have? I just had to hope that my work pleased the queen, that I would produce not just a passable portrait, but a masterpiece. One that would not only save my own life, but make me immortal, if only by artistic reputation.

"And so, I kept working, as did the others. It's a strange experience, using your talents under mortal duress. It can poison your passion, make you despise the very thing you love. Some of my colleagues couldn't take the pressure. They started making mistakes, losing a grip on their talent. Their failure was a ticket to madness, and death. Luckily. the relationship I had with my work was intimate, almost unassailable. I immersed myself in the process, until even the chaos and carnage around me seemed distant and meaningless. There was only myself, and my masterpiece; the rest of the world was nothing but inchoate darkness. I hardly even noticed when the last of my colleagues was killed, leaving me alone. I just kept on working.

"Soon, I was finished. I was so very proud of my work! It'd taken me just over a year. I felt – or at least, a part of me felt – that the greatness of my artistic accomplishment justified all of my suffering, and the long terror of my imprisonment.

"I showed the finished product to the queen. She seemed very pleased, and complimented me on my skill – right before she tore the work to pieces, and threw it on the fire.

"You can hardly imagine my grief! I'm ashamed to say it, but I grieved more for that painting than I did for any of the talented men and women who'd been murdered in my presence that year. I wept like a child, and fell to the floor. When I asked the queen why she'd destroyed it, she said she'd changed her mind. She no longer wanted a portrait of herself – she wanted a portrait of *herself and her son.* I couldn't help but let out a miserable laugh. To destroy a thing of beauty for such a ridiculously trivial reason – it was almost inconceivable! Only later did I realise she'd ruined the painting because she knew it was precious to me, and she'd wanted me to suffer. Not because she hated me, but just because she couldn't help herself.

"With a crushed spirit, I began the second painting. The young Barbus -- then such a quiet, pale, skinny little boy -- was brought in to model for me. He hardly said a word, and seemed to live in terror of his mother. At the time, I felt sorry for him, but had I known then what he'd become, I wouldn't have felt any pity at all. In fact, I like to think I would have wrung his little neck the first chance I could."

As Ashleigh's words seeped into her mind, Honey tried to imagine her husband as a timid little boy, but found the task impossible.

The painter continued.

"It took me another year to finish the second painting – another twelve months of imprisonment and fear, during which I was forced to bear witness to Queen Barba's rages. Even more terrifying than her temper was her libido. She had a habit of seizing servants and soldiers for sudden acts of coupling, acts which her mates were unlikely to survive. Sometimes she literally *ate* her way through them. I suppose I should count myself lucky she never took a fancy to me. Then again, she had a grander destiny in store for yours truly!"

Ashleigh laughed bitterly, then went on.

"When I showed her the second painting, she was very, very pleased. She smiled and complimented me in such a civil manner that I almost forgot what she was. In a moment of daring, I asked for my payment, saying I was sorry to depart, but that I'd best be going home to Starfall, where my relatives were missing me.

"The queen just looked at me, and laughed. It was then I realised what a part of me had known all along: she had no intention of letting me leave. She told me I would stay on as official court painter, with the fullness of her patronage behind me. There was a project that needed my attention, she said – a collaborative masterpiece of art first begun in the time of her ancestor Goatius Xex.

"She was talking, of course, about the Atrocity Exhibit. I was sickened, appalled, much like you must've been, Honey. And yet, I must also admit to being awed by the talent on display. The artists of Gutgirt had been some of the greatest of their time! It pained me to see so much genius yoked to such hideous purpose. How could I allow myself to suffer a similar fate? How could I allow my talents to be poured into something so vile?

"I decided I had to escape. For a while I played along, working on the death scenes of Banjoul, Barba's fifth husband, all the while planning my getaway." He paused, and sighed. "But why waste time recounting *that* story? It's obvious my escape attempt failed. When the Crimson Fangs caught me, the queen made sure I would never flee again. Here, look –"

Ashleigh drew away the blanket that covered his lower half, revealing the stumps of his legs, cut off below the knees.

Honeydew gasped. "That's awful!" she said.

"Not nearly as bad as what she threatened to do if I tried again. 'Should you even seek to *crawl* out of here,' she said, 'I will have you sewn to a chair.' She meant it, too. Her engineers made drawings of the fiendish device, complete with funnels, tubes, and removable chamber pots – the sort of thing a man might be sewn into, and stay in for life.

"Naturally, after that, I gave up any thought of escape. Instead, I waited for Barba to die, hoping her cruelty would end with her, and that her son would be a kinder, more sympathetic ruler." He let out a bark of cynical laughter. "Some hope that was! He might've been mild in the beginning, but once he took up her mantle, and put on that terrible crown, he became each bit as awful! Worse, in fact! He's so consumed by bloodthirst he can't keep his own palace running properly. This" – he gestured to the workshop – "used to be filled with poets, embalmers, technicians, you-name-it. Now there's just me and Marius, forced to do everything ourselves. It's a heavy burden for a legless old man and a beardless young boy."

Honey glanced over at Marius, who continued to sketch the dead bride. "Is he your son?"

"Not by blood," said Ashleigh. "But I suppose I'm the closest thing to family he has. I'm not sure what happened to his parents. He refuses to talk about it. Or, indeed, much of anything at all. But he's a talented artist. One day, he'll make a fine replacement for me, though I wish he'd get the chance to ply his trade somewhere else. This palace is no place for a child. No place for anyone, especially not a beautiful young woman like you. But they were all young and beautiful, before they ended up in here..."

Unthinkingly, his eyes turned towards the preserved cadaver in the centre of the room. Even in death, the woman was indeed very beautiful, with a nubile figure and fiery red hair.

"Did you meet her, too?" asked Honeydew. "Before she died?"

"Hmm?" said the old man, as though his thoughts had wandered off. "No, I never met her. I never met any of Barbus' other brides. You're the first one ever to find your way here."

"But...but I thought you said most of them came to the gallery, to sate their curiosity?"

"Oh, yes. It's the same sick game Barbus and his family have been playing for many generations. But this room isn't part of the gallery. The door you came through is a secret one, designed to be opened only from this side. We're supposed to keep it shut, but there's not enough ventilation, and I don't want young Marius here choking on the preservative fumes. Though, if the king finds out you've seen us, he'll punish me for leaving the door open by doing something horrible to Marius. He always punishes Marius to get to me. He knows I don't care that much about my own life anymore, so he targets the boy."

Honey saw Marius tremble in fear for a moment, before going back to silently drawing with his charcoals.

"I'm sorry," she said. "I've put you both in danger."

"As long as you don't tell anyone, then nothing will happen. You can keep a secret, can't you?"

"Of course. I won't say a word."

As she turned to leave, he asked, "Where are you going? I told you, this place is run like a shambles these days. Hardly anyone ever comes to check on us. Why not stay a while? We could use the company, and I'm sure you must have questions.'"

"Actually, I do," said Honey. "If the Crimson Kings and Queens all have impenetrable skin, then how come Barbus' mother was able to cut her own throat?"

The old man peered at her quizzically. "You mean you don't *know*? Though I suppose it makes sense. The Xexes have been spreading false information for centuries, telling people it's a gift of their bloodline, or a blessing from the demons, or the result of a fairy spell, or some other such nonsense. But the *truth* is, the source of their power is their crown. Or, more specifically, the blood-diamond that sits in the centre of that crown."

Chapter 4: The Story of the Crown

"It started with Goatius Xex, the line's founder," Ashleigh said. "Who, as you know, was once nothing but an ordinary mercenary – ruthless, to be sure, and not without skill, but ordinary nonetheless."

Honey nodded hungrily, eager to hear more of this portentous information.

"Somewhere near Seven Skulls, up in the cold north, his unit got ambushed. Only Goatius survived, fleeing alone through the white snowy wastes, till he was forced to take shelter in a cave. There, he found a demon, frozen in the ice, immobile but very much alive. It spoke directly into Xex's mind, demanding freedom. Xex, mercenary that he was, offered a counter-bargain; in exchange for setting it free, the demon would grant him power, making him invincible in battle. The demon agreed, and so Xex gathered wood and built a roaring bonfire in front of the demon's icy prison.

"Inch by inch, scintilla by scintilla, the ice began to melt, revealing the demon's living form. They say its skin was red, its eyes were like shining jewels, and that its manhood was like a great crimson serpent.

"The demon tore out of the melting ice and howled in rapture at its freedom. Then Xex had the nerve to ask for his prize. Some say, when the demon seized him, it did so with its massive clawed hand; others say it used its serpentine phallus, twining around Xex's neck like a noose. Its stinking breath blew into his face as it growled. Imprisoned for centuries, it hungered terribly, and in more ways than one. Why not slake its appetites?

"Desperately, Xex reminded it of their bargain, and the demon relented. For whatever reason, the creature chose to keep its word. It tore out one of its own shining eyes and gave it to Xex, who watched in astonishment as the eyeball transformed in his hand, taking the shape of a brilliant, flawlessly-cut crimson blood-diamond. As soon as he held it, he felt the object's power surging through him, granting him strength and invulnerability – among other things. He thanked the demon, who laughed and vanished into the snow, never to be seen by the mortal again.

"The next time Xex fought in battle, he wore the gem in a pouch around his neck. To his delight, he found the sense of vigour it gave him wasn't just in his mind. He could tear his opponents limb-from-limb, with nothing but his hands; he could uproot whole trees from the ground and use them as clubs; he could wade through an ocean of blades without once getting cut.

"With his newfound power, he quickly earned riches and fame. No doubt you know how he and his mercenary band, The Plague, helped the king of Shimmerland defeat the plutocrats of Porkwood, and how Xex was given the kingdom of Gutgirt for his troubles.

"But there was more to the story. The diamond, which he'd by then had mounted into a ring, contained more than just a fraction of the demon's power. It held a fraction of the demon's malice, as well, malice much greater than that of a man. Some even think the demon got rid of its malice deliberately – that it had been imprisoned by its very own brethren for the sickening scope of its cruelty, and that after a few hundred years of being trapped in the ice, it'd decided to reform its horrid ways by ripping its cruelty right out of its head, and placing it inside of a receptacle. So when Xex came along, the demon decided to kill two birds with one stone, and give the mortal his reward, along with a hidden little twist. Either that, or the power of the demon was simply inseparable from its cruelty, and that by asking for said power, Xex had been asking for a measure of savagery as well. In any case, the gem was poisoned. Within a few years, Xex went from a ruthless killer-for-hire into an absolute monster. He visited horrors untold upon his foes, though, in the context of warfare, Xex's monstrosity was seen as acceptable, even laudable. As long as he got results – as long as he hammered cold nails of fear into the hearts of the enemy – then Xex was a conquering hero, rather than a pervert with a passion for cruelty.

"It was only *after* the fighting ended that Xex's new appetites started causing trouble. A man like Xex – a man like Xex had *become* – was not suitable for peacetime.

"He married a beautiful young woman, whom by all accounts he loved very dearly. But his love became tainted. His behaviour towards her grew more and more cruel. He ultimately cooked her alive and ate her for dinner, after having her raped by his elite soldiers, former members of The Plague now calling themselves The Crimson Fangs. So great was his perverse enjoyment of his wife's annihilation – a rapture beyond any normal conception of pleasure or pain – he decided to commemorate the experience in art. Thus beginning this secret museum, to become known as the Atrocity Exhibit."

"So...so he was being controlled by the gem?" said Honey. "The *gem* turned him into a monster?"

"I think it's more complex than that," Ashleigh said. "After all, does alcohol *make* a man cheat on his wife, get into fights, piss in the square, and act like a fool? No, it merely encourages him, giving him license to fulfil all the urges he already has inside. That's how the gem works. It calls to the cruelty within them, drawing to the surface that which dwells in the innermost reaches of the heart."

He paused for a moment, as if letting his words sink in, then continued.

"In time, Xex became so rabid that his own daughter, Xexia, pulled the ring from his finger and slit his throat. Then she had the gem set into a crown, and proclaimed herself Queen of Gutgirt. Her actions began a tradition; since that day, all the rulers of Gutgirt have either been killed by their children, or slaughtered themselves. Indeed, it's the only way they *can* be killed, since they're invincible as long as they wear the gem. No-one not of the Xex bloodline can remove or so much as touch it."

But I knocked the crown from Barbus' head! What does that mean? wondered Honey.

"And so," said Ashleigh, "the Xexes have ruled for three hundred years, invincible and monstrous. Dozens have tried to assassinate them, but all have failed, suffering a hideous and paralysing pain the very moment they laid hands upon the crown. Trust me, I've seen it. Back when I was new to the court, one of the other painters made an attempt at Barba. He'd no sooner touched the thing than he collapsed to the ground, screaming and shitting himself in an agony that had stolen all control of his body. Barba picked him up like a bothersome rodent and threw him out a window."

He paused, and sighed.

"Since they cannot be killed," he said, "they continue to carry out their horrors, growing more and more awful, each generation crueller than the last. I suspect the gem is not just a repository of the *demon's* malice, but a storehouse of all the malice of anyone close to it. I think it absorbs the taint of cruelty from their minds, the way a pair of underpants takes up the stink from someone's arse. But the gemstone can never be washed, can never be cleaned – it can only get dirtier and dirtier, until all the filth it accumulates rips a hole in the very cosmos."

Ashleigh paused again, and shook his head.

"Forgive me – I'm starting to wax esoteric. But it's true Barbus gets worse by the day. Even his beloved Crimson Fangs often avoid the palace, for fear they fall prey to his arbitrary rages. He lives surrounded by terrified soldiers and servants, any of whom would kill him if they could. He sits on his throne made of blood, utterly alone, ruling only through the callous mechanics of fear."

At this the old man stopped speaking, slouching in his chair as if wearied. It seemed, at last, that his thoughts were at an end.

Honey knew it was time for *her* to speak, to reveal the strange secret of her wedding night. True, Barbus had threatened her with torture and death, but what was the point of holding back? She'd already decided to risk everything, even her life, to escape from the Crimson King's clutches.

"What if I told you *I* had been able to touch the king's crown?" she asked.

Shaken from his reverie, the old man sat upright and peered at her intensely, the embers of what might have been long-forgotten hope flaring in his eyes.

"How?" he whispered. "Tell me!"

"When Barbus was...when he was consummating our marriage, I struck at his face, and knocked off his crown. He went totally berserk, killing all the guards in the room, and swore to do utterly unspeakable things to me if I ever touched it again, or told anyone. But I don't understand. You said no-one not of the Xex bloodline --"

"At some point in the past, your family tree must've crossed over with that of the Xex!" Ashleigh said. "The Crimson Kings have all been notorious rapists. Suppose one of them had their way with one of your ancestors?"

Honeydew directed her thoughts to her childhood. Her parents had forced Honeydew and her sister to study the royal biographies and chronicles concerning the family history, until they'd internalised the saga. Not a true saga, of course, but a warped and idealised one, crafted by obsequious poets and pet historians, just as their portraits were likewise the products of distortion, calculated to make their subjects look more beautiful, noble, and regal. Even through all that spin, she was able to lay hold of the truth.

"My great-great-great grandmother Lemongrass!" she cried, her eyes turning bright with understanding. "She went on a diplomatic mission to Gutgirt, and gave birth soon after. Her daughter, my great-great grandmother, was supposedly a legitimate child, fathered by Lemongrass' husband. But the baby was born with raven-black hair, in spite of the fact almost everyone else in our family has had silver hair, like mine – that's where we get our family name, Silverlock. She must've been a bastard, conceived through rape, and her mother decided to conceal her true origins! Then my sister and I ended up inheriting her blood. We even had the dark hair – at least for a while. When we little, our hair was black as pitch! It only turned silver later on."

"There you have it," said Ashleigh. "You and Barbus are cousins. And now the question is – what do you plan to do?"

The answer was simple. Knowing the secret of Barbus' weakness – as well as the secret of her own twisted bloodline – there was only one option available: remove her husband's crown, snuff out his life, and bring his abominable reign to an end!

Armand rushed into his secret room to behold the site of a massacre. A sea of severed limbs and torn clothing covered the floor. His dolls had been destroyed!

"Fancy a tea party, husband?" asked Oda, who sat at the table, mockingly sipping some tea from a beautiful cup. The chairs to either side of her were occupied by decapitated dolls.

"Why, Oda?" sobbed the king, as tears began to drip from his eyes. "Why would you do this?"

"Because it isn't right for a man, let alone a king, to be playing with dolls," she said.

"Surely it's okay for a man to keep some amount of softness, some amount of his childhood, sequestered inside! Do we have to be utterly calloused, utterly ruthless, utterly hard? Surely there's a time we can unwind, and let our inner children out to play..."

"No there fucking isn't!" snapped Oda, flinging the teacup across the room, so that it shattered into pieces and spilled cold tea across the severed heads and limbs of her husband's imaginary friends. "Men are *supposed* to be hard. Tempered, like steel! They're supposed to penetrate things – with their swords, or with their dicks! But you're all soft, Armand. You're a fucking soft-cock. I hate you!"

But Armand wasn't listening; he was too busy descending to his knees and lamenting the doom of his dolls, which he picked up and cradled one-by-one, muttering their names as the tears kept flowing down his cheeks.

"Oh Muffin Dove the jester, what has she done to you! Oh Oscar the Bear, you were once the fluffiest of all – now your stuffing's all over the place! Oh Mary, sweet Mary, sister of the sun, your dress is in tatters, your eyes are on the floor!"

Oda curled her lip in disgust. It was then she realised her husband would have to be dealt with– not just for her, but for the sake of the kingdom. He just wasn't kingly material.

Chapter 5: Regicide

Barbus returned from his campaign a week later, reeking of blood. Honey was tempted to attack him at once – but she knew better than that. She needed to bide her time and look for an opening.

It wasn't easy to find one. He was clearly wary of her, staying at a distance, so he could keep an eye on her. When he had his way with her, he tied her or pinned her arms with his terrible strength, preventing her from moving. She wondered why he didn't just kill her, and get rid of the threat. Was he thrill-seeking, perhaps, getting off on the danger she presented? Maybe a part of him knew he was a monster, and wanted someone to stop him. Or maybe he just couldn't bear to let her go. Could it be he loved her, in some twisted and horrible way?

Honey didn't know, nor did she want to; all she knew was she wanted him dead. Her grim resolution helped her to weather his cruel violations. When he forced her to cum against her will, she often tried to think of Armand. Other times, to her later regret, she imagined Barbus' death – imagined ripping off his crown and gouging out his eyes, his blood jetting all over her. When an orgasm hit her in the midst of that imaginary gore, she felt, just for a solitary moment, as though she were riding the cock of Vengeance incarnate, rather than submitting to her husband's demands. The world fell away; she slipped free of the bonds of space, time, and mortality, and entered a transcendental paradise of murderous ecstasy.

But it only ever lasted for a moment, and afterwards made her feel ashamed, so she tried just to think of Armand, whom she still longed to be with one day.

She had to put up with many more days of terror and abuse before she saw her opening. Just in time, too; Barbus' games were getting more and more violent. Having already claimed her other holes, he'd taken to having his way with her mouth. He thrust himself deep into her throat, until his balls were on her chin and his pubes in her nose. That she kept throwing up didn't seem to dampen his desire; if anything it made him even harder. Nor did it bother him when she tried to bite, since his flesh there was also impervious to harm. He'd fuck her throat without mercy, until she was covered in saliva and bile, her dark eyes were streaming with tears. Then he took to pinching shut her nostrils, so she couldn't even breathe. She'd fight hopelessly, desperately sucking for air, but only ever able to suck on his violating prick. Her vision grew thin; her senses grew faint; stars exploded in front of her eyes as she started to suffocate. A few times, she blacked out, and woke up alone, splattered with vomit and cum. Other times, he kept choking her, and letting her revive, over and over, until time itself seemed to disperse and lose any meaning, and she felt she were trapped in a realm of unending torture, repeating itself over and over, like the scenes of a fever dream.

She was sure he would kill her this way, given time. It was humiliating enough to suffer his meat in her mouth, to swallow his horrible seed, as though she were a human receptacle of filth. But to die of it – and to have it recorded in oils, for all of posterity? She imagined poor Ashleigh, painting her blue-faced cadaver, with a dick down her throat. She imagined her epitaph:

Here Lies Queen Honeydew Xex, who choked to death on dick

She wouldn't – she *couldn't* -- let that be the story of her!

Finally, she found an opportunity. She'd suffered her husband's abuses for long enough to learn his routine; there was only one moment each day in which he seemed to be vulnerable. She just had to hang all her hopes on that moment, and gamble with her life.

Oda wasted no time in plotting to get rid of her husband. The first step she took was to find a partner in crime. She was mostly alone in Shimmerland, apart from her ladies-in-waiting, and she needed someone local, someone with contacts in the region.

She selected Lord Pickerwood, one of Armand's cousins. Ambitious and arrogant, yet lazy and of average ability, Pickerwood had been passed over for numerous important appointments, both by Armand's parents and by Armand himself. He was therefore restless, embittered, and covetous – murderously so. It didn't take Oda long to size him up and let him in on her plan. To help cement their alliance, she took him as her lover, as well as co-conspirator. He was rougher in the sack than Armand, which pleased her a little, though still she longed for the iron-hard embrace of King Barbus, the man of her dreams.

Be patient, she told herself. *You'll have him eventually.*

Her plan was simple: to murder Armand and make it look like natural causes, then inherit the Kingdom of Shimmerland. Once she was queen, she could make a proposal to King Barbus, offering her kingdom as dowry. How could he resist such a prize?

One foreseeable obstacle, however, was Honeydew, Oda's own sister. She would also have to be put out of the way. Not murdered, of course – Barbus could simply divorce her and send her back home to Chalkwood. Such things weren't unheard of, although it would go against the advice of the royal astrologers, and therefore the will of the demon Zabazap. Nonetheless, Oda felt sure Barbus would be more than willing to defy tradition – especially if it meant acquiring a whole other kingdom, without the use of force!

As far as Oda could tell, the only other obstacle to the fulfillment of her dreams was how to kill Armand and make it look natural. He was young, renowned for good health, though there was a history of heart failure in his family; it was said his grandfather and great-uncle had both dropped dead well before their time. Fortuitously, Pickerwood had access to a certain undetectable poison, brewed by the hags of Gingerra, which would simulate a heart attack, and leave no other traces. But how to administer the potion? Armand may have been a sap, but he wasn't a fool; all of his food was scrupulously tested before it passed his lips. Thus Oda found herself pacing the room in which she'd made a secret assignation with Pickerwood, while her lover and co-conspirator reclined upon the bed, watching her.

"Forget it, babe," he said. "We'll just have to find some other way of bumping him off. Maybe rig up some dodgy scaffolding, like what killed his parents?"

But Oda was too stubborn to give up so readily. She kept on pacing and cudgelling her brains for an answer, until eventually her eyes lit up with the cold light of murderous knowledge.

"I've got it!" she said. "I know something he likes to eat that doesn't get tested beforehand!"

"What's that?" asked Pickerwood.

Oda smiled coyly. "Something you've often eaten as well, Woody my dear."

Over the next few weeks, Oda set about making herself immune to the poison she intended to use on her husband. She began by ingesting a tiny, almost infinitesimal amount, then upped the dosage gradually, until her tolerance was such that she could handle a dose which, were it not for her built-up immunity, would've been fatal.

At last the day came when she was ready. She took off her clothes, opened her legs, and spread a lethal dose of the poison on her pussy. The transparent potion would be easily mistaken for her natural juices, and its bitter and vaguely metallic taste was already quite similar to that of her cunt. Thus prepared, she held her pose on the bed and called for Armand. He arrived shortly, fresh from his secret room, where he was no doubt still repairing the damage she'd done to his legion of dolls.

"Come to me husband," she said. "I want you."

Armand looked surprised to see her spread out on the bed with her gash on display – surprised, but not displeased.

"I'm glad to see you want to resume our conjugal relations, my sweet," he said. "You haven't been in the mood for quite some time. In fact, I was even starting to worry there might be something going on with you and my cousin Pickerwood..."

"That creep? Don't be ridiculous! No, I've just had a lot of headaches, that's all. But right now I want you. So come to me, please..."

She writhed on the bed, running her hands up her chest and keeping her legs spread wide. But instead of rushing to the bed, Armand lingered, smiling.

"I'm glad you've decided to be intimate with me again," he said. "I know a lot of harsh words were traded between us. But I forgive you for what you said, and for what you did to my dolls..."

For fuck's sake just eat me already, thought Oda. *Eat me and die!*

"I'm glad you forgive me," she said. "I want everything to be right with us. Come on, come to me. I don't want to speak with words any more. Talk to my other set of lips!"

He got on the bed and knelt with his mouth just inches from her cunt.

"May I eat your pussy, my queen?" he asked.

Oda had to fight to stop herself from groaning with frustration. *Why does he always ask before doing anything?* she wondered. Surely her spread legs and saucy innuendo had already served as a sufficient invitation! His timidness was just another reason why he had to die. Oh how she longed for a man who would take the pulse of her lust with a glance, and take her accordingly – or, better yet, a man who would take her whenever he wanted, and make her a slave to his brutish desire.

"Yes," she said. "Eat me!"

He nodded, lowered his head – and started gently blowing on her.

"Don't breathe on it," she said. "Eat it!"

"But a bit of gentle blowing heightens arousal, and expectation...it says so in Madame Cunnicle's *Manual*..."

Even if she weren't trying to kill him, and were just trying to get some head, she never would've fancied a spot of gentle blowing! As far as she was concerned, that was all just a lot of stupid faffing. She wanted a ravenous tongue, lapping like that of a serpent – lapping like that of a hound!

"Skip the blowing and put your mouth on me!" she said.

He nodded again – then started nibbling her toes, then kissing his way up her legs.

Oda clenched her fists and made aggravated faces her husband couldn't see. Why was he taking so long to get down to business? The agony of suspense was almost unbearable. It was almost as if he were trying to torture her!

Slowly he kissed and licked his way up, moving ever closer to her poisoned cunt. Paranoid fancies flitted through her mind as she waited. What if he'd somehow discovered her plot? What if this was all just a game? What if he was toying with her? She imagined him kissing his way to her cunt, then quickly pulling back and calling for his guards to throw her in the dungeon. Her heart hammered, her blood raced.

Calm down! she thought. *Just wait a little longer. And don't freak out – he'll notice something's up!*

If Armand noticed her pounding pulse rate, he must've through it was due to erotic arousal, rather than murderous tension. Upwards he inched, until he was face-to-face with her glistening gash.

"You're so wet already," he said. "I told you the blowing increases anticipation. Madame Cunnicle knows what she's talking about."

She felt him spread her lips with his fingers, holding them taut. Then he moved closer –

Finally! she thought as his tongue made contact.

"That's it," she said, feeling a wave of relief wash over her, just before a new wave of murderous excitement took its place. "Lick me all over!"

She paid very close attention as he lapped her, wanting to be sure he ingested the bulk of the poison. Her juices were flowing now, her heart pumping wildly. There was only one step left to carry out her plan, and make Armand's death look like natural causes.

"I can't take it anymore," she said. "I want you inside me!"

He obliged and slipped inside of her, absorbing even more of the poison through the pores of his prick. He rutted on top, peering down at her, his eyes filled with pleasure and something like love. Oda wrapped her legs around him, pulling him in deeper, making him fight her for each and every thrust.

"That's it," she shouted, "fuck me!"

A galloping excitement raced through her. She felt like she were jumping off a precipice. A part of her couldn't believe what she was doing – as if she were watching from above, like a disembodied spirit. Suddenly she wondered – *was* this what she wanted? Was she *utterly* sure she wanted to end him?

Last moment doubts fluttered through her mind, making her heart race even faster. Just then, he didn't look at all like a worthless, wimpy wretch, but a handsome young lover, toiling for her pleasure. There was innocence and love in his eyes. A smile was on his face.

A smile that became a rictus of agony. He froze mid-thrust, his eyes springing wide with pain and surprise. A single hand shot to his breast, clutching at his faltering heart. He gave a sudden croak –

Then collapsed onto her, twitching.

Oda lay there, breathing heavily, trying to control her anxiety. A part of her felt sickened and shocked by what she'd just done. But what was the point of regrets now? She was balls-deep in this deadly conspiracy – just as a dead man was balls-deep in her. She had no choice but to continue, and hope that these nerves would soon fade.

"Help!" she cried. "Someone, help! There's something wrong with the king!"

Guards rushed into the room, and found the king of Shimmerland dead atop his beautiful young wife, having seemingly taxed out his heart in the act of making love to her.

Barbus strode towards Honeydew's room, eager to enjoy her again. He loved her in his own way, just as he'd loved all of his wives – with a passion indivisible from cruelty.

He opened the door and peered inside. The curtains were drawn on the four-poster bed, but he could see a silhouette through the diaphanous fabric. It looked as though Honeydew was sitting there, waiting for him. The three guards within his line of sight faced diligently into the corners, as they'd been ordered to. He didn't bother checking on the fourth. His mind was a screaming red ruin these days, in which only the loudest of signals got through – signals to fuck, and kill, often at the very same time.

He strode to the bed, ripped open the curtain –

And narrowed his eyes in shock. Instead of his wife, the fourth guard knelt on the bed, holding a sword as if ready to strike.

What the fuck?

A figure sprang from the top of the canopy, snatched at his crown, and ripped it off his head.

Honeydew dropped to the floor, clasping the crown. Her plan had been simple, but dangerous. At first she'd been wary of enrolling the guards – what if they should tell on her?

But then she remembered what Ashleigh had said – the guards and the servants were victims just like her, who lived in constant terror of the king's random cruelty. The only ones loyal to Barbus were the Crimson Fangs, and even they'd moved their quarters away from the castle for fear of their lord's indiscriminate anger.

It'd therefore been quite easy for Honey to talk the four guards into helping her. Her plan was the only hope anyone had for survival.

"Get him!" one shouted, as Honeydew rolled across the rug, holding the crown.

The soldier on the bed thrust his sword. Barbus caught the blade in his bare hands, stopping it from entering his guts. It sliced his fingers and palms to the bone. He let out the scream of a man who hadn't felt pain in a very long time. As his blood gushed, his eyes went wide with horror, even as the eyes of the guards – and those of Honey herself – filled with hope.

But the king wasn't finished yet. He may no longer have had the strength of twenty men, but he still had the strength of a maniac fighting for his life. His scream became a roar of savage anger, and he shoved the blade with his lacerated hands, pushing his attacker away. The soldier fell back on the bed, while Barbus turned and ran after Honey, seeking his salvation, seeking his power – seeking the Crown.

Honey ran into the corridor, pursued by her husband, who in turn was pursued by the other three guards. They'd been slow to react at the outset; paralysed, perhaps, by the fear they still felt. But now, having seen Barbus bleed, they were eager to finish the job. They set after him like hounds, shouting their murderous oaths.

"Kill him!"

"Kill the tyrant!"

"Kill the monster!"

Barbus kept ahead of them and raced towards Honey. He was taller than her, and faster as well. She knew she couldn't outpace him for long. He'd be on her in moments.

But she couldn't let that happen – she couldn't surrender the crown!

She turned to face him as he sprinted towards her, his bleeding hands outstretched toward the crown. She lifted it up –

And hurled it through the air. Barbus skidded to a halt as it arched over his head. He tried to leap and catch it, but the crown flew too high and sailed out a window behind him. He ran towards the opening, as though intent on recapturing the crown even if it meant diving from the castle's upper towers. In a fury, Honeydew leapt on her husband's back and clawed at his face. Her fingers grazed his eyes. He screamed and threw her off, then continued to advance towards the window, blinking his lacerated eyes.

The soldiers blocked his path with their swords. One stabbed him in the stomach, another chopped at his arm, and then all the swords were a flying blur of blood and steel, driving the king to his knees.

Barbus fell, his body a lacerated ruin, chunks of riven muscle hanging off the bone and rivulets of blood running fast from a dozen deep wounds. The guards kept on hacking at him in a frenzy, as one might attack something loathsome to the senses, like a cockroach or a venomous spider. His head lolled back as he lay on the ground; he looked up at his wife with terror in his eyes.

Honey peered down at him – and grinned. Whatever compassion she might have felt for him was drowned in an ocean of hate. Savage excitement shook her to the core. His suffering was music to her soul. She wanted to add to it. She wanted to crouch beside him and rip out his eyes with her own bare hands!

The urge, the terrible urge for cruelty, suddenly reminded her of a dreadful episode in her youth, the one she'd dubbed the Day of the Flies. It stopped her cold. She banished the savage grin from her face, and watched with taut lips as he bled out and died.

She stood above his carcass, paralysed by shock and relief, until she was shaken from her reverie by an outburst of shouts.

"All hail Honeydew!" cried the guards, kneeling before her. "All hail the queen!"

Oda stood in the throne room, the corpse of her husband laid out before her on a bier. There was much loud lamenting from the nobles and knights who surrounded the body. Even Oda herself was crying. They weren't just crocodile tears; she'd found herself plagued by feelings of regret ever since the murder. The image of Armand's dying face kept flitting through her mind. She'd started thinking strange and uncharacteristic thoughts, like that maybe Armand hadn't really been *that* bad, and that perhaps she could've even learned to love him, given time. But now, his young and beautiful body, once so full of health, was a mouldering waste, to be fed to the worms so many years before its proper time. A tragedy if ever there was one.

Why am I feeling these stupid emotions? she wondered. *This is what I* wanted!

She told herself this fit of strange compassion would end. That this had all been a necessary step to fulfill her desires. That Armand had been a stupid, weak, limp-dicked fool, and that soon she'd forget all about him – especially when her true love, Barbus, accepted her proposal!

She was shaken from her reverie when those around her took a knee, and in the flowery formula of Shimmerland, proclaimed their undying allegiance to the Oda, the widowed queen.

Thus it was that both sisters brought about the deaths of their husbands in the same afternoon, and became the sole rulers of their respective kingdoms, opening the way for the mayhem and devastation that would follow.

Chapter 6: Aftermath

News of the Crimson King's death spread quickly through the palace. Soon soldiers and servants alike were proclaiming their loyalty to Honey. But the coup wasn't quite over yet; there was still a deadly faction loyal to the king – the Crimson Fangs. Using the royal seal, Honey sent them a message, telling them to muster on a certain field at the first light of dawn the next day. The field was bounded by a deep, dark forest – the perfect place for an ambush. When the Crimson Fangs arrived, drunk or hungover from their previous evening's debaucheries, they failed to notice the soldiers hiding in the bushes with crossbows at the ready. Honey was with them. When she was satisfied all the Crimson Fangs were gathered, she gave the signal for the slaughter to begin.

A storm of crossbow bolts shot from the forest and skewered the Fangs. Dozens shrieked and fell off their horses; the rest wheeled in dismay as soldiers rushed them on all sides, swinging their axes and hefting their swords. The Fangs fell easily, some of them trying to surrender, or begging for their lives. They weren't really an elite military unit, after all, just a band of murderers and drunks.

As Honey watched them die, she felt another surge of undoubtable joy, just as she'd felt when she'd stood over Barbus' body. It was a sort of carnivorous excitement, she fancied, the sort of thing a wolf or a lion might feel – active, intense, and utterly possessing. It made her want to run into the melee and hack off some heads herself. It made her want to do other things, too – bloody and inchoate things she didn't want to think about in detail.

She took a deep breath and shook off the urges. She wondered where all of this cruelty was coming from. Perhaps it was a part of her nature, inherited from the tainted branch of her family tree that derived from the horrid house of Xex. Or maybe it just came from the Void, like the essence of Chaos itself. In either case, she decided to keep it locked away.

With the Crimson Fangs dead, Honey was undisputed ruler of

Gutgirt. A great public meeting was called to announce the change of leadership. One of the soldiers suggested the king's naked body be brought forth into the square. The people needed to see evidence of his death with their own eyes – otherwise they might think the whole thing some cruel prank, the king just waiting in the wings, ready to enact awful vengeance on anyone who cheered at the news of his demise.

And so, his mangled body was displayed before the people of Gutgirt, who gazed upon it in stunned and frozen silence. Some seemed unable to believe their good fortune. Others stared at the corpse as though it were a slumbering serpent that might rise up and bite them. Then one brave soul approached, touched the stiffened limbs and deep wounds, and cried out, "He's dead, he's really dead!"

The square exploded with sounds of jubilation. People cheered and danced, hailing Queen Honeydew. But then, a gruesome side to their joy surfaced. Decades of festering hatreds were unleashed upon the body of the king as knives slashed it to pieces. Barbus' cock was cut off, as were his balls; swords were rammed up his arse and shoved down his throat. He was dragged and kicked through the streets, then dumped into an open cesspit, where his former subjects took turns to shit and piss all over him, until he was nothing but an inchoate cluster of filth and ruination.

Honeydew found herself untroubled by the people's revenge. A part of her even rejoiced in it, though she tried to ignore that part, and focus on nicer things. Soon, the revelry was in full swing. Animals were butchered for a gigantic feast; musicians came out and filled the streets with song; the square became one gigantic party. She danced with the soldiers who'd helped her kill Barbus, all of whom were already enjoying a heroic reputation. Then she danced with young Marius, whom she'd set free from the palace. She even danced with old Ashleigh, holding his hands as he sat legless but beaming in his chair. At the climax of the festivities a great bonfire was set up, in which all of the exhibits from the Crimson Museum were summarily burned.

Ashleigh wept as he watched the work of a lifetime was consigned to the flames, but he wept with joy rather than sadness, for his life – and his art – was finally his own once again.

The festivities went on for days. Honeydew felt like a woman reborn, delivered from the certainty of suffering and death, to the pinnacle of freedom and fame. She'd had the horrible crown locked away in the treasury at once, refusing to even lay a hand on it.

The only thing to darken her mood was the news, newly arriving, of the death of young King Armand of Shimmerland.

In contrast to the celebration happening in Gutgirt, the kingdom of Shimmerland was a place of lamentation. The streets were filled with wailing and weeping. Armand's body was conveyed through a great mass of mourners, who covered it with roses and bathed it in tears. It was taken to his family's ancient crypt, where the foremost court poets offered him eulogies that went on for days, extolling his beauty, generosity, and kindness.

The funereal spirit made Oda unhinged, and deepened the guilt she felt. She told herself the price the deed had exacted on her soul would be worth paying, as soon as she fulfilled all her dreams by marrying Barbus. And yet, even as she clung to these dreams, they began to look strange and unreal, like figures once seen in darkness now newly transformed by the light. Nevertheless she kept hold of them, as if her very sanity depended on it.

Then the news came of Barbus' death. In a bloody palace coup, organised by Honeydew no less!

Oda was beside herself with fury. Her own sister had dashed all her dreams! Armand had died for nothing, and Oda would forever be alone. She had to exact her revenge!

When the funeral was over, she summoned the nobles of Shimmerland, and announced her intentions for war.

Chapter 7: Council of War

"My sister is a witch," announced Oda. "In exchange for great power, she has sold her soul to a creature from Beyond. I've seen this creature visit her often, in the innocuous form of a *butterfly*. I've kept her secret all these years, out of a sense of familial piety. But now she's gone too far, and I can shelter her no longer. Lords, I even believe *she* was responsible for the death of my beloved Armand!"

The nobles traded glances and muttered to each other, some clearly sceptical.

"Do you have any proof, Your Highness?" asked a wizened old baron called Grundig.

"The proof of my sister's witchery is in her very deeds. She was able to kill Barbus Xex, a man who had impervious flesh and the strength of twenty men. How could she have done that, if not by the power of sorcery? She sucked out his power while he slept, then got his guards to assassinate him, men whom she'd no doubt bewitched. She clearly has sinister and far-reaching plans, but her success depends on stealth, treachery, and scheming. If we swoop on her now, with the fullness of our military might, I'm sure she'll be helpless, and Shimmerland can be rid of a terrible threat!"

The nobles glanced around and muttered again, looking not entirely convinced. Technically they were Oda's vassals now, and sworn to obey, but she'd only been queen for a couple of days, and her reign was still insecure. In order to make this war happen, she needed their unflinching support.

Her lover Pickerwood stepped forward to help with her sales pitch.

"Gentlemen," he said. "Let's be honest, shall we? For centuries, Gutgirt has been growing on our border like a chancre on our balls. Its rulers aren't even noble-born, but commoner scum, descendants of a

man with origins so utterly ignoble he only had two bloody names –
Goatius Xex! The only reason our great king Glitz – may the star demon shine on his soul in the underworld – *ever* decided to ennoble
that man, and grant him a kingdom, was because he was scared! Just
as we all have been scared to the marrow by the Crimson Kings ever
since. That's why we've ignored their aggressive expansion. That's why
we've ignored their random acts of violence. That's why we've been
giving them our children in marriage, like human sacrifices sent to be
slaughtered for their pleasure! All of these things we have done out of
fear. And rightly so, because power like theirs deserves to be feared.
But now? King Barbus has died without any heirs, and the power of
the Xexes has died along with him. Which means *now* is our chance
to finally get rid of the plague that is Gutgirt. There is no better time
to strike than this moment, while their kingdom is still in a shambles,
and Honeydew is yet to consolidate her strength. We'll never have a
better chance!"

The nobles conferred amongst themselves with a series of whis-
pers and significant glances. Some had been affronted by the boldness
of Pickerwood's speech, but all had been impressed by its logic.

"As for Honeydew being a witch," Pickerwood went on, "that I'm
unable to confirm or deny. But I will say this – the people of Shimmerland are hurting, my lords. They mourn for their king. What better
outlet for their emotions than a war – especially if the purpose of that
war is to topple the woman who murdered their lord with her sinister
magick?"

The nobles glanced at one another one final time. The looks in
their eyes and predatory smiles on their faces said it all – Shimmerland was going to war.

But Oda didn't want this to be just any sort of war. She wanted it
to be like one of the wars she'd read about in the bloodiest pages of her
history books. She wanted *total* war – a war to annihilation.

"Pickerwood is right," she said. "Gutgirt is a sore that needs to be cleansed from our border. Its lands must be emptied, to provide our own people with breathing space. Therefore I propose the following measures: all Gutgirtian women and children will be seized and sold into slavery in foreign lands. Their men who do not die in battle shall have both of their hands cut off, thus leaving them a nation of lonely cripples unable even to wank. Without the means to feed themselves, they'll soon die off, allowing our people to move in. Within a generation or so, the land of Gutgirt will be no more. There will only be Shimmerland, stretching out far to the west!"

Oda fell silent, allowing her words to sink in. Some of the nobles seemed uneasy with the cruelty she proposed.

"Of course," she added, "these new lands will need to be ruled and protected by noble lords, like all others. Those who choose to share in this war will share in the spoils, and find their own territories greatly expanded!"

She watched with satisfaction as a number of eyeballs lit up with greed. There was no longer any doubt in her mind; she would have her total war, and Gutgirt would be swimming in blood. Then Honeydew would pay for destroying her dreams!

Chapter 8: The Hand-Lopper

The army of Shimmerland stormed into Gutgirt, sacking dozens of towns in a series of lightning-fast raids. Their soldiers fought without mercy, their grief for their king transformed into murderous hate. Thousands of Gutgirtians were massacred, while those who survived often wished they hadn't. The women and children were taken to be sold into slavery, as per Oda's command, while the men had their hands lopped off, leaving them crippled and virtually helpless. Many died from shock, loss of blood, or infection, leaving only a meagre percentage to lament their abominable fate.

Oda rode behind the bulk of the army in her coach, surrounded by her personal guard. The thrill of the war went a long way to soothing her conflicting emotions over Armand's demise. All of her anger – even that which had once been reserved for herself – was now solidly directed at her sister.

As she saw the towns burning, her heart raced with excitement. She felt like one of the heroines in her favourite book, *The Six Centuries of Suffering* by Alcott Vizette, leading armies in grandiose quests for revenge, leaving thousands of corpses in their wake.

I'm back on track, she thought to herself as she sat in the coach, drinking in the smell of smoke. *For a while the death of that loser Armand unsettled me. But now I'm back to my normal self – I'm back to pursuing my dreams!*

Unfortunately, she still wasn't in the thick of the action. She wanted to wade through blood and bear witness to carnage, just like her heroines did. So she demanded to be taken to one of the conquered towns, where captured men were having their hands cut off, and her vassals obeyed.

It's time, thought Oda as they arrived at her requested destination. *I'm finally going to see some real gore!*

To her chagrin, her parents had never allowed her to attend the executions back in Chalkwood; they'd said they were far too grisly for a young girl. She'd had to settle for pulling the wings off of flies, but it wasn't the same. Now, at last, she would slake the burning appetite for death she'd been fostering for so many years in her own fervid dreams! She stepped out of the coach – and into a whirlwind of sensory horror.

She stood in a field of trampled crops with a ransacked town beyond it. The mingled aromas of ashes, blood, faeces, and urine assaulted her nostrils. Curses, shouts, and agonised screams filled her ears. In the centre of the field was a pile of severed hands. Two groups of prisoners huddled to either side of it, one group without hands, one group with. The soldiers of Shimmerland surrounded them, resplendent in their red and green cloaks.

Oda watched as a man was dragged to his feet and led towards a
bloody tree stump, where the hand-lopper waited, a giant of a brute
with an axe and a crude black mask. The prisoner fought and cursed,
only to be beaten half-stupid by the soldiers, then dragged on limp
legs to the block, where they stretched out his arms by the rope that
bound his wrists, then gathered around him and held him in place.

The next few moments were a blur of intense, bloody images – the
sight of the axe as it flashed in the sun; the terror in the eyes of the
prisoner turning to pain as the blade went through his wrists, severing
his hands, the blood spurting out in ungovernable torrents. Then the
flat of a red-hot blade was pressed against the ragged red flesh, searing the wound, stopping the flow, and filling the air with the stench of
burning meat. The man fell unconscious from shock, and was dragged
towards the second group, many of whom had already died from their
injuries. They lay there turning stiff, while the flies buzzed around
them, buzzards and ravens circling overhead, hungrily sniffing at the
gore.

Oda ran behind the coach and was violently sick. She hadn't been
prepared for the full invasive horror of it – the stench, the filth, the
sheer viscerality. It wasn't like it was in her head, *or* in her books. And
the terror of the prisoners had gotten to her. The fear in their eyes
had reached right into her soul and plucked at her heartstrings, to the
point where she'd caught herself wanting to yell for the lopper to stop
with the lopping!

What's wrong with me? she thought. *Where is this stupid compassion coming from?!*

She wondered if it was part of her nature, written in the stars before she'd been born. Or perhaps it just came from the Void, like the
essence of Chaos itself. Either way, it was a problem. How could she
live out her sanguinary dreams while throwing up and feeling bad for
her victims?

For a second she reeled both inside and out, assaulted by doubts that cut to the marrow of her being and threatened to overturn all she'd built since the days of her childhood. Then she righted herself, and told herself it would all be okay.

It's just first-time jitters, that's all, she thought. *All brutal tyrants probably get them at first. After seeing a few more mutilations, you'll probably adjust to all the horrible smells, and stop getting bothered by the looks in their eyes. That's probably when you'll start to enjoy it, just like the ladies and lords of the old Screaming City!*

Thus reassured, she wiped off her mouth, got back in the coach, and signalled for her convoy to continue on its way, following the bulk of the army as it headed for Gutgirt's capital, Crimsonia.

News of the invasion travelled fast, an image of events emerging as Honey listened to reports from a series of haggard and blood-splattered messengers. The Shimmerlandian army was rampaging through town after town, carrying out dreadful acts of pillage and massacre, subjecting survivors to further disgraces of slavery and mutilation

Honey's alabaster skin turned even paler as she listened to the tales of slaughter and panic from the bloody frontier. She could scarcely believe her sister was responsible. Oda may have always had an eerie obsession with death and destruction, but this was something else. This was a pogrom, a genocide – the killing of a nation!

And then there was the terrible accusation that Honey herself had killed Armand with witchcraft! The very notion was sick, perverse, an inversion of reality. For whom had loved Armand more than Honeydew? Certainly not Oda, whom Honey suspected may have slain the king herself. Was there no end to Oda's savagery?

The accusation of witchcraft was a dire one indeed. The customs of the land required witches be dealt with most harshly – iron blindfolds hammered onto their faces, to stop them from using the evil eye; steely stoppers jammed into their mouths, to stop them from muttering spells; their fingers cut off, to stop them from making arcane gestures; and then, to top it all off, they would be burned until nothing but ashes remained!

By calling her a witch, Oda was calling for Honey's demise. Honey knew their relationship had been strained for some time, but how could Oda bear her such colossal ill-will as to seek out her torture and death? What force, what motive, could have poisoned her against her own twin so utterly?

Perhaps it's Barbus' death that's set her off, she thought. *Oda always did have a perverted attraction to him. But surely that's not why she's doing all of this. It couldn't be!*

Honey struggled not to believe her own conclusion, even though part of her knew it to be true. Could her sister really be so cold, so ruthless, so crazy, as to murder a nation and burn her own twin, all for the unrequited love she felt for a vicious, tyrannical murderer?!

I have to stop thinking about this and focus on something practical, thought Honey, *otherwise I'm gonna go crazy!*

She turned to her newly-appointed general, a fresh-faced young man called Raindrop. There had been older officers once, but Barbus had killed them all in fits of violence.

"What do you think, general?" she said. "What are our chances of beating Oda's army?"

"I'd say it all depends, your Majesty," he said, after a significant silence.

"Depends on what?"

"On what measures you're willing to take," he said. "The Gutgirtian army has suffered decades, even centuries, of serious neglect. Our numbers are small, our equipment is old, and the soldiers lack training and experience. You see, the, uh, the *execrated one* --" this being her late husband's current epithet, none in the kingdom wishing to so much as speak his name, "-- didn't use his army as an army, but more like a personal cheering squad. Our job was to follow him to the battles, wave the banners, beat the drums, and call out his name as he slaughtered the enemy."

"Surely you must have done something more than that!"

"When the battle was over, we helped with the clean-up – dispatching wounded enemies, looting bodies, burning towns, that sort of thing. But when it came to the fighting, he did all that himself. We were just along for the ride. I suppose you could say we were...irrelevant. Which means, unfortunately, that we're quite unprepared to deal with this threat.'

"What exactly are you saying, general?"

"I'm saying there's no way on earth we could beat the Shimmerland army. Even if our troops were better trained, there's just not enough of us. As far as I can see – as far as the other officers can see – our only alternative would be ... well ..." Raindrop averted his gaze, looking at the floor, as if too loaded with sorrow and shame to meet her eyes.

"What is it, general – what's this alternative?" asked Honey, although she feared she already knew the answer.

"The Crimson Crown, your Majesty," he said, raising his sad blue eyes to hers.

Honeydew's heart hammered with dread; her fingers grew tense on the arms of her throne. With difficulty, she managed to swallow a lump of saliva that felt choking and hard in her throat.

"I'm sorry, your Majesty," said Raindrop. "But the Crimson Crown has been the bulwark of Gutgirt for centuries. Without it, we're nothing. Perhaps if this attack had come in a year, or even in a few months, we might've been able to do things another way – build ourselves up, train more troops, acquire better gear. But, as it stands...well, we're helpless, your Majesty – we're helpless without our Crimson Queen."

Honey nodded gravely, and swallowed again. On the outside, she looked stoic, but inside, a nauseating tide of anxiety crept its way up from her guts.

"Thank you, general," she said, "for your honest advice. I'd like all to leave me now. Everyone except my privy council."

Raindrop bowed, and departed with his fellow officers. The throne room emptied, until Honeydew and her five councillors remained. Those five were the only people in Gutgirt she really knew and trusted: the four guards who'd helped her kill Barbus, and Ashleigh the painter, who sat in a handsome new wheelchair.

For a while, Honey was silent, her mind whirling with horrible questions. Did she dare put on that cursed crown? If she did, then what would become of her? Would she be poisoned by its influence? Would she turn into a monster like Barbus and the rest of his blood-thirsty kin – *her* bloodthirsty kin?

I'm not a cruel person, she thought. *Maybe I'll be immune to it?*

No sooner had this thought run through her head than she knew it was just wishful thinking. She knew there was cruelty inside of her, just as there was cruelty in everyone. She'd felt it when she'd stood over Barbus' body; she'd felt it when she'd watched the Crimson Fangs being massacred; she'd even felt it as a young girl, on the Day of the Flies.

For the first time in years, she allowed herself to fully remember that awful day. The palace had been almost empty, most of the adults having gone off to witness the brutal execution of a traitor who was to be torn in two by a pair of straining horses. She and Oda had been too young to attend, Honey happy she didn't have to witness such a horrible thing, and Oda livid she didn't get to share in the gory excitement.

So, Oda had decided to carry out her own executions, catching flies and sentencing them to death for various crimes, like 'having poopy feets,' 'making an annoying buzzing noise,' and 'landing on a princess.' One-by-one, she tore them apart, ripping off their wings, pulling their bodies in half so their vile-coloured guts spilled out across the pads of her fingers and their bisected bits did separate death-dances before going still.

Eventually, she offered one of the flies to Honey.

"Here," she said. "You be the executioner this time. This guy's being punished for trying to molest me. He flew up my dress!"

Gingerly, Honey took it, feeling its precarious life helplessly buzzing in her hand. She at once became conscious of a fearsome but delectable power, the same sort of power she felt when her sister made her play at being a bandit or an ogre, only much more palpable. For this wasn't make-believe; she was about to do a murder, albeit a very, very small one.

"Come on," whispered Oda. "Squish him – pull off his bits!"

Honey hesitated, egged on not just by Oda's words, but by a desire to indulge in this act of arbitrary cruelty. It came from deep inside, from a part of herself she neglected, avoided, and didn't want to own, a part that was usually weak, but suddenly strong. She raised the fly and twisted its form until it split apart, and lay squirming in her fingers, its two parts connected by a strip of slimy guts. Honey felt a sense of giddy pleasure – followed by immediate remorse. She ran off, wept, then buried the fly in a beautiful jewellery box she took from her mother's bedroom. Then she swore she'd never do such a horrid thing again, and never let her sister bring out her bad side.

Since then she'd turned her back on anything resembling cruelty, focusing on nice things. But somehow that cruelty was still inside of her, despite all her kindness and compassion, the way dark night still resides in the day in the form of deep shadows cast by the sun.

And, since there *was* cruelty inside her, then the crown, once worn, could try to feed and enhance it, until, perhaps, what had begun as a rivulet of savagery transformed into an ocean, and she found herself drowning in a great crimson sea.

Could she fight against that process, stand against the crown's seductive power and maintain her sense of self? Or would she be lost in it, transfigured in blood, like all the Crimson Queens that had come before her? Ashleigh said the crown didn't control people as though they were puppets; it *influenced* them, *seduced* them, like booze, drugs, or sexual desire, pushing them to do things a part of them already wanted. It twisted them not by making them something they weren't, but by making them more of what they *already were*, by exaggerating the darkest facets of their souls until that was all that remained.

Honey tried to picture herself warped into something unrecognisable, like Barbus and his ancestors, and the other pale-skinned killers who'd leered from the paintings in the Crimson Museum. She found it hard to imagine *she* could ever change so much. How could she grow into something so alien? Surely the tiny seed of cruelty inside her would never be enough to furnish such a forest of depravity!

But what if it was? A terrified part of her feared the very worst – that her mind, her very self, would be lost to the power of the crown.

And what if she *didn't* use the crown – what then? The army of Shimmerland would continue to rampage through her kingdom. Her people, her subjects – the ones that had accepted her like a surrogate mother, despite the kingly blood on her hands; the ones who depended on her for their protection – would be slaughtered, mutilated, and enslaved, until nothing of Gutgirt remained but a sickening legend.

Even then, Oda's revenge would continue, until Honey herself was gagged, blind-folded, deprived of her fingers, tied to a post, and burned into an eddy of ashes.

Just what sort of choice was that? She could either risk losing her mind, or risk losing everything, including her life. But would her life be worth keeping if she lost her very self?

Oh, what a fucked-up dilemma! she thought, feeling sure no-one else had ever fallen prey to such a twisted situation.

She tried to think her way out of it – and ended right back at the beginning. On and on, the horrible questions kept running through her head, each one feeding into another, sometimes with slight or novel variations, until they inevitably circled, like a serpent devouring its tail. There *was* no thinking her way out of this. Action and decision were the only path to sanity ... albeit, perhaps, of the temporary kind.

She turned to her councillors and poured out her heart to them, telling them all of her fears and concerns, even though all of them already knew, as well as she did, what was at stake. Together, they examined her dilemma, without adding any new knowledge, nor any new hope. No-one had any secret wisdom, no marvellous plan. The dilemma remained unyielding.

"We're sorry, Honey," said Ashleigh. "But there's nothing more to be said. This is a terrible choice – one that only you, and you alone, can make."

Chapter 9: The Crimson Queen

On the opposite side of the field, their back to the woods, waited the army of Shimmerland, resplendent in livery of bright red and green.

On this side, gathered in front of Honey's carriage, was the army of Gutgirt, clad in its traditional crimson regalia.

The contrast could not have been more blatant; the Shimmerland force was at least ten times larger. If it came to battle, the Gutgirtians would find themselves routed and slaughtered in no time at all.

She studied the enemy force, nearly mesmerized by its sheer and utter massiveness. The sky was overcast, and the silvery sun shone coldly on the armour and weapons of the Shimmerland soldiers, lighting them up, so they looked like serried trees in a forest of steel. Seen from a distance, they seemed almost featureless, inhuman, nothing but murderous machines clad in a semblance of humanity. The noise they made as they shouted and hammered on the rims of their shields was enough to shake the ground and scare the birds from the sky –

even those that were waiting for a carrion feast.

Honeydew shuddered, and tried not to panic. She wasn't a coward by any means, but neither was she a seasoned commander or soldier. The sight of such a large army at the ready filled her with dread. Instinctively she wanted to run, hide, even to negotiate terms of surrender. Unfortunately, all of their requests for a parley had so far been denied by Queen Oda. Honeydew looked for her sister in the multitude, but couldn't see any sign of her, not even a whisper of her dyed black hair.

Oh sister, thought Honey. *Could it be you've doomed us both? Why must you be such a miserable BITCH?*

"Are you ready, Majesty?" asked General Raindrop.

The words shook Honey loose from her reverie. She turned to him, and nodded. The general gestured, and his men brought forth a trunk fitted with a slew of hefty locks. One-by-one the locks were disabled, and at length the lid was thrown open, revealing something that terrified Honey almost as much as did the Shimmerland army – the Crimson Crown. Its gem shone with a demonic lustre, as though it were home to an everlasting fire the colour of blood.

"Get yourselves back," said Honey.

The soldiers obeyed, retreating to a safe distance as she slowly approached the gleaming crown. She was dressed for war in a suit of armour that had once belonged to Barba, the last Crimson Queen. As it turned out, they were both of a similar size, and the armour fitted Honeydew perfectly. It was of a starkly gothic style; the ridged metal plates painted glossy red, as if the armour had already been steeped in blood. The armour was complete save for a helmet, so that Honey's face was bared to the wind, and her long white hair lay unbound, falling across the back of her cuirass almost like a cape.

Honey felt uncomfortable in the armour. It wasn't heavy – not physically, at least. In fact, it seemed to have been fabricated mostly for show. For what would a Crimson Queen need armour for, anyway, when her skin could not be cut? No; it was not the physical heaviness of the armour that oppressed Honey's spirits, but rather what the armour represented – the murderous legacy of Xex, and all that went with it.

She knelt before the chest. The gemstone in the crown seemed to throb in her presence, like Barbus' cock had throbbed with eager blood.

She reached out and touched it. Even through her gauntlet and the glove underneath, she felt a sudden surge of electric excitement carry into her flesh.

Terror rose in her breast along with the excitement. A part of her wanted to throw the crown away and never pick it up again, even if that meant the people of Gutgirt would be doomed. Worse, another part of her – a mischievous, unwanted facet – bade her put the crown on for the thrill alone. She tremored with fear and desire as she held the crown before her.

You can do it, she told herself. *All you have to do is wear the crown until the battle is over. Then you can take it off, and keep it locked away until it's needed again, which hopefully will be never. That way you can stop yourself from becoming warped, and twisted, like Barbus...*

Such were the comforting thoughts she told herself as she set it upon her head.

"AGH!"

She cried out as the crown settled into place. For a moment she felt like currents of lightning were shooting down through her skull, into her brain. They joined with her thoughts in a frenzied dance, filling the space behind her eyes with zigzagging bolts of crimson.

Just as abruptly, the pain stopped. Honey stood, feeling sharp – sharper, perhaps, than she'd ever felt before. Her fear was still there, but it was weaker now, overshadowed by a blossoming arrogance that leapt from the void of her soul like lava from the depths of the earth.

When she thought of battle, she no longer wanted to run, hide, or parley for peace – in fact, the very thought of peace made her want to hock up a loogie and spit in someone's eye.

A surge of feral excitement thrummed through her body, so strong she felt she could almost direct it from her fingers in obliterating red bolts. She felt like a wolf or a lion must feel. The crown hadn't *put* these feelings in her head, she knew, but rather teased them up from below, where they'd lain like the roots of long reeds in a marsh. She was no longer herself, and yet she was more herself than she'd ever been before.

"Your weapon, Majesty," said Raindrop, drawing her attention to the gigantic club of solid black iron waiting on the back of a large ox-drawn wagon nearby.

In the past, the very sight of that weapon had terrified her. She'd thought of the carnage it'd wrought in the hands of King Barbus and others. How many brains it must've broken – how many hearts it must've crushed! Yet now, though the sight of the weapon appalled her, it excited her equally as much with its ruinous weight, its incredible length, its terrible *girth* – it was thicker than a lamp post!

Do I dare to pick it up? she thought.

Of course I do! came her immediate inner response.

She took hold of the club, expecting its ruinous weight to defy her, to make her muscles ache and give up. Instead, with a sense of astonishment, she lifted it with relative ease. It was heavy, to be sure, but its weight was comfortable, desirable, giving her a sense of the power she held in her hands. Anything less would be too light; anything more would be too heavy. It felt just right. She raised it up, feeling another surge of excitement. Up until now she'd been just a delicate young woman – now she had the strength of twenty men! Instinctively she thought of the times she'd been bullied and victimized – most notably by Barbus. With this strength, she'd never be a victim again! She could crush a man like Barbus with her skinniest fingers! The power was intoxicating, and she wanted to use it in the crudest and most vulgar manner possible – by smashing people's heads in!

The soldiers started chanting. "All hail the Crimson Queen!"

Their calamitous shouts lifted Honey to a brand-new plateau, a bubbling frenzy threatening to claim her, to transform her thoughts into nothing but inchoate redness. Her body was thrumming with power – she felt like a bowstring, ready to SNAP!

Keep it together! she told herself, even though her thoughts were like a herd of wild horses getting ready to stampede. *You're here for a reason – don't forget that! You've got one mission, and one mission only – protect your people! Send the Shimmerlandians running with their tails between their legs!*

Luckily, on this matter, her feelings and thoughts were in utmost agreement. With a war cry so savage it scared and surprised even her, Honeydew ran towards the ranks of the enemy, hefting the gigantic club. Her steps felt light; her speed was incredible. She shot across the field like a colt, and as she closed on the confused Shimmerlandian ranks, a flash of instinct told her to jump.

She did more than jump, hurtling through the air like a gigantic flea to land in the centre of the enemy formation. She brought the giant club down before her with a horrific CRASH!, flattening a long line of soldiers. She barely had a chance to reflect on how she'd just killed ten men before she was raising the club and spinning it around, shattering bodies and sending them flying, creating a circle of death in which she could move. With the club extended fully, she spun through them like a one-woman whirlwind, breaking ribcages and bashing off heads. She couldn't see the full extent of the gore, only a streaming blur of blood that followed her eyes like a ribbon as she twirled.

Dizzy, she stopped spinning and stumbled to a halt, resting the tip of her club on the ground. Looking back, she found herself at the end of a zigzagging path of broken bodies that cut through the enemy ranks like the tracks of a rhino through a wheat field. Not all the men were dead; many were screaming or wheezing, broken but alive as they lay in her wake.

As she reeled, the Shimmerlandians seized upon their chance. Several men threw themselves on her lowered club, trying to stop her from raising it again. She did so anyway, groaning with effort. For a moment it rose, covered with the scrambling, shouting bodies of fully-armoured men. But the weight was too great; Honey had found the limitations of her terrible new strength. She dropped the burdened club – but not before turning it so that the men who'd been clinging atop it were now on the bottom, crushed beneath the great weapon as it crashed back to the ground. Their armour crumpled like paper mâché and blood splattered out from the separating seams.

More rushed in, trying to get in close now that Honey was momentarily unarmed. She drew her sword, a fat-bladed thing with a wedge-like edge built for delivering devastating chops and standing up to terrible punishment, and swung it at the first Shimmerlandian who reached her. His head came off, not neatly severed, but bluntly and violently wrenched from the neck, much like the bud of a flower flies from the stem when kicked with the tip of one's shoe. Her blade came down again, flattening an armoured skull. Blood shot out through the eye slits of the crumpling helm.

Again and again she swung the blade, like a butcher disgruntled with a stubborn piece of meat, smashing and annihilating all who came within reach. Still they crowded round, stabbing at her naked face and eyes, only to find to their horror that she could not be cut. Screams erupted from their ranks, and many Shimmerlandians turned and fled, spreading a sense of panic that swept like a wind. As enemies fled from her fury, Honey found herself with room to move easily again. She charged at the backs of those attempting to run, bashing in their heads with the wedge-like edge of her blade, or hacking at their spines, so they fell at her feet partly paralysed, struggling with their arms but immobile below the waist.

The whole time, she acted on a sort of wild instinct, while a part of herself was still conscious and aware, watching her rampage as if watching someone else, feeling alternating washes of terror, revulsion – and excitement. Dimly she was aware of her Gutgirtian army, assaulting the disordered front ranks of the demoralised enemy force. She could hear them shouting her name –

"Honeydew, Honeydew, Honeydew! All hail the Crimson Queen!"

Their shouts gave her even more fervour. She hacked and hacked, till the air was misted with blood and she could smell it so thickly in her nostrils it blocked out every other scent with its bitter-sweet sickliness. A part of her wanted to throw up. Another part – perhaps the part in foremost communion with the crown – liked the scent so much she desired to lap at the blood like a wolf. With so much blood on her face, she soon got her wish, if only inadvertently. It dripped into her mouth, tasting of bitterness and iron. A part of her felt ill, while another part savoured the flavour, wanting more, more, MORE!

She cleaved another foe, and her overworked sword snapped in half, leaving her with only her hands. But, with the strength of twenty men, even her dainty white fingers were weapons!

She clapped her hands on either side of an enemy's head. His helm collapsed and his skull cracked like an egg, forcing blood and brain to go shooting through the holes in his visor. The gore splattered afresh all over her face. She stopped, blinded, senses cocooned by the hot wetness clogging her nostrils, coating her lips, overwhelming her with its scent and its taste. She tried to wipe it away but her blood-covered gauntlets weren't suited to the task. Even when she managed to scoop it out of her eyes so she could see, it was still on her lips and in her nose, preventing her from breathing, lest she breathe it in too. A part of her was sickened, repulsed by the thick, cloying film; another part *wanted* to let it in, to bathe in it both inside and out. With a cry of mingled joy and revulsion, she opened her mouth and let it rush over her tongue. The blood was disgusting, with a hint of deliciousness thrown in, like any other type of acquired taste. She swallowed it down, sucked in a blood-tainted breath, then licked her lips. She told herself it was only to clean her mouth, because her gauntlets were too clumsy to do so, but a part of her was howling with joy at the texture and taste.

What's happening to me? she wondered, though she already knew.

She'd felt these sensations before, on a much lower scale. She'd felt them when she'd tortured that fly as a child; when she'd stood over Barbus' body; when she'd watched the Crimson Fangs get destroyed. The complex of feelings was always the same – a sense of great power that gloried in itself; a bestial hunger for agony and blood; the pleasure of selfishness unbound; and, last but not least, the delicious frisson of doing the forbidden. In other words, it was cruelty, pure and simple. It had always been inside of her – she was simply just letting it out.

She charged her fleeing foes. How could they possibly escape? Her speed was terrifying. She leapt through the air and landed among their ranks, ripping off their heads and punching through their chests until her hands were in their bodies, basking in their wheezing, dying breaths, clutching their still-beating hearts before popping them like bits of fruit. She pulled out their entrails; she ripped open their ribcages; she held them down and stuck her invincible fingers inside of them like little bony spears. She laughed; with each vicious kill the pleasure inside grew more bloated, more expansive, more consuming. She could feel it welling up inside of her, like water from an overfilled pool, washing over all of those places of cautious restraint and regret, all of those instincts that might seek to censor or stop her behaviour, all being deluged in blood and the pleasure of blood. She could feel herself losing herself, and a part of her liked it. She could feel herself *gaining* herself, and a part of her was terrified, a part that was steadily retreating to the outermost darkness of her mind, like a boat drifting out into the blackness of a never-ending sea.

All the while, she was ripping, bashing, tearing, hollowing, separating, bludgeoning, impaling, destroying, until her world was a dripping kaleidoscope of gore and the blood was all over her face, caking her skin and dyeing her hair, which was no longer white, but a glistening crimson, just like her armour, but her armour, she thought, was getting in the way, preventing her from feeling all that hot, spurting blood on her skin, and so, seized by a sudden wild impulse, she ripped off her armour, then the clothes underneath, until she was naked on the battlefield. For a moment she looked like a terrible apparition, with a wet crimson head atop a body white as alabaster.

What am I doing? she wondered, as a feeling of vulnerability broke through her abandon. But the feeling quickly faded, drowned by a wild exhilaration. *What have I got to fear?* She asked herself. *I'm invincible! One of these soldiers could fuck me with a sword, and it wouldn't even hurt – it might even feel good!*

She grinned, part of her shocked and disgusted, the other half oddly turned-on, by what she'd just thought. Her cunt, she noticed, was wet, her clit so engorged with hot blood it had thrown off its hood and pushed itself out towards the rush of the battlefield wind.

What's wrong with me?

But the rest of her didn't care. She leapt back into the melee, tearing bodies asunder, panting with pleasure as the blood, hot and sticky, went splashing down her nakedness and running its way between her legs in a trickling rivulet, caressing her clit on the way.

Desire took hold. She ripped a ragged helmet from a downed opponent's head and sat on his face.

"LICK!" she shouted, clasping his skull in her hands and planting her thumbs atop his eyes to give him incentive. He tried to resist, screwing shut his lips and trying to wriggle his mouth from the path of her gash. It was no use, of course – she had him held tight, thrusting her cunt into his face, so that her clit was on his stiff upper lip. As he struggled he brushed it, giving her tremors of delight. She ground herself against his face and pushed him closer, making sure he knew he had nowhere to go. Finally he opened his mouth – and bit her as hard as he could.

Honeydew shrieked – in delight. Her clit was invincible; his teeth couldn't cut it. The sensation was shocking, almost painful, but still undeniably good. She squirmed atop his face as he uselessly gnawed at the man in the boat. But it didn't take long for Honey to get bored.

"Enough teasing," she shouted, turned-on but growing impatient. "LICK!"

To make her command more emphatic, she scraped her fingers across his skull behind the ears, ripping the flesh. He let out a muffled scream and trembled between her imprisoning thighs. Giving in at last, he stuck out his tongue and started licking, tasting the gore-tainted juices of her cunt. His tongue pushed deep into her gash, then flickered up over her clit and started lapping it wildly. Honeydew bucked atop his face like she was riding a bull, shrieking with abandon, so wound up she felt the orgasm coming almost at once. Dimly she realised *this* was the first time in her life she'd ever initiated any sort of sexual activity that wasn't masturbation.

She howled as the orgasm gripped her. At the same time, she pressed with her thumbs into the captive man's eyes until they ruptured from the sockets like bits of vile jelly. His agony made him convulse between her legs, but she'd already climaxed, and didn't want any more licking, so she tightened her thighs like the jaws of a vice till his head crumpled inwards between them, bathing her labia in brains.

She stood, feeling a sense of liberation, as though she'd been reborn. She could almost hear her conscience screaming in horror, but the sound was very faint, as though it came only from a distant, dying star in the outermost depths of the Void. Her cry of savage laughter drowned it out completely as she rushed into the carnage, seeking more fun.

Oda peered through the window of her royal coach, beholding with utmost horror the ruin that was claiming her army. A single figure tore through the ranks, while the rest of the Gutgirtians followed in its wake, taking advantage of the terror and carnage it created.

At first Oda wasn't sure who that dread figure was. Could it be Barbus, returned from the dead? Perhaps he'd never died at all, and the whole thing had been a giant black joke, the sort he was famous for? Or maybe one of his relatives had showed up to claim his mysterious power. It was only when Oda heard the name "Honeydew!" being chanted that she knew who was slaughtering her men, though she could hardly believe it.

It wasn't till the carnage came closer, and she saw her twin sister striding naked through the mayhem, transfigured into the likeness of a demoness, her body splashed in blood from head to toe, her silver hair dyed by the gore so that it fell down her back like a slippery red waterfall, while the Crimson Crown throbbed atop her head like a beacon of death – it wasn't till she saw all these things that Oda understood what was happening.

She watched with wide and paralysed eyes as the carnage got closer, spreading like a wave through the ranks of her army. The closer it got, the more it assaulted her senses. The smell of blood was everywhere, bittersweet and sickly. Instinctively it made her want to vomit. Even worse was the smell of piss and shit, for the dying had a habit of voiding their bowels, unleashing a gigantic reek that commingled with the scent of the gore, creating a unique perfume that seemed to punch her in the nose with its utter disgustingness. Oda had to clamp her fingers on her nostrils and breathe through her mouth, but even then she kept feeling like she might just throw up.

And then there were the sounds – the cries of those in pain, the shrieks of those in terror, the howls of those visiting triumphant destruction on their foes, all mingling together in a terrible symphony, so that the myriad sounds would assault Oda's psyche first with sympathy, then with fright, and finally with uttermost horror.

And the sights! Bodies torn to pieces; entrails exposed; severed limbs dangling from ribbons of sinew! Even worse than the gore were the faces of the dying, all naked and raw in their extremity of terror and pain, filling Oda's heart with a sympathy she just couldn't quell.

In a devastating moment of truth, Oda experienced a revelation that had been hanging on the edge of her consciousness for weeks, ever since she'd murdered Armand. It'd come close to surfacing a few days previous, when she'd witnessed the mutilation of the Gutgirtians, but she'd held it at bay, half-sensing its significance, but fearful of what it might do to her identity. Now it came howling from the void of her mind like a meteor intent on destruction.

She realised, in one searing moment, that her lifelong obsession with suffering and death had been nothing but a fantasy, born of childish ignorance; that her very existence, up until this moment, had been little more than a misguided dream; and that the reality of all of her previous desires was not only repulsive to her senses, but utterly abhorrent to her true inner will.

"Oh!" she cried in the depths of her epiphany. "What cruel hearts are made for deeds such as these!"

She signalled the retreat, then fled from the battlefield, and from her sister, who continued to rage among the routed like a ravening wolf, seeking out foes to devour.

It would be two whole years before the sisters came together again, on the very same field, albeit in very different circumstances.

Chapter 10: Widow Wood

The twin princes Rigney and Pim stood in the field, watching as the queens arrived.

First came Queen Honeydew, the Crimson Queen, riding from the west on a stallion the colour of coagulated blood. The red jewel glimmered on her crown, and her lush crimson garments rippled in the wind. Long white hair streamed out behind her. That hair, it was said, was stronger than iron, and could never be cut. According to rumour, she used it to strangle people sometimes, using a braid like a noose or strands like a garrotte. It was only one of the novel executions and cruelties ascribed to her burgeoning legend.

She smiled as she rode in alone, perhaps remembering the day, two years previous, when she'd slaughtered ten thousand soldiers of Shimmerland all by herself on this very spot.

Prince Rigney shuddered as he saw her. He fancied he could almost smell the scent of blood on her breath. Her murderous cruelty repulsed him, as did her great reputation for wantonness. She was famous for sleeping around, and even more famous for killing half the men she lay with. It was said she drank their blood, and even ate their flesh. When Rigney imagined her cunt, he imagined it with teeth.

Please, he thought, *not her – anyone but her!*

His brother Pim had an altogether different reaction as he watched Queen Honeydew ride into the field. His heart began to hammer and his prick got hard. He was in love! Honey was all he desired – powerful, lusty, capricious. He longed to be engulfed – even destroyed – by the fire of her love. He even longed to partake of those dreadful midnight orgies she was rumoured to orchestrate, when she and her elite military unit – the Crimson Claws – had their fun with captives of war by the light of burning cities and devastated towns.

Her, thought Pim, *please, great demon, give me to* her!

As Honey took her place on the field, a coach drove in from the east, surrounded by a plentiful military escort of Shimmerland soldiers in bright red and green. A slender veiled figure could be seen at the window, gazing through a gauzy window covering, so that she was little more than a dark silhouette.

It was none other than Queen Oda of Shimmerland. Since her inglorious defeat at the hand of her sister, Oda had become something of a recluse, devoting her time to helping the needy. Her benevolent rule was famed throughout Typhon. People said you couldn't find a beggar on the streets of Shimmerland even if you tried – Queen Oda the Kind had clothed, fed, and housed them all!

As Prince Pim beheld Oda's silhouette, he felt nothing but disdain. What a boring, insipid, tedious woman she was. How dull she looked beside her blazing red sister – like a match stick placed next to a bonfire! A woman like her, so retiring and demure, so plain in her habits, would never be enough to arouse his rarefied desire.

Not her, he thought. *Anyone but her!*

His brother, Prince Rigney, had a different reaction. As he saw Oda his heart began to sing as though it were filled with a host of happy choristers. He was in love! Queen Oda was everything he wanted in a woman – modest, caring, and in need of true love. Her wishes in regards to romance were well-known – she was looking for a man like herself, honest and benign, to whom she could cling with the faithful ardour of a dove.

Her, thought Rigney, *Please, great demon, make Oda mine!*

For, of course, the princes were there in that field to meet their prospective brides. They'd only been born a few minutes apart, and the only real difference between their charts was a slight obscuration of Heolow's Moon that had occurred during Rigney's arrival.

All that remained was for the royal astrologer to divine the perfect match for both brothers, by studying the horoscope charts of the queens and reading the great demon's will.

The two princes watched anxiously as the queens made their way towards the royal astrologer, presenting him with their horoscopes in elaborate leather scroll cases. As they did so, they came within a few scant feet of each other – in closer proximity than they'd been since the day they'd been married off to Armand and Barbus.

Oda was visibly shaking. It seemed as if she'd stay sheltered behind her white veil, and refuse to make eye contact. At length, however, she drew back the veil and looked the Crimson Queen in the eye.

"I'm sorry, Honey," she said. "For what I did. For what you've become."

Honeydew snarled, causing her sister to step back in fear.

"Pity me again," said the Crimson Queen, "and I'll rip your fucking head off, treaty or no treaty. Understand?"

Oda nodded.

"Good. Just keep sending me those luscious young men every month, or I'll finish what I started two years ago, and raze your stupid kingdom to the ground."

Oda nodded again, then, with a brave look in her eye, said, "It's not too late for you, Honey. You can still come back!"

"Shut that fucking cesspit of cum you call a mouth," said Honey, snarling once more, "or I'll eat you up and queef you out."

Oda flinched away, and put her white veil back in position, while the royal astrologers started calling on the great demon Zabazap as they pored over the horoscopes. Musicians played to entertain the people while the calculations were made; wine was handed out in disposable clay cups. Oda and Honeydew stood aloof from proceedings and from each other. Their eyes, so pointedly averted, never once met.

At length the calculations were complete, and the leader of the astrologers stepped forward, throwing wide his arms in an imperious gesture.

"We have consulted the stars," he cried, "and divined the will of the great demon Zabazap! Rigney will be married to Honeydew, and Pim will be married to Oda!"

The princes were each overcome with horror. How could things have gone so wrong, they wondered – how could the will of the demon be so misguided and malicious?

Pim looked at Oda, demure in her veil, shrinking from the presence of her powerful sister. Was *this* really the creature he was going to marry?

At the same time, Rigney looked at Honeydew, quaking as he did so. She was grinning at him like a hungry hyena. Would he even survive his wedding night?

Oh, great demon help me! thought both of the brothers in unison.

A great peal of thunder exploded from the sky, and a streak of silver lightning shot down, striking the earth like a dagger and blasting up huge clots of earth. Arcs of zigzagging fire spread out from a crater newly created, whilst at the centre of the impact lay an oval of blinding silver fire, as though the bolt of lightning had failed to disperse, and instead was loitering around, preparing for some further purpose.

All those in attendance watched as the silvery light coalesced into the form of a beautiful man with androgynous features. His violet hair was billowing and cloudy, like a nebula, his alabaster skin marked with luminous lightning bolt tattoos. His robes of silver and black seemed to have been sewn from the substance of the starry void itself.

The royal astrologers looked at the figure, looked at each other, then sank to their knees, shouting, "The great demon Zabazap – he's descended among us!"

"That's right," said the figure, in a soft and syrupy voice that was a little too deep to be a woman's, but almost too soft to be a man's. "I'm Zabazap. And I've had it up to here with you stupid bastards abusing my name!" He glared at the astrologers with shimmering eyes of silvery wrath. "Where do you get off, claiming to interpret my will? I never gave you any signs. The stars are just stars, for fuck's sake – they're not messages for you! As if I've got the time, or the inclination, or even the *power* to go around re-ordering all the celestial bodies every time one of you is born, in order to tell you what to do! It's ridiculous! And sadly ironic, I must say. Why, my brethren and I fought a war for you people – a war to liberate mortals from deific tyranny! We killed off the gods. Do you have any idea how hard that was? We did it to set creation free! And what do you do? You go around looking for someone to tell you what to do! Well it ain't me, you hear? It ain't me, babe!"

A resounding silence filled the field. Some of the astrologers were weeping.

"But... but mighty demon," said the chiefest of them, "we've been invoking your name for centuries!"

"I know," said the demon with a sigh. "Believe me, I know. I've been hearing you the whole bloody time, like a fly buzzing around just behind my left ear. But I've been busy, okay? This is the first break I could find in my schedule to come here and set you people straight. And so, without further ado..."

The demon reached out his hand, splayed his fingers wide, and from the tip of each sent out a bolt of silver lightning at the royal astrologers. They burst into flames and fell to the ground, riddled with zigzagging wounds. The horoscopes of the queens and the princes burned up as well. The onlookers stared in shock and horror – all save for Honeydew, who seemed unperturbed, and instead stood there smiling and licking her lips, amused, for sure, by the deaths of the astrologers, and perhaps even peckish from the smell of their charbroiled bodies.

"Well that's it, then," said the demon. "I'm off. And remember – the stars are just stars! Don't go saying otherwise, and don't go abusing my name – or I'll come back and slaughter you all!"

For a moment there was silence, then someone in the crowd called out, "So who are we supposed to marry, then?"

"I don't care," said the demon. "Whoever the fuck you want!"

So saying, he turned back into a lightning bolt, and flew in reverse into the great starry heaven. And so it came to pass that astrology was mostly abandoned in those regions, and marriages based on mutual attraction were arranged.

As for the queens and the princes who were gathered that day, Oda married Rigney, and Honey married Pim, and they all lived happily until death did them part – even Prince Pim, who was eaten alive by Honey shortly after their wedding night, and died in the throes of a masochistic ecstasy, but not before impregnating his wife with the seed of a son, who would grow to be the last, and the worst, of all the Crimson Kings –

But that is a story for some other time.

This has been the story of Honeydew and Oda, who, through a dalliance with cruelty and murder, both found their true inner will.

The Unwithering Flower

Chapter 1: Dreams of Avarice

It is the Aeon of Chaos. All the gods are dead, and demons frolic in the void.

Narseh stood grinning on the deck of the galley. He was a man of average height, with a swarthy complexion and a hawkish nose. The point of his manicured beard looked like the tip of a dagger in silhouette. He wore a saffron turban, a lime-green kaftan, and a set of jewelled slippers with crescent-shaped toes. A crescent-shaped dagger rested on his hip, continuing the motif.

The whole ensemble was typical in style for a man of his origins. Narseh came from Alhazred, the Land of Smokeless Fire, where rainbow flames dance across the desert at dusk, cold, silent, and scintillating, said to be stirred from the embers of the fire that had destroyed the old universe. Others said the flames were pieces of the ancient djinn, whose bodies lay scattered but yearning for life once again.

Narseh didn't care either way. He wasn't the romantic or sentimental type, and the unremitting grin he wore as his galley hugged the coastline was not one stirred up by memories of his homeland.

The coastline was rugged and dark. He could almost smell the wild goats as they frolicked and rutted on the mountains that rose from the water. It was a more pleasant scent than the stench of sweat and urine wafting from the galley's lower deck, where dozens of slaves sat toiling at the oars, chained to the benches and unable to rise, not even for the purpose of relieving their bladders.

The sound of their labour was a dull, dismal symphony. The shouting of the foreman and the cracking of his whip provided percussion;

the groaning of the galley slaves provided a chorus; the creaking of the oarlocks and the sloshing of the waves were the song's sombre notes.

Yet neither was it the suffering of his chattel that made Narseh smile. He was not a cruel man, merely an indifferent one, and he would just as soon deal in happy slaves as in miserable ones – profit margins permitting, of course.

He glanced across the sea. Its glassy curves shimmered back at him like the facets of a poorly-cut diamond. For a moment he fancied himself standing atop such a gigantic gem, and tried to calculate the wealth he might gain from selling it – not all of it, of course, just fragments cut down into saleable portions. The rest he'd retain and transform into a house, a dazzling and transparent castle.

The fantasy, though pleasant, was not the reason for his grin. Such idle dreams of opulence flitted through his mind all day long, the way other men might fantasise about sex. Mere dreams of wealth could not move Narseh to smile, only its acquisition, actual or imminent.

As he kept watching the horizon, he finally caught sight of the cause of his joy – the port of Hedonia, City of Delights. Others called it simply the City of Whores. It lived up to either name, a coastal hub where sex was for sale in every conceivable variety.

Of course, many seaside towns focused on such trade. But Hedonia was special. The people took their work very seriously. For them it was not merely some prosaic means of making money, but a discipline to be practised with all the application of alchemy. Ancient pleasure guilds trained their initiates in secret carnal arts long passed down through generations of chicken-heads and dynasties of prostate-ticklers. Thus the prostitutes of Hedonia had a singular reputation, and were to the whores of other regions as a regiment of knights to a rabble of conscripts.

They were the reason Narseh smiled. Not because he planned on having sex with any, of course; he never paid for anything he might get for free. No, he smiled because he planned to acquire some prostitutes and take them back to Alhazred. He'd already liquidated a great deal of his assets in order to do so; the wealth was locked away in his hold in the form of a trunk full of diamonds, silver, and gold.

He could see it all now. He'd find himself a few good specimens of either gender, some young ones for beauty, some old ones for experience (though not too old, of course). Then he'd sail back to his homeland with his precious new cargo of hoes, where their value would quadruple. He could sell them off, or keep them and go into the whoremaster business himself, forcing his stable to divulge their carnal secrets to a slew of fresh initiates. He could start a Hedonia away from Hedonia, a franchise with a formula for ecstasy.

Yes, that was why Narseh was smiling, because he expected that soon – very soon – he'd be making a great deal of money.

The galley slowed as it drew towards the ramshackle jetties sprawling from the harbour. The sun sank redly above, tinting the vista the colour of blood. To Narseh it seemed as though he were staring through the facets of a gigantic ruby, taking in the city's slanted rooftops and flocks of circling pigeons.

There sure are a lot of pigeons, he thought.

Then he saw they weren't pigeons at all, but murders of crows. He inhaled through his nose to taste the fragrance of Hedonia, imagining a bouquet of perfumes to mask the scent of sex, but what he got instead was the stench of almighty decay, like a battlefield abandoned in summer to a conquering army of flies.

He inspected the port with horrified eyes. There were far fewer ships than he'd anticipated, and many of those were in the process of hastily departing. His limited view of the streets showed them mostly deserted, though they should've been bustling with bodies for sale. A single figure, dressed in a very un-revealing ensemble of black robes and leather mask in the likeness of a bird's beak, pushed a wheelbarrow filled with contents bundled and crooked and covered in a ragged black sheet. When the wheelbarrow jarred on a loose piece of paving, a body slipped out, buzzing with flies and fat with decay.

Oh fuck, thought Narseh. *It's a plague!*

Chapter 2: The Stench of Opportunity

Narseh felt like crying and tearing his beard out by the root. He'd come all this way, only to find the city riddled with plague. The prices of slaves would be vastly inflated. Worse yet, any chattel he purchased might be crawling with disease. They might die before he got them to Alhazred, or transmit their sickness to the galley slaves. Then he'd be sailing on a plague-ship, reeking not only of urine but of death. He might even end up having to row it himself!

The prospect was ghastly, so too the prospect of his own very possible demise. But both took a back seat to his fears about his finances.

Perhaps I should set sail immediately, he thought. *Just call the whole thing a loss!*

The very idea was anathema. Surely there was a way he could get a return on this venture! He stood on the deck, wracking his brains and staring at the hastily departing boats.

I've got it! he thought.

He could offer the unfortunate people of Hedonia an escape from the plague – for a price, of course. It wouldn't be as good as acquiring a hold full of specialised whores, but it might just allow him to recover the cost of his journey and make a little profit on top. He decided to go out in search of the wealthy and the desperate. Not in person, obviously – he'd send an expendable slave to do the rounds of the city in his stead, selling passage abroad.

It was a decent scheme. He no longer felt like crying, or tearing out his beard, though he was far from ecstatic. He was just about to go below deck and start putting his plan into action when he saw another galley pulling in besides his.

The vessel was silent, save for the groaning of oarlocks and the sloshing of oars in the surf. He heard no accompanying grunting of galley slaves, no clinking of chains, not even the rhythmical whipping of the lash against backs. The statue of a four-armed demon with the head of a bird and an onyx-black beak was mounted on the bow of the vessel. Surrounding it were pictograms littered with the macabre imagery of entrails, buzzards, and skeletons twisted into stylized shapes.

Such peculiar aesthetics proclaimed the ship as being from Khem, the land of the necromancers, who peopled their empire with animate dead.

The galley drew up along the jetty across from him, and a woman appeared on deck. She had a fine-featured face, with skin a shade darker than Narseh's. In spite of her beauty, Narseh's attentions were drawn not to her soft fulsome lips, nor to her cute button nose, but to the splendid-looking garments she wore. Her veil and matching dress were cut from dazzling silk in the colours of lapis and gold. Golden bits of jewellery encircled her wrists, ankles, and waist. The catches and buckles looked like serpents intertwisting and biting one other.

By contrast, one of her garments truly stood out from the others, not for its beauty, but for its utter repulsiveness. Hanging from her back, like a vulture's black plumage, was a cloak made from slivers of mortuary shrouds. Narseh could smell its foul odour even above the stench of the city. Its stitches were caked with the scum of decay, as though they'd been steeped in a cauldron of corpses. He recognised the garment as ritual garb, worn only by the necromancers of Khem. It served as a marker of their status, as well as a magickal fetish that helped steep their presence in the energies of death.

He nodded to the woman, smiling. He was always very friendly with strangers who looked very rich, and her jewellery alone was worth a small fortune. He wasn't sure exactly what he wanted from her yet, but the lustre of gold had him flitting to her presence like a bee to a pollinating flower.

"Greetings, fine lady," he hailed, concealing his disgust at her foul-smelling robe, as well as his general unease about necromancers, who had terrible powers he didn't understand. "Narseh Az-Pinah at your service. Merchant of the high seas."

He preferred not to say 'slaver of the high seas,' though that was the business he primarily engaged in. Slave-trading, unfortunately, had a bit of a branding problem, its practitioners viewed by many as sinister and grubby individuals. Some even thought the occupation was a crime against inherent human dignity! Total nonsense, in Narseh's opinion. Dignity wasn't inherent – you had to buy it, like everything else! Slaves couldn't buy and didn't own anything, ergo, no dignity for them. Hypothetically-speaking, even if they *did* possess dignity, their masters would technically own it all anyway, just as they owned their slaves' clothing, organs, and teeth. Still, it wasn't too much of a stretch to call himself a merchant; he'd buy and sell anything that might make him a profit.

The woman regarded him for a moment, long enough to have him wondering if perhaps she didn't speak Ozich.

Then she did reply. "Wena," she said. "Wena of Khem."

"A delightful name," said Narseh, "and one I must confess I've never heard before. So, Wena, what brings you to this perilous port? Here to buy corpses?" He knew the necromancers often did so, going abroad in times of catastrophe, seeking to plump up their empire's force of domestic undead.

In a way it made him jealous, the very idea there might be a form of labour even cheaper than slavery. If there was, then zombies were it. They didn't need to eat, sleep, or do any other things that cut into a man's bottom line. On the other hand, they couldn't reproduce, unlike living slaves, who could, would, and did, bringing forth a free generation of chattel, born into bondage from the very beginning. The fact that a stock of zombies could only be increased by the active collection of corpses was enough of a flaw in the whole necromantic operation to keep Narseh from weeping with jealously. Corpses weren't as easy to come by as might be imagined. Most people revered their dead loved ones, cremating their bodies with all due ceremony, and would rather jump on the pyre themselves than let the corpse of Dear Uncle Joe get transformed into a zombie. Thus, plague towns and other places where death was running rampant, where there weren't enough living to bury the dead, where bodies were disposed of in bulk by miserable corpse-carters who could easily be bribed to offer up their whole charnel inventory, proved ideal for the enterprising necromancer.

If that was Wena's purpose here, Narseh could see no conflict or intersection in their interests. After all, he had no corpses to sell – unless he wanted to slaughter his galley slaves, though he doubted the return would be worthwhile. Thus, he imagined he'd soon be bidding goodbye to this beautiful woman, and her beautiful gold.

"I'm not here for dead bodies," she said.

Does that mean she's here for live ones? wondered Narseh, looking her up and down again. She was a woman, after all, and he did sense a certain tender longing about her. Had she come to get ploughed by the gigolos of Hedonia?

It wasn't uncommon for wealthy ladies to engage in such sex tourism. The skills of the Hedonian man-whores were as legendary as those of their female counterparts, after all. As Narseh understood it from his research, many even bore coded tattoos on their biceps that spoke of their sexual abilities.

The image of a serpent stretched out between the sun and the moon, for instance, denoted the length of time they could maintain an erection. The longer the serpent, the longer the man-whore in question's crimson crowbar would stand at the ready. Certain rare specimens boasted the image of a serpent encircling sun and moon, meaning they were capable of keeping their meat in heat for a full day and night. Images of fruit or other foodstuffs, such as pineapples or mangoes, attested to the relative sweetness of their semen, as determined by a licensed tribunal of cum connoisseurs. The image of discrete grains of sand in an hourglass told of how long each had to wait after cumming before getting hard once again. Simple Ozich numerals – often running well into the double digits – indicated the number of climaxes each could reach in a day before being spent.

Additionally, the images of animals announced their affiliation among the Hedonian gigolo guilds, known for the size of their equipment or their mastery of certain techniques. The list of guilds included, he recalled, the Anacondas (no prizes for guessing their specialty); the Rhinos, whose members' members had a striking upward bend; and the Woodpeckers, who prided themselves not on length, nor on girth, but on speed of penetration. All such tattoos were inked in a similar style by licensed professionals. And woe to those who might try to lie through the use of illicit tattoos, for should their deception be uncovered, then their unlawful ink would be flayed from their bodies by the merciless Hedonian Sex Police.

Yes, Narseh knew all of these facts from his research on Hedonia. Yet, despite the great prowess – not to mention the freakish anatomical attributes – ascribed to the Hedonian hustlers, he couldn't see why a beautiful woman like Wena would pay for it. At least, not in her native land of Khem, where necromancy was normal and accepted; anywhere else, men might be repulsed by her profession, in spite of her looks. But in Khem she'd never run out of suitors, would have lovers aplenty – they'd be lining up around the block!

So what would she be doing in Hedonia, looking for some strange?

"Nor am I here for the gigolos, if that's what you're wondering," she added, seeming a little offended by his speculative perusal.

"I'm terribly sorry if my silence just now carried any untoward implications. But this is Hedonia, after all." He stepped down from his galley to the jetty between them, and after a brief pause she did likewise. Narseh bowed, took her hand, and kissed it gently, managing not to recoil from the morbid reek of her robe. "Might I ask, if you're not here for dead bodies – or live ones – what it is that you are doing here?"

"I'm in exile," she said. "They kicked me out with nothing but my galley, my jewels, and a couple of servants. Which means I have to make a living somehow. I thought here, where there's plague, my talents might prove lucrative."

"I didn't know necromancers could heal the sick," Narseh said.

"Oh, we can't. But we can use the Eyes of Death to see if there's sickness inside people. I can tell them if they've got the plague or not, for a modest fee."

As she stared at him, her beautiful emerald eyes became filmy and whitish, like those of the dead. Narseh shuddered under her scrutiny. Was she scanning him for plague, right then and there?

"Don't worry," she said as her eyes returned to normal. "You're healthy. Very healthy, in fact..."

For a moment, her gaze lingered lower than his eyes. Narseh almost didn't notice – he was too busy thanking the Candle King for his clean bill of health.

"Ah, yes, thank you for that free sample of your services," he said. "Tell me, though, have you ever tried this little scheme of yours before?"

"Well, no, not really..."

"I see. I'm afraid I've got some bad news for you: there's no way you'll make any money with it."

"Why not?"

Still suppressing his disgust at her putrescent cloak, Narseh put his arm around her shoulder in a comradely fashion, and gestured to the city around them.

"Think about it, my dear," he said. "If a person's feeling healthy, they're not going to *want* to know if they're sick or not. All that matters to them is that they feel good right then, and they don't want to question that. They just want to go on living their lives, hoping everything will turn out all right. And the people who're *already* feeling ill? They don't need your services, because they already *know*! Which means you've no market to sell to, no market at all.'

"What about the local government?" she asked. "I could help them identify the sick ones, and put them in quarantine to stop the spread of the disease."

Narseh sighed, beginning to think her more than a little naïve. Whatever had they taught her at necromancy school? Certainly nothing about business or practical matters!

"Ah, Wena," he said. "You might be able to see with the Eyes of Death, but I see with Eyes of Gold Coins, and I'm afraid you're mistaken on that score as well. Those who run the government are probably already in hiding on their country estates, waiting it out. That's a fact I'd put money on, and I'm not a man who gambles lightly. Meanwhile, though, those very same masters of the city have their agents out in the streets, collecting their taxes as usual, taxes which've no doubt started dwindling most terribly, given all the death going on. So the *last* thing they'd want is to put a whole chunk of the city's population in quarantine. That'd diminish their revenues even further!"

"You mean they'd rather keep people working till they die?"

"Of course! Think about it. How long can a plague-ridden person walk around like normal, before the sickness goes and topples them over?"

Wena peered out into the streets, using her Eyes of Death to observe the vectors of plague moving about through the populace, bubbling like soup in people's organs and veins.

"A few days," she said. "Maybe a week, at the most."

"Exactly," said Narseh. "Just consider, all that labour lost. Hedonia has a twenty percent tax on prostitution, its primary industry. Imagine the thousands of whores who'd be put into quarantine for a week before they died. How many hand jobs and blow jobs and other sorts of jobs could they have done in that time, and all getting taxed at twenty percent? Then add in all the barbers, the stone masons, the mat weavers, the seamstresses, and so on. The rulers of the city would never agree to lose all that revenue, just to save on a few paltry lives. Let alone pay you for it. Trust me, I've dealt with a fair few governments in my time – monarchies, democracies, pornocracies, you name it. They all have one thing in common – they only ever care about cold, hard *cash*."

Wena sighed, perhaps realizing he might be correct.

"Well, I'm here now," she said. "There's got to be something I can do..."

At the sound of creaking footsteps behind them, Narseh whirled, coming face-to-face with a pair of Wena's servants, lugging her luggage down to the dock.

The servants were undead. That much was obvious, in spite of the cloaks they wore to disguise their true natures. They smelled of dried roses and preservatives, with just a hint of decay. Their desiccated bodies were wrapped in saffron silk winding sheets, their excavated eye sockets fitted with jewels. The finery was typical for the undead butlers of Khem's necromancer nobility, who liked to keep their servants attired in a manner that reflected the glory of their station. Even in exile, it seemed Wena liked to keep up appearances.

Narseh admired the jewels in the dead men's eyes, seeing his own face reflected in the facets. Oh how he loved to behold his own image in that beautiful environ of crystal! The sight often made him imagine a whole other world, a gemstone world, where his flesh was embodied in riches everlasting. But such fancies were not thoughts for today. No; today his mind was mired in the practical – and suddenly whirling with excitement.

He peered at the zombies, then back to the street, where a cartload of corpses was being offloaded from a brothel. His mercantile mind made a simple calculation, and he knew he had the answer, not just to his own monetary ambitions, but to Wena's want of gainful employment, as well. He couldn't believe he hadn't seen it right away!

"My marvellous Wena," he said with a smile, "I think this might be the start of a beautiful friendship!"

Chapter 3: The Unwithering Flower

A few months later...

Aktus wandered the streets of Hedonia, grumbling to himself as he went. The stench of death hung heavy in the air, but that wasn't why he was cranky. He was used to the aroma. He and his mercenary band, the Axes of Aarseth, had just spent six months fighting under contract for the kingdom of Myconia, helping them to conquer the neighbouring region of Pecoz.

Ah, the fighting had been fierce, the bodies piled ten-deep by the end of it, wafting up a death-reek even more potent than that of the city he strolled through at present. In the end, Myconia had won, and Aktus had made off like a bandit, not just with the agreed-upon payment for services rendered, but also with sacks of gold and goblets he'd plundered from Pecoz when "Havoc!" had been cried. Once all that had been done with, all he'd been able to think about was dipping his wick in the seasoned, sultry sybarites who dwelt in the legendary City of Whores.

Which led to his present ill-humour, for they'd arrived to find Hedonia in the wake of a plague, if not still being ravaged by some vestige of it. Many of the brothels remained shut. Those few whores out and about looked decidedly unhealthy, their bodies dotted with barely-healed buboes, their skin pale and sweaty in the glare of the lanterns that lit up the realm after dusk. Corpse-carts went rattling through the streets, oozing yet more stench as they carried off the last of a logjam of bodies. From the houses and alleys came a chorus of weeping and post-viral coughs.

It was very, very different from the sounds Aktus had been told to expect in Hedonia, which were supposed to amount to nothing less than an ever-flowing symphony of carnal delight, made up of bedposts creaking, voices moaning, and the overlapping slapping of body parts.

Some of his comrades had wanted to abandon the city at once. But Aktus was stubborn. He'd come all this way, and wasn't ready to give up on his quest to drain his balls in a Hedonian brothel. So they'd split up to search for an oasis of pleasure in this ill-fated plague-pit.

Perhaps that was one just ahead of him?

He stopped outside a building lit by a single red lantern. The place was called The Quimcushion, and had a picture on the sign of a pillow that looked like a pussy getting stabbed at by dozens of needles. The graphic didn't exactly appeal to Aktus' appetites, but the buildings on either side – the Red Thread and the Wolf Den, respectively – were both locked and shuttered. So he ascended the steps, only to be blocked at the entrance by the doorman, an oafish looking chap with cauliflower ears and a row of replacement wooden teeth.

"Sorry mate," said the bouncer, "all full tonight."

Aktus glared at the man. Were they really full up, or did the doorman just not like the look of him?

It wasn't hard to imagine why. Like the rest of his comrades in the Axes of Aarseth, Aktus cultivated a particular appearance. His hair was long and smeared with black dye that made it appear wet, thick, and bedraggled. The inchoate image of a skull had been painted on his face with black and white makeup, giving him the aspect of some leering sort of ghost. It was an image designed to bring terror to the foes of the Axes, and they wore it both on and off the battlefield, hoping the style would one day be considered iconic.

"Oh shit!" people would say. "There go the Axes of Aarseth!"

Thus men would flee, and women would moisten, at the thought of the mercenaries' might. As it was, however, few in this region had even heard of the Axes, often taking them for weirdos, dressed up, perhaps, for some fancy-dress gathering. Nonetheless, Aktus didn't like getting discriminated against because of his appearance. It made him want to poke those judgemental eyes with his thumbs until the juice came out like jelly. He thought about doing just that to the bouncer right now – it'd be easy enough.

Then he changed his mind. Perhaps the man wasn't keeping him out because of the makeup he wore. Maybe the place really was full? Most of the brothels were shut or boarded up, after all.

He growled his displeasure and departed, passing block after block of more boarded-up bordellos. Finally, his vision alighted on a wash of brilliant light. A building stood ahead of him, fronted with dozens of lanterns, all of them red. On the sign was a flower with a pussy in the centre. The paint had been lacquered, so the petals and the lips looked perpetually wet. A sign on the wall read:

The Unwithering Flower.
Cleanest brothel in all of Hedonia
Our girls do it all, no question, no complaint
Reasonable rates, all guests welcome!

Aktus shrugged and stepped inside. The place smelled of cheap paint and sawdust, as though it'd recently been refurbished. Behind the desk in the foyer sat a man with a swarthy complexion, a turban, and a luscious black beard tapering to a point. Being well-travelled, Aktus recognised him as a native of Alhazred, where tongues of rainbow fire go dancing with the desert siroccos after dusk.

"Hello and welcome, my friend!" the man said with a smile on his face. "I am Narseh. I take it you're ready to experience the pleasures of The Unwithering Flower, home to the cleanest, most obedient whores in all of Hedonia?"

"Reckon I am," said Aktus.

"Excellent! You'll have to pay upfront, of course."

Aktus' eyes went wide as Narseh listed the price.

"The sign said the rates were reasonable," he protested.

"Oh but they are! Haven't you noticed there's been a bit of a plague? Sadly, the whores of Hedonia have been decimated, which means it's very much a seller's market right now. But don't think I'm trying to swindle you. Just wait till you get a load of our girls! They'll do anything you want them to, anything at all – just say it, and they'll do it, they won't even blink. You'll think they've got no will of their own!" Narseh paused, and cleared his throat. "Assuming you want a girl, of course. We've got boys here as well, even a hermaphrodite. We're thinking of bringing in a jaguar, for the more jaded clientele..."

"A girl will be fine," said Aktus.

"Great!" said Narseh, and held out an expectant hand.

Aktus reached into his moneybag for a fistful of silver. Narseh counted the coins, squirrelled them away in his robes, then smiled once again.

"Please follow me," he said. Pausing, he glanced at the massive, two-headed axe slung across Aktus' back, its blades barely concealed by a thick leather sheath. "Perhaps you'd like to stow your weapon in the lobby?"

"Never!" said Aktus. "The Axes of Aarseth never hand over our weapons!"

"Good for you, I suppose. Just don't go chopping up the girls, or I'll have to charge you extra. Okay?"

Aktus nodded, not quite sure if the man was joking or not.

Narseh led him down a hallway and into a room, where he told him to wait.

"She'll be along shortly," he said. "If you don't like the look of her, let me know, and I'll fetch you another."

Aktus nodded again and Narseh disappeared, leaving him alone. He paced the room, examining the décor. In the centre was a bed with crimson covers. On the walls, frescoes of sex acts stretched from floor to ceiling, creating a kaleidoscope of coitus, cunnilingus and fellatio, with images of dripping pink pussy lips and arcs of spurting jism providing a border.

With the images getting him right in the mood, he utterly failed to notice the macabre hieroglyphs cunningly obscured by the lurid façade. Images of entrails, buzzards, and twisted skeletons hid amongst explosions of cum, tufts of pubic hair, even labial folds. Anyone would have had a hard time detecting them, let alone someone whose blood was rushing southwards, as Aktus' presently was.

He stripped off and waited with a throbbing erection. Soon, the door opened and a woman walked in, wearing a rose-coloured robe.

Aktus awaited her fearful response. After all, he was six-foot-four, with a body striped with scars and a face caked with ghastly corpse-paint. Instead, she just smiled at him, fastened the door in her wake, and threw off her robe. His eyes opened wide as he beheld her naked body. She was nubile, and pale, with luscious dark hair.

Her perky breasts bounced as she strode to him and dropped to her knees. She started sucking immediately, making hungry, moaning sounds, as though she were partaking of some unearthly delight, rather than a mercenary's unwashed cock. She took him in deeper and deeper, as far as he could go.

Her gag reflex must be totally dead! he thought.

The hungry, moaning sounds continued as she impaled her oesophagus over and over on his prick, until Aktus was shuddering and spurting and clutching her head in his hands.

She got up, licked her lips, then took hold of his prick and led him to the bed, where she nursed him to hardness again. Then she lay there, like a doll, waiting to be posed. He spread her legs and thrust himself inside, finding her gripping and wet. She made yet more hungry, moaning sounds, shuddering as if from a series of orgasms.

Had Aktus been a more attentive lover, he would've realised she was faking it, that her sighs were like a soundtrack on repeat, her spasms of pleasure nothing but a pantomime. He might've even seen that there was something very strange, even something very *wrong* about her. But he neither noticed, nor cared. He was too busy climbing a mountain of pleasure – and exploding all over the summit.

He fell back on the bed in the aftermath of orgasm. She lay in his arms, almost utterly still. Her body smelt strongly of flowers. The scent was in her hair, her skin, even in the juice from her pussy and the spittle from her mouth. The odour struck him as a little peculiar, but he didn't really question it. Instead he considered how much time he had left, and how much more he could do to her before it ran out. Would he be able to go up the back passage, he wondered?

She'll probably refuse, or ask for more money, he thought, but when he broached the subject she merely bent over and spread her cheeks wide.

He slid inside. Her arsehole was lubricated, too, as if she'd been prepared for this. It was also immaculately clean, as if she'd been scrubbed from the inside. After he came again, he lay there, too exhausted by his triple performance to go another round. Still, she knelt beside him, sucking on his now-flaccid member, in spite of the places it'd been, till a knock rattled the door.

"Closing time!" called Narseh's voice.

The woman sprang up immediately and put on her robe. At the door, she turned back and smiled, then departed. Only then did it occur to Aktus that, in spite of all her moaning, she hadn't said a word.

Another satisfied customer! Narseh thought as he hustled the mercenary out into the street. The man looked weak in the knees, dazed with post-coital ecstasy.

Once he'd shut the door and bolted it, he descended into the depths of The Unwithering Flower, to a secret chamber where his prostitutes were gathering. One by one, they settled their bodies onto the benches that dotted the chamber like funeral slabs.

As was quite fitting. They were all dead, of course.

Chapter 4: Closing Time

Narseh inspected his resting stable of hoes. In the dim light, they looked very dead indeed. Only the magick of the hieroglyphs, hidden in the frescoes on the walls, gave them their semblance of life. Narseh wasn't entirely sure how it worked, but somehow the hieroglyphs cast a spell to deceive the eyes of the unwitting patrons. Of course, their other senses had to be fooled as well.

The girls had to *feel* alive, for one thing, not just look it. Luckily, Wena had been able to arrest their decay with some other sort of spell, which stopped them from bloating or falling to pieces. A third spell lent warmth to their otherwise cold, clammy flesh.

Since they still smelt like death, and lacked a means of self-lubrication, further solutions were required. Removing and replacing their internal organs with a mixture of sawdust and flowers gave them a floral scent, like those of Wena's servants. Before each session with a client, aromatic oils were applied liberally to their various orifices.

As for their sexual performances, Narseh had no clue – that was all Wena's doing. Somehow she'd programmed their bodies with a rote set of acts, the same way her butlers were programmed to heave around her luggage or stand guard at her door.

Narseh clapped his hands. "Chop, chop!" he called. "Let's get this show on the road!"

His former galley slaves hurried into the room. They'd been given new jobs as brothel attendants. Or perhaps they were mortuary workers? He supposed there wasn't really a word for what they did. This venture of theirs seemed utterly unprecedented. What did that make him, he wondered – a pimp, a mortician, or a grave-robber? A pimptician? A necro-panderer? It really didn't matter. What mattered was the coin clinking into his coffers – which it was.

The business itself had been easy enough to set up. With hundreds of buildings left vacant in the wake of the plague, no one had questioned when they'd simply moved in to one, Narseh acting as if he owned the place. As for his stable of strumpets, he'd snatched them up at a steal. Some of them he'd literally stolen, looting the plague pits by night for the sexiest corpses. Others he'd purchased for a pittance from madams and pimps who'd been only too happy to turn a final profit, however meagre, from the bodies of their whores.

He watched as his minions went to work on the cadavers, douching out their pussies and arseholes, then scrubbing them with sponges on sticks. Narseh's mouth wrinkled with disgust. All that goo sluicing out. He was glad he had slaves for this sort of work!

Even harder to clean was the cum accrued from the performance of fellatio. It dribbled down their throats and seeped into the sawdust stuffing that filled their torsos. The only way to deal with the mess was to open them up and scoop out the soiled bits directly. The zombified whores had to be so treated every other day, or the smell would seep out and arouse the suspicions of the patrons. Narseh had thought about banning fellatio to save all that hassle, but what sort of brothel worth its salt would ever do that? He'd be the laughing stock of Hedonia if he dared take the mouth off the menu!

His slaves busily undid the sutures on the bodies of the girls, scooped the soiled stuffing from within, dumped it in a bin, and replaced it with fresh batches of sawdust and roses.

"Watch it, moron!" snapped Narseh, as one added way too many petals to the mixture. "Those are expensive. Use more sawdust, or I'll dock your pay!"

"But you don't pay me, boss."

"And I never will. Not with that attitude!" He strode away, grumbling to himself. But it was all for show, of course. The cost of the flowers was nothing compared to how much money he was making overall.

The plague had killed off over a third of the city's population. Many of the brothels were still closed or running at less than half capacity, even as the customers began to trickle back in from abroad, creating a surfeit of demand the beleaguered bordellos couldn't meet. So, in steps Narseh to the rescue, with his stable of ravishing beauties – provided one saw them in the optimal light.

It was the perfect setup. Squatting in the building, they therefore paid no rent; their employees were dead, and needed no wages or food. The only real expense was that blasted twenty-percent prostitution tax. But since Narseh grossly underdeclared all his profits, even the taxman wasn't much of a problem.

He grinned from ear-to-ear as he stepped into the necromancer's chamber – which, given recent developments, was his chamber, too.

"Hello my sweet," he said, beaming with happiness.

Wena lay on the mat, not passed out, but clearly exhausted. Her two undead butlers stood like statues by the door. The rest of the zombies from her galley had been hidden in the hollows of the brothel's walls, entombed but ever vigilant, just waiting for their mistress' command. Narseh liked to think of them as bouncers on call. They'd certainly be handy, should trouble arise.

She murmured a greeting, still lying prone on the floor.

"You know it's a shame we can't stay open longer," said Narseh, as he transferred coins from his pockets to the overflowing treasure chest in the corner. "We'd make even more money!"

"I need to rest," said Wena. "Maintaining all those spells is exhausting."

"Of course it is, my sweet," said Narseh. "And you certainly deserve some downtime. Here, let me help you into bed."

He knelt beside her. For a moment her zombie butlers tensed, as they always did, alert to any possible threat to their mistress. She pacified them both with a glance as Narseh picked her up and carried her over to the bed. She felt light in his arms. It seemed she'd lost weight since the brothel had opened just a few months ago. He supposed it must be tiring work indeed that she was doing, meditating ten hours a day to keep all the spells running smoothly. Still, he wished she didn't need quite so much rest. It was cutting into their profits!

He laid her on the bed and sat beside her, stroking her face.

"You have a rest now, my sweet," he said. "We've got another full day ahead of us tomorrow. I'm off to do some accounting..."

As he made a move to rise, she held him by the wrist. "Don't go," she said, a look of languid lust in her eyes. She guided his hand down to the warmth between her thighs.

"I thought you needed a break?" he said. "You should probably avoid too much strenuous activity..."

"I need *this*," she said. "I want this. The magick, it's not just physically exhausting, it's mentally draining, as well. I need some brightness. I need some life! So do you, you know. You can't just think about profits all day."

The fuck I can't, thought Narseh.

"Come on," she said.

She drew up her dress and pressed his hand firmly against her. She was hot and wet. He bathed his fingers in the moisture, teasing her gently. She gave a relaxed sigh and started squirming her body on the bed, slowly getting hotter and wetter, until she pushed his hand away, primed for something deeper.

"Get undressed," she said. "Let me see you."

Narseh stood up and began to disrobe.

Once again, as Wena lay watching him, she found herself wondering why she was so attracted to this man. His looks certainly provided part of the answer. His naked body was handsome and lean in the light of the lanterns. He took off his turban, letting his long, dark hair fall down past his shoulders.

What else did she admire? His silver tongue, perhaps. He always seemed to know just the right thing to say, and could read other people in ways that she couldn't. After all, she'd spent her youth being trained as a necromancer, taught to deal with the dead things, not the living. He, on the other hand, was worldly, well-travelled. His way with people fascinated her, and his charisma was undeniable.

His greed, though... sometimes she wondered if there was anything in him other than a love for accumulating money. Was he falling for her, as she was for him – or was he merely managing another investment?

Or maybe I'm just desperate, she thought.

After all, few people outside of Khem would get in bed with a necromancer. Perhaps loneliness had made her seek out his affection, the way a starving dog might fawn upon the lousiest of masters for a meagre scrap of food. For a moment, as he stood silhouetted before the lantern, his face transformed into a mask of black shadow, she saw only the darkness in their union.

Then he climbed upon the bed and smiled in the light. Wena melted. Surely there was true love and brightness inside of him. Surely he was loving her, too – not just with his body, but his soul?

In spite of her exhaustion she jumped into his arms, casting off her dress and fondling his prick as they kissed. She tried to mount him in the lotus position, so she could look into his eyes and kiss him on the lips as they fucked, but he gently disentangled their legs and coaxed her up on all fours. She let him, being rather fond of doggy-style, too.

Reaching back, she guided him inside of her, murmuring softly as he entered. Narseh knelt behind her, his hands on her hips, building up a gentle momentum. She glanced over her shoulder at him with lusty eyes, seeking to fire his own passion even brighter. He met her gaze eagerly and pumped harder, making her quiver. Then her face turned away as she let out a series of almost-silent moans.

Appealing though the sight was of Wena's slim, dusky body stretched out before him, tapering away from her rump, Narseh looked past her to the treasure chest in the corner. The sight of gold and riches always made him hornier. That's why he'd chosen this sexual position – he wanted to stare at his burgeoning wealth as they went at it.

He could see his own reflection in the gemstones littering the horde, and in the contours of a statue atop the lot. It depicted a naked and beautiful courtesan. Just a moulded image, of course, which couldn't compare to the flesh-and-blood woman trembling on his prick. And yet, as their rutting wore on, he found himself spending more time looking at the statue than at Wena, taking in its gleaming thighs, its jewel-tipped breasts, the reflection of the firelight dancing across its sleek, gilded surface like mercury. In his preoccupation, he almost didn't notice when Wena succumbed to a shuddering orgasm.

He felt her get wetter and wider around him. Glancing down between the peachy round cheeks of her butt, he saw her cute arsehole twitching from spasms of pleasure. Her whole body quivered and shook. Satisfied that she was satisfied, he launched a crescendo of thrusts that had her shuddering again before he spurted inside of her. The orgasm deadened his vision, as it so often did, dimming every sense except that which resided in his prick. Still he kept sight of the horde, even as the rest of the room dimmed into darkness, so that the gemstones, and the coins, and the gold figurine hung like luminescent ghosts in the void of his climax.

He slowed to a stop. Wena slipped off his prick and rolled over onto her back. She smiled and wriggled with residual delight.

She really is getting thin, he thought, spying the outlines of her ribs against her skin.

Then his eyes were drawn to her pussy, where cum dribbled out in a white rivulet.

"You're sure you won't get pregnant?" he asked.

She shot him an irritated look; he'd soured her mood. "You ask that every time," she snapped.

"It's just that a pregnancy might distract from our work..."

"And I told you not to worry about it. Okay?"

"Fine, fine," he said, stretching out beside her, though she suspected he still wasn't entirely mollified.

Wena sighed. As a necromancer, unwanted pregnancies were rarely a concern. Many of her counterparts in Khem couldn't even conceive; their bodies were too heavily infused with the energies of death. Those who could often brought forth abominations, grave-born things that were half-living, half-dead. Since Wena had been banished before her training was complete, her womb wasn't yet thoroughly steeped; she could still conceive normally – if she wanted to. It was entirely her choice. She had enough magickal awareness to recognise the moment of conception, and enough necromantic power to abort any offspring at once, should that be her will.

And should her magick somehow fail to do the job, the city of Hedonia was a hub of abortionists and apothecaries who'd be only too willing to help. Thousands of unwanted foetuses were snuffed every day, flushed down the drains or tossed into the streets to provide the wild dogs with a ready source of protein. There must have been millions of them, she thought, floating like tadpoles in the sewers below. If she reached out with her Death Sight she might sense them all swarming there, an ocean of accumulated anti-birth.

But she didn't want to sense them. This whole change of topic was making her upset, plunging her thoughts into darkness.

"How long are we going to keep doing this?" she asked.

"As long as you want me too, my sweet," said Narseh with a randy-looking smile.

"Not the sex, silly. This business."

"As long as we can get away with it."

"I'm serious, Narseh. We can't go on like this forever. The longer we continue, the more chance there is someone will notice the hieroglyphs, or see through the magick. Anyone with second sight who happens by would figure out the truth straightaway. If the frescoes are damaged – even if the *paint* starts to peel – then the spells will be compromised. If people figure out they've been having sex with corpses, we'll be lynched from the nearest fucking lamppost!"

"We'll be fine. I have the frescoes checked for damage every day. And if anyone does figure out the truth, I'll just bribe them to be silent. Money talks, remember?"

"It's not just the difficulty in maintaining the illusions," she said. 'The longer I sustain a spell of this magnitude, the more deathly energies will build up. In the walls, in the soil, in the very air. The miasma's getting thick as it is. So much necromantic power can have horrible side effects, and I wasn't really taught how to handle them. I got kicked out before I could finish that part of my training..."

"You worry too much, my love," he said. "You're just getting gloomy from exhaustion. Sleep, rest, and tomorrow you'll feel better." He stretched out a blanket to cover her body, then leaned in and kissed her on the mouth. "I'll be back soon," he said. "I just have to go balance the ledger."

For a moment, she clung to his warmth, then let him slip away into the shadows. But, unable to sleep, she tossed and turned beneath the covers. She couldn't shake the feeling that something was about to go very, very wrong.

Chapter 5: Boys' Night Out

Aktus was in the hotel bar, nursing a pint of black lager, when two of his comrades emerged from their quarters and came shambling to his table, sitting down with a grumble. Even through their corpse-paint he could tell they were hungover. They propped their axes against the wall and ordered up drinks. The fearful bar staff jumped to attention, while the rest of the patrons gave the mercenaries a wide-berth, wary of their sinister makeup and their ever-present axes.

"Where're the others?" Aktus asked as the drinks arrived and the two sat there swigging.

Their company totalled ten, a pretty meagre sum by the standards of mercenary bands, which often had hundreds or thousands of members. Still, what the Axes of Aarseth lacked in numbers they made up for in might. Each was as deadly as a full score of lesser soldiers, and commanded an income to match. On account of this, they were called the 'Twennies,' or 'Twenty-men.' Their massive axes were too heavy for most others to even pick up, let alone wield. Mastering those weapons had taken them years of harsh training, until their arms had grown thick as some men's thighs, and their bodies were towers of muscle and strength. They cut through ranks of infantry like sickles through wheat.

"Still in bed," said Immo, the largest of the group, not just in muscle but in fat. His face, though streaked with corpse-paint, seemed jolly nonetheless. He laughed as he continued. "They all struck out last night. Got so frustrated with blue balls they came back here and drank till they dropped. I doubt they'll be up for a couple more hours!"

"How did you do?" asked Aktus.

"Not so great. Wandered around for a while, then finally managed to find myself a shrivelled old whore. She said she'd been the best in Hedonia, back in her day, though you sure couldn't tell that by looking at her now. A real double-bagger, that's for sure. She even brought her own bags! One for me, another for her. We must've looked like two condemned criminals, having a tryst before our date with the hangman. Still, the blowjob was good. Her wooden teeth came right out of her mouth!"

Gorgo, the third of their number and the tallest, made a sickened sound and spat a mouthful of lager on the floor. His features were gaunt. Rings of black paint made his eyes look almost skeletally sunken.

"What about you?" asked Aktus, turning towards him.

"Not so great either. I ended up having to settle for a ladyboy."

Immo laughed. "Are you sure you '*settled*?' Maybe that's just what you were after all along!"

"Fuck you," said Gorgo.

"Oh, don't be like that. Nothing wrong with ladyboys. Let's face it, even when you're with a girl, you only end up trying to fuck them up the arse anyway. At least with a tranny you know what's on the menu! Saves a lot of beating around the bush, so to speak."

"Is that what you did with this vintage old sexpot of yours?"

"I certainly tried, but the years hadn't been kind to her down there. Too many sessions of anal gymnastics left her full-prolapse. It was like trying to throat-fuck a snake."

Gorgo groaned and looked nauseous, not just from his hangover. "You're disgusting," he said, but Immo just laughed. Gorgo turned to Aktus instead. "How about you?"

Aktus beamed, then regaled them with a tale of the pleasures he'd experienced at The Unwithering Flower. Immo and Gorgo hung on his words as he gave them a blow-by-blow description of the blowjob he'd received, followed by the rest of his sexcapades. By the time he'd finished they looked a lot less hungover, and a great deal more animated.

"I guess we know where we're going tonight!" said Immo with a broad grin.

It was, indeed, several hours before the rest of their company put in an appearance. By then, having been steadily drinking while they

waited, Aktus was drunk, Gorgo was wasted, and Immo well on the way to soused.

The others put in a good effort to catch up, and before long they stumbled together down the Hedonian streets, bumping into strangers, roaring, singing, laughing in the lantern-lit dusk. Aktus had to struggle to find his way back to the Unwithering Flower, his friends mocking him, saying he must've passed out and imagined the whole thing, that he'd probably had sex with a hobo in a state of delirium. He was just about to throw a punch when he saw the tell-tale glow of a dozen red lanterns and the image of a flower with a pussy in the middle.

"There!" he said.

They hustled to the doors, then Immo stopped them with a slurred warning.

"Gotta compozhe ourshelves," he said, staggering to keep his balance. "Don't wanta sheem too pishted, or they won't lettusssh in. Shavvy?"

Agreeing, they all took a moment, straightening their backs and sucking down sobering breaths.

With the dream-like confidence of someone very drunk, Aktus felt – nay, he *knew* – that he could clear his head and reverse the effects of the alcohol with nothing but pure, unmitigated willpower. He focused his mind. Suddenly the world seemed brighter, sharper, his vision more focused. His body felt steady, as sober as could be. He took a step –

And reeled right into Immo, who laughed. "Fuck it," he said. "Letsh go in."

The doors opened, and in blundered a whole host of drunk, dangerous, heavily armed men. Narseh took a wary look at them, then saw their moneybags were bulging!

He smiled widely and spoke to the one he recognised. "Hello again, my friend! I see you've come back to sup some more nectar from the Flower! And brought company!"

"I sure have," said Aktus, swaying on his feet. "Do we get a group discount?"

Narseh chuckled. "No discounts, I'm afraid. But I'm sure your joy will be doubled by the presence of your comrades."

One of the mercenaries pushed forth from the back of the ranks.

"Are you shaying we're gonna fuck each other?" he growled.

"Of course not," said Narseh. "I merely meant that it will be a comradely exercise for you, since you're all here together. Yes?"

The mercenary glared suspiciously at him a moment longer, then shrugged, his drunken anger seemingly diffused.

"Coins on the counter, gentlemen," said Narseh.

They reached into their moneybags and started slamming down silver. Some were so drunk they gave him too much, which he pocketed regardless. Others had miscounted and given too little; from them he demanded the remainder, and pocketed that, as well.

"I take it you'll be keeping your weapons with you?" he asked, remembering Aktus' habit from the previous evening.

"Where we go, they go," one of them said.

"As you please. Follow me."

Narseh led them through the halls, showing each to a room. Before long, he was alone in the corridor – or so he thought, until a hand reached out from the darkness, grabbing his shoulder with terrifying strength.

Chapter 6: Half-Mast

He whirled. Behind him stood one of Wena's undead butlers, clutching his shoulder with the ignorant strength of the dead.

"Get off me, you oaf!" he ordered, attempting to brush off its grip.

But the implacable corpse was too strong. It all but dragged him down the corridor and into Wena's chamber. Only then did it let go.

Upset at being manhandled, Narseh kicked the unfeeling zombie in the shin, then glanced down at Wena, who sat in a circle of incense sticks in the centre of the room. He knew from her look of intense concentration she was busy meditating, maintaining the spells. Her beautiful face was beaded with sweat from the effort.

"What do you think you're doing?" he snapped, gesturing towards her undead servant. "We can't have those *things* out there wandering the halls! What if someone saw them?"

"I don't like the look of those mercenaries," she said, without looking up at him.

"I'll admit that their makeup is a little peculiar –"

"It's not the makeup I'm worried about, Narseh. They're drunk, dangerous."

"I'd say far more of the former than the latter. Those boys are plastered! They're too drunk to know where they are, let alone figure out what's going on."

"I hope you're right."

"Of course I am. As I've told you, you worry too much, my dear."

He bent to kiss her on the cheek, then went to empty his pocketfuls of coins into the treasure chest. His heart grew more buoyant with every single CLINK!

Immo fell across the bed after failing a titanic struggle to remove his own trousers. Finally, he managed to wrestle them off, and lay there with his senses spinning. The room's decorative frescoes whirled before his eyes, creating a kaleidoscope of lips, hips, and thighs. Within the blur were hints of hieroglyphs he couldn't quite see, sinister images of buzzards and skulls.

He ignored them and played with his prick instead, finding it limp and unresponsive from the gallons of lager he'd imbibed.

Poor girl's really gonna have her work cut out for her, he mused.

Just then, the door opened and a woman stepped in. He tried to make out her features, but the world kept billowing before his eyes like a curtain in the breeze. With an effort of will he got it to stay still long enough to see that she was pretty and pale.

No bags needed this time, he thought with a smile.

She slipped off her robe and strode over to the bed, smelling of roses. At once, she went to work between his legs, sucking his flaccid little cock into her mouth and stroking it nimbly with her fingers. It stayed limp for a while, then grew semi-erect, so that it hung between her lips like a piece of pale rope. Still she kept sucking it, coaxing it, stroking it. Her eyes looked hungry as they stared into his, bloated with a likeness of lust. She moaned as if tasting a delicacy, as though his half-awake snake were giving her some kind of blazing oral orgasm.

Is she mocking me? Immo wondered, feeling his jovial persona begin to unravel.

Any other woman would've given up by now, and told him to forget it. "These things happen," she would've said, shrugging. "Sober up and come back later." But this one kept plying his limpness as though it were the stiffest, most fabulous cock in the world.

Of course, it didn't occur to him that this was all just a rote, pre-programmed display; he read mockery in those blank, soulless eyes. She was laughing at him inwardly, he was sure, acting as though he were a stud when he couldn't get it up. This was a whole new species of ridicule!

"Get offa me!" he shouted, pushing her from the bed.

She fell to the floor. For a moment she knelt there, looking blank. Then she started playing with herself, teasing her nipples and fingering her lubricated pussy. She started moaning wantonly, as if trying to arouse him, as if oblivious to the anger in his eyes.

Fucking bitch is still taunting me! he thought.

Immo got to his feet, swaying as he did. He reeled, and saw the walls reeling with him. The frescoes' images swirled all around, mocking him in turn with their depictions of coitus and fellatio, of penetrated pussies and steel-rod erections.

"FUCK!" he roared.

He groped for his axe and swung its leather-sheathed head at the wall. Whether deliberately or not, he managed to smash the blade straight thought the centre of a pussy, shattering the flimsy plaster and destroying the hieroglyphs hidden amid the labia.

The room suddenly seemed darker. The scent of flowers was joined by a whiff of decay. Immo knew that smell from the battlefield. It stirred up a surge of adrenaline, clearing away his vertigo and focusing his mind through its alcoholic haze.

It came from the girl, who still knelt on the floor, fingering her pussy and plucking her nipples. Between her breasts was a suture he was sure hadn't been there before. It ran to her navel, as though her body had been opened up and sewn back together. Her skin was not only pale, it was bloodless, and grey.

When she looked up at him, her unfeeling eyes were made of glass.

Immo let out a horrified yell and started pulling at the leather sheathing his axe's broad blades.

Chapter 7: Stiffs

"We've got a breach," said Wena. "One of those idiots just smashed up a fresco!"

"How's he reacting?" asked Narseh. "Can we bribe him?"

Closing her own eyes, she looked through those of the dead girl. She saw Immo standing before her, naked and enraged, stripping the sheath from his axe.

"I think he wants payment in blood!" she said.

"Then we'll have to drain *his* coffers of it first," said Narseh. "Deal with him!"

Wena sent her full consciousness into the corpse. She felt its cold flesh all around her as though it were her own. She even felt the cum-soaked sawdust filling its chest.

She forced the dead meat to its feet and stood facing the mercenary, just as he whipped off the leather and laid bare the gleaming blade. He swung. Wena ducked her dead puppet beneath the blur of blue steel and rushed him, grabbing his balls in one hand and his throat in the other. She squeezed with undead might until his trachea snapped and his testicles burst between her surrogate fingers.

The effort left her drained, not to mention distracted. For a dizzying moment she lost all control of her spells. Throughout the halls and the rooms of The Unwithering Flower, the magickal light flickered and dimmed, allowing naked death to peek out from the gloom.

Aktus was ploughing his whore from behind when he first heard the distant cries. He thought briefly about investigating, but the sounds had been muffled by the walls, were probably cries of pleasure anyway, and his own pleasure was far too imminent.

So, he kept pumping, until the light in the room faded like a guttering candle and his whore's floral scent became mingled with rot. Her moans fell silent. Her skin went pallid and dry.

Fuck! he thought, pulling out of her suddenly cooled pussy and scrambling to the back of the bed.

She turned and looked at him with a slack, dead face. As the lights shimmered again, her lips curved in a glistening smile, and she began crawling across the covers towards him.

"Oh fuck!" Wena gasped, her eyes popping open. "Oh fuck, oh fuck. I lost it, Narseh. I lost it!"

"Lost what?"

"Control of the spell. Just for a few seconds. But they would've seen everything!"

A series of horrified shouts rose up from the brothel, confirming her fears.

"We need to contain it," said Narseh. "It's time to clean house. Understand?"

Wena nodded grimly, and shut her eyes again.

Gorgo lay on the bed in blissful ignorance, eyes closed so he could focus on the blowjob he was getting.

His eyes had been closed for a while. Consequently, he hadn't seen the light grow dim, nor had he seen the cadaverous face of the creature sucking his cock. He hadn't heard the shouts and the screams of his comrades, either, for his room shared a wall with a noisy pub next door.

Thus he lay in blissful ignorance, marvelling at the skills of his fellator. She was taking him deeply, right to the root. There was no touch of teeth –

-- until now.

The teeth bit down savagely, shearing him off. He screamed, eyes open now, seeing the blood from his stump blasting across a face that looked utterly dead. He'd wanted to give her a facial, of course – just not like this!

He saw the ragged remnants of his member protruding between

her desiccated lips. Then he passed out from shock and started bleeding to death.

Aktus stared in confusion at the smiling girl crawling toward him. She wasn't moaning anymore, wasn't making any noises at all.

Was this all some weird hallucination, he wondered? Had someone spiked one of his drinks with psychedelics? His fellow Axes were fond of such pranks ...

But the stench had been so real! He still felt it clinging to his nostrils! And what about the shouts he'd heard from down the hall? What about the other red flags, like the weird muteness of the women, and their peculiar emotionlessness? Something was definitely wrong here!

From her crawling crouch, the woman suddenly sprang towards him with jaws open wide. He threw himself sideways off the bed, letting her land on the pillows behind him. Scrambling to his feet, he dashed across the room, just as she took another lunge. She missed him by a hair and crashed against the wall. The light had begun to flicker and strobe, making her look beautiful one moment, cadaverous the next. Her sultry smile appeared and disappeared with the coming and going of the light, like a face in a frenzied game of peek-a-boo.

She leapt at him.

"Fuck!" he shouted.

His axe sat propped against the wall. He picked it up, and without having time to whip off the sheath, struck her in the head, hoping that bludgeoning force would be enough to do the job.

The blade hit her hard, sending her reeling. One of her eyes popped out and rolled across the floor. As the light flickered low again he saw that it was made of cut glass. The skull behind the hollow socket was totally empty.

"Fuck!" he roared again.

She rushed towards him in a frenzy, grasping at the axe. The sheath was still on it. For a moment they wrestled with the weapon between them. Then the sheath tore loose, and the dead girl stumbled backwards, holding it. She bit and clawed at it fiercely, as though she were rending human flesh.

Aktus gaped in horror. In her sickening state of undeath, she had lost the ability to differentiate people from objects. Then he swung the naked blade and took her apart at the middle.

As the light shone bright, she seemed to die just like anyone else, collapsing to the ground in a welter of blood. Then the light guttered down again, revealing a bloodless cadaver, from which sodden bits of sawdust and petals spilled out, like a mulch of autumn leaves, soaked not with rain but with semen.

The scent of stale cum joined the reek of decay. Aktus tried not to vomit. He heard the screams rising up anew all around him – the screams of his comrades, the Axes of Aarseth!

"I'm coming, brothers!" he shouted, running to the door.

It was locked.

More freakish sorcery! he thought.

He knew, in spite of his drunkenness, fear, and adrenaline, that the vilest of magick was at work in this brothel. Into his mind flashed an image of the man from Alhazred.

"You bastard," he growled. "I'll fix you!"

He cleaved and chopped through the door and forced his way into the hall, into yet more flickering light and the perfume of roses tainted with the odour of death.

Another door exploded into rubble and Sadek, one of Aktus' companions, fell sprawling with a dead woman clinging to his back. His eyes had been ripped from their sockets, and the woman was gnawing at the side of his neck, bathing herself in a gush of arterial blood.

"Bitch!" shouted Aktus, shearing off her head with a single blow.

She kept moving regardless, mauling Sadek with her hands in lieu of her mouth. Since his friend was already as good as dead anyway, Aktus hacked both of them in half. Dismembered, the woman grew finally still, spilling sawdust and roses from her bisected ribs.

Aktus grit his teeth. His brothers were dying!

Though, by the sounds, some were still alive. He could hear them fighting to survive. He rushed to the closest room and swung his axe at the door. It bit through wood, then flesh, then bone. The blade came back bloody, and a body hit the floor.

Aktus stared in horror through the splintered ruins. One of his bros had been backed up against the door, struggling with a dead thing; now he was a dead thing himself, cleft through the spine by Aktus' own unwitting axe.

"Fuck!" shouted Aktus, and then a prostitute zombie crashed through the wrecked door, trampling the body of his comrade underfoot.

He split her down the middle, from forehead to groin. She collapsed with a predictable outpouring of potpourri, sawdust, and jism.

Aktus rushed for the next room, from which came yet more shouting.

Better use my shoulder this time! he thought, having learned a cruel lesson from the accidental butchering of his comrade.

He stepped back and got ready to shoulder-charge the door, but before he could, a figure burst from the wall behind him, reeking of death and wrapped in bright saffron.

Chapter 8: Frenzy

"How's it going out there?" asked Narseh as he paced about the room.

"Badly," said Wena. "These guys are tough. I've got five of them down, but the rest are still going. They've already killed a dozen of the girls!"

"*Killed?* How can they be killed? They're already dead!"

"Destroyed, then. The magick is broken by bodily dismemberment. I can't animate corpses if they're in a dozen pieces! Narseh, we need to go, *now*. Even if we manage to kill everyone here, people will come looking for them. Then there's the screaming –"

"You're overreacting," he said. "I'm sure it's not as bad as you say. Why don't I take a peek for myself?"

"Narseh, no!" she shouted. "Don't go out there!"

But he'd already hurried from the room.

The creature in saffron silks cinched its arms around Aktus' chest before he had time to react. It bit at his neck, but its teeth had rotted out long ago, leaving only mummified gums that grasped at the flesh without breaking the skin.

The real danger came from its arms. They squeezed like a vice, cracking one of his ribs. If he didn't act fast, he'd be crushed! He still had his axe, but his upper arms being pinned against his sides prevented him from swinging it. He dropped the useless weapon and grabbed the creature's wrists. They were withered and wrapped, like those of a mummy, but coursing with the pitiless power of a solid steel trap. Aktus knew he had only one chance – to throw all of his strength into one last attempt to break free, before it was too late.

He gritted his teeth and pulled with all his might at the mummified hands, trying to loosen their grip. His muscles bulged, the sinews on his neck standing out like straining ropes. He thought he might tear his own body apart with his exertions. Then he felt the undead arms loosen a little. With a growl of wild fury, he bent at the waist and hurled the withered monster off his back. For all its uncanny strength, the thing was surprisingly light. It crashed to the floor and split its skull on the boards. Eyeballs made of lapis lazuli popped from its head and shot across the hall like a pair of rogue marbles.

But it still wasn't finished. It writhed on the ground, trying to right itself. Aktus picked up his axe and started hacking, refusing to stop until the creature was in motionless pieces. Herbs from its hollowed-out insides flew everywhere, making him sneeze.

Another of his comrades shouted in alarm from somewhere up ahead.

"I'm coming!" called Aktus. It was the sort of exclamation commonly heard in a Hedonian brothel, if not in this particular context.

Aktus raced down the corridor, rounded a corner, and found Borgo fighting with more of the things from the walls. One of them had hold of his axe, trying to pull it away; the other drew back its hand for a gut-punch.

"Borgo, watch out!"

His warning came too late. The mummy's fist plunged into Borgo's guts and came out entangled with intestine. Borgo, done for, slumped to the floor, his face going paler than his corpse paint.

"RAAHH!!" Aktus let out a bloodthirsty roar and charged in, swinging.

"What're you doing standing around?" Narseh snapped, as he rushed through the mortuary room where his slaves had paused to listen to the terrible sounds coming from the rest of the brothel. "Get back to work!"

The slaves resumed half-heartedly cleaning, while he hurried into the hall. A bloodthirsty cry from around a corner was followed by a series of hacking sounds. Taking a careful peek, he saw one of the mercenaries – the one who'd come twice now to the brothel, and more times inside of it – looming over two dismembered mummies. His naked body was splattered with blood, sawdust, and rose petals. He was panting like an animal, his muscular chest heaving wide with every breath, like a barrel of sinew and bone fit to burst. When he looked up from the slaughter, he locked eyes with Narseh.

Oh shit, Narseh thought.

Aktus, fresh from the heights of his murderous frenzy, saw the man from Alhazred peering around the corner. His bloodthirst rekindled. He forgot all about trying to save the rest of his comrades. He had only one urge now – to catch that awful, bastard proprietor of this murderous establishment, and unfurl his bleeding guts like the threads of a tapestry undone. He roared and gave chase as his enemy fled.

"Get out of the way!" shouted Narseh, pushing slaves to the side as he ran back into the mortuary room.

He slammed the door and bolted it behind him, then stood a moment fearful and panting, before turning to the slaves with a display of cool command.

"Right," he said. "Time to bow out. Exit, stage left. You lot, ready the boats. You two, stay by this door. If that maniac gets through, hold him off. Don't worry – I'll make a sacrifice to your souls in the afterlife!"

As they scattered to do his bidding, he raced to Wena's chamber, already regretting his generous offer to reward his dead slaves in the underworld. Then again, he hadn't specified just what the sacrifice would be. Perhaps some apples, brought at a discount, just before the closing of the market?

He found her wide-eyed and anxious, waiting for him, one of the room's ornate tapestries torn from the wall, revealing a staircase behind it, which connected to the tunnels that served as their secret escape route. A cold draft issued from the opening, reeking of death.

"You were right," said Narseh. "It's bad out there. Time to gather our takings and close up shop. Get those undead idiots of yours to carry the chest."

Wena nodded, and sighed with relief. She gestured to the zombies, who picked up the heavy treasure chest.

"Wait!" cried Narseh. "It isn't full! It can hold more!"

Frantic, he dashed around the room, snatching up coins and bits of jewellery and tossing them in. With Wena's help, it was soon overflowing. She made to close the lid, couldn't, and began to haul out the large and bulky golden courtesan statue.

"No!" He stayed her hand. "We'll tie it! Twist the bedsheets into ropes!"

Once the chest was secured, he still didn't head for the exit, but kept gathering up more of his precious treasure. He stuffed coins in his pockets, hung chains around his neck, loaded rings on his fingers and bracelets on his wrists. He even jammed coins into his slippers.

I guess I finally look the part of a pimp! he thought, though he had no time to admire the effect. Instead, he likewise began filling Wena's pockets and adorning her body with as much jewellery as he could.

Then, from the direction of the mortuary room, came the racket of splintering wood and a mercenary's furious bellow.

"Come on!" Wena threw on her putrescent cloak, regarding him with wide, desperate eyes. "We've got to go!"

The zombies were already maneuvering the heavy chest slowly down the stairs. Narseh glanced around, heartsick with horror as he saw all the wealth still littering the room.

But another loud CRASH! and the terrified screams of his slaves decided him. He seized Wena's outstretched hand, and together they descended into darkness.

The two men who stood guard with surgical knives screamed in terror as Aktus chopped through the door and they saw his wrathful face. He was about to cut them down when they threw away their weapons and surrendered.

"We're just slaves!" one of them pleaded.

The other pointed. "The one you want, he went thattaway!"

Aktus barked like a dog and pushed past them both, following the indicated directions. He arrived in a lavish chamber filled with incense and scattered bits of treasure. From a dark opening in the wall came the perfume of death and a cold, biting wind. Rough-hewn stairs led down. Aktus took them without even blinking.

Narseh peered around. The solitary torch he'd managed to light showed him a wide, circular tunnel, with a path on either side and a waste-water trench flowing down the middle. It wasn't as filthy as he might have imagined, and was in fact the relic of some past civilization whose buildings had long ago been razed to the ground. The present-day inhabitants of Hedonia lived atop the old ruins, and disposed of their waste in cesspits on the outskirts of town. Thus the sewer itself was mostly unused, filled only with what rubbish from the streets the rains had washed down a few antique gutters.

Slovenly barbarians, he thought, shaking his head. There was indoor plumbing aplenty in Alhazred. He even had a bidet back home!

But Alhazred was an orderly, regulated society. It was hard for an entrepreneur like himself to make a fortune there, with so many rules restraining free trade. That's why he'd come to these savage eastern lands in the first place, where chaos created opportunity.

It also created danger, as was most tellingly shown by his present predicament.

He hurried along the tunnel's side walkway, holding Wena's hand. A pity she was so clingy, especially right now. They could each have been lugging a sackful of coins instead of gripping each other's sweaty fingers! Bad enough he also had to be burdened carrying the torch, but they needed to be able to see where they were going.

They arrived at a junction. To the left, the old sewer continued; to the right, a roughly-hewn passage built by smugglers or pirates in ages past led to a small, hidden jetty by the side of a cliff. There, waiting in readiness for an eventuality just such as this, Narseh's own galley was docked, right beside Wena's.

All they had to do was reach their boats, and they could sail out to sea, leaving their murderous pursuer behind them.

They hurried along the passage, shivering as they went. Overflowing waste-water from the sewer trickled ahead of them, following a gutter worn into the stone floor. Some manner of wet, stinking residue resembling liquefied flesh clung to the walls. The air grew steadily colder, reeking of decay. It seemed as if the very earth itself were a corpse, its bowels rotting around them.

A rat darted past. Narseh almost shrieked as he saw it in the torchlight. Its ragged pelt was full of holes, exposing bones underneath. It was just as dead – and yet just as alive – as Wena's servants.

"What the fuck's going on down here?" he hissed.

"The necromantic energies," she said. "I told you they were building up. They can have some pretty weird side-effects."

"No kidding," said Narseh, trying to keep casual, even as chills ran down his spine. He caught himself squeezing her hand despite his best efforts and could only hope she didn't realise how anxious he was.

They hurried on as fast as the slow-moving treasure-laden zombies allowed, listening for sounds of pursuing mercenaries with axes.

Finally, they emerged into a large, lightless sea-cave, which had been sealed off by those same long-ago pirates or smugglers to serve as a hideout. A wall of jagged rocks blocked the former cave entrance, with only a concealed doorway giving clandestine access to the jetty outside.

Where once the tide had come and gone, now a giant pool of stagnant water formed an underground lake, created by decades or centuries of accumulated sewer runoff. It reeked worse than anything Narseh had yet had the misfortune to smell, but he knew their boats, and their escape, waited just beyond it.

"Come on," he said, tugging at Wena's hand.

But she stood frozen to the spot, staring in horror at the stagnant pool.

Chapter 9: Anti-birth

"Don't. Move," whispered Wena.

Her senses warned her of some awful presence, something horrible and vast, lurking just under the surface. Some conglomeration of death, congealed perhaps from the corpses of rats or fish, insects, human hair, toenail clippings ... anything dead that had sluiced through the sewers to stew in this vile bath of necromantic miasma.

Whatever it was, it was no doubt inimical to life.

It was also, she knew for certain, impossible to control. Unlike zombies, created by formulaic spells passed down since the age before this one, the thing in the pool was a by-blow, a mutant.

She might've made it, albeit inadvertently, with the excessive energies that had spilled from her spells, but it sure wasn't hers to command.

"What's wrong?" asked Narseh.

"There's something in the water," she said, her voice low. "We have to be really, really quiet."

They crept around the edge of the pool, moving as silently as possible. The zombies moved quietly too, clasping the treasure chest between them. But the walkway was slick with putrescence, and wet from the lapping of the water, and Narseh's soft slippers were not made for such treacherous terrain. His feet slipped out from under him, and he fell arse-first toward the ground, upon which the coins stuffing his pockets seemed destined to make a great noisy CRASH.

Wena acted on instinct, calling on the power of her cloak. The strips of black shroud-cloth from which it was made came to writhing life and whipped around Narseh like the coils of an octopus, catching him mid-fall. The coins in his pockets clinked and jangled from the movement, and although the sounds were dim, they rang through the cavern regardless, like notes of distant music.

With her cloak, she set Narseh back on his feet. For once, he didn't seem to notice the putrid foulness of its fabric. Motionless, they stared at the water. Wena's heart raced as she saw a cluster of bubbles break the surface, heralding movement from below. She felt it, too, with her necromantic senses, the way a fisherman feels a quivering tension on his line when something has bitten below.

But was the thing in the water waking up, or merely rolling over in its sleep, stirred but not roused by the noise?

Tense, hideous moments passed as they watched the bubbles gradually cease. The thing remained dormant. Wena could sense its great quietude, pregnant with death.

She took a deep breath and released Narseh from the cloak. Holding hands again, they continued their silent course toward the exit. The slope leading up to it was crooked, rough, and coated in slime, looking even more treacherous than the walkway had been. Wena made for it regardless, but Narseh pulled her back, pointing to the zombies.

"They go first," he said. "I'm not letting that treasure chest out of my sight!"

Wena nodded to her butlers. They began climbing the slope with agonizing slowness, lugging the ungainly weight of the treasure chest between them. They were not elegant creatures at the best of times, and their burden, combined with the steepness of their ascent, and the slippery surface, was taxing their agility to the limit. Wena and Narseh watched and waited, glancing nervously between the zombies and the surface of the pool.

A bloodthirsty bellow echoed through the cavern as a naked corpse-painted axeman spattered with sawdust, rose petals, and blood came charging from the tunnel.

He'd reach them in no time! They had to escape – but the way was still blocked by the two shambling zombies!

"Do something!" urged Narseh.

"Like what?"

"I don't know, blast him with a lightning bolt!"

"I can't fucking do that!"

"You're a sorcerer!"

"That doesn't mean I have lightning powers!"

The axeman ran at them, skirting the edge of the pool. His bare feet had no problem at all negotiating the slippery slime; he was used to wading through entrails on the battlefield.

Wena looked again to the water, surprised to find herself actually hoping for bubbles. The creature within, whatever it was, was now their only hope of deliverance. Surely it would respond to the maniac's shouting!

But it didn't. Clearly, its slumber was deep. Below the waters, the sounds of the mercenary's roars must have been muffled to a distant, humming vibration.

"Fuck!" whispered Wena.

The zombies were still only two-thirds of the way up, blocking their escape. That giant axe came closer and closer, like a pendulum of death counting down. Desperately, Wena reached into her pocket and pulled out a diamond the size of a baby's clenched fist. She went to throw it into the water, thinking to stir up the beast, but Narseh held her back.

"Are you mad, woman? Use the lesser currencies!"

They both began tossing coins, sending ripples spreading across the surface in overlapping, colliding patterns, stirring currents that might disturb the monster beneath. Meanwhile, the axeman closed in, to fifty feet, then forty, then thirty –

Then stopped short as a monstrous mass reared up from the depths, streaming vile rivulets of stagnant water.

Dead things, she had thought, sluiced down into the sewers to fester and congeal in this awful cauldron, but what she saw now was not made up merely of rats, fish, and discarded toenail clippings. No, here were the unwanted bastards of the City of Whores, a host of half-formed embryos, myriad abortions brought together and melded into one by the necromantic energy tainting the cavern. Its overall appearance mirrored that of its integral parts, giving it the shape of a gigantic foetus with a translucent head and vestigial, rubbery features.

Still submerged to its navel, it loomed twenty feet above them. Only the zombies did not react with disgust; even Wena had to fight not to vomit at the sight or the stench of the abomination. She and Narseh huddled, clinging to each other, trembling and terrified.

The axeman froze for a moment, too, gaping with shock. Then he let out another war-cry, hefted his axe, and continued his charge toward Narseh, ignoring the beast.

It did not ignore him, but hurled itself onto the walkway with a great splash of rancid water, blocking his path and reaching for him with its flipper-like arms. Enraged, he swung at it, hacking so deep into its chest the full blade of his axe disappeared. Although he must have struck through to its hidden, awful heart, it only shuddered, then enfolded him in its grasp and embraced him to its bosom.

The gesture was essentially a hug, though not a very gentle one.

The axeman shrieked, his bones pulverized as it squeezed. He went limp. His axe, dislodged, fell from his dead hands to vanish into the pool.

The creature shook him curiously, his body flopping like a broken doll. It then let out a thousand tiny anguished screams from the thousand tiny mouths that dotted its body.

Wena felt a tear dribbling from her eye. The monster may have been inimical to life – but perhaps all it wanted was love.

Mewling, it began to suck on Aktus' head as though it were a nipple.

"Looks like our friend's got a new job as a wet nurse," said Narseh, sounding as though he were trying to dampen down a tremor in his voice. "Let's get out of here, before it tries to suckle on us too!"

Wena's butlers were no longer blocking the ascent, so they ran for the exit and the jetty beyond, eager to hustle to their galleys and set off for brighter shores, leaving the plague-haunted city of Hedonia behind.

Chapter 10: Tales Within Tales

Some time later…

Narseh finished speaking and reclined on a pile of bright cushions, taking a draw from his hookah. Before him sat a very rich fool, his eyes wide with wonder.

"An amazing tale!" said the fool. "I almost can't believe it! First you arrive in Hedonia to help ferry desperate people away from the plague. Truly a noble endeavour! Then you uncover the existence of that nefarious brothel – what was it called – The Unwithering Flower? – which you discover is secretly being run by a necromancer, using magick to trick unsuspecting people into having sex with corpses! Who could conceive of such a repugnant, treacherous act? And on top of that, murdering beautiful young women to provide all the bodies? Ghastlier still! Yet you *still* took it upon yourself to infiltrate that whorehouse of horror and uncover those sickening shenanigans. You even managed to defeat the necromancer's axe-wielding henchmen, rescue the maiden they'd most recently kidnapped, and escape through that underground cove, bypassing the necromancer's pet monster by distracting it with coins. Truly a feat for the ages! But what, may I ask, happened next? What of all the gold and jewels you discovered in the necromancer's chamber? Were you able to keep any of it?"

Narseh sighed out smoke, and shook his head sadly.

"I'm afraid not," he said. "The maiden had swooned at the sight of such horrors. I had to carry her delicate body to safety by myself, which meant I didn't have space in my arms for anything else. The rest was lost into that slime pit, to dwell with the monster forever. Thus, I returned to our glorious Alhazred poorer than ever, my coffers all but empty. The only treasure I managed to bring home from my journey was the maiden. Who, of course, became my seventh wife, so I still feel myself rich. For, surely, love is the greatest treasure of all. Wouldn't you agree?

"Indeed!" said the rich fool, looking enchanted. "Oh, Narseh, truly you're a man of courage and enlightenment! I'd like to offer you a gift in exchange for this incredible tale. Perhaps in such manner may the cruelties of fortune be somewhat reversed, and you'll receive the due thanks that your efforts deserve."

The fool gestured to his retinue of servants, who strode forth carrying armfuls of riches, including vessels of silver and gold, bolts of brocaded silk, and sacks of fine tobacco.

"'Please allow this to replace a portion of the treasure you lost," said the fool.

"Ah, sir, You are too kind," said Narseh humbly inclining his head.

"Not at all! Though now I suppose I should leave you to your rest. You do have seven wives to satisfy, after all! But perhaps I could hear another of your amazing tales next week? If you've got time, that is...?"

"I think that could be arranged," said Narseh.

They rose, and bowed to each other, and the fool and his servants started filing from the chamber. As Narseh surveyed his new riches, a slave stepped forth from a discreet corner.

"Shall we put this with the rest of your treasure, master?" he asked.

Narseh slapped him over the head, hard. The sound of it echoed in the high-domed room.

"Idiot!" he hissed. "That gullible shithead might not yet be out of earshot!"

"Sorry, master," said the slave, who then waited for the sound of the villa's front door closing, and asked the same question again.

"Yes," said Narseh. "Now you may put this with the rest."

He unlocked his great vault and watched the slaves add the fresh pile of riches to the treasure horde inside.

His coffers were most definitely not empty, contrary to what he had told the rich fool. Nor was that the only lie or bent truth he'd told. Almost the whole story had been horribly distorted. For one thing, his seventh wife was no helpless young maiden from Hedonia, but an experienced woman from Khem.

And yet, there were a few grains of truth to the tale he'd just spun. He *had* rescued a woman from Hedonia, and she was surely virginal. For who could ever penetrate her body of glittering gold?

Narseh smiled at the golden statue of the courtesan crowning his treasure horde. Then, giving thanks to the Candle King, he dived into his coins like a pig into swill.

His seven wives would have to wait, as they so often did – the gold was calling his attentions tonight!

Narseh will return for more fantastic journeys!

Narseh the Slaver and the Lucre of Death

The Nefarious Journeys of Narseh the Slaver, Part 2

It's the Aeon of Chaos. The gods are dead, and the demons roll marbles made from their eyes.

Chapter 1: Among the Tombstones

Narseh the slaver strolled through the graveyard with a bouquet of flowers in hand. He glanced at the gravestones as he walked. Many were corroded with age. Some had collapsed into piles of dirty rubble. Those still standing bore laconic and sinister epitaphs. One simply said 'here I lie; soon you shall join me.' Another catalogued the impressive career of a local magistrate, whose *curriculum vitae* ended with a description of his current occupation: 'worm food.'

Narseh held back a shudder. Like most people he didn't like to think about mortality, and harboured a natural terror of death. But even greater than his fear of dying was his fear of dying *before* he became outrageously and fabulously wealthy.

People often said 'you can't take money with you when you die.' Narseh knew them to be fools. For he had consulted with certain experts regarding the transmigration of souls and the mysterious realm of the underworld. From them he had purchased the rituals which would allow him to transplant his wealth into the afterlife when the time of his death arrived.

He had the whole thing planned out. As soon as he died, all his worldly assets would be liquidated into gold, jewels, silks and tobacco, then placed inside a giant magickal circle. From there they would be teleported into the realm of the dead, where his soul would be waiting to collect the cache. He wouldn't have to carry all that loot by himself; he'd left detailed instructions for his wives and slaves to kill themselves the moment he died, so that they too might continue to serve him in the afterlife. And in the event that they should demur from such a morbid request, and linger on beyond him in the realm of the living, he had placed some assassins on retainer to garrotte them.

Thus Narseh hoped to retire to the afterlife in fabulous style. The problem was he just didn't have enough money yet. He was rich, to be sure – but not rich enough to sustain himself throughout the long, untold aeons he might end up spending in the underworld.

His anxiety deepened as he walked among the tombstones in the wealthier section of the graveyard. Most were decorated with statues of the morbid demons who dwelt in the lands of the dead. Most commonly depicted was the Lady of the Scythe, a terrible and beautiful figure who stood with her eponymous weapon raised above her head. She was always shown naked, save for a belt from which tiny human beings hung on hooks like the strips of a revealing leather skirt. Her statues were smeared with ritual ashes, for her true physical body was said to have congealed from the countless cremains of a gigantic funeral pyre.

It was demons like her, Narseh had been told, whom he would have to bribe in order to secure safe passage and fine accommodation in the underworld. Because the underworld, apparently, was much like the realm of the living – a chaotic, greedy place in which there were all sorts of people who needed to be bribed. Local warlords, ferrymen, demons – the list was endless! Who knew how much money they'd ask for? If Narseh wasn't careful, he'd end up spending most of his resources just paying them off. And if he didn't accumulate enough capital before that fateful day, he might end up just another member of the deceased bourgeoisie, condemned to a droll eternity. Even worse – he might end up a pauper, with hardly two sticks of gold to rub together!

The very thought was almost enough to make him tear out his beard in terror. He had to secure his great nest egg before it was too late. Feeling the presence of death all around him, standing in the shadow of the Lady's wicked scythe, he offered up a prayer to the Candle King.

'Oh great Candle King,' said Narseh. 'Please don't let me die yet. Don't snuff out my life – not until I'm fabulously rich! I'll garland your altars with gold if you just let me live until then!'

Narseh fell silent, waiting for some sign the Candle King had heard him. There came only the rustling of wind through graveside weeds. Narseh took that as a positive sign, and quelled his anxiety. Besides, he didn't have time to be worrying about mortality – he was here to make money.

With a renewed sense of purpose he strode through the cemetery, peering at the gravestones as he went, as though he were searching for a specific grave. In truth, he was searching for a funeral service he knew to be taking place that afternoon.

He came upon it soon enough. There, in the wealthiest section of the graveyard, was a freshly dug grave with casket in place. A small group of people stood gathered around it: a pair of dirty gravediggers, a rite master, and a middle-aged woman in luxurious attire. The latter was the wife and only heir of the dead man, one Kinevel Kruze. The widow sobbed, wiping her eyes with a handkerchief. Her grief was very fresh, for her husband had died only one day before. The speed of his burial might have seemed unusual in other lands, but here in the province of Hillshadow such practices were standard, for ancient tradition demanded the dead be inhumed within twenty-four hours, lest their souls grow attached to the landscape and torment the living.

Narseh knew all of these details from his careful research. Allow-

ing a brief and sinister smile to flash unseen across his lips, the slaver knelt before a random grave in close proximity to the funeral. Pre-
tending to pay his respects, he placed his bouquet of flowers on the
grave and composed his face into a sorrowful mask.

'Oh my dear long-lost cousin,' he said dramatically, before pausing
to scan the name of the deceased, which he hadn't yet looked at.

'Oh fuck,' he hissed.

The dead man's name was not 'Fuck,' of course; it was Paerulicent
Amberkance Perfleeticat the Third. A ridiculous name which Narseh
would now have to remember and recite in order to maintain his deception. He sighed, wishing he'd taken more time to scan the writing
on the tombstones.

Too late now, he thought, and continued to address the dead
stranger in tones both dramatic and doleful.

'Oh my dear long-lost cousin, Paerulicent Amberkance Perfleeticat
the Third. Such a tragedy I never got to know you. So sad we were separated by the wide Ozich Sea. Still, I'm glad I can offer you these flowers. Perhaps they'll bring you some comfort, down there in the underworld...'

'Though not for long,' he whispered. 'Since I'm going to steal them
right back!'

Narseh chuckled under his breath, then wondered again about the
strange economics of the Underworld. Would the dead Paerulicent receive the bouquet in the afterlife, only for the flowers to vanish from
his hands the moment they were stolen back from the grave? Or would
they remain with him forever, transfigured into roses for the dead?

The wailing of the widow roused Narseh from his musings. Her
cries were followed by the droning of the rite master as he called upon
the great cosmic demons to please watch over the deceased – and to
please refrain from eating his soul. Soon the gravediggers were shovel-
ling earth atop the casket while the still-weeping widow was consoled
by the celebrant. One by one the clods fell, until the grave was filled

with wet, bulging dirt. The diggers tamped it down with the backs of their spades, then bowed to the widow and departed in silence. For a time she remained there, wiping her tears and peering at the grave, till the rite master placed a comforting hand upon her shoulder and led her away toward the cemetery gates.

Narseh remained on his knees, waiting, feeling a pulse of excitement within.

The moment is at hand!

No sooner had those thoughts passed through his head than a muffled sound arose from the ground, as of someone beating a fist against the sealed coffin lid.

Chapter 2: The Second Death

Narseh raced to the freshly-filled grave and fell to his knees beside it. Gritting his teeth, he plunged his manicured hands into the soil, clawing it towards him.

How utterly repulsive, he thought. Not only was he pawing at the worm-laden soil of a grave, even worse – he was performing manual labour!

Such work was for underlings and slaves, not a well-bred merchant such as he. And yet, for his deception to work, he would have to get his hands dirty – at least a little. He swallowed his pride, thinking of the wealth he would receive if all went to plan. The thoughts washed away his unease. For Narseh the slaver would swim through a sewer if a pile of gleaming gold were at the end of it.

He continued to dig, while the muted sound of hammering continued to arise from below, sounding more and more desperate with each passing moment.

'Help!' shouted Narseh. 'Somebody help!'

The two gravediggers rushed into view, still carrying their shovels.

'Hey!' shouted one of them. 'What's all this carrying on?'

'Someone's alive down there,' said Narseh. 'Listen!'

Narseh suspended his digging, while the gravediggers bent their dirty ears toward the sounds from below. Loose soil quivered as the body in the casket beat upon the lid.

'Butcher's balls!' shouted one of the gravediggers, while the other remained frozen in shock.

'Start digging you idiots,' shouted Narseh, 'before the poor man runs out of air!'

The gravediggers hefted their spades and dug like madmen. Narseh stepped back, cleaning his hands with a silken kerchief, avoiding the soil as it flew from their shovels. Messy mounds of earth rose up beside the grave, while the thudding from the casket grew louder and louder, accompanied by terrified cries from within. The diggers worked harder as they heard those fearful shouts, sweating and grunting from their efforts, till their shovels slammed hard against the coffin's naked timber. Tossing their shovels by the graveside, they knelt in the pit and pried off the lid.

The figure within was bloated and pale; from his flesh came a whiff of decay. He sat up at once, panting, glancing around.

'It's about bloody time,' he said. 'I very nearly died in there!'

'We thought you *were* dead,' said one of the gravediggers. 'That's why we buried you! If this man over here hadn't heard you...' he gestured to Narseh, who stood at the edge of the grave looking down.

'So this is my saviour,' said the man in the casket. 'Help me up, will you?'

He reached out with a pale, puffy hand. Narseh knelt and helped him out of the grave, feeling the hackles on his neck stiffen as he did so. Touching that flesh was even worse than touching the grave dirt – even worse than his short stint of manual labour! And yet, it was a necessary sacrifice for the riches to come.

Finally the dead man stood up beside the grave, shooting Narseh a gratified smile.

'Thank you, kind sir,' he said. 'I'm not sure I can ever repay you, but I'm going to try all the same. If it wasn't for you, I'd have died in that horrible hole!'

'Actually,' said Narseh, gesturing to the gravediggers with feigned humility, 'it was these two men here who did most of the work...'

'I'd say that's the least they could have done,' said the dead man, 'since they're the ones who buried me alive in the first place!' He shot them a disdainful glare. 'Absolute negligence! You're lucky I'm not a vindictive man, or I'd have both of you fired, and brought up on criminal charges!'

'Sorry, sir,' said one of the gravediggers. 'But everyone said you were dead. They even had a funeral. Your wife was here, weeping by your graveside just minutes ago!'

'Well, I'd say it's high time we set the record straight, wouldn't you? Come on, take me to the town. I need to see the magistrate about this alleged death of mine! While I'm there, I'll arrange for my saviour here to get his just reward.'

'Yes sir,' said the gravediggers. 'Right away, sir!'

They ran off to retrieve a vehicle, leaving Narseh and the dead man in silence. The dead man shot Narseh a wink; Narseh winked back, then resumed his humble and innocent façade.

Soon the gravediggers returned in a mule-driven wagon. Narseh and the dead man climbed into the wagon bed and sat amidst the clinging smell of grave dirt. One of the diggers whipped the reins, driving the wagon through the cemetery gates and onto the dry earthen road which led to the town of Blackheart's Crossing. Parked by the highway were Narseh's own vehicles, a trio of luxurious coaches with black steeds in harnesses of bronze-studded leather. Slaves sat in the drivers' seats, waiting for their master's command. Narseh bid them to follow, and they lashed the reins, pursuing the wagon in a haze of rising dust.

It didn't take them long to reach the town. The place was a colony, built on conquered soil by the Republic of Kurolow. Like many such places it had been built to a formula, with a plaza in the centre surrounded by governmental buildings.

Narseh glanced at the towering structures dismissively. The town was not as shabby as others in this part of the world, but it could hardly compare with the grandeur of Alhazred, the place of his birth, where the towers of the Seven Sultans shone like jewels in the night, and plumes of rainbow fire danced through the deserts at dusk, smokeless and whirling on the sultry desert winds.

The vehicles stopped before the courthouse, and the dead man leapt from the wagon.

'Come on,' he said. 'Let's get this matter sorted. I don't much like being legally dead!'

Narseh and the gravediggers followed the dead man as he rushed into the courthouse past a pair of armed guards who looked quite surprised to see him. The guards followed after, and soon the whole group emerged into a large stone courtroom where a trio of magistrates were presiding over a trial. The trial was evidently not a grand matter; a scattering of spectators dotted the pews, and a solitary defendant stood with a hang-dog look in the desolate space before the judges' bench.

'Mister Amansovis,' said one of the magistrates. 'I hereby find you guilty of –'

The judge froze mid-sentence as the dead man rushed into the hall.

'Kruze?' said the judge with a look of surprise. 'Is that you?'

'It most certainly is!' snapped the dead man.

'But you're supposed to be dead!'

'I know. That's why I'm here!'

The gobsmacked magistrates glanced at one another, while the people in the pews began to whisper excitedly.

'Kruze is back!' they said.

'I thought he was dead?'

'We should've been so lucky!'

Kinevel Kruze had been a well-known member of the town, but not a well-liked one. His extravagant wealth had been equalled only by his hateful disposition. By his own stern request – and to the sorrow of none – the general public had been banned from attending his funeral. Presently he strode into the space before the judges, while Narseh and the gravediggers followed behind.

'I'm here to have my death certificate nullified!' snapped the dead man.

'Indeed,' said the judges. 'But we're rather in the middle of something...'

Kruze shot a glance at the defendant with the hang-dog look.

'In the middle of what?' he snapped. 'The piddling trial of some peasant cattle molester? By the dead gods below, I've come back from being buried alive!'

The judges glanced at one another, and nodded.

'Very well,' said the chief magistrate. 'In light of this incredible occurrence, I'm going to postpone the matter of the People Versus Amansovis, and open the court to this more important matter. Mister Kruze, please tell us the tale of your astonishing return from the grave.'

The bailiffs dragged away the distressed-looking Amansovis, while the dead man addressed the assembly.

'I will tell you my tale. But all I can tell you is that which I remember clearly. Yesterday – if indeed it really was yesterday, for the passage of time is somewhat muddy for me at the moment – I remember taking ill, and wanting to lie down. Then came a period of interminable blackness, as if some deep and mighty sleep had overcome me. The next thing I knew I was waking in darkness, surrounded by the stench of the grave, bounded by the timbers of a coffin sealed with nails. Filth sifted down upon my head through the splits in the timbers. I could hear the very worms crawling in the earth! I tried to break my way out of the casket, but the space was so confining I could barely move my arms. All I could do was bash my fists against the lid!'

He held up his hands, showing the scratches on his pale and puffy flesh. The audience, riveted, listened in amazement as the dead man continued.

'I screamed as loud as I could, for I fancied I could already feel the stagnant air beginning to run out. I'd begun to give up hope, when suddenly I heard a voice calling down through the earth, muffled by the dirt, but there all the same. It was the voice of that man there – that man, my saviour!'

The dead man whirled and pointed at Narseh.

'That man took note of my plight. That man dug the earth with his own noble hands. That man summoned these two moronic gravediggers from their bout of lazy drinking, and forced them to unearth me from the grave in which they had mistakenly laid me. If it wasn't for him, I'd be doomed. If it wasn't for him, I'd be worm-food. Saviour, please – tell me your name!'

'My name is Narseh Az-Pinah, from the land of Alhazred.'

The three judges glanced at one another, then turned to the witnesses.

'Is this true?' asked the chief magistrate.

'Yes, Your Honour,' said Narseh, affecting a humble demeanour.

'Yes, Your Honour,' said one of the gravediggers. 'Except that we weren't off drinking when it happened. We were starting to dig another grave...'

'A likely story,' hissed the dead man.

Ignoring both Kruze and the diggers, the judge turned to Narseh.

'It seems you're quite the hero, mister Az-Pinah. But tell me if you please, just what was a foreigner like you doing in a graveyard, here in Blackheart's Crossing?'

'Well,' said Narseh, 'recently I've been doing a bit of genealogical research, you see, during which time I discovered that a branch of my family hailed from this area. Being a man of some modest means, and dedicated above all to honouring the spirits of my poor departed kin, I undertook a mission to visit their places of rest, so I might supply them with gifts to enrich them in the afterlife. I was visiting just such a grave when I heard mister Kruze here struggling in his coffin...' Narseh put his hand on his heart, endeavouring to look as righteous as possible.

'Your familial piety is clearly to be commended, Mister Az-Pinah,' said the judge. 'But who, may I ask, was this long-lost relative of yours?'

Narseh paused, struggling to recall the ridiculous name from the grave he had randomly chosen. Panic rose within his breast as he suffered a bout of sudden mental blankness. Try as he might he couldn't recall the name, though it seemed to linger torturously on the edge of his thoughts. Seconds ticked by. He felt the scrutinizing gazes of all three judges fixed keenly upon him. A solitary droplet of sweat began to crawl down his forehead, and the room seemed somehow hotter. His entire precious scheme – perhaps even his liberty, his life – was now hanging by a thread of stubborn memory.

Fuck! he thought. *Curse your stupid name, Paerulicent Amberkance Perfleeticat the Third!*

With a sense of relief he composed himself, and repeated the name out loud for the judges to hear.

'You're sure he's a relative of yours?' asked one of the magistrates.

'Quite sure,' said Narseh. 'Although, to be fair, many of the records I've consulted are mouldering from age, as well as being filled with scribal errors. Still, I'd much rather pay my respects to a foreigner by accident, than miss out on honouring my very own kin through an excess of scholarly caution.'

'Well said,' said the dead man. 'Well said indeed. Truly you're a man of great character! Which is why I'd like to amend my will at once. Honoured judges, let the record state that Mister Narseh Az-Pinah of Alhazred is to receive half of my estate when I die!' A collective gasp rose up from the audience, while the dead man continued. 'And the other half is to be given to this fair town!'

A gasp of total shock rose up from the spectators. Could Kinevel Kruze, the notoriously miserly misanthrope, really be bequeathing his wealth to the people he'd treated with contempt for so long? The dead man strolled around, gesturing grandly.

'My brush with the grave has taught me a valuable lesson,' he said. 'When I was lying down there in the cold, sodden earth, feeling the dust of dead bodies defiling my lungs, I realized what a rotten human being I've been all these years. I want to make up for it. I want to give something back!'

'That's a very noble sentiment,' said the judge. 'But are you sure about all this? What about your wife?'

'Forget that stupid cow,' snapped the dead man. 'She's the one who buried me alive in the first place! I don't want to give her a crumb, the ungrateful bitch. No, my money shall go to Mister Az-Pinah, and to the town of Blackheart's Crossing.'

'I beg you to reconsider,' said Narseh. 'Surely your poor wife should be forgiven –'

'No!' snapped the dead man. 'I'll hear no argument. My mind's made up!'

Narseh fell silent. The magistrates glanced at one another, and shrugged. They didn't want to argue too strongly – not when the dead man was trying to enrich their own coffers.

'Very well,' said the chief judge. 'Let the record show that Kinevel Kruze is alive, and that his estate upon his *actual* death shall be split equally between Mister Narseh Az-Pinah of Alhazred, and the town of Blackheart's Crossing.'

The scribe wrote the judgement in a ledger. No sooner had he done so than the dead man put a hand to his chest, let out a terrible groan, and fell to the floor with an echoing CRASH!

A bailiff rushed to check the dead man's breathing and pulse. With a look of alarm he turned to the judges. 'He's stone dead!'

Another gasp rose up from the audience.

'Poor man,' said Narseh. 'The strain of being buried alive must have killed him in the end.' He paused, glancing slyly at the magistrates. 'Still, I trust the court will honour his final request?'

Narseh grinned as his slaves loaded the last of Kruze's loot into the back of a carriage. Barely a week had gone by since Kinevel Kruze's second death, and already his estate had been liquidated, with half of the proceeds going to Narseh and the rest to the town's local government. Kinevel's widow had complained quite a lot in the interim, of course, but the judges hadn't listened.

Still smiling, Narseh climbed into the coach and strode between the stacked-up crates of gold, tapestries, and jewels. Beyond the crates was a door leading to a secret compartment, cunningly concealed amidst the cabin's baroque decor. After glancing around to make sure no one was watching, Narseh opened the door by use of a secret lever, then slipped inside, sealing the entrance behind him. There, sitting in the glimmer of a feeble lantern, was his girlfriend Wena.

Wena's emerald eyes stared up at him brightly. She hailed from the land of the necromancers, but had been banished by her brethren before being taught all of their magickal arts. Nevertheless she had managed to learn a few sorcerous tricks – including how to raise the dead into a semblance of life and take control of their bodies, just as she had done with Kinevel Kruze, who'd been dead as a doornail when they'd put him in the ground.

She rose up at once, embracing Narseh tightly. She was dressed in a cloak made from strips of black mummy wrap. The fabric had been soaked in putrescence and dried in the sun. Dried effluvium clung to the stiffened strips of linen, some of which bristled from her shoulders like the plumage of a vulture. Steeped in the energies of death, the garment served as a focus for her sorcery. It also stank horribly, though Narseh was more or less used to that by now.

What he wasn't quite used to was the stench of her body. She'd been cooped up in the coach for a week now, concealed from prying eyes, lest the people of Blackheart's Crossing should notice her presence and thereby uncover Narseh's trickery. Her only direct contact with other people during this time had been when Narseh's slaves had tended to her needs under cover of darkness, bringing her food and emptying her chamber pots. Greeted with her now, Narseh found her unwashed aroma, combined with the foetid bouquet of her cloak, almost unbearable. He recoiled from her embrace, and Wena stepped back, looking wounded.

'You've left me alone all this time,' she hissed, 'and now you won't even touch me?'

'I'm sorry, my dear,' he said. 'It's just that you're so very...*stinky*.'

'How do you think *I* feel?' she whispered. 'I've been stuck in this bloody compartment for days!'

'I know, my dear,' he said. 'And I'm so very sorry. It must have been awful for you, alone in this closet by yourself. It was a grim time for me, that's for sure, sleeping by my lonesome in that expensive hotel across the street. But it had to be done, for the sake of the job. Here, come to me...'

With a loving air he smiled and embraced her, braving the stench. For a moment she was sullen and limp in his arms. Then she squeezed him back tightly, and looked into his eyes.

'How did I do?' she asked.

'You were marvellous,' said Narseh. 'Your performance as Kinevel Kruze was amazing. Our job here is done, and we'll soon be away.'

She smiled and pulled him down for a kiss. Her breath was rank, but Narseh kissed her all the same. He had to keep her happy, after all – she was the key to his current success. And somewhere in his black soul was a spark of affection, like a crack in the facets of an ebony sapphire.

'What now?' she asked, when they finally broke off the kiss.

'First, I think we need to take you to a place where you can bathe, my dear,' he said, wrinkling his nose in an exaggerated manner.

Wena giggled in his arms.

'Then,' he said with a smile, '*then* we'll be off someplace else, to find another dead man to fleece!'

Wena frowned. 'I'm not staying in the coach this time, Narseh.'

'That's okay, my dove. We'll find a way to have you stay with me this time, I promise.'

Her frown began to soften, but only a little. 'Are you sure we should do this again, quite so soon?'

'Indeed, my dear. This scam worked a treat! We only made one minor mistake.'

'What's that?'

'We shouldn't have given any money to the state. We should've seized it all!'

'But giving that money to the council got them playing on our side!'

'I know,' he said. 'Believe me, I know. You should have seen the greed flashing through the eyes of those judges...!'

It was almost like looking in a mirror, he thought. Then he added: 'Still, it's not really fair they should reap the rewards of our labour, now is it? After all, *we're* the ones bringing back the bodies. They're just sitting on their arses.'

'But if the magistrates don't support our case, then we'll end up with nothing! What if the dead man's heirs should contest the new will? What if we have to go through a trial? The longer we get stuck in some town, fighting in court, the greater the chance they'll uncover the trick!'

'You worry too much, my sweet,' he said, stroking her cheek. 'This scheme is foolproof. Nothing can go wrong!'

Wena smiled back and stayed silent, even while the sound of alarm bells clanged in her head.

Chapter 3: The Hashishan

The hashishan flitted like a shadow through the tunnels of the derelict sewer system. The place was as dry and as dusty as a tomb. Very few people even knew of its existence, though it ran beneath the streets of the town like veins beneath the skin of a cadaver.

Moving by the light of a solitary taper, the hashishan spied his destination up ahead: a timber ladder ascending to a trapdoor. The bricks around the trapdoor, though pitted and old, were not yet as weathered as those which surrounded them, suggesting the door had been built many decades or centuries after the sewer itself had first been completed.

The hashishan stopped a few feet short of the ladder. He placed the taper in his teeth and removed a pipe from his pocket. The pipe was a luxurious piece, its ebony surface engraved with cavorting demons whose bodies seemed to be congealing from stylized billows of smoke. The most conspicuous figure of all was that of Soaefoth, the demon sloth himself, in whose perennially stoned and sleepy eyes lurked glimmers of eldritch might and ancient deicide.

The hashishan gazed at the familiar image for a moment, then placed the pipe between his thighs as he removed from his cloak a small leather pouch from which issued a moist and minty aroma. The smell grew stronger as he opened the pouch to reveal a quarter-ounce of black and resinous weed. He sniffed the weed with delight, then stuffed a single bud into the pipe before returning the pouch to his pocket. Taking the taper from betwixt his teeth and placing the pipe to his lips, he fired up the bud and began to inhale. The taper's flame dove into the bowl, plunging the tunnel into almost total darkness. The bud's outer surface flickered and flared like the skin of a meteor skimming the heavens. Smoke tendrils stretched through the filter and into the hashishan's well-trained lungs, where they coiled and sat, soaking deep into the scarred airways, till at last their dregs were exhaled in a roiling plume which looked almost solid in the shadows of the sewer.

Sweet euphoria cradled the hashishan's head. The black weed was strong. It might have made another man sleepy or lazy, but the hashishan had been trained to use the narcotic differently. Focusing his mind through the haze, he entered a self-induced trance.

Much of his psyche grew dormant. His jabbering thoughts, his preoccupations, his fears, even his present anxiety as he stood on the cusp of his murderous mission – all these things and more melted away into the dark recesses of his consciousness, until all he felt was an uncanny sense of his immediate surroundings.

The dry air of the sewer felt suddenly cooler and more tangible. He could feel its subtle caress on his skin with immaculate precision, as if each and every hair on his body were a separate sensory organ attuned to the atmosphere around him. He seemed to depart from the prosaic flow of ordinary space and time, becoming a stranger to himself, a stranger in a new, weird world where anything could happen, and where *he* could do anything – he could steal, he could sneak, he could murder, all with a smooth and disassociated ease.

Replacing the pipe in his pocket and the taper back betwixt his teeth he began to ascend the wooden ladder. Gingerly he did so, for the frame and the rungs were old and rotting. They creaked with protest even from the burden of his slender weight.

Soon he reached the trapdoor and carefully began to push it upwards. The metal felt scabrous with rust. The hinges creaked softly. Flakes of iron fell upon his face. Holding the trapdoor upraised, he slipped through the crack before closing the portal softly behind him.

The hashishan had emerged into a cramped, dusty corridor. Looking down, he saw the remains of the chain and padlock that had once secured the trapdoor, lying rusted and broken with age. They seemed to have lain undisturbed for a very long time. So far, everything his employers had told him was accurate. Thanks to them, he knew he was now above ground, in a secret passage concealed within the villa of the man he'd come to murder.

Onwards he crept down the corridor. Soon he arrived at a door on the left. Feeling calm but alert he snuffed out the taper, opened the door, and stepped into silvery shadows. He'd emerged exactly where his employers had told him he would – in the old miser's trophy room. Moonbeams filtered through a series of iron-barred windows, shedding their gleam on the pelts and severed heads which adorned the room. Here was a lion's pelt splayed on the ground; there was a rhino's head mounted on a wall, its horn adorned with intricate carvings; here was the body of a neonate white wyrm, its lamprey-like mouth fixed into a permanent gape by the taxidermist's art. All the pieces were immaculately clean, for the miser was not miserly at all when it came to the upkeep of his trophies and relics.

The hashishan crept from the room into the network of hallways beyond. The villa was opulent and massive, but mostly unpeopled, save for the miser and his small staff of servants, most of whom were presently sleeping. The miser had guards, but only a few of them. They talked loudly as they made their rounds, and their footfalls echoed ahead of them, allowing the hashishan to easily avoid them. Onwards he crept through the corridors, bypassing rooms filled with the harvest of avarice. There were luxurious bathrooms with large marble pools, chambers with silver and gold statues on display, and beautiful atriums inlaid with mosaics of jewels and precious stones.

Soon he arrived outside the old miser's study. The door was ajar, and the light of a fitful lantern spilled into the hallway, ruffling the shadows on the walls. The old man was up late pouring over his papers, just as the hashishan's employers had predicted.

The hashishan drew closer to the door. Now that he was so close to his goal, he could feel a sense of excitement and dread begin to bubble up from the depths of his mind, threatening to taint the perfection of his trance. He paused, focused his mind, and banished all emotion. Once again he felt nothing but crystalline awareness, mixed with his murderous imperative.

He peered through the doorway into the study. Seated at a desk inside was the miser himself, perusing his ledgers and books. The man's name was Muragar Zak. He was hoary but healthy in his age. An old man like that might live to be a hundred years old, hence why his embittered descendants had hired the hashishan. But Muragar's death had to look natural, or at least like an accident, otherwise suspicion might be cast upon them. Luckily the hashishan had means of making the death look prosaic. In his pocket, next to his pipe and his bag of weed, was a vial of potent venom milked from the fangs of a Thunian singing snake. A single droplet introduced into the bloodstream was enough to bring about an almost instant cardiac arrest.

The hashishan took out the vial, carefully unstoppered the cap, and dipped a small needle into the acrid-smelling liquid within. His weapon was ready; now all he had to do was administer the sting. But how to get close? He couldn't cross the room without exposing himself to the risk of being seen. If the old man caught a glimpse of him – even for a moment – he might just have enough time to sound the alarm before the hashishan closed the distance. And even if the old man was unable to summon his guards, he could still try to fight back against the intruder. The hashishan was confident he could easily triumph in any such conflict, but that wasn't the problem. Any scuffle, no matter how brief or one-sided, could result in tell-tale bruises or marks being left on the old miser's body, making the death look suspicious. No, he had to get close by some other means. There was nothing else for it – he'd have to use the Demon Arts of Death.

He focused his mind, picturing the demonic runes his master had taught him. Some practitioners of the Demon Arts – like the knights of the Order of Chaos – carved the runes on their weapons, and made use of them that way. The hashishan often laughed when he thought about such amateurs. For his master had taught him to internalize the power of the runes completely. Now they were so much a part of the hashishan that they seemed to be branded on his soul, or enshrined in the palace of his mind, like frescoes in cerebral halls.

He pictured the full sequence of runes he needed, then stepped into a thick patch of darkness on the wall. The darkness gave way like cool air. He found himself walking in a murky netherworld, surrounded by infinite shadows. The air was almost unbearably cold. The overlapping shadows contorted, taking on the likeness of stupefying tapestries, each covered with an intricate pattern. The hashishan experienced a moment of terrible vertigo. It felt as if each fleeting, shadowy pattern were tugging at him, trying to pull him toward it. Each pattern, he knew, was a door to a corresponding pocket of darkness which existed somewhere in the universe. Many were the doors which might lead to a place of certain doom, or to some distant corner of the fathomless cosmos, where a person could wander till death, lost and alone. In truth, there was only one path he wanted, one path he'd trained his bloodshot eyes on since traversing the breach into the shadowverse. He followed that path –

And crawled out into the shadows beneath the miser's desk. His body trembled from the residual coldness of the realm he had traversed, and tiny icicles clung to his clothing. Too much longer in the shadowverse and he would have risked death from exposure. Only powerful beings like cosmic demons could travel those highways of darkness for any length of time, for their bodies were immune to the cold and their minds were resistant to the maddening patterns of the myriad shadow gates. As for the hashishan, he was only a mortal. He hunched into a ball, reeling from the shock of his journey. He clenched his jaw to stop his teeth from chattering, and fought to control his quaking limbs. The miser's legs were just inches away, close enough to make the kill – and yet his quivering hand could barely keep a hold on the poison-tipped needle.

The miser stirred in his chair, as if somehow aware that something was wrong. There was no more time for the hashishan to marshal his strength. With trembling hand the stabbed the needle towards the old man's naked foot. It struck between the toes. The miser's voice rose up in a cry –

But only for a moment. The rising sound died. The miser convulsed in his chair. The hashishan slipped out from under the desk and stood beside his victim. The old man was clutching at his heart with a white-knuckled hand. His eyes rolled back to the whites. He seized, then shook, then slumped onto the desk. Rivulets of ink spilled across his ledgers as his falling body overturned the inkpot.

The hashishan craned his ear. The villa was silent. He embedded the needle's poisoned tip into a cork, wrapped both up in leather, and carefully placed the resulting parcel into his pocket, planning to dispose of it later. He watched the miser's chest for movement, but it was utterly still. He took a small mirror from his pocket and held it to the miser's mouth, looking for any sign of breath escaping the lips. There was none. He checked the old man's radial artery for a pulse. There was none. He checked the carotid, and found nothing there either.

The miser was dead. Emerging partway from his narcotic trance, the hashishan permitted himself a satisfied smile. His work here was done. The old man had died of a heart attack, and no one would notice the venom in his veins, nor the tiny pinprick on his foot.

All that remained for the hashishan was the relatively simple task of escaping the villa without being seen. Then he'd simply have to lie low and wait until it was time to take payment for his services. Usually, he only took a job if at least half of the money was provided upfront. But this job was different. The miser's heirs, united in their murderous conspiracy, had offered the hashishan five times his normal fee. The only catch was that they couldn't afford to pay him until the old man's estate had been divided among them, for such was the miser's stinginess that all of them were presently living in poverty. The hashishan had accepted the arrangement without much complaint. For the amount being offered, he was happy to postpone his payday, at least for a little while. And should his employers – or anyone else – try to get between him and his fee, he'd simply kill them all, and take what was owed from their lifeless bodies.

Chapter 4: At Midday I'll Possess Your Corpse

'It's perfect!' said Narseh as he knelt before Wena in the coach's secret compartment. 'There's a funeral going on right now. I heard about it earlier, when I was taking my lunch in the town. The man was a rich old miser. He had himself a gigantic villa, all filled up with riches he'd been hoarding for years. His descendants haven't even got a crumb!' He paused, smiling mischievously. 'I bet they're excited. I bet they're looking forward to a great big payday. Well, sucks to be them – because we're gonna swoop in and take the whole lot!'

'Are you sure?' asked the necromancer. 'I mean, maybe we should only take half. Or two-thirds. They'll be a lot less likely to put up a fight, if we leave them with something...'

'Nonsense, my sweet. It's all or nothing!'

'But surely they'll fight it in court...'

'Let them fight,' he said. 'It won't do them any good. We'll make this one foolproof. This time I want you to make that corpse look as truly alive as you possibly can. Make his heart beat in his chest and his veins throb with blood. Convince them the dead man is of sound mind and body, and acting of his own free will. Then, and only then, will our benefactor "die" once again. Can you do that?'

'Yes,' she said. 'But – '

'No buts,' he said, pressing her lips shut with his finger. 'We're not at home to Mister Negative, my sweet. Besides, I have absolute confidence in you.' He smiled and gazed into her eyes, until Wena felt confident too. 'And now I must away to buy some flowers, and take up my position in the cemetery. Wait for the signal, then do as before.'

He rose, then stooped to give her a parting kiss on the mouth. Wena wrapped her arms around his shoulders, holding him close and kissing him fervently back. She reluctantly let go as she felt him pull away.

'Don't worry about a thing, my dear,' he said. 'I believe in you. We're going to get all of that money. And when we're done, we'll take a break for a while and just be together, you and me.'

'You promise?'

'I promise,' he said.

They shared a warm smile, and Narseh slipped from the compartment, pulling the door closed behind him. Wena sat alone in the light of a feeble red lantern, waiting. For a time the smile remained on her lips. His presence and his words had melted her misgivings, filling her with confidence. But now that he was gone, doubts began to creep into her mind once again, doubts that had plagued her on and off since the two had first met.

Was Narseh just using her, stringing her along for the sake of her necromantic arts? Did he even really love her at all? He told her he did, but she couldn't be sure. Perhaps all he really loved was money, and the process of acquiring it. He kept dragging her into these criminal schemes. Often she tried to protest, but somehow he always knew just what to say to get her back onboard. Sometimes she felt as though she were trapped in his orbit, like the moon around the earth, bound by the power of his words and the gravity of his will.

Perhaps she was weak. Perhaps she was merely in love. His smile made her melt; his caresses got her wet. And she couldn't deny that their crimes were often exciting, not to mention rewarding. And yet, there was a part of her psyche that screamed out in protest. A part that disliked being trapped in his orbit. A part of her, perhaps, that even resented her lover. It was silent when Narseh was near, as if smothered or negated by the pleasure of his company. But when he was gone – as he was at that moment – she felt that rebelliousness well up inside her, like the pangs of a stomach ache.

Maybe our relationship is poisoned? she wondered, and not for the first time.

Then she thought of his words, about his pledge that they would both take a break once this job was completed. She hoped it was true. She longed for a brief respite from all this scheming, scamming, and stealing. An oasis of pleasure in a desert of greed, where there would only be love and its joyful expression.

A knock on the door of the compartment jarred her from her thoughts. Narseh's slaves had been watching the cemetery gates, waiting for the funeral to finish and the mourners to depart. Their knocking was her cue to take possession of the corpse!

Wena closed her eyes and began to meditate. With practiced ease her psyche slipped loose from her physical body and hovered invisibly above it. Some sorcerers could travel almost anywhere like that – across the starry void, between dimensional membranes, even through the stubborn mists of time. But being the soul of a necromancer, Wena's astral spirit could only travel like a magnet drawn toward the energies of death.

Wena's astral form flew from the coach toward the cemetery. Like a ghost she passed through the bodies of mourners emerging from the gates. Some of them flinched or recoiled, as if a chill wind had suddenly caressed them. Wena sensed them from the inside as her astral form briefly occupied the same space as their internal organs. Their insides were opaque to her sight, but she could feel their beating hearts, their breathing lungs, the warmth of the blood as it pulsed through arteries and veins. Her essence fled from such things, conditioned as it was to seek the miasma of the dead.

Wena's essence flew through the graveyard like a bird of prey. Each time she flew above a grave she felt herself drawn towards the worm-eaten flesh of the body below. Her astral form, long tainted by the art of necromancy, instinctively longed to anchor itself in the flesh and bones of the dead.

Resisting the pull of each cadaver, Wena flew on towards her true target. Soon she saw Narseh ahead, kneeling before a grave with a bouquet of flowers in hand. She passed through his flesh, briefly wondering if she could somehow sense the spark of his love for her somewhere within him. All she felt was the pulse of his blood, quickened by the thrill of the score that awaited.

A dozen feet from Narseh lay the miser's fresh grave. Wena flew down into the soil and felt the strong pull of the corpse, which due to its freshness was teeming with necromantic energy.

Wena let her soul sink into the corpse and settle into place. She felt the dead flesh around her psyche like a suit. It teemed with newborn rot. The miser's corpse had only just begun to break down. In a few more days it would be bloated with gases, parts of it swollen like pieces of nightmare fruit. The stench would be appalling. For now, however, it could still be mistaken for the body of a living man – especially with a little help from Wena's magick.

She quickly went to work arresting the process of decay. Perhaps if she had studied harder during her abortive stint at necromancy school she would have discovered the traces of venom still lingering in the corpse's veins, and would have known the old miser was a victim of foul play. Instead she noticed nothing untoward, and simply completed her spell, stalling the process of decomposition and imbuing the corpse with an illusory semblance of life.

'Help!' she shouted in the voice of the dead man, as she hammered with his fists against the lid of the coffin.

Chapter 5: Return of the Miser

'Woo-hoo!' shouted Ninia Zak, granddaughter of Muragar Zak. 'The old bastard's dead!'

She raised her goblet in a toast. The rest of the heirs toasted back. There was Ninia's younger brother, Gerebrah Zak; her even younger brother, Dalmion Zak; her younger sister, Soronia Zak; and her two cousins, Yellen Zak and Merekin Zak. Together they represented all the living adult members of the Zak family. They also represented the members of a criminal conspiracy responsible for Muragar's assassination at the hands of the hashishan. Ninia was the ringleader. It was she who had convinced the other five to go along with the plan. She was thirty years old, and tired of being poor. Why should the whole family languish in poverty while Muragar sat fat atop a giant heap of silver and gold? Ninia's children deserved better. They all deserved better.

It hadn't taken much work to get the others to go along with her plan. And so here they were, shouting with joy and clinking their goblets. Not that the goblets made an actual clinking sound. The vessels were cheap timber cups which sometimes left splinters in Ninia's mouth. It was true – she and her co-conspirators couldn't even afford decent tableware!

But soon that would all change. Now that the old man was dead, it was only a matter of time until his estate was divided amongst them. Then they would drink from vessels of gold in the old miser's villa, in which they would dwell like a true family, and that vast edifice, which for so long had been a realm of silent avarice, would transform into a place of laughter and life. It was a dream come true! And Ninia had made it come true, through her very own boldness and firm resolution.

She couldn't be happier. She smiled at her family, and they smiled back.

The moment was shattered by a rapping at the door. Ninia's younger brother Gerebrah opened it, revealing a neighbour who stood panting on the steps as though he'd been jogging. His eyes were wide with amazement.

'You won't believe it,' he said. 'Your grandfather's alive. Someone dug him up from the grave. He's over in the courthouse right now!'

Silence fell over the room as the conspirators traded looks of shock and apprehension.

'Is this some sick joke?' asked Ninia. 'Because it isn't very funny!'

'I'm not joking!' said the neighbour. 'Come see for yourself if you don't believe me!'

The Zaks traded wary glances, then headed off at once to the courthouse, leaving their children at home. It took them a while to arrive, for their ramshackle houses were located in a poor part of town far from the majestic buildings of state. When they finally rushed through the doors of the courthouse, all of them froze in amazement. There, before the judges, was the rotten old miser himself, in the process of addressing the court. Standing beside him was a stranger with a turban and a crescent-shaped beard. Judging by his clothes, Ninia guessed the stranger must have hailed from Alhazred, the land of smokeless fire. And yet, Ninia had greater things to worry about than this man's provenance. Her grandfather seemed to be alive! Could it be the hashishan had fouled up the job? No, that seemed impossible. Ninia had seen Muragar's body for herself. She'd even checked his pulse. He'd been dead as a doornail! Bewildered, she watched the dead man raise his hand and continue to address the court.

'And so I,' said the dead man, 'Muragar Zak, being of sound mind and body, and under no compulsion whatsoever, hereby bequeath all my worldly positions, at the time of my death, to my noble friend and saviour, Mister Narseh Az-Pinah.'

The spectators whispered in amazement.

'What the FUCK!' shouted Ninia, unable to control herself.

The dead man glanced at her, then turned to the judges.

'Your Honour, can you please tell this woman to be quiet?'

The judges peered back at him with worried expressions.

'Mister Zak,' said one of them, 'surely you recognise your very own granddaughter?'

Oh shit, thought Wena as she peered through the dead man's eyes at the group of shocked strangers in the doorway. *The guy's family's here – and I don't know their names, or anything about them! If I'm not careful, I could ruin it all.*

She glanced at Narseh, catching a glimmer of concern in his eyes. She knew she had to fix this – fast.

'I see no family before me!' yelled Wena in a voice not her own. 'This bunch of ingrates are the ones who sought to bury me alive. From now on I shan't speak their names, nor even look at them at all if I can help it. They're dead to me, the lot of them!'

Murmurs of surprise spread through the courtroom, while Narseh tried to hide a creeping smile.

'And now,' said the dead man, 'I'd like to get this matter over with conclusively. I invite any physician in attendance to check both my physical and mental health at once. I want there to be no doubt whatsoever in the eyes of the court that my state of mind is perfectly sound, and that my brush with death has only made me stronger in will.'

The judges nodded. Soon a physician arrived and escorted the dead man to an antechamber. Ninia Zak waited in agonized suspense. Her mind whirled with confusion. How was this possible? She'd seen the miser's corpse just yesterday. And yet here he was, right before her eyes, talking, walking, and breathing.

Is it some kind of sorcery? she wondered. *Or is the old man just too mean to die? Maybe something went wrong with the assassin's poison. Maybe it just made him look dead for a while!*

Dozens of possible scenarios flitted through Ninia's mind. And yet, what occupied her thoughts most of all was the prospect of losing all that money. She could almost *feel* all that cash slipping through her fingers like ephemeral sand. Fervently she hoped the old man would somehow fail the physician's exam.

Let him be pronounced a lunatic, she thought. *Let the whole thing be revealed as a sorcerer's scam! For surely no sorcerer could fool a learned physician...*

While Ninia fretted, Wena sat in the antechamber, dressed in the flesh of the dead man, undergoing a battery of tests. First the physician asked her a series of general knowledge questions, such as what year it was, who the reigning archon was, what important events had occurred in the region, and so on. Wena passed the test with flying colours. She was glad he hadn't asked more specific or localized questions, or indeed any questions about the dead man himself, about whom she knew very little. Then he showed her pictures of animals and objects, asking her to name them. She aced that test too. So far, it was child's play.

After that came the physical exam, which was far more difficult. Wena had to pump stagnant blood through the dead man's vessels to simulate a heartbeat. She had to suck breath into his stiffened airways, then pump it back out to simulate his breathing. She had to warm his cold flesh, moisten his dry lips, banish the burgeoning stench of decay. The effort was draining – but in the end, it paid off.

'Muragar Zak is of sound mind and body,' said the physician as they returned to the courtroom.

Ninia Zak felt her heart sink.

'In that case,' said the senior judge, 'I have no choice but to endorse Zak's new living testament. Let the record bear witness!'

The courtroom scribe entered the decree. No sooner had he done so than Muragar Zak grasped his chest, screamed, and hit the floor with a CRASH!

The physician sped to the body, checking it for signs of life. A few moments later he looked up and shook his head.

'He's dead, Your Honour,' he said.

The spectators gasped. So did Ninia.

'Such a tragedy,' said Narseh. 'The stress of being buried alive must have killed him in the end. Still, I trust the court will honour his request. Seeing as how he was of sound mind and body...'

'No way!' shouted Ninia, rushing to the front of the court with the rest of her relatives. 'We're the family. It's only fair that we inherit! We'd like to contest the will.'

I knew this would happen, thought Wena as she lay on the floor, still cloaked in the dead man's flesh, peering through his fixed eyes.

Narseh turned to Ninia. 'My heart grieves for your loss, Mrs...'

'Ninia Zak,' she said.

'Mrs. Ninia Zak. Such a tragedy that you should lose your dear grandfather twice in one week. And, to be honest, I find his final testament somewhat unseemly. To deny one's own family their rightful inheritance, even for the heinous act of burying one's body alive, seems overly punitive to my mind. Certainly *I*, given the choice, would never even dream to deny you your birthright. Indeed, for me, this unexpected offer of wealth feels much like a burden...'

'Then hand it over!' she said.

Narseh shook his head with an appearance of sadness. 'Would that I could. And yet, I fear that I must honour this man's most solemn request, regardless of my own feelings, lest I might anger his spirit in the underworld...'

I can't believe this shit! thought Ninia, glaring at Narseh. *Who is this bastard?!*

She turned to glare at the judges.

'You can't possibly do this,' she said. 'Even if grandfather *was* in his right mind – and I'm not really sure that he was – still, this request – this request is appalling! To give all that money to a stranger, to a foreigner, it's – it's unthinkable! It's against all the laws of tradition!'

'And yet that *is* what he asked for,' said Narseh. 'And who are we to defile a man's last living wishes on this earth?'

The judges motioned for silence, then whispered to each other. At length they turned back to the parties before them.

'Whilst it is true that Muragar Zak made this request of his own free will, it is indeed very irregular, and goes against precedent. Because of this, we would like to schedule a full and proper hearing, to take place next week. In the meantime, Muragar Zak's possessions will be held in trust by the state, until such time as this matter be resolved.'

Fuck, thought Narseh.

Yes! thought Ninia.

Narseh cleared his throat. 'A sage judgement, Your Honours,' he said. 'Your wisdom is truly commendable, and I shall abide by your ultimate decision, whatever it may be. And yet, there is one concession I might ask for...'

'Yes?' asked a judge.

'Well,' he said, 'it's just that I'm a man of modest means, you see.' Narseh held his hands together like a humble orphan begging for food. 'As you know, I'm currently on a sojourn to visit the graves of my many long-lost relatives. This endeavour, though dear to my heart, has unfortunately used up almost all of my wealth, so that all I have at present are the clothes on my back, some sundry possessions, a few dozen slaves, and the trio of coaches parked outside. Thusly I fear I can't afford to pay for any lodgings. If I'm to stay in this town throughout the course of this trial, I'd be forced to sleep in the back of a carriage, in stifling and humid confinement, which, as I'm sure you'll agree, is scarcely a fit place for any human being to reside in, and would certainly prove to be an unfair disadvantage when it came time for me to take part in the proceedings of this honourable court. And, since I'm assuming my opponents in this case all have their own stable lodgings...'

'What're you getting at, Mister Narseh?'

'Well,' he said. 'Might I be able to stay in the dead man's villa?'

Ninia gritted her teeth at the thought of this unctuous stranger staying in the home her family had built. It felt like desecration! Then she remembered the secret entrance she and her brothers had discovered while playing there as children. The same secret entrance the hashishan had so recently used – and which he could easily use again, should the need arise. A sinister smile flashed across her face, ever so briefly.

'The Zak family is happy for the stranger to stay at our villa,' she said.

The three judges, who had not yet finished their deliberations, shrugged at one another and granted her seemingly gracious request.

'Very well,' said one of them. 'Mister Az-Pinah will have use of the villa throughout the course of the trial until a final verdict is reached. But none of the objects therein may be disturbed. Is that clear?'

'I wouldn't dream of it,' said Narseh with his hand over his heart.

'Then this matter is adjourned for the moment. We shall proceed on the Ides of Iscariot!'

A few moments later, Ninia emerged from the courthouse with the rest of the Zaks. They watched as the man from Alhazred climbed into a fancy-looking coach and drove off towards the villa.

'What now, sis?' asked Gerebrah Zak.

'Now?' said Ninia. 'Now he have a talk with the hashishan!'

Chapter 6: Plans like Smoke

The hashishan sat on a rickety chair in Ninia's kitchen. Ninia and the rest of the conspirators were gathered around him in the cramped and dismal room. The hearth shed fitful light on their faces. They all looked anxious – save the hashishan, whose expression was tranquil. The smoke from his pipe hung thick in the air, for the windows and doors had all been sealed lest some neighbour should spy on the conspiracy. The smoke was potent; Ninia could already feel the beginnings of a second-hand high. She coughed into the crook of her arm, and wondered how the assassin could function with such a powerful narcotic in his system. Every time she'd seen him, he'd been smoking his pipe.

The guy must be high all day long, she thought. *He's probably got an incredible tolerance.*

So far he hadn't said much at all, and neither had they. Presently he peered at the Zaks, noting their anxious expressions. His bloodshot eyes were a startling blue.

'Is there a problem?' he asked.

'You bet there's a problem,' said Ninia. 'The man we hired you to kill wasn't dead!'

She launched into a hurried explanation of the afternoon's events – how her grandfather had apparently awoken in the grave, only to be rescued by a stranger from Alhazred, to whom he then bequeathed all his wealth, just before dropping dead in the middle of the courthouse.

'Most peculiar,' said the hashishan.

'No shit it's peculiar!' said Ninia.

'Still,' he said, after exhaling more smoke, 'there's no way your grandfather was alive.'

'But we saw it with our own eyes!' said Gerebrah Zak. 'Plus, I've heard of things happening like this before. People seem dead, but they're only asleep. Then later they wake up, sometimes even after they've been buried...'

'Impossible,' said the hashishan. 'Muragar was dead when I left him. And trust me, boy, I know. Death is my business.'

'Then how do you explain it?' asked Ninia.

'The only explanation is sorcery. As far as I know, there are only two types of beings capable of raising the dead like that. The first are cosmic demons. The second are the necromancers of Khem.'

'But this guy's not from Khem,' said Ninia. 'He's from Alhazred.'

'Then he must have an accomplice, or a patron, working in the shadows.'

'So you're saying he's a thief?' said Gerebrah. 'That this is all some kind of magickal scam?'

The hashishan nodded.

'Well then we have to expose them. Right?' said Gerebrah, glancing around.

Ninia shook her head. 'We're not going to expose them,' she said. 'We're going to kill them. These bastards have to pay for what they've done!' She turned to the assassin. 'They're staying in the villa right now. I want you to sneak back in there and slaughter them all, then make their bodies and their coaches disappear, along with some of grandfather's wealth. The judges will conclude that they were thieves who've fled in the night. Then grandfather's estate will be transferred back to us, and we can pay you what we owe.'

The hashishan took a long drag from his pipe as he considered her proposal.

'That's a lot of slaughter,' he said. 'It's going to cost you a lot – *quadruple* what you already owe.'

Ninia winced. That was a lot of money. And yet, it was nothing compared with the vastness of Muragar's fortune.

'You've got a deal,' she said, extending her hand.

The hashishan shook it, and smiled.

Narseh strode through the villa, peering at the wealth on display. Racks of embossed silver plate; trunks of gold and jewels; statues of marble, carnelian, and jade – the riches seemed endless. A pair of his most educated slaves followed him with ledgers, taking a detailed inventory of the villa's many treasures, along with their approximate value. So far the overall figure was very, very high.

Narseh turned to Wena, who'd been smuggled from the coach to the villa in the folds of a carpet.

'We've hit the jackpot, my sweet!' he said with a smile.

'Are you sure we should be celebrating yet?' she asked. 'There's still the court case to consider...'

'Bah!' said Narseh. 'There's no way the court will overturn the will completely. The best those wretched relatives can hope for is a percentage – half, at the most. And long before that can even happen, we'll gather up the best of the treasures and bury them outside the town, so we can dig them up later. Face it, my dear – no matter what happens, we'll be making a killing!'

He smiled at her again, and Wena smiled back, though her worries remained.

'But aren't you concerned at all?' she said. 'And don't you think it's odd that they agreed to us staying here so quickly? What if they're planning something rotten?'

Narseh scoffed again. 'You worry too much, my dear. Besides, even if they are planning something, what can they do? I've got slaves standing guard at every entrance. And you've got sentries of your own to watch over us – and your guards don't sleep.'

He gestured to the pair of undead servants who followed in the necromancer's wake. Their bodies had been dried in natron and wrapped in emerald linen which matched the hue of Wena's eyes. Their own eyes had been scooped out and replaced with polished onyx. Their organs had likewise been removed, replaced with a mixture of sawdust and dried roses, which covered their musty odour with a sweeter perfume. Each zombie wore a cloak, and carried a khopesh. Their presence was indeed a comfort to Wena, for they would never tire, never sleep, never shirk from duty so long as she lived, and they themselves could only be destroyed through total dismemberment. They were in many ways the perfect guardians. And yet, she still felt worried.

Narseh caught the look in her eyes and clasped her hands in his.

'Stop fretting, my sweet,' he said. 'Come on – let me show you the master bedroom!'

He led her through the halls. The zombies followed after, while the slaves stayed behind to continue the stocktake.

Soon they arrived at a sumptuous chamber. The marble walls were adorned with silken brocade which shimmered in the light of a crystal chandelier. In the centre of the room was a four-poster bed with velvet curtains and piles of plump cushions on a fat feather mattress. And yet the most breathtaking sight of all was the huge pile of treasure piled around the bed – stacks of polished gold, heaps of silver plate, and mounds of gemstones which gleamed in a dozen different colours.

'Beautiful, isn't it?' said Narseh. 'I had the slaves bring it here earlier. Of course it will all have to be taken out soon, and buried for safekeeping. Still, I thought it might be nice to recline amidst the fruits of our labours. Don't you?'

Wena glanced around, feeling a pulse of excitement at the sight of all that treasure. Perhaps Narseh's greed was infecting her? And yet, more than she wanted the gold she wanted *him*. She wanted his passion, however grudging and rare it seemed to be.

She kissed him on the lips. This time he did not recoil, as he had in the coach – for this time her body was washed and her stinking cloak was on a hangar by the villa's front door.

Soon they were lying on the silken bedsheets. Wena was naked save for her black wig. Narseh was completely naked. He'd even taken off his turban, allowing his dark locks to cascade down his shoulders and over his chest.

Wena eyed him hungrily. He might have been greedy, but he wasn't a glutton. His body was lean from his restless lifestyle. He lay on his back with his prick standing up. She grasped it, feeling the pulse of warm blood beneath the skin. His hand found her cunt and fingered her throbbing clit. Both of them were ready.

She straddled his lap, and was about to mount him face-to-face, when he took her by the waist and began gently turning her away.

'Face the other way, please,' he said. 'I want to see your peachy rump…'

Wena paused. She liked being able to look him in the eyes when they made love. But she also liked pleasing him, and he seemed so keen to get a look at her butt. She turned around to face the shuttered door, then guided him inside her, humming with delight as she felt him within. The exquisite shock of entry was a novelty that never grew old. Moaning she rode him, slowly at first, then faster and faster, feeling the pleasure build higher and higher.

Meanwhile Narseh lay with his head on the pillows, watching her move. She was slender and dark. Her butt was firm and taut, like a ripening peach. He gripped it with his hands and ran his fingers up her waist, caught up in the luxury of looking at her. She was so very beautiful. And yet…

And yet there was all of that treasure nearby. His gaze moved past her, taking in the sight of silver and gold. Lying on the bed, he couldn't see the floor, just piles of gleaming riches sprawling out toward the walls.

He imagined the bed was adrift on an ocean of wealth. He imagined the rocking of the bed was the gentle susurration of those gleaming, golden waves. He focused his eyes back on Wena; he focused his eyes back on the gold; then he unfocused them completely, so that Wena was a black silhouette backed by an ocean of riches. It seemed to be the best of both worlds, and he moaned with delight.

Wena moaned too. Her movements grew erratic as the climax shook her body. Narseh surrendered and exploded inside her. As the orgasm gripping him, his vision grew even more blurred, and for a moment Wena vanished from his gaze, her dark silhouette eclipsed by the gleam of the gold.

Afterwards they lay on the bed, drinking wine and eating sweets. Wena smiled at Narseh, flushed in the afterglow. Her worries were gone for the moment, silenced by an onslaught of pleasure. Just for a second, she felt like there was nothing that could possibly go wrong.

The hashishan lurked in the shadows of the trophy room, watching the doorway. He'd gained access to the villa using the same secret entrance as last time. But from here on it seemed this mission would be harder than the last one. The hallways were crawling with armed guards. Judging from their clothing they were slaves from Alhazred. Chattel, but deadly nonetheless. The hashishan had watched them for a while now, building up a picture of their movements and trying to estimate their numbers. They patrolled in pairs, strolling the corridors with irritating frequency. Presently two of them were passing through the hallway outside.

The hashishan reached for his blade – then stopped. Cutting them down would be easy enough, but these people were supposed to disappear into the night; there couldn't be bloodstains, not if he could help it. So what then? He could sneak up behind them, break the neck of one, then finish the other. But there might be a scuffle, or a scream. He couldn't have that either. He had to kill them both at once – silently, and bloodlessly. There was only one option: the Demon Arts of Death.

He crept into the hallway behind the strolling figures. At the same time he visualised a sequence of runes, invoking a technique known as the Snake Father's Knot.

Keeping the runes in his mind, he fixed his gaze on the shadowy ceiling above the two slaves. He beckoned to the darkness – and the darkness responded. From the pool of shadow above the two guards came a pair of serpents made from manifest darkness. Their forms were black as pitch, but obviously tangible. They hung from the ceiling, their bodies still joined to the darkness that had birthed them. Lazily they wriggled in the air, as though awaiting a purpose – or an instruction.

The hashishan focused his mind and gestured at the serpents. Each snake coiled itself into the likeness of a noose. Gesturing again, as if conducting some serpentine orchestra of death, the hashishan bid the snakes to descend.

The guards thrashed, but could not scream as the snakes wrapped around their necks and dragged them up into the air. Coils of solid darkness dug into their necks, cutting off not only their breath, but the flow of arterial blood to their heads. In shock they dropped their sabres to the ground. The weapons landed on the plush carpet with a muffled thud.

Still commanding the serpents with his gestures, still holding the runes in his mind, the hashishan advanced until he stood beside the struggling figures. They kicked and clawed at the serpents, but their efforts were futile; the Snake Father's Knot was stronger than any earthly rope.

It wasn't long until both men began to succumb to the perverse and gruesome effects of strangulation. One man had an obvious erection, while the other was pissing himself. Urine tricked down his leg onto the carpet. The hashishan drew back to avoid the splatter. Finally both men fouled their trousers – and grew utterly still.

The hashishan maintained the technique for a few moments longer, making sure the men were dead. Then he banished the runes from his mind. The serpents dissolved back into the shadows of the ceiling, dropping the dead men to the floor. They landed with a stifled thud, their arms and legs askew.

The hashishan took a deep breath and wiped the sweat from his brow. Using the Demon Arts was mentally and physically draining; he felt as if he'd just run a short marathon, whilst somehow playing chess with a master. He was tired – and yet, he had work to do.

One by one he dragged the corpses into the trophy room, holding his breath lest he smell the foulness in their pants. From there he dragged them to the trapdoor, and hurled them down into the secret tunnels under the villa. With his victims thus disposed of, the hashishan returned to the trophy room, and waited in the shadows once again. His job was to eliminate everyone who occupied the villa, and this seemed like a good way to start.

Wena pulled away from Narseh's embrace. She was tipsy from wine, but her necromantic senses were sharp enough to detect the presence of death somewhere nearby.

'What is it, my dear?' asked Narseh.

'I'm not sure,' she said. 'I thought I could feel something – something dying.'

Narseh shrugged. 'It's probably just a rat in the walls. Don't trouble yourself. This is our special time, remember?'

For a moment Wena remained stiff, her head swimming with worry. Then her lover crawled between her legs and laid his tongue on her lips, and she thought about nothing but pleasure.

The hashishan tipped another body through the trapdoor, then wiped his sweaty forehead. One by one he had slaughtered the guards on patrol. Desperate fingers had clawed at nooses; eyes had bulged; twitching bodies had shat themselves in spasms of death, until the reek of their foulness hung thick in the hall. Now there were no more patrols, just eight soiled bodies in the tunnel below.

The hashishan sat in the trophy room, feeling exhausted. The use of the Demon Arts was taxing indeed. He took some sweets from his pocket and gobbled them up, renewing his strength and satisfying his hunger. Then he took out his pipe. He figured he deserved another hit after his efforts. Besides, there was still a lot of work to be done, and he needed to maintain his murderous trance.

He sucked on the burning buds until nothing was left but a film of resin, then crept into the hallway. It was time to find the man from Alhazred. Where might he be? Where would the hashishan stay, if he were living at this villa? Probably somewhere unassuming, where no one would look. But his target was a different man, with different priorities. Ninia Zak had described him as flashy in appearance and flowery in speech. He fancied himself, and was fond of life's luxuries.

He's probably in the master bedroom, thought the hashishan.

And so he made his way there, scattering breadcrumbs of death in his wake as he slew what servants remained. He snapped a slave's neck as the man sat writing in a ledger; he strangled a sentry stationed in a doorway. He crept through the shadows with nary a sound, until he was peering round a corner at the entrance to the master bedroom.

Necromancy, he thought. *I knew it!*

For there, outside the door, were a pair of undead monsters wrapped in green linen.

The hashishan drew his sabre from its scabbard. He'd tangled with creatures like this in the past, and knew there was only one way to end them, short of slaying their master: total bodily dismemberment. He would have to chop them up. At least he needn't worry about bloodstains. The creatures were withered, and the blood in their veins was as dust.

He stepped into the corridor, raised his blade, and pictured a set of especially ragged-looking runes. Together they unlocked a technique which some called the Creeping Death, but which the hashishan's master had poetically referred to as 'Tzintillion's Stray Glance.'

He swung his sword through the air. A ripple of razor-sharp energy flew off the edge of the blade and severed the legs of the closest zombie. The creature went down, weeping dust from its wounds in lieu of blood. At once it began crawling towards him, while the other one charged, swinging its khopesh.

The hashishan parried – but only just. The creature had the horrid strength of death, and had almost broken his guard. He leapt back, avoiding another brutal swing. The creature was powerful, but lacking in finesse. He hacked through its wrist, and its hand hit the floor, still gripping the khopesh.

He didn't stop there. Swinging his blade in a series of elegant arcs, he hacked off its legs and its head, then finished it off with a disembowelling strike. Flowers and sawdust exploded from the lacerated abdomen.

Meanwhile the legless undead had crawled into range. It swung at his foot – but missed as the hashishan leapt back. He circled the zombie's prone form, hacking it to pieces as he went, as though he were chopping dry timber.

Wena's eyes flicked open. She'd fallen asleep in the aftermath of fucking, but something was pulling her awake. Instantly she knew what it was – her zombies were in trouble! She could feel their bodies coming apart, along with the spells that gave them a semblance of life.

A bolt of sobriety shot through her limbs. She was sleepy and tipsy no longer. She grabbed Narseh's shoulder and shook him awake. He peered at her groggily, and started to speak, but she clamped a hand over his mouth.

'We're under attack,' she whispered. 'My zombies are dying!'

Narseh's eyes widened in shock. From the hall outside came the muffled sound of chopping. Then the chopping stopped – and there was nothing but silence.

Narseh and Wena traded a terrified glance, then rose from the bed. Narseh seized his crescent-shaped dagger. Wena took her sickle from the nightstand. The two of them stood side-by-side, dressed only in their robes. They glanced around the chamber. The barred windows were high and narrow. The room's only exit was the door ahead of them, which just then flew open, admitting a man in black armed with a sabre. He stank of death and weed smoke.

'So you're the necromancer,' he said, fixing his eyes on Wena.

'The lady's occupation is none of your business,' said Narseh. 'And I'd thank you to leave, sir. This is private property.' He tried to make his voice sound as commanding as possible, but he couldn't hide the tremor of fear in his tone. The dagger shook in his grip.

'It sure is private property,' said the hashishan. 'But that doesn't mean it's yours.'

He advanced in a fighting stance. The curve of his blade was like a toothless smile on the face of death.

'Don't come any closer!' shouted Narseh, brandishing the dagger. He turned to Wena. 'Quick, my sweet – blast him with a lightning bolt!'

'I told you already I can't do that!' she hissed.

The hashishan stepped closer; Narseh gulped, then brandished the dagger again.

'Stay back!' he shouted. 'I'm warning you!'

The hashishan swung his sword twice. Two razor-sharp ripples of energy flew from the blade toward Wena and Narseh – and knocked the weapons from their hands with pinpoint precision.

Narseh raised his hands. 'Now let's just calm down here. Surely we can work this all out...'

Once again he tried to sound confident, but his voice had risen in pitch, and sounded almost girlish.

'There's nothing to be worked out,' said the hashishan. 'I've come here to kill you.'

'Then why did you disarm us? You could have cut our heads off with that trick. Clearly you want to make a bargain –'

'There can't be any blood,' said the hashishan as he drew even closer.

'Wait!' shouted Narseh. 'You're clearly a professional. Who was it that hired you? The Zaks? Whatever they're offering you I'll match it. I'll even add five percent!'

'Five percent?' repeated Wena. 'We'll double it!'

In spite of his terror, Narseh recoiled from such a generous bribe.

'Don't listen to her,' he said. 'She's hysterical!'

The hashishan continued to advance.

'Alright,' said Narseh. 'Ten percent. But that's the absolute limit!'

Again the hashishan said nothing, and took another step forward.

'Fifteen percent,' said Narseh. 'You won't get any better than that!'

The hashishan drew closer still. Narseh took Wena's hand and leapt onto the bed, making a run for the opposite side of the room. The hashishan swung his blade, sending another crescent of razor-sharp force flying through the air. It sliced through a bedpost and slammed into the wall, slicing the marble itself. Dust erupted from the cut. Wena and Narseh froze in their tracks.

'Don't run,' said the hashishan. 'Or I'll cut you in half, blood or no blood, then shampoo the carpets.'

The two lovers glanced at one another in terror.

'Kneel on the floor,' said the hashishan. 'I'll make it quick.'

Still holding hands, Wena and Narseh knelt on the floor. Their interlocked fingers trembled. Standing before them, the hashishan removed a vial of black venom from his coat, followed by a solitary needle. Narseh saw it glitter in the moonlight, and began to weep.

'No,' he said, turning his gaze toward the ceiling. 'NO! It can't end like this. Candle King, I beseech you, don't snuff me yet! Please! Please, I'll to anything! I'll pile up the treasures on your altar. I'll send you slaves, concubines, armies of odalisques, spices, gemstones, mountains of tobacco, just don't snuff me out, not yet. I'm not rich enough. I'm too young to die. I've got so much to take. I've got so much to *give*! Please, please, don't snuff me OOOOOUUT!'

Narseh wept and rambled, wringing his hands and tearing at his beard.

Wena placed a hand on his shoulder. She was scared too, but still in control. Being a necromancer, she'd been surrounded by death all her life. Perhaps that's why she feared it less than he did. Then again, perhaps she was simply less craven. Either way she tried to comfort him, but he seemed to be off in some other reality.

'Begging won't save you,' said the hashishan. 'Stupid superstitions won't save you.'

'Then what will?' said Wena. 'Surely there's something.' She gestured around them. 'Just look at all this wealth! Let us live, and you can have it all. Even more, if you like. There's plenty to be had...'

'I know,' said the hashishan. 'I was planning to steal some, after I kill you.'

Wena clenched her teeth. There had to be something she could do to get out of this mess. The assassin was a businessman, surely. There had to be some kind a bargain she could make with him. But what? Narseh was the one who was good at bargaining, not her. He was the one who could persuade people, talk to people, change people's minds. But right now he was useless.

'Candle King, Candle King, save me!' he cried, as snotty tears ran down his beard.

Wena felt her heart begin to sink as the hashishan removed the cork from his vial of black venom. She was almost ready to start wailing with her lover. Instead she took a breath, and steeled herself. Narseh was useless right now, so she had to take over his role. What would he do? What would he say, if he wasn't an incoherent mess?

The hashishan dipped the pin into the poison. Wena's heart hammered in terror. Then an idea shot straight into her brain, like a bat into a cavern at dusk.

'Wait!' she said.

The hashishan peered down with his sleepy eyes. 'Yes?'

'You're an assassin,' she said.

'No shit.'

'And your job's very dangerous, I bet.'

'Comes with the territory.'

'And I bet it gets gruelling, dealing out death day after day. And it's not like you're fighting in wars, where it's kill-or-be-killed, and your foes have a chance to fight back. You take them by surprise. Stab them in the back, kill them in their sleep. I'm sure it must play on your mind. That's why you're high right now, isn't it? To deaden your conscience. To tamp down your compassion...'

He glanced at her silently. She could tell she'd struck a nerve.

'What if I said you could take a break from all that?' she said. 'That you could still use your skills, but without any risk, and without having to hurt anyone at all?'

He peered at her in silence for a while, holding the needle.

'I'm listening,' he said.

Wena explained her scheme. The hashishan listened, but he was so hard to read, Wena couldn't tell if she were winning him over. His face was just so blank...

At length Wena was finished. For a time the hashishan remained silent, as if mulling things over. Wena's heart began to lift as he put away the poisoned needle – then sank once again as he pulled out a dagger and grabbed Narseh by the beard.

'NO!' shouted Wena as the blade went slicing down.

'It's done,' said the hashishan.

Ninia sighed with relief, then smiled at the rest of the conspirators, all of whom were gathered in the room. The hashishan, who was seated at the same rickety chair he had used during his last visit, tossed something bloody and black on the table. Peering closer, Ninia saw it was the beard of the man from Alhazred, no doubt removed from his cadaver. She picked it up, feeling a sinister thrill as she held it. Then, with the air of someone who'd forgotten something important, she rushed to shut the doors and windows. As always, she didn't want anyone spying on their meeting.

'Tell me what happened,' she said, sitting across from the hashishan. 'Did you slaughter them all?'

The hashishan nodded as he loaded his pipe and fired it up. Between each puff he spoke in great detail of the murders he'd committed and the deadly Demon Arts he'd used to commit them. Ninia listened intently, while the room became filled with clouds of potent smoke. It smelled somewhat different than last time. Even the buds looked different, being not black but crimson in colour.

Ninia paid it no mind. Nor did she mind getting a second-hand high – not when all her dreams were about to come true. She was finally about to get her hands on the old miser's money! She giggled to herself in delight.

I must be getting a bit stoned, she thought.

There was no doubt about it. Her body felt languid and strange. As she glanced around the room she saw the shadows of her relatives detach from their bodies and buzz with electric red light. Before she knew it she had fallen from her chair, and lay giggling uncontrollably. Her relatives fell down beside her, laughing like hyenas on the grubby kitchen floor.

The hashishan stood up, tapping the ash from his pipe. His bloodshot eyes were cold. Ninia felt a surge of terror. Her body was numb. The fingers on her hands were curling up like the petals of dying flowers.

'What's...what's happening?' she managed to ask, between the fits of uncontrollable laughter.

The hashishan held up a crimson bud, much like the ones he had just smoked.

'This is Javasava Red,' he said. 'It's quite deadly. But I've been smoking a bit every day for the past seven years, so I'm immune to the effects. I doubt the same can be said for you.'

'But...but why?' stammered Ninia, even as her world became black.

'Because I'm a businessman. And I've had a better offer.'

'But what about honour? We had a deal!'

The hashishan repeated the mantra his master had so often spoken:

'Nothing is true. Everything is permitted.'

He turned and strode from the house. Wena and Narseh were waiting outside. Narseh was touching the place where his beard had once been.

'Took me months to grow that out,' he grumbled.

Wena smiled at him. 'I think you'll look handsome clean-shaven.'

That night the Zak family mysteriously vanished. Searching their house, agents of the court found a vial of black venom, which prompted them to once again exhume the corpse of Muragar Zak. In his veins were found traces of the toxin. It was surmised that the Zaks had poisoned the old man, albeit inexpertly, which had caused him to fall into a death-like slumber, after which he had awoken for a time before succumbing to a heart attack. Warrants were issued for the arrest of the Zaks, and the miser's estate was handed to Narseh, who liquidated it promptly and departed the town, joined by a stranger with bloodshot eyes.

Chapter 7: The Plague of Undead

Shavran huddled in the hall with the others, listening in terror to the racket coming from outside.

Shavran was the mayor of Haresburough. A few minutes earlier he'd been going about his business as usual – collecting bribes, getting free blowjobs from hookers, and so-on – when a horde of zombies had poured into the streets, baying for blood. Some were bloated and fresh; others were old, with skin like withered paper unfurling from their bones.

Shavran had fled to the hall with the rest of the townsfolk. Presently the monsters were outside, groaning and banging on the door. The people within were shaking or screaming in terror, clutching the few meagre weapons they'd managed to get hold of. As the sounds of hunger and terror rose to an almighty pitch, a skeletal fist punched through the door, creating a hole through which the faces of the dead could be seen. There they were – a sea of sockets without eyes, lipless grins, rotting teeth eager to bite through living flesh.

'Fuck!' shouted Shavran. 'Save us! Somebody save us!'

In the next few moments his plea was miraculously answered.

First came the sound of galloping horses and the groaning of carriage wheels. Then the dead things began to fall, cut down by ripples of razor-sharp force till none were left standing. The air grew silent save for the whinnying of horses and the gasping of the people in the hall.

'You can come out now,' said a voice from outside.

Gingerly Shavran stepped up to the door and peered into the street. There, standing atop a hill of dismembered zombies was a man dressed in black, wielding a sabre. Behind him was a carriage. Sitting in the driver's seat was a man in a turban with a short growth of beard.

'Greetings fair citizens!' said Narseh. 'May I ask who's in charge here?'

'That would be me,' said Shavran, still reeling from the shock of the undead assault and this sudden reversal of fortune.

Narseh leapt down from the carriage and strode towards the hall. Gingerly he tiptoed past the bodies, avoiding the puddles of ooze and bits of mangled flesh. At length he reached the mayor, and held out his hand through the hole in the door. Shavran shook it limply, still trying to get over his shock.

'My name is Narseh Az-Pinah,' said the stranger. 'And this is my comrade, Zativa. We're professional zombie hunters. And we couldn't help but notice that your town's become the target of the Undead Curse.'

'The...the Undead Curse?' stammered Shavran.

'That's right,' said Narseh. 'The Undead Curse. Haven't you heard of it? It's sweeping the land like a wave, hopping from one unlucky town to another! I'm afraid this is just the beginning.' He gestured to the corpses on the ground. 'There will be many more monsters than this. Wave after flesh-hungry wave! But lucky for you, my friend and I can help. All we ask for is a small, meagre payment, simply to off-set our operating costs. We'd do it for free, but a person has to eat, you know?'

'Of course,' said Shavran. 'We'll be happy to reward you.'

'Good, good,' said Narseh. 'Now, why don't you open that door, and you and I can have a talk about our fee structure?'

Epilogue: A Fantastic Tale

Some time later...

Narseh sat on a pillow in his palace, taking a drag from a jewel-studded hookah.

'And that,' he said, exhaling the smoke, 'was how I defeated the Great Undead Plague.'

'Amazing!' said one of the guests who'd come to listen to Narseh's fantastic tales. 'I almost can't believe it! Let me go over things again, just in case I've missed anything out. There you were, travelling through the Republic of Kurolow to pay homage at the graves of your many long-lost relatives, when you heard a man banging on the lid

356

of his casket. You did the right thing and saved him, of course, after which he took you to the courthouse, willed you his entire estate, then suddenly dropped dead. You tried to have the will overturned, thinking it was very unfair that the poor man's descendants should be so disadvantaged. But in order to overturn the will, you had to stay in the town for some time, and go through the necessary motions. And not having anywhere to stay, you accepted an offer to reside in the old man's giant villa. But little did you know the whole thing was a sinister trap!

'Because the man in the coffin was a sorcerer. He wanted to escape from death by possessing a strong, virile body. But all of his descendants were feeble and weak. So he came back from the grave just long enough to will you his estate and trap you in his web. Being the site of his terrible magick, the villa was haunted by his spirit, which tried to possess you. Luckily your mind was too strong, and you managed to fight off his influence. The sorcerer, enraged, took possession of his granddaughter, and used her to hire a hashishan to murder you. But after a thrilling and incredible sword-fight, you managed to defeat the hashishan, and, rather than killing him, you graciously chose to spare his wretched life, after which he pledged to serve you faithfully forever. At that point the spirit, even more enraged, cast a terrible spell that unleashed undead hordes from the earth. Rampaging monsters began to roam the land, eating human flesh. Unable to sit back and watch, you took it upon yourself to send the foul monsters to the grave once again, facing terrible danger in the process.' The man paused, and took a breath. 'Have I listed all the details correctly?'

'Pretty much,' said Narseh. 'Although I must point out that slaughtering zombies is very expensive, and I didn't have the heart to ask for money from the poor, defenceless people whom I rescued. As a consequence, I'm afraid I used up a great deal of my capital in the endeavour. I still haven't quite recovered from the financial blow...'

Narseh stared sadly at the floor, which was inlaid with brilliant arrangements of lapis and turquoise.

'Such a sad world we live in,' said the guest, 'in which righteous men are so often left destitute, while liars and cheats are left to prosper without end. Well not this time, my friend! I for one would like to give you some gifts, not only to repay you for the tale of this thrilling adventure, but to offset all the hardships you've suffered whilst helping the unfortunate.'

'I should like you give you gifts as well,' said another of the guests.

'Me too!' said another.

The men stood up and clapped their hands, whereupon their slaves poured into the room, carrying wealth fit for an imperial procession – brocaded silks from the land of distant Leng, bearing the visage of the Saffron Sage; silver plate from the pornocracy of Thune, embossed with entrancing erotica; sacks of tobacco; pelts of exotic beasts; and various objects of wondrous appearance and incredible monetary value.

'You're too kind, gentlemen,' said Narseh, wiping his eyes. 'I fear I might weep. Perhaps you might leave me alone, so I don't make a fool of myself?'

The guests nodded graciously and departed the palace, whereupon a sly smile spread over Narseh's lips. The story had been bullshit, of course – well, mostly bullshit. He really *had* stopped a plague of undead, albeit one of his and Wena's creation. Luckily his audience had been chosen from the stupidest – and wealthiest – people in Alhazred.

He called to his slaves, who began to carry his new treasures to the vault. Narseh followed behind, passing the altar of the Candle King, which was empty of offerings as usual.

Soon he stood in his vault, staring at a sea of gleaming treasure which stretched from one wall to another. It was more than a man could spend in several lifetimes.

Narseh shook his head and sighed. He didn't have nearly enough! Especially not enough to finance his retirement in the afterlife. Soon he'd have to go back to work once again, and take another voyage across the wide Ozich Sea.

Narseh will return in more nefarious journeys!

OTHER BOOKS FROM
BJ SWANN

ZHUULTON OF ZHUUL AND THE FEAST OF THE CENTIPEDE

ZHUULTON OF ZHUUL AND THE CONSPIRACY OF RAVENS

BARON BAD TRIP

TEMPERANCE HOLOCAUST

HOLOCAUST HEARTS

OUR LADY OF THE SCYTHE: DEMON ACADEMY

swannbedlam.com